RNF

D0236539

Rhydyfelin
Poplar Road
01

THE TREACHEROUS TEDDY

THE TREACHEROUS TEDDY

JOHN J. LAMB

WHEELER
CHIVERS

This Large Print edition is published by Wheeler Publishing, Waterville, Maine, USA and by BBC Audiobooks Ltd, Bath, England.
Wheeler Publishing, a part of Gale, Cengage Learning.
Copyright © 2009 by John J. Lamb.
The moral right of the author has been asserted.
A Bear Collector's Mystery.

ALL RIGHTS RESERVED
This is a work of fiction. Names, characters, places, and incidents either are the product of the author's imagination or are used fictitiously, and any resemblance to actual persons, living or dead, business establishments, events, or locales is entirely coincidental. The publisher does not have any control over and does not assume any responsibility for author or third-party Web sites or their content.
The text of this Large Print edition is unabridged.
Other aspects of the book may vary from the original edition.
Set in 16 pt. Plantin.
Printed on permanent paper.

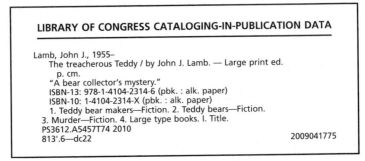

LIBRARY OF CONGRESS CATALOGING-IN-PUBLICATION DATA

Lamb, John J., 1955–
    The treacherous Teddy / by John J. Lamb. — Large print ed.
    p. cm.
    "A bear collector's mystery."
    ISBN-13: 978-1-4104-2314-6 (pbk. : alk. paper)
    ISBN-10: 1-4104-2314-X (pbk. : alk. paper)
    1. Teddy bear makers—Fiction. 2. Teddy bears—Fiction.
3. Murder—Fiction. 4. Large type books. I. Title.
PS3612.A5457T74 2010
813'.6—dc22   2009041775

BRITISH LIBRARY CATALOGUING-IN-PUBLICATION DATA AVAILABLE

Published in 2010 in the U.S. by arrangement with The Berkley Publishing Group, a member of Penguin Group (USA) Inc.
Published in 2010 in the U.K. by arrangement with The Berkley Publishing Group, a member of Penguin Group (USA) Inc.

U.K. Hardcover: 978 1 408 47820 2 (Chivers Large Print)
U.K. Softcover: 978 1 408 47821 9 (Camden Large Print)

Printed in the United States of America
1 2 3 4 5 6 7 14 13 12 11 10

*Dedicated to the memory of our sweet
and beloved
four-footed kids . . .
Baby Bear, Kristen Noel, Laddy (AKA
Kitchener), and Cammie*

ONE

I like the gentle patter of raindrops against the window. The sound is soothing, but tonight it made me edgy.

It was early evening on a Thursday in the first week of November, and after nearly three weeks of unseasonably warm and dry weather in the Shenandoah Valley of Virginia, a light rain had begun to fall. I was upstairs in our workroom, putting the finishing touches on my newest teddy bear, while unsuccessfully trying to keep my mind off the fact that the first few hours of a rainstorm turns the roads as slick as a politician's answer to an unwelcome question. Ordinarily, I don't worry about highway conditions while sitting at home, but tonight my wife, Ashleigh, was out in a patrol car, working as an auxiliary deputy for the Massanutten County Sheriff's Office.

I glanced at the police scanner on the shelf

above the big worktable. The device had been quiet for about the past ten minutes, but I knew the silence couldn't last. Gene Kelly sang in the rain, but folks around here speed in the rain, and it's the rare storm that doesn't produce at least one horrific traffic collision that looks as if a tactical nuclear weapon caused the damage. As a consequence, I knew it was merely a matter of time until the sheriff's dispatcher sent Ash out to a major crash scene. Then I'd have something new to fret about.

I realized that I was learning something my wife had discovered more than twenty-seven years ago: being married to a cop was often scary. Unfortunately, I wasn't handling the stress as well as she had.

My name is Brad Lyon and I used to be a homicide inspector with the San Francisco Police Department until a murder suspect's BFB — big freaking bullet — pretty much destroyed my left shin. The orthopedic surgeon did what he could to repair the damage and I diligently rehabbed my leg, but it was a long and painful exercise in futility. I was forced into early retirement from the PD three years ago when it became clear that I'd always have a bad limp and need a cane if I wanted to walk any more than a few feet. Afterward, we'd relocated to Ash's hometown of Remmelkemp Mill, Virginia, where we now lived in a hundred-year-old farmhouse beside the South Fork of the Shenandoah River. Then, under her gentle tutelage, I'd followed my wife into an improbable yet satisfying second career as a teddy bear artist.

I wasn't the only one reinventing my life, however.

Over the past two years, Ash and I had assisted the local sheriff's office with a couple of murder investigations, and those experiences had whetted my wife's previously unsuspected appetite for police work. She'd become a volunteer deputy sheriff and quickly demonstrated that she was a born street cop. Indeed, her performance was so outstanding that Tina Barron, the sheriff of Massanutten County and a good friend of ours, had recently asked my wife to join the force as a full-time deputy.

Ash had declined the offer, but I knew my wife was utterly hooked on cop work. Our discussions over morning coffee were once mostly about teddy bears and the shows we were going to attend. Now the topics were just as likely to be interrogation techniques or crime scene analysis, as my wife picked my brain. I just hoped she hadn't passed on the permanent position with the sheriff's office because she thought I'd be unhappy with our reversed roles.

That wasn't the case. In fact, I was damn proud of her and wanted to provide her with the same opportunity she'd given me when we were first married. Back then, Ash had put her life and personal goals on hold to raise our two children, who are now grown and I'm glad to report are self-sufficient and successful adults. Our son, Christopher, is a vintner at a winery in Missouri, while his older sister, Heather, followed in my footsteps and is a detective with SFPD. Ash deserves all the credit for how our kids turned out. She managed our household while I pursued a rewarding career. It was finally her turn to chase a dream and I'd support her in whatever way I could, which I suppose included learning to deal with my apprehensions.

I forced myself to concentrate on the Bernina sewing machine and the small pieces of black fabric that I was stitching together to create a miniature sports jacket for Bear-atio Caine, my teddy bear incarnation of the crime lab lieutenant played by David Caruso in the television program *CSI: Miami.* Back when I first started creating stuffed animals, I came up with the somewhat quirky idea of making bears modeled after characters from cop TV shows and movies. I never expected there'd be a huge demand for my "Claw and Order Collection," and I was right. Still, I was having fun, and my bears had found a modest following among collectors who either were married to cops or worked in law enforcement.

Made from reddish-orange mohair and standing twenty inches tall, Bear-atio Caine was the most challenging bear I'd ever undertaken to create. It was my first effort using a Loc-Line mechanism — essentially a plastic skeleton, which allowed greater freedom in posing a teddy bear, especially the head. This extra flexibility was vital. When Caruso plays the sad-eyed detective on television, one of his signature stylistic touches is to tilt his head at a variety of peculiar angles. I wanted Bear-atio to be capable of this same macawlike suppleness.

I finished sewing the jacket pieces together, carefully folded the collar and lapels into their proper positions, and put the tiny garment on the bear. Even by my own harsh standards, I had to admit the jacket looked pretty good. All I had left to do was make some miniature black slacks, affix a pair of tiny sunglasses on the bear's muzzle, and then pose Bear-atio with his paws on his hips — another delicious Caruso acting tic. Bear-atio would be finished in time for the teddy bear show we were hosting at the church community center in town on Saturday.

The scanner emitted the tiny bleep that signaled the beginning of a radio transmission. It was Ash, though the device's small speaker made her voice sound tinny. She said, "Mike-Eleven to dispatch."

"Go ahead," said the dispatcher, sounding bored. I knew the dispatcher's name was Gloria, and she liked to spend her shifts doing crossword puzzles.

"I'm making a traffic stop on a red Nissan Sentra." Ash read off the Nissan's license plate and said her location was on Port Republic Road, about a half mile east of Doe Hill Road.

Our Old English sheepdog, Kitchener, was lying at my feet. He'd become so accustomed to hearing Ash's disembodied voice coming from the little box that he didn't even bother to lift his head to look at the scanner anymore. I envied his laid-back attitude. Then again, maybe he'd have been more attentive if he knew how many accounts of cop killings begin with the words *The officer was making a routine traffic stop.*

After a few seconds of silence, Gloria

came on the air and said, "Dispatch to Mike-Eleven, I need you to clear your stop. We have a priority call."

"Will do. Go ahead with the information," said Ash.

"Negative. Give me a call on your cell phone and I'll explain."

"Affirmative."

"Now, that's interesting, Kitch," I said, reaching down to scratch him behind his ear. "Usually, the only reason you dispatch a call over the phone is because you think a suspect is monitoring the police radio and you don't want to let him know the cops are on the way to his location."

Kitch cocked his head and gave me a questioning look. It was obvious he'd picked up on my fresh surge of uneasiness. It's been my experience that the kind of crook who eavesdrops on police radio frequencies is also a prime candidate to resist or flee the cops. My first instinct was to warn Ash of the potential danger, so I sat up and reached for the portable telephone on the table. Then I withdrew my hand, suddenly feeling chastened. If I called Ash to kibitz about how she approached the call, it would say that I didn't trust her abilities, which I did. My wife was a good cop, and I realized it would probably be best if I turned the scanner off and stopped obsessing over her safety.

Yet I could no more do that than dance a Highland fling, so I returned my attention to Bear-atio, who still needed a pair of pants. Using the fabric tape measure, I confirmed that my mohair sleuth's waist size was twelve inches and that trouser length would be about ten inches. Meanwhile, the scanner remained silent and I had to assume that Ash had received her instructions and was on her way to the call.

I unfolded some more of the same black fabric from which I'd made the bear's jacket and smoothed it out before laying down the first of two pieces of a tissue-paper clothing pattern. Once the pattern was pinned to the fabric, I used one of our pairs of razor-sharp scissors to begin cutting out the piece. That's when the radio emitted a bleep.

A man's voice said, "Game Warden Unit Five-Seventy-Eight to Mike-Eleven, the poaching suspect just spotted me and he's rabbiting."

Ash replied, "Copy and I'm in the vicinity. Where do you want me?"

"The track he's on comes out right where Kobler Hollow Road loops back against the base of the mountain. Can you intercept?"

"Affirmative. Confirming the suspect

vehicle is a black, older-model Dodge pickup truck? Anything else I should know?"

"At least one gun in the truck, but Chet is peaceable."

"Nice to know. I'm just coming up on Kobler Hollow Road now. ETA is less than two minutes." Ash sounded as if she were enjoying herself.

"Which means she'll get to the road before you do, Chet." The game warden was now obviously talking to the fleeing hunter. "I know you're listening to us, so do yourself a favor. Shut it down when you get to the road. You've got a load of trouble as it is."

I allowed myself to relax a tiny bit, now that I knew the nature of Ash's mysterious call. Though the poacher was armed, I knew the chances were effectively nil that he'd violently resist the cops. There was no reason to. Hunting is an integral part of the culture around here, so local juries seldom convict anyone for poaching. I involuntarily glanced toward the east-facing window. Kobler Hollow was across the river and about three miles away, at the base of the Blue Ridge Mountains. It was a tiny agricultural community that, despite its proximity to the busy U.S. Highway 340 and Remmelkemp Mill, felt isolated.

The scanner chirruped and then I sat bolt

15

upright in the chair as Ash half-shouted, "Mike-Eleven to dispatch, my car was just sideswiped!"

"Are you injured?" asked the dispatcher.

"Negative, and now it's a hit-and-run. I'm in pursuit," Ash said loudly so that she could be heard over the patrol car's yelping siren. "We're northbound on Kobler Hollow Road, heading toward Highway Three-Forty."

"Mike-Eleven, did Chet hit you with his pickup?" demanded the game warden.

"No, it was a dark blue Saab sedan with a partial license of Three-Bravo-Juliet. I don't think they were Virginia plates. Do you need me to come back there?"

"Negative. Hit-and-run on a sheriff's cruiser trumps a poaching charge. We'll get Chet some other day."

"Mike-Eleven, your location now?" the dispatcher asked.

"I'm about a hundred yards behind the suspect vehicle, which is turning . . . northbound onto Highway Three-Forty," said Ash, who sounded a little calmer.

"Copy. Mike-Six is still on his call at Rockingham Memorial Hospital, so I'm notifying the state police to roll back-up."

"Copy."

Ash didn't sound concerned that there

16

wasn't another police unit immediately available to assist her, but it scared me. I'm not certain why, but I went over and pushed the window open. Maybe I needed confirmation from my own ears that this potentially lethal drama was unfolding while I sat snug in our home making a teddy bear. If so, I received the proof immediately. Off to the east, over the sound of the rain, I could faintly hear a yelping police siren. Talk about feeling useless.

Ash came on the radio again. "Still in pursuit, speed . . . over a hundred, and we're just passing Island Ford Road."

"Passing Island Ford Road. Be advised, the closest state police unit is coming from Mount Video," the dispatcher replied, using the local pronunciation for Montevideo, a community about ten miles to the west.

"Then I guess I'll have to stick with this guy until backup arrives," said Ash. "We're coming up on an eighteen-wheeler and . . . stand by . . . oh!"

The next few seconds of silence were simply torturous. I could no longer hear the siren outside and didn't know whether that meant Ash's car was now out of earshot or had just been involved in a wreck. Slamming the window shut, I grabbed the phone and began to punch in the numbers for the private line into the county's emergency services communications center. I knew I was overreacting, but I was going to tell Gloria to put down her freaking crossword puzzle book and radio my wife to check on her safety.

Fortunately, Ash came back on the air and I disconnected from the call. My wife sounded angry. "Mike-Eleven to dispatch, I'm breaking off the pursuit. All we have is misdemeanor offenses and someone is going to die out here if I keep chasing that guy. He just missed hitting a car head-on while passing that truck."

"Pursuit being terminated," the dispatcher said.

"Suspect vehicle last seen northbound on U.S. Three-Forty, approaching Berrytown Road."

"I'll pass that along in a BOL to the state police. Do you want them to continue to your location?"

Even with the scratchy radio reception, I could hear Ash sigh. "Negative. No point."

I slumped back into the chair and silently thanked God that my wife possessed both the good sense and courage to stop pursuing the Saab. All too often, cops who become involved in dangerous vehicle pursuits forget to weigh the risk to the community against the benefit of capturing someone who's committed a minor offense, which is exactly what a hit-and-run was. No car fender ever made is worth a human life, so Ash had made a wise choice and a ballsy one, too. Although we'd almost finished the first decade of the twenty-first century, many of the male cops around here still hold a pretty dim view of women in law enforcement. Ash had to know that some of her fellow deputies would claim she'd terminated the chase because she been too afraid to continue.

Ash was transmitting again. "Mike-Eleven to the game warden unit, any chance we can still go after your guy?"

"Negative. He's in the wind and I'm call-ing it a night," said the game warden.

"Sorry." My wife sounded even more downcast. "Mike-Eleven to dispatch, before I come to the station to make my report, I'm going to head back to Kobler Hollow Road. I want to check out the house where the vehicle came from. Maybe they know the guy."

"Copy."

"And you might as well call the sheriff and tell her that I dinged up a car."

"The sheriff has already been advised," Gloria said smugly.

Gritting my teeth, I thought, *You little witch. When the radio went dead, you couldn't be bothered to check on my wife's welfare, but you didn't waste any time ratting her out for damaging a cruiser.* I suddenly regretted not having completed that ear-scorching call to the dispatch center.

Now that the excitement was over, I finished cutting the fabric for Bear-atio's slacks. I'd just begun to slowly stitch one of the legs together when Ash's voice came over the scanner again.

"Mike-Eleven to dispatch, I'll be out at one-sixty-two Kobler Hollow Road. The mailbox says it's the Rawlins farm."

"Copy, out at the Rawlins farm." The dispatcher sounded distracted, and I wondered if she was struggling to come up with a four-letter word for *indolent.*

About thirty seconds passed, and when Ash came back on the air, the poorer sound quality of the transmission told me she was using her handheld portable radio. In an urgent voice, she said, "Mike-Eleven to dispatch, I have a possible murder victim here. Send me Code Three backup. We need to check the house for other victims and suspects."

The game warden cut into the frequency before the dispatcher could reply. "Unit

Five-Seventy-Eight to Mike-Eleven, I'll be there in a couple of minutes."

I thought, *God bless you, Unit Five-Seventy-Eight,* as I turned off the Bernina. I wasn't going to finish Bear-atio's slacks tonight.

Then Gloria came on the air, sounding flustered. "Do you need the rescue squad?"

"Not unless they can bring this poor man back to life, dispatch." Ash's voice was acid. "But contact Sheriff Barron and my husband and tell them to respond to this location immediately."

Two

I changed into jeans and a long-sleeved flannel shirt and pulled out a pair of sturdy work boots. It hadn't been raining that hard or for very long, but it doesn't take much moisture to turn the soil around here into the sort of glutinous mud that can suck the shoes right from your feet.

Next, I retrieved my Glock pistol and shoulder holster from the sock drawer and slipped the rig on. As a civilian investigative consultant for the sheriff's office, I had a permit to carry a concealed weapon. It wasn't a requirement of my duties to be armed, but a quarter century of cop work has taught me that it's better to have a gun and not need it than to need one and not have it, especially when working a fresh homicide. Believe it or not, sometimes killers *do* return to the scene of the crime.

Grabbing my rechargeable flashlight and blackthorn cane, I led Kitch downstairs and secured him inside his big plastic crate. Our dog suffers from separation anxiety, and one of his ways of dealing with stress is to chew on things, which can be a little hazardous in a house packed with expensive teddy bears. The crate's metal-grate door faced toward the television, and I turned the tube on for Kitch. He'd be happy. The shopping network QVC was airing a "Food Fest" program, and at the moment they were selling bacon-wrapped filet mignon steaks.

I paused at the front door to put on my heavy parka and San Francisco Giants ball cap, and once outside I heard an emergency vehicle siren begin yelping from the direction of Remmelkemp Mill. I strongly suspected it was Sheriff Tina Barron on her way to assist Ash. I climbed into our Nissan Xterra, slipped a Cannonball Adderley jazz CD into the player, and headed toward the Rawlins farm. There was no need for me to rush. The corpse wasn't going anywhere.

The rain began to taper off a little as I crossed the river and then turned south onto U.S. Route 340, otherwise known as the Stonewall Jackson Highway. Although I couldn't see the Blue Ridge Mountains, I knew they were to my left and less than a mile away. Fortunately, there wasn't much traffic on the road, but I didn't relax or increase my speed. There was no need for both members of the Lyon household to be involved in accidents tonight. That train of thought naturally led to Ash. I knew I would have to resist my natural inclination to give her a hug or otherwise make any sort of fuss over her having been in a hit-and-run. My wife was on duty, and cops don't behave that way toward one another.

Besides, I had a feeling that she'd be in no mood for a pep talk or to be comforted. One of the first things that must have occurred to Ash when she found the dead body was that she'd possibly allowed a murderer to escape — not that her decision to terminate the pursuit wasn't appropriate, given the limited information she'd possessed at the time. However, my wife is a perfectionist, and I knew it was likely she was furious with herself for having — at least in her mind — dropped the ball. That wasn't the case, and if she brought the subject up, I was going to pass along a messy fact about cop work that I'd learned many years ago: You can handle a situation perfectly, and things can still turn to crap.

After traveling about four miles, I arrived at the intersection with Kobler Hollow Road and made a left turn. Despite the poor illumination, I noticed what looked like fresh fishtailing skid marks on the wet pavement and wondered whether the Saab or my wife's patrol car had made them. Incredibly, the night seemed to become even darker. The narrow road was so closely hemmed on both sides by tall evergreen trees and dense hedgerows that it was like a tunnel.

Finally, I saw the flashing blue lights of a stationary patrol car. As I got closer, I saw that it was a gray state police cruiser blocking a gravel lane that led from the road toward the mountain. The mailbox next to the driveway bore the name RAWLINS in white reflective letters. The state trooper got out of his car and walked over to my SUV as I came to a stop.

Lowering the window, I held up my sheriff's office ID card and said, "I'm Brad Lyon. Sheriff Barron probably told you I was coming."

"She did. Go ahead and park over there." The state trooper pointed to the gravelly shoulder on the opposite side of the road.

"Any reason why I can't drive in?"

"No room. The driveway isn't that long and it's pretty much bumper-to-bumper with police cars."

So I'd have to walk — or more accurately, limp — the rest of the way in. I parked the

25

SUV and discovered that the state trooper hadn't exaggerated. The one-lane driveway was lined with tall holly shrubs and was jammed to capacity with police cruisers from the sheriff's office, state police, an SUV that belonged to the game warden, and even a couple of cop cars from two of the nearby small towns.

Somewhere in the near distance, a dog was frantically barking, and when I arrived at the other end of the driveway I realized the sound was coming from inside the Rawlinses' white, two-story Cape Cod–style house. There was a massive whitewashed barn opposite the home, and a light mounted high on the side of the barn lit the small yard with a dim bluish-white glow. Parked in front of the house was a sheriff's car with its headlights still on. I assumed it was Ash's cruiser and that the murder victim, whom I couldn't see from my current position, was lying on the gravel driveway in the dual cones of light. Glancing back at the house, I noted that the porch light was on, as was at least one light inside the home on the first floor. The glowing exterior lights on the porch and barn suggested the victim had died after nightfall.

A flashlight blinked on and off from the direction of the barn, and I realized I was being signaled. There was a carport-like structure attached to the barn, and inside the open enclosure were a cluster of dark silhouettes. Tina had wisely established her command post away from the body, which still wasn't visible.

As I stumped toward the carport, three officers detached themselves from the group and nodded to me on their way back to the patrol cars. I saw from the shoulder patches on their uniforms that they were cops from Elkton, Grottoes, and the state police. If Tina was already sending her reinforcements back to their home jurisdictions, it meant she was confident the murderer was gone.

It was dark beneath the carport, yet I had no trouble identifying two of the three remaining people awaiting my arrival. Dressed in a brown and tan deputy sheriff's uniform, with her wavy blond hair worn in a bun, Ash had her arms folded across her chest and her head tilted downward. Even in the gloom, I could see she wore a forlorn expression. Standing next to Ash was Sheriff Tina Barron, who wore a parka with the hood pulled up, concealing her curly brunette hair. The third person was a tall, lean, gray-bearded man attired in a game warden's uniform, who I assumed was Unit

27

Five-Seventy-Eight. Outside, the rain was falling a little harder, the droplets drumming on the carport's aluminum roof.

Tina said, "I'm glad to see you dressed warmly. We're going to be out here a while."

"So it's a confirmed homicide?" I asked.

"Yep. The ME is en route from Roanoke, which will give us plenty of time to process the scene and collect what little evidence hasn't been washed away by the rain. The camera and evidence collection kit are in the trunk of my car," said Tina, giving my wife a worried glance. "We can start whenever you're ready."

Ash had remained silent, which was a bad sign. Even though I'd decided against offering my wife any overt signs of affection, I reached out to give her gloved hand a reassuring squeeze. I just couldn't help myself. She looked so sad. Ash gripped my hand tightly, and I was glad I'd trusted my instincts.

"How are you doing?" I quietly asked.

"Lousy," Ash grumbled.

"I understand how you feel, but you made the right call to terminate the pursuit."

"Oh, great. So you heard how I screwed everything up."

"Honey, you know that I always monitor the scanner when you're working. You didn't

28

screw up. If you'd pushed that chase any further, someone would've died. I'd have done the same thing you did."

Tina nodded vigorously. "That's what I've been telling her."

Ash looked up at me with bleak eyes. "But I let a murder suspect get away."

"We don't know that for sure." Tina tried to sound encouraging.

"Especially since your victim is Everett Rawlins," said the bearded man. He extended an open right hand toward me. "I'm Game Warden Randy Kent, and I guess you must be Brad Lyon."

As I shook hands with Randy, I decided to wait until we were alone before quietly expressing my appreciation for his backing up Ash so quickly. In her present disheartened mood, there was a good chance that Ash would misinterpret it as a tacit statement that I'd thought she'd needed rescuing. So instead, I said, "Good to meet you. Why is our victim's identity so important?"

"Because two weeks ago, Ev Rawlins swore out a complaint against Chester Lincoln, charging poaching, trespassing, and the attempted shooting of a domestic pet." Randy nodded toward the house, where the dog had begun to bark again. "That would be Longstreet."

29

"Longstreet?" I asked.

"Ev's dog. He's a hundred-pound Rott-weiler, and I secured him in the downstairs bathroom when we checked inside the house."

"And I've already called animal control to come and take Longstreet to the shelter," Tina added. "It's sad. I think he knows his master is dead."

Randy resumed his tale. "Ev told me that he just happened to be walking Longstreet one night when he came upon Chet doing some illegal hunting. He said that Chet took a shot at the dog for no reason."

I chuckled at the improbable tale. "More likely Ev told Cujo it was all-you-can-eat night on the mountain and sent him after the guy."

"That's what I think, too. But it's Ev's word against Chet's." Randy glanced toward where I presumed the body lay. His voice became doleful. "Or at least it was until tonight."

"And this Chet is the same guy you were trying to stop?" I asked.

"Yeah, Chet Lincoln. I have a warrant for his arrest. Maybe Chet thought he had a score to settle. It was no secret that Ev was dead-set on pressing charges."

"Not much of a motive for murder,

though, is it? From what I've seen, nobody around here goes to jail for illegal hunting."

"Most of the time that's true." There was a trace of sourness in Randy's voice. "But lots of folks have had their fill of Chet trespassing on their property, and they know he's killing way more game than he could ever eat."

Tina cut in. "Which brings me to the question I was about to ask when Brad arrived. How did you find Chet out here?"

"Ev called me on my cell phone at about five-forty-five this evening. Biggest mistake I ever made was giving him the number, because he used to call me day and night. Anyway, he told me that he'd seen headlights up on the ridge." Randy jerked his head in the direction of the Blue Ridge Mountains.

"And the only reason someone would be up there after dark and in this bad weather was if they were hunting," said Tina.

"Exactly. I was hoping it would be Chet, so I responded."

"And isn't it an *amazing* coincidence that you saw Mr. Lincoln on Mr. Rawlins's land right about the time the murder occurred," said Tina.

"But that doesn't explain why the Saab took off out of here like a bat out of hell,"

Ash said impatiently. My wife doesn't curse, and the fact that she'd employed even a mild profanity told me how upset she was. She turned to the game warden. "Chet may have been up on the ridge, but did you ever see him near the house?"

"Well . . . no. He was coming back up the slope when I saw him," Randy replied.

"And did he have a hunting bow?"

Randy shrugged. "I couldn't tell. He was too far away, and you can't always make out the details when you're looking through a night-vision scope."

"A hunting bow? Honey, you just lost me," I said.

"You haven't seen the body?" Ash asked.

"Not yet."

"Poor Everett has an arrow sticking out of his chest."

Fortunately, I recognized the quaver in my wife's voice before I blurted, *So, he got the shaft.* Instead, I said, "You sound as if you knew him."

"I did. He was a grade ahead of me all through school. His sister, Melinda, and I were friends." Ash sighed. "I guess that's the other reason I'm so upset. It's a shock to look down at a dead person and realize it's someone you used to have water balloon fights with."

any evidence that Everett

I don't think there's much of
re going to find a weapon under-
ody." Ash squinted at me. "You
mean? It just doesn't add up."
eared his throat. "Deputy Lyon

all me Ash."
Ash, considering that, as you
it, it *is* hunting season, could this
an accident?"
ely," said Tina as she pulled back
s hood. "If we'd found Mr. Raw-
the woods, maybe I'd consider it
ty."
ce he's in his driveway, next to his
d there were exterior lights on . . ."

dded. "Whoever shot that arrow
ctly where he was aiming."
that were true," said Randy. "But
ed in these mountains for nineteen
you'd be flat terrified if you knew
y of the hunters are chugaluggin'
mode-huggin' drunk."
is why they sometimes mistake a
r best buddy for a deer," I said.
gave a humorless chuckle. "Or miss
y're shooting at because they're so

"I'm sorry you had to experience that." I squeezed her hand.

"So am I, which is why I want to find out who killed him," Ash said sternly.

"And you think it was the person in the Saab?"

"What other reason would he have had for rocketing out of here and hitting my cruiser?"

"I don't know," said Tina. "However, we can prove that Mr. Lincoln had the motive, means, and opportunity to commit murder. Add the fact that he fled the scene and we have to look at him as a prime suspect."

"I suppose," Ash said grudgingly. She turned to Randy. "But you told me over the radio that Chet was armed with at least one gun."

"I didn't actually see it, but Chet always has a hunting rifle in his truck," said Kent.

"Does he ever use a hunting bow?"

"I don't know if he's ever used it, but I saw a hunting bow one of the times I was at his trailer."

"What are you getting at, Ashleigh?" Tina asked.

"Why take a chance on killing someone with a bow and arrow when you've got a high-powered rifle? It doesn't make any sense."

"Unfortunately, it does, my love," I said. "A rifle shot can be heard for miles, and maybe Mr. Lincoln didn't want to make any noise while he was killing Mr. Rawlins."

T

Ash pondered what
then shook her he
sorry, but I have to
the middle of nowhe
and the woods are f
anything that moves.
worried about his rif

"That's an exceller
alizing once more th
into a first-class dete
me wonder about sor
went out to confront
his triple-XL-sized gu

"Maybe because
wouldn't miss Longs
Tina.

"If that's true, it m
was a good chance C
Yet he went out there
a little suicidal, unless

"What?" Tina asked.

"Is th
armed?"

"No,
chance
neath h
see wha

Randy
—"

"Pleas

"Oka
pointed
have be

"Not
her par
lins out
a possib

"But
house,
said As

Tina
knew e

"I wis
I've wo
years ar
how ma
and cor

"Whi
relative

Randy
what th

"I'm sorry you had to experience that." I squeezed her hand.

"So am I, which is why I want to find out who killed him," Ash said sternly.

"And you think it was the person in the Saab?"

"What other reason would he have had for rocketing out of here and hitting my cruiser?"

"I don't know," said Tina. "However, we can prove that Mr. Lincoln had the motive, means, and opportunity to commit murder. Add the fact that he fled the scene and we have to look at him as a prime suspect."

"I suppose," Ash said grudgingly. She turned to Randy. "But you told me over the radio that Chet was armed with at least one gun."

"I didn't actually see it, but Chet always has a hunting rifle in his truck," said Kent.

"Does he ever use a hunting bow?"

"I don't know if he's ever used it, but I saw a hunting bow one of the times I was at his trailer."

"What are you getting at, Ashleigh?" Tina asked.

"Why take a chance on killing someone with a bow and arrow when you've got a high-powered rifle? It doesn't make any sense."

"Unfortunately, it does, my love," I said. "A rifle shot can be heard for miles, and maybe Mr. Lincoln didn't want to make any noise while he was killing Mr. Rawlins."

THREE

Ash pondered what I said for a moment and then shook her head. "Brad, honey, I'm sorry, but I have to disagree. We're out in the middle of nowhere, it's hunting season, and the woods are full of guys shooting at anything that moves. So why would Chet be worried about his rifle being heard?"

"That's an excellent question," I said, realizing once more that my wife was turning into a first-class detective. "And that makes me wonder about something else. If Everett went out to confront Chet, why did he leave his triple-XL-sized guard dog in the house?"

"Maybe because he was afraid Chet wouldn't miss Longstreet this time," said Tina.

"If that's true, it means he thought there was a good chance Chet might open fire. Yet he went out there himself. *That* sounds a little suicidal, unless . . ."

"What?" Tina asked.

"Is there any evidence that Everett was armed?"

"No, and I don't think there's much of a chance we're going to find a weapon underneath his body." Ash squinted at me. "You see what I mean? It just doesn't add up."

Randy cleared his throat. "Deputy Lyon—"

"Please call me Ash."

"Okay, Ash, considering that, as you pointed out, it *is* hunting season, could this have been an accident?"

"Not likely," said Tina as she pulled back her parka's hood. "If we'd found Mr. Rawlins out in the woods, maybe I'd consider it a possibility."

"But since he's in his driveway, next to his house, and there were exterior lights on . . ." said Ash.

Tina nodded. "Whoever shot that arrow knew exactly where he was aiming."

"I wish that were true," said Randy. "But I've worked in these mountains for nineteen years and you'd be flat terrified if you knew how many of the hunters are chugaluggin' and commode-huggin' drunk."

"Which is why they sometimes mistake a relative or best buddy for a deer," I said.

Randy gave a humorless chuckle. "Or miss what they're shooting at because they're so hammered on hard liquor that they can't see. To tell the truth, I'm amazed we don't have more accidental shootings."

"What if that's what Mr. Lincoln wanted us to think?" said Tina. "Unfortunately for him, there's no way of getting around the fact that Chet was seen a couple hundred yards from where the man who was going to put him in jail was found dead."

I said, "There's no question, it's damned suspicious, Tina. But we can't rule anything out yet, including the Saab."

"I don't know. It's hard to believe that some guy would drive here in an expensive car and then use an old-fashioned weapon like a bow and arrow to kill Mr. Rawlins."

"Maybe he was Saab-in Hood," I innocently suggested.

Tina rolled her eyes, Randy emitted a tiny groan, and I was relieved to see Ash smile slightly.

I turned to my wife. "Where was the car when you first saw it?"

Ash thought for a second. "About halfway down the driveway. It was dark and I wanted to make sure the gravel driveway wasn't the road leading up the mountain that Chet was on. So I slowed down and used my car's spotlight. When the light hit the Saab, it took off like a rocket."

"Which way was the car facing?"

"Toward me."

"So it was leaving the house when you arrived."

"Maybe, but I can't say whether it was moving or not when I first saw it."

"Did you get a look at the driver?" Tina asked.

"No, it all happened so fast and I think the windows were tinted." Ash sounded irritated. "The Saab sideswiped me as it came out of the driveway. Then it was off to the races."

"And was this a newer-model car?"

"I'm not an expert, but I'd have to say it was very new. A four-door."

"Probably the Nine-Five Sedan," Tina said meditatively. Then, when she saw that Ash and I were gaping at her as if she'd begun speaking in Swedish, she demanded, "What?"

"Since when have you been an expert on Saabs?" Ash asked.

"Well . . . Sergei and I were in Charlottesville last weekend and we stopped at the dealership. He's kind of thinking about trading in his pickup truck for something . . ."

"With enough seats for you *and* your kids?"

Tina smiled shyly.

Ash said, "Oh, that's wonderful. I'm so happy that everything is going well for you and Sergei."

Sergei Zubatov was my best friend in Remmelkemp Mill, but I hadn't been seeing as much of him since June, when he began dating Tina. Back during the cold war, Sergei had been a member of Soviet military intelligence, otherwise known as the GRU. Nowadays, he owned and operated Pinckney's Brick Pit restaurant, home of some of the finest North Carolina–style barbecue you'll ever find.

"Whoa. I can't believe Sergei is trading in his four-wheel-drive behemoth for a family car. What's next, a trip to Disney World?" I asked with an incredulous laugh.

Tina suddenly wore a deer-in-the-headlights expression. She shot a panicked glance at Ash, who quickly said, "*I* didn't tell him!"

Realizing I'd inadvertently uncovered a secret, I grinned and said, "No! Sergei — our lovable cynic, Sergei — in the Magic Kingdom? Oh, Tina, you have to get me a picture of him wearing Mickey Mouse ears. I'm begging you. Name your price and I'll write the check when we get home."

"And now you know why we kept it a secret from you." Ash squeezed my hand warningly.

Despite the gloom, I could see that Tina looked genuinely troubled. "Sergei knew that if you found out, you'd tease him unmercifully."

"And you're nervous that if I torment him too much, he might change his mind about the trip? Don't worry, Tina. If it's that important to you, I can keep my mouth shut," I said.

Ash gave my hand another squeeze coupled with an amused look that said, *I suppose there's always a first time for everything.* I wasn't insulted. The truth is I have a bad habit of putting my mouth in gear before engaging my brain.

Tina relaxed slightly. "Thanks. Now, getting back to the Saab that Ash was chasing . . ."

"And lost," Ash muttered. "I'll check the Saab website when we're done here to confirm whether it was a Nine-Five model."

"What about the license plate?" I asked. "You said you didn't think it was from Virginia."

"I'm pretty sure it wasn't, but all I can tell you is that it had a white background with either black or dark blue letters."

"And the Three-Bravo-Juliet sequence?"

"You remember the partial plate?" Ash

was surprised.

"I pay very close attention when my wife announces that she's chasing a car on a rainy highway at a hundred miles an hour."

"Yes, Three-Bravo-Juliet were the first three characters on the plate. I'm certain of that."

"Lots of cops wouldn't have even gotten that much information. You did a good job."

"If you say so." However, Ash obviously wasn't convinced.

Tina turned to the game warden. "Randy, you can clear if you want and send me your report in the morning."

"Thanks, but I think I should hang loose until animal control gets here. He may need a hand with Longstreet," said Randy, glancing meaningfully toward the house, where the dog was still barking.

"Rain's letting up a little," I said. "If you don't mind, I'd like to go over and take a look at our victim while you guys get the camera and evidence collection kit from the car."

"Meet you there," said Tina as she, Ash, and Randy headed for the sheriff's patrol car.

Pulling up the hood of my parka, I limped across the yard and around an intervening fat cluster of yew bushes, toward the spot where the dead body lay. Although there was some illumination from the patrol car's headlights, I turned my flashlight on for a better look. If Everett Rawlins was only a year older than Ash, that made him forty-nine, but his sparse gray hair and weather-creased face made him look much older . . . almost as old as I looked. I guess both farming — like him — and getting shot — like me — have a way of prematurely aging you.

Everett Rawlins lay diagonally across the driveway on his back, with his left arm outstretched and his right hand on his upper abdomen, an inch or so away from the arrow that protruded from his chest. Taking a closer look at the left hand, I was surprised to see a simple gold wedding band on the victim's ring finger. Nobody had mentioned that Rawlins was married, and I wondered where his wife was.

There wasn't much blood showing, and I couldn't tell whether that was because he'd bled internally or because the rain had washed the gore from the gravel. The dead man's head faced toward the house, while his feet were pointed in the direction of a black wall of tall pine trees that stood on the east perimeter of the yard about thirty yards away. Based on the body's position, it looked to me as if the arrow that had killed him might have come from the evergreens, which made sense. It was an ideal spot to ambush someone coming out of the house.

The victim's wet clothing also told a tale. Rawlins wore blue jeans, a threadbare plaid flannel shirt, and relatively clean work boots. He wasn't dressed for the wet and chilly weather, which likely meant he hadn't intended to be outside for very long.

As Ash, Tina, and Randy arrived with the evidence collection gear, I said, "Hey, I see he's wearing a wedding ring. What do you know about his wife?"

"Her name was Lois; she died a couple of years ago," said Tina.

"Everett's girlfriend from high school, Lois Wetterstedt?" Ash asked.

"I guess. They were married a long time."

"Just to satisfy my morbid curiosity, what was her COD?" I asked. COD stood for *cause of death.*

"Bad luck. The winter before you and Ash moved here, we had a really bad ice storm."

Randy Kent nodded in agreement. "It was nasty. There was so much ice, some folks were stuck in their homes for a week."

"Lois Rawlins went out to the barn for some reason and a huge tree limb all loaded with ice fell on her." Tina hooked a thumb toward a large deciduous tree with an asymmetrical array of naked branches. "I'd like to think she died instantly, but . . ."

"Oh, how horrible," Ash murmured.

Tina looked down at the dead man. "Mr. Rawlins was out in one of his fields, taking forage to his longhorns, so he didn't find her until he came home later that afternoon."

I grimaced. "Talk about walking into a nightmare."

"Yep. He started blaming himself and never stopped."

"Poor Everett," said Ash. "Did they have any kids?"

"Just one son, Kurt. If I remember correctly, he lives somewhere in northern Virginia, near D.C.," said Tina.

Using my cane for support, I slowly knelt on the wet gravel to take a closer look at the arrow. I'd never seen anything like it. I was expecting the sort of wooden projectile I'd shot at hay bales during summer camp almost forty years earlier, but this arrow's shaft was slate-gray and looked metallic. Then something else caught my eye. The passage of the arrow through the shirt hadn't left a clean hole in the fabric. Instead, there were four small cuts in the flannel that radiated outward at ninety-degree angles from the shaft.

Randy crouched down beside me. "Something catch your eye?"

"These little cuts." I pointed to where the arrow protruded from the shirt. "They almost remind me of the kind of stellate tearing you usually see on a contact gunshot wound."

The game warden grunted. "I'll wager this is a broadhead arrow. Think of a hollow arrowhead made out of four reinforced razor blades coming to a sharp point."

"Which would account for the slices in the fabric."

"Uh-huh. You use broadheads when you're hunting bear or other big game."

"Such as humans, in this case. Sounds lethal."

"They are. I won't be surprised if we find this arrow went straight through him."

"Turned into a shish kebab. That's a hell of a way to die . . . not that there are any good ones." I pushed myself to my feet. "Where would you buy arrows like that?"

"Any one of a dozen hunting-supply stores in this part of the valley," said Randy, standing up, too. "Hardcore bow hunters usually buy the individual parts and make their own. But, like I said before, I've never known Chet to use a bow."

"So tell me, just what sort of animals did

Chet hunt for around here?"

"There's deer all over the mountains, but I'm assuming he came to Ev's land looking for black bears."

"Why would they be here?" Ash asked.

"There's an old sand quarry down that road." The game warden pointed toward a dirt lane that led from the farmyard. "It's been abandoned since the nineteen sixties, and the bears hibernate there."

I said, "And it sounds as if Chet came here repeatedly, which raises an interesting question: Just how many dead bears does a guy need?"

"You aren't going to believe this, but there's a huge market for bear gallbladders." The disgust was palpable in Randy's voice. "The organs are used to make snake-oil cures for male impotence. I can't prove that Chet is the one doing it, but . . ."

"You've found dead bears that have been gutted," I guessed sourly. It was a foolishly sentimental notion, but I've loved bears ever since Ash began making teddy bears. Yeah, I know they're wild animals, that *Gentle Ben* was just a TV show, and that hunting is supposed to be a sport. But the idea of killing one of those magnificent creatures for no other purpose than to harvest an organ was just obscene.

"I've found a few. The rangers up in the national park have found others," said Randy.

"Oh, that's just vile," said Ash as Tina nodded in agreement.

"It's easy to blame Chet, but he wouldn't be out here if there weren't customers," said Randy.

"That's the same excuse dope dealers use," I sighed, then motioned toward the line of pine trees. "I don't know a thing about archery. How difficult a shot would it have been to hit Everett from there?"

"That's almost point-blank range for an experienced bow hunter," Randy replied. "And here's something else to consider: It's dark, so you can't see it from here, but a hill begins just beyond those trees . . . the same hill where I saw Chet jump into his truck."

Tina peered at the trees. "You think that's where Mr. Lincoln was hiding?"

"It looks as if Rawlins was facing in that direction when the arrow hit, but that doesn't necessarily mean anything. For all we know, he might have managed a couple of steps before he fell," I said.

"But if Mr. Lincoln was lying in wait there, that shows premeditation —" began Tina.

"Which would turn a 'hunting accident' into first-degree murder," Ash finished. Hanging her head a little, she continued in a chastened voice, "I'm beginning to think maybe I was wrong about the Saab being involved."

I put my hand on her shoulder. "Honey, it's way too early to rule anything out, especially since we have no proof that Chet has any skill with a bow and arrow."

Tina's portable radio squawked, and she pulled it from her belt to listen to the message. She acknowledged the call and then turned to us. "The animal control guy is here. You want to get started with the crime scene photographs while Randy and I help corral Longstreet?"

"Sounds good," I said.

"Be careful," Ash added.

Ash opened a black nylon case and handed me the department's new Nikon digital camera. I'd have been just as happy working with old-fashioned film, but I could see the advantages of going digital. The new camera allowed you to review each photo as you took it, and best of all, the pictures would be ready just as soon as we could get to the computer at the sheriff's office. Back when I started in cop work, you might wait the better part of a day before the photo lab developed your crime scene pictures.

Longstreet shifted his barking into overdrive as Tina, Randy, and the animal control officer went into the house. Meanwhile, I leaned my cane against the patrol car and began snapping orientation photographs of Rawlins's body, while Ash kept notes of each picture I took. It started to sprinkle again as I moved in for some closer shots of the victim. Suddenly, the barking stopped and I relaxed a little when there was no scream of pain followed by gunfire.

As I bent to take a photo of Rawlins's boots, Ash said, "Maybe I'm just not cut out for police work."

"Huh?" I lowered the camera to look at her.

"After the pursuit, I got so jittery, my hands were trembling."

"That's just adrenaline palsy, sweetheart. It used to happen to me all the time. What's more, you didn't sound scared during the pursuit."

"I didn't?" Her face brightened.

"No." I reached out to brush my fingers against her cheek. "You did a great job and I'm proud of you."

"I just wish your leg were well enough so that we could work a patrol car together."

"Probably a bad idea, honey. We'd always

be looking for a place to park and neck. Now, I'd better get back to work." Inching forward with my legs spread on either side of the body, I moved into a position where I could take an overhead shot of Rawlins's chest wound. I took the picture and then said, "Hmm, this is interesting."

"What's that?"

"You don't really notice it until you stand right over him, but this arrow came in at a slight downward angle. You see?"

Ash moved so that our heads were close enough that I could smell her Pure Grace perfume. At last, she said, "You're right. It's at a definite angle. Whoever shot the arrow was at a slightly higher elevation than Everett."

"Or the arrow was on the downward portion of an arc, which would have to mean it was a long-distance shot. That's hard to imagine in this darkness."

Ash gave me a supporting hand as I carefully stepped away from the body. Then she glanced at the tree line and said, "Those pines are at the same level as the rest of the yard. The arrow probably *wasn't* shot from there."

"I agree. So, where the hell did it come from?" I scanned the yard.

"How about the second-floor window of

the barn? No, that's too high."

"We'll check it out, though. But I'm beginning to think it came from somewhere near the bottom of that hill." I pointed to an invisible spot in the blackness, just above the tops of the pine trees. "Which is just down the slope from where Chet parked his truck."

FOUR

There was shouting from inside the Rawlins house, and then the front door sailed open with a window-rattling crash. Longstreet was first through the door, followed immediately by the animal control guy, who was desperately trying to maintain his grip on the steel catchpole. The huge dog was furious over the tightening noose around his neck and turned to snap at the kennel cop. A second later, Longstreet saw us standing over his fallen master and things looked as if they were about to go from bad to worse.

The snarling Rottweiler started in our direction, his progress slowed only slightly by the animal control officer, who couldn't find any firm footing on the gravel. Randy darted forward to give the guy a hand as Tina yanked her gun from its holster and prepared to shoot the dog if it attacked us. Meanwhile, I was desperately trying to remember if I had one of Kitch's Milk-Bones in my coat pockets.

"He's just scared and upset," said Ash. Squaring her shoulders, she took several steps toward Longstreet and then stopped and put her hands on her hips. The dog stopped, looked up at her, and seemed to relax a little.

My wife, the dog whisperer, I thought admiringly. Ash had grown up in a home full of large dogs, and during our marriage we'd owned a husky and then a Bernese mountain dog before we'd gotten Kitch. Every one of our four-footed furry kids suffered from selective deafness when it came to me, but they always listened to Ash. She was the pack leader.

Ash held out her hand. "Give me the catchpole."

"I don't think that's such a good idea, ma'am," said the animal control officer.

"It'll be all right. He can tell that you're scared of him."

"You're damn right I'm scared of him."

"Well, I'm not. Now, give me the catch-pole," said Ash.

The animal control guy shot a nervous glance at Tina, who reluctantly nodded. He handed the steel pole to Ash as Randy backed away. Longstreet was panting hard

53

now, and it was obvious that the noose around his neck was too tight. Ash pressed the release mechanism on the catchpole to loosen the cable a little. The dog didn't try to attack her or escape. Instead, Longstreet looked up at Ash with coal-black eyes that were both sad and grateful. I began to relax and noticed that Tina had holstered her pistol.

"We need to let him go over and smell Everett," said Ash. "After that, I'll take him out to the truck."

I slowly backed away from the body as Ash led the Rottweiler over to the corpse. Longstreet snuffled the body and then nudged Rawlins's left shoulder with his broad muzzle. The dog whined when his master didn't respond. A few moments earlier, I'd been frightened of the dog; now, I felt sorry for him. Ash bent over to scratch Longstreet between the shoulder blades and quietly tell him that his daddy knew he was a good dog. Then she led the docile Rottweiler away from the dead man and down the driveway. Randy and the animal control officer followed them at a discreet distance.

Tina came over to me and I said, "That was nearly a doggone tragedy."

She ignored the pun. "It's also another example of why I need Ash as a full-time deputy."

"Yeah, she is something special, isn't she? But Ash doesn't want to become a full-time cop. I'm sorry, Tina. I don't know what to tell you."

"How about that *you're* interested in the job? Even with your bad leg, I'd rather have you than any of the duds who've been applying for the position," Tina said with a heavy sigh.

"Thanks, I think."

Tina winced. "That's not how I meant it."

"I know, relax. This whole deputy thing is going to work out. Now, I want you to look at something very interesting."

I was showing Tina the slight downward angle of the arrow in Rawlins's chest when Ash and Randy returned. Both of them looked unruffled and — more important — unbitten, so I assumed that they'd secured Longstreet without incident. The game warden crouched down to take a look at the arrow and, after a moment's inspection, agreed with us. The killer had likely been somewhere on the lower slope of the hillside when he'd fired the arrow.

"We need to search that hillside for evidence, but I don't see how we can do it tonight," said Tina. "It's just too dark."

"So we come back early tomorrow morning, when I can at least see what I'm trip-ping over," I said.

"What next, then?" asked Ash.

"Well, we don't need to take any more photos of Everett until the ME gets here. I'd suggest we get some pictures of the inside of the house," I said.

Randy pulled a folded sheet of paper from his coat pocket and handed it to Tina. "I figured you'd want the hard copy of Chet's driver's license and vehicle info. The physi-cal description is still pretty accurate, except for the black hair. It's all gone now."

Tina turned on her flashlight to look at the sheet. "I see he lists a Remmelkemp Mill P.O. box for his address. Where does he actually live?"

"On Shawnee Camp Road, over on the east slope of Massanutten Mountain," Randy said. "He has a single-wide mobile home out in the woods near the end of the road. I know he probably won't be there, but I'm going to swing by his place on my way home."

"Call us if you see him," said Tina.

"Count on it. Oh, and a word to the wise if and when you do visit Chet's house . . ."

"What's that?"

"Chet is as bald as a cue ball, but nobody is ever gonna confuse him for Mr. Clean.

You'll smell the house before you see it, so you might want to wear a hazmat suit." Randy's tone suggested that he was only half joking. The game warden then gave us a casual wave and headed down the driveway.

Tina said, "I'll stay out here with the body, if you guys want to look for any evidence in the house."

"Sounds good," I said.

"Before we go inside, let's take a walk around the exterior," said Ash. "Someone I love once told me that we don't know how large the crime scene is until we look."

The rain started to come down harder as we went to the front of the house. Even in the dim light, I could see evidence that this had been a well-maintained home. The porch was tidy and the custom front door featured a large oval of leaded and stained glass configured to look like a white rose. Even the vinyl siding looked fairly new. I took some photos and then headed around the corner of the house.

Now that we were out of Tina's hearing range, I said, "You did a great job there with Longstreet."

"It wasn't *that* big a deal," said Ash.

"Sorry, love, but I've got to disagree. So does Tina. That's why she's thinking about

57

offering you the full-time deputy's position again."

We stopped to look at the side of the house. There wasn't much to see. Just four windows, more white vinyl, and a row of plump holly bushes growing in the flower-bed next to the house. I handed Ash my cane and took some photos while waiting for my wife to say something.

Ash finally said, "Brad, honey, I really enjoy being an auxiliary cop and I know that Tina is having trouble finding a new deputy, but I just don't want the job."

"Why not?"

"Why not?" Ash has a way of cocking her head and gaping at me when I've said something she considers irredeemably stupid. "For twenty-five years the only times we saw each other were on weekends — when you weren't called out to some murder — or when you took vacation. And how often were those canceled because you were needed at a homicide trial?"

"More times than I'd care to remember," I said quietly.

"Don't feel bad. It's simply the way things were. But now I have the chance to be with you, and that's all I really want. Besides, I want to open Ursa Major with you, and I couldn't do that if I were working as a full-time deputy."

Ursa Major was our proposed name for the teddy bear shop and museum we wanted to open. The idea for the business was Ash's brainchild. She'd unexpectedly come up with the notion back in late September, while dusting some of the antique and award-winning bears from our collection. Ash had idly commented that it was a shame other people couldn't enjoy our bears, which sparked an epiphany. A few days and obviously a great deal of thought later, she revisited the issue and revealed to me her plan to open a teddy bear emporium that would double as a museum. The business would primarily feature stuffed animals made by the Massanutten Teddy Bear Artist Guild, a crafting club she'd established the previous year, but would also carry a selection of bears made by some of our favorite artists. Her hope was that Ursa Major would become both a tourist attraction and a successful bear shop.

I was skeptical at first, but her enthusiasm won me over and we developed a business plan. Things had progressed quickly, and we'd identified a possible site for our business — an abandoned Victorian-era home on the outskirts of Remmelkemp Mill. We'd already toured the house once and planned to meet the real estate agent tomorrow to take a second look at the property.

Ash took my hand. "I enjoy working patrol once a week as an auxiliary, but I don't want to give up the freedom to pursue our dreams. I've waited too long for this part of our lives."

"Was it worth the wait?"

Ash leaned over to kiss me on the cheek. "Absolutely. Now, let's get back to work."

We walked around to the back of the house, where we found what I assumed was Everett Rawlins's Ford F-250 pickup truck parked a few yards from the back door.

Ash nodded toward the truck. "When we searched the house for other victims and suspects, I checked the hood. It was cold, so he hadn't driven anywhere for a while."

I took a couple of photographs, and then we moved to the east side of the house, which faced toward the mountains. Again, there wasn't much that was noteworthy. There were another four windows, an electric utility box, and some more holly bushes. The only thing that even slightly caught my eye was a bit of damage in the vinyl siding, about six-and-a-half feet up the wall and near the front corner. It looked as if the bracket from a flag holder had once been mounted there and then been torn off by high winds. The same thing had happened at our house, back during the late spring when a hellacious thunderstorm struck the region. I took several pictures of the wall, and then we returned to the front of the house.

We mounted the porch steps and went into the home, where we were greeted by both the faint spicy smell of what was probably chili and the sound of Liza Minnelli and Joel Grey singing a sardonic ditty about the joys of money. There was a coat closet near the front door and I opened the door. Inside, I saw a pump-action shotgun leaning against the interior wall.

"Well, that's one way to handle annoying door-to-door solicitors," I said, taking a picture of the weapon.

"Actually, it's pretty common for folks to have a weapon like that handy," said Ash. "Back when I was growing up, we still had bear on our side of the river. Daddy kept a double-barreled shotgun in our front closet."

"You want to check to see if it's loaded?"

Ash nodded and removed the firearm from the closet. As she began removing cartridges from the shotgun, she said, "It's a twelve-gauge, loaded with rifle slugs."

"Which will make a doughnut-sized hole

in a man. So why didn't Ev take his minia-ture antitank gun with him when he went outside?"

"Because he was in a hurry?"

"Or didn't feel there was a threat."

"So maybe we're back to this being a hunting accident?"

"It's way too early to tell, my love. But you know how much I hate a mystery."

Ash worked the gun's pump mechanism to ensure she'd removed all the rounds. "What do you want me to do with this stuff?"

"Put the shotgun back in the closet and the rounds on the upper shelf. We'll collect it as possible evidence later."

We went into the living room, where, as expected, the sofa and easy chair faced in the direction of the television. I noted a small logo in the lower right-hand corner of the screen that indicated it was tuned to the Turner Classic Movies channel, which was airing *Cabaret.* A rectangular end table stood next to the easy chair and on it was a television remote control, a copy of *TV Guide,* a nearly empty bottle of Yingling beer, and a soup bowl that was about half-full of what looked like canned chili. *A lonely man's lonely meal,* I thought. Leaning against the inside rim of the bowl was a spoon, which suggested Mr. Rawlins had been interrupted during his supper.

Nodding toward the TV, I said, "So what's wrong with this picture?"

"How do you mean?" Ash asked.

"*Cabaret*? You knew Everett Rawlins. Does that seem like the kind of movie he — or any other guy around here — would watch?"

"As a matter of fact, no. That probably means he was watching something else when he went outside."

"Exactly, which might help us establish a tentative timeline." I took several photographs of the room and then picked up the *TV Guide*. Finding the listing for Thursday night, I said, "*Cabaret* started at seven. Before that, it was *She Wore a Yellow Ribbon*. Interesting choice for a double feature."

"Is that a John Wayne movie?"

"Yeah. It's a classic guy film from an era when that didn't mean it was full of car crashes, naked bimbos, and jokes about flatulence."

"Well, John Wayne definitely sounds more like the sort of movie Everett would watch." Ash looked thoughtful. "So, we've probably narrowed down the time of death to between five-forty-five and sometime before the movie ended at seven P.M."

"Yep." I leaned over to press the mute button on the TV remote. "Do you see anything else significant?"

"The unfinished dinner . . . if you can call a beer and canned chili a dinner. Poor Everett. He probably never learned to cook, and with Lois gone . . ."

"He made whatever was easiest. This guy was living my worst nightmare," I sighed, suddenly recalling how close I'd come to losing Ash back in September when we were visiting California. "Anyway, something made him get up and leave his meal to go outside."

"Maybe he saw Chet's headlights up on the ridge."

"From this chair?" I sat down in the recliner and craned my neck to look out the adjoining window. "You might be able to see the bottom of the hill from here, but not the upper part. The porch roof is in the way."

Ash turned and headed for the kitchen. "Maybe there's another explanation." I pushed myself up from the chair and followed her. "What have you got?"

"Take a look at this." Ash pointed to some items on the white tile counter. "The kitchen is pretty clean. Yet we've got a crumpled-up, chili-stained paper napkin and an unopened bottle of beer."

"Which might mean he was in the kitchen getting another bottle of liquid bread when things went south. Good obs."

Ash leaned over the counter to look out the window. "Maybe not. You can't see the upper part of the hill from here either. The porch roof is still in the way. Could that mean Everett saw someone in his yard?"

"And that person ran to the hill? That fits the evidence we have right now, but . . ."

"What?"

"If you're going to ambush someone, do you make a point of ensuring that your victim sees you before you spring the trap?"

"Brad, honey, none of this adds up."

"I know, so we keeping digging until it does. Now, if you'll move, I'll get some pictures of the kitchen."

I completed the photos, and then we moved on to the dining room, the laundry room, and then what looked to be Rawlins's office at the back of the house. Unlike the kitchen, the office wasn't tidy. Paperwork was piled in haphazard stacks on the desk and chairs and in front of the dark computer monitor.

"Ransacking?" Ash asked.

"No, it's too neat for that. It looks more as if he was trying to find some kind of document." I pointed to the open drawer on an old metal filing cabinet.

"I'll bet Lois handled all the bills and paperwork."

"Which probably meant he didn't know where anything was."

I photographed the office, and then we started upstairs. I don't move fast under the best of circumstances, and stairs slow me down to the speed of a DMV clerk. Ash took my cane and I kept a death grip on the banister as I carefully mounted each step. The slow journey to the second floor afforded me a glimpse of the Rawlins family's life in an array of framed photos on the wall. There was a faded color portrait of Everett and Lois's wedding, a picture of a much younger Everett wearing a navy uniform, a shot of a grinning Lois holding an enormous pumpkin, and several photos of a boy I assumed was their son, Kurt, as he grew up.

Upstairs, we checked the master bedroom, the bathroom, and Kurt's boyhood bedroom. We didn't find anything that qualified as murder evidence, but we did locate a .357 magnum revolver in Rawlins's nightstand drawer. However, the handgun was unloaded, which suggested Rawlins hadn't considered himself in any sort of danger.

There was a buzz of static, and then Tina's voice sounded from Ash's portable radio. "Mike-One to Mike-Eleven, can you come out? The ME just arrived."

Ash keyed the mike and said, "We're on our way out."

We went downstairs and out into the yard, where the commonwealth's medical examiner's van was now parked behind Ash's patrol car. Tina and another dark-haired woman were standing in the gentle rain beside the van. As we got closer, I recognized the ME as Dr. Dolly Grice, whom we'd met the previous year when I'd discovered a murder victim at the local history museum. Grice had impressed me as intelligent, observant, and prone to the macabre humor common among those who routinely deal with the dead. We shook hands with the ME and then went over to Rawlins's body.

Dr. Grice did a double take when she saw the murder victim. "Whoa! So, where is the *rest* of the Seventh Cavalry?"

"I take it you haven't seen many people killed this way?" Tina asked.

"Actually, I've handled a couple deaths where arrows were the COD, but I've never seen one where the arrow was still sticking out of the body. The other hunters always yank it out and try to stop the bleeding."

Dolly pulled out a camera and snapped two photos.

"Which brings up something we hadn't considered," I said. "Even if this began as an accident, it turned into a crime when whoever shot the arrow didn't render first aid or call for the paramedics."

"And that makes it manslaughter," said Tina.

Dr. Grice put her camera back into her satchel and then knelt to examine the body. "I'm just speculating, but this looks like a Cupid-from-hell shot, right into the base of the heart. The victim was probably dead within a few seconds."

"If he was shot in the heart, how come there isn't much blood?" Ash asked.

"It's probably all still in his chest cavity. Internal exsanguination." The ME shifted her position and began pulling on a pair of latex gloves. "Can someone give me a hand here?"

I began to clap, but stopped when Ash gave me an I-can't-believe-you're-doing-that look. She said, "How can we help?"

"You can start by telling your husband to behave," Dr. Grice said with a chuckle.

"I've tried. It doesn't work."

The ME tossed Ash a pair of latex gloves. "Then help me roll our victim over a little.

68

I want to see if we've got a through-and-through wound."

Ash immediately knelt on the gravel near the corpse. It was a rewarding moment for me. The last time we'd processed a murder scene, she'd been somewhat squeamish about touching the dead body. It was a natural reaction, but Ash obviously intended to conquer that weakness. The two women carefully rolled Rawlins over onto his left side, revealing the dead man's back. There was no sign of blood or of the arrowhead protruding from the shirt. Ash continued to hold the body on its side until Dr. Grice and I finished our photographs.

"That's kind of strange." Dolly sounded thoughtful. "In every other case I've worked like this, there was evidence that the arrow made at least a partial exit from the opposite side of the body."

"What would account for this one not going through?" Tina asked.

Dr. Grice shrugged. "The only thing that makes sense to me is that maybe the arrow was fired from a significant distance, which would cause it to lose velocity."

"Less force equals less penetration," I agreed.

"Hopefully, we'll know more tomorrow morning, after the autopsy," said Dr. Grice, waving for her two attendants to come and prepare the body for transportation to the regional ME's office.

"It's going to be a little difficult getting him into a body bag," I said.

"Aren't you going to remove the arrow now?" Ash asked Dolly.

"No. I don't have the equipment to do it, and we might lose trace evidence. It's better for us to wait until the autopsy," the ME replied. "Oh, and Brad?"

"Yes, Dr. Grice?"

"I noticed that you didn't torture us with any of your usual bad puns. Are you running out of material?"

"No . . . no," I said pensively. "I just stopped because I thought it made me look like I was overconfident and full of myself. You know . . . arrow-gant."

FIVE

The two morgue techs swiftly manhandled the cadaver into the vinyl body bag, but the protruding arrow prevented them from zipping the bag shut. Then Dr. Grice came up with the clever idea of using the arrow as a support pole and draping a second body bag over Rawlins. The final result was grotesquely suggestive of a pup tent. It was a good thing I remembered the victim had been one of Ash's childhood friends before I wisecracked that Rawlins sure didn't look like a happy camper.

The attendants shifted the body onto a gurney and then lugged the stretcher to the van. Meanwhile, Dolly consulted her PDA and then told Tina the autopsy would be at 10:30 the following morning. Tina jotted the information down in her notebook.

Dr. Grice said, "Do we have contact info on next of kin?"

"Mr. Rawlins had a son named Kurt, who

I think lives in northern Virginia. I want to say in Fairfax, but I can't be sure," said Tina.

"There was an address book near the phone. You want me to go in and look?" Ash suggested. Tina nodded, and Ash jogged inside, then returned a minute later. Tearing a sheet from her notebook, she said, "Kurt lives in Merrifield."

Dr. Grice took the sheet from Ash. "That should be everything I need for now. We'll see you tomorrow, Sheriff."

As the ME van departed, Tina looked toward the expanse of blackness where the hill stood. "So we can't say for sure if we actually have a murder here."

"That's true, but we have to process the scene as if it were," I said.

"I know, but if the arrow was fired from a long way off, the hunter might not even have been aware he hit Mr. Rawlins." Tina turned to face us. "Maybe this *was* an accident."

"But that doesn't explain why the Saab was here and then took off," said Ash.

"Or what made him go out into his front yard at the precise moment some supposedly booze-soaked bow hunter let an arrow rip," I added. "Bottom line: It's too early for any conclusions. There's just way too much we don't know yet."

A cell phone began to trill, and Tina pulled the device from her coat pocket. She squinted at the tiny screen and then shyly said, "Let me take this call. I'll only be a second."

She took several steps toward the barn and quietly answered the phone. I glanced at my watch. It was slightly after nine, which meant Sergei had probably just arrived home after closing his restaurant for the night. She snapped the phone shut about a half minute later and rejoined us, looking pleased.

"That was Sergei," said Tina.

"From that happy look on your face, I'd have never guessed. So . . . what did you guys talk about?" I said teasingly.

"None of your business," Tina cheerfully replied. "But he wanted me to pass along a message to you, Ash. He needs a final count by tomorrow afternoon on the number of box lunches you're going to want for the teddy bear show."

It was Ash's idea to provide lunches for the artists participating in Saturday's Massanutten Mountain Teddy Jubilee, which was going to be held in her hometown of Remmelkemp Mill. It had been tough luring well-known bear makers to a newly established teddy bear festival, especially

73

when travel expenses were so high. So Ash had offered incentives such as low table fees and a free meal. It was a good plan, but I believe that most of the artists who'd decided to participate did so just because they liked Ash. Whatever their reasons for coming, the Teddy Jubilee was going to feature an impressive roster of attendees, including the award-winning Martha Burch, Donna Nielsen, Pam Kisner, and Darlene Allen.

Ash gently popped her forehead with her palm. "I meant to go by the restaurant and talk to Sergei earlier this evening."

"I told him that you'd been a *little* busy tonight," said Tina. "So, when do our out-of-state bear artists begin to arrive?"

Ash said, "I'm picking up Martha Burch at Dulles in the morning at eleven-thirty. That means I can only work a couple of hours tomorrow before I have to go."

"I'm assuming I'll have Brad, so it isn't a problem. Besides, I can't wait to meet Martha. The Ice King is just amazing."

Tina was referring to one of the stuffed animals in our collection. The Ice King was an exquisitely handsome polar bear dressed in blue regal clothing and wearing a sparkling crown made from faux ice crystals. We'd always loved and admired Martha's work, so I'd asked her to create the Ice King as a Christmas present for Ash. The bear instantly became one of the most cherished pieces in our collection, and it grew even more precious in the following months, when the Ice King had been nominated for both major American awards for teddy bear artists: the TOBY (Teddy Bear of the Year) and the Golden Teddy.

I said, "Yeah, I'm available almost all day. The only thing we have pending is an appointment at four with the real estate agent to look at that house again."

"God, I hope I'm back from the airport by then." Ash was becoming stressed.

"It's going be okay, honey."

Tina knew of our interest in the Victorian home and said, "It would be the perfect location for your shop."

I nodded. "We think so, too. But the price is still a little high. What's more, the place is going to require a huge amount of refurbishing, and I'm not exactly a handyman."

"Sergei and I will help."

"Thanks, Tina. That's good to know."

"And Daddy will lend us any kind of power tools we need," Ash added. Ash's parents live on the farm just to the west of our house. Her dad is Laurence AKA "Lolly" Remmelkemp — yep, the town is named after my wife's family — and he owns an amazing collection of power tools. Some are almost older than I am, but they all work.

"Since I'm not exactly a Tool Time sort of guy, I hope he hangs around to give me some pointers in their use," I said.

"Daddy will be happy to help. We won't need a stud finder, though." Ash gave me a sweet and chaste smile. "I'm already pretty good at that."

Usually, I'm the one delivering the double entendres, so it took a second or two for Ash's comment to register. I gave her a look of mock disapproval. "*You* have been hanging around me way too much."

"I'll say." Tina tried to sound scandalized, but the effect was spoiled by a giggle. "Now, I think we'd better get back to work. Is there evidence in the house that we need to collect?"

"Some, but nothing that looks really useful."

"We'll go get the evidence storage bags," said Ash.

We went back inside the house and I began by offering Tina our interpretation of the scene, including the apparent inconsistency of Rawlins being unable to see the upper slope of the hill from inside the home.

Tina couldn't make any more sense of it than we could as she walked from window to window peering out. After that, we collected the shotgun and ammunition from the closet as well as Rawlins's half-empty dinner bowl, the used paper napkin, and both beer bottles.

Ash said, "I realize why we want the shotgun, but does this other stuff have any evidentiary value?"

"Based on what we know right now, probably not. But it's better to be safe than sorry," I said.

We next went back to Everett Rawlins's office. Feeling my leg beginning to stiffen up and ache in the cool damp weather, I asked Ash to go beneath the desk to unplug the computer and unhook all the cables. She agreed and suggested I sit in the office chair for a few minutes. It was wise advice, but my first reaction was to put on a brave face and insist that I was fine. I'm a vain man and hate feeling as if I'm being a wimp. However, I also knew that if I pushed my leg tonight, I'd be in no shape to tackle our search of the hill the following morning. I sat down, reflecting yet again that being crippled sucks.

Tina gestured toward the piles of paperwork. "What about all this stuff? Should we bother collecting it?"

I swiveled the chair to face her. "It's your case and your call, but I think it's obvious that Mr. Rawlins was searching for something. If this does turn out to be a murder, our motive might be hiding in one of those stacks."

"Agreed. Let's collect it."

As Tina and Ash loaded the documents into a pair of cardboard boxes, I grabbed the computer and followed the two women as they lugged the boxes outside. The rain seemed to have all but stopped, and off to the west, a few glittering stars were visible through a gap in the clouds. It looked as if the modest storm was already clearing out.

Once we'd secured the evidence in the trunk of Tina's patrol car, Ash turned to me and said, "Honey, there isn't any point in you going up and down those stairs again. Why don't you stay here and photograph the damage to my car, while Tina and I go upstairs and get the gun?"

"I don't like admitting it, but that's a good idea. My shin is really beginning to ache," I said mournfully.

"I can tell. Sometimes you just push yourself too hard."

"I know, but that doesn't mean I have to be mature about it."

Ash patted my arm. "That's my Brad."

Tina and Ash went back into the house, and I began taking orientation photographs of my wife's patrol car. I moved to the right front fender and took some close-up shots of the comet-shaped dent. The police cruiser was predominantly white in color, which made it easy to see the dark blue paint transfers from the Saab. I decided to let the crime lab worry about collecting some of the tiny paint chips.

While examining the dented fender, I suddenly realized that I'd overlooked something. The angle of collision suggested that the left front part of the Saab had collided with Ash's unit. If so, there was a good chance that the Saab's headlight or running light might have been broken. Yet I hadn't even bothered to look for glass shards in the road when I'd arrived, even though I knew a crash had occurred there. Irritated that I'd violated my own maxim of never underestimating the size of the crime scene, I smacked my palm with my cane.

I heard Ash and Tina come out onto the porch and noticed that they'd extinguished all the house's interior lights. Tina locked the front door and came over to where I stood as Ash went to put the revolver in the other cruiser.

Tina said, "You noticed the paint transfers?"

"Yeah, but I'm not comfortable trying to recover them. Ash's car needs to be sent to the crime lab."

"That's what I figured. I'll get a flatbed wrecker to meet us at the station."

"Good, but before we do that, we need to go back out and take a close look at Kobler Hollow Road."

Ash rejoined us and asked, "Why?"

"There may still be some evidence out there. The paint can give us class characteristics, but it's almost impossible to link that transfer to a specific vehicle. However, broken headlight glass . . ."

Ash's eyes widened. "Oh! The Saab's left front headlight might have been smashed when it hit me."

"Exactly. If there's broken glass and if we find the Saab, the crime lab might be able to match some of the pieces."

"Then let's get to work," said Tina.

I walked back out to the road while Ash and Tina drove their patrol cars. The women parked their cars facing toward the general area where the collision occurred and then turned on their vehicles' high beams and door-mounted spotlights. But even with that illumination, we still needed our flashlights.

Dividing the road into three parallel search paths, we began our careful search for something I couldn't state with certainty would even be there. Fortunately, we got lucky.

Tina's search course ran down the middle of the road, and she was the first one to spot the constellation of broken glass pieces on the wet asphalt. She said, "Check this out. I'm pretty sure this is auto headlight glass."

We gathered around the debris and I said, "I think you're right."

Ash glanced over to where the driveway met the road. "And this is about where the Saab hit me."

"Great work, Tina. Now, let me get some photos and then we'll collect this stuff."

Once the glass fragments had been gathered up and packaged in an evidence envelope, Tina said, "So, what time do you want to come back out here tomorrow morning?"

"As early as possible. First light," I replied.

"I agree. No later than six-thirty," said Ash. "That way I'll have time to clean up before I leave for Dulles."

"Okay, then we'll meet here at zero-six-thirty. Go ahead and wear grubbies. There's no point in getting our uniforms filthy," said Tina.

We made our way back to the sheriff's

department, where I helped the women carry all the stuff we'd seized into the evidence room. Ash then glumly informed me that she had reports to write and that I should go home. Once she was finished with the paperwork, she'd catch a ride to our house with the midnight-shift deputy.

However, Tina told her to go home. My wife resisted the idea at first, but there was no point in Ash staying up half the night to write a homicide report for a death we couldn't say for sure was murder, especially when she was due back at work so early the following morning. Furthermore, Tina reminded Ash that we had the department's report-writing program loaded into our personal computer, and if she really needed to, she could write her reports in the comfort of home anyway. We both thanked Tina and headed for the SUV.

It was nearly eleven P.M. when we got home. I took Kitch out into the yard for his final potty call while Ash went upstairs to change out of her uniform. Once Kitch was finished, we went back upstairs, where I found Ash in our craft room examining Bear-atio. Her blond hair was now free from the constraining bun and she was wearing a pink flannel nightshirt.

She said, "*This* is very good work. Do you

think you'll have him finished by tomor-row?"

"I *am* done with him." I knew Ash was referring to Bear-atio not wearing any trousers, but I feigned puzzlement.

"Doesn't he need a pair of pants?"

"I don't see why. You like detectives without pants."

"I like *one* detective without pants." She put Bear-atio down and came over to give me a long, slow kiss. "But that's because I'm a stud finder. Now, let's go to bed."

Six

We were awakened at five-thirty A.M. by Andrea Bocelli's superb voice coming from our alarm clock/CD player. It was still dark outside and we could hear the waterfall-like sound of the wind as it rushed through the pine trees that stand on the ridge just west of our home. I glanced at the digital thermometer and noted that it was thirty-eight degrees outside. Winter was coming.

I fed Kitch, and then Ash and I ate a breakfast of country sausage, scrambled eggs, and toast made from ciabatta rolls. Knowing I was going to be on my feet for a minimum of a couple of hours, I took some ibuprofen and hoped the pills would suppress the pain in my shin for a little while. I felt guilty about putting Kitch back into his crate, so I let him do a prewash on the plates before putting them in the sink and promised him that we'd play in the yard when I got home.

Meanwhile, Ash went upstairs to put her police gun belt on over her jeans and grab her parka. She brought my cane and shoulder rig down with her, and I slipped the holster on. Then I grabbed my knit wool cap from the hat rack, and after saying final good-byes to Kitch, we went out to the SUV.

We drove to the Rawlins farm, where we found Tina's patrol car parked in front of the house. Now that it was almost daylight, I could see the hill that we'd been talking about the previous evening. It was closer than I'd envisioned, and I noted with dismay that the slope was covered with thick forest and what looked like dense undergrowth. With its palette of pine tree–green and mixture of autumnal orange, maroon, and russet, the hill was lovely — but I dreaded the impending hunt for evidence.

As we huddled in the yard, Ash asked, "Did anybody find the Saab?"

Tina shook her head. "There hasn't been a word about it. So, where do we want to start?"

I glanced up at the wooded knoll. "I hate to admit it, but there's no way I can help you search that hill. It wouldn't be more than thirty seconds before you'd have to call the rescue squad to come and carry me out."

"So why don't you take some more photos down here while Ash and I go up and take a look around?"

"I suppose that makes the most sense."

"The camera is on the front seat." Tina nodded toward her patrol car.

"And I'll leave you my portable radio so that we can stay in communication." Ash handed me her walkie-talkie.

"Yeah, just in case I have to be like that old lady in the TV commercial and yell, 'Help, I've fallen and I can't get up,' " I grumbled.

Ash rubbed my arm, and then she and Tina started toward the hill. I watched them until they'd moved beyond the line of evergreens and were lost to sight. Meanwhile, the sun began to rise over the Blue Ridge Mountains, flooding the yard with bright light. I retrieved the camera and got busy taking photos of the driveway, barn, and exterior of the house. Although I knew these daylight orientation photos were important, it still felt like make-work, especially when I failed to find any new evidence.

I'm not certain why, but when I finished the pictures I went over to the place where Lois Rawlins had died. The tree was enormous, with gnarled meandering branches that reminded me of the century-old chinquapin oak in our front yard by the river. Almost three years had passed since the tragedy, but it was easy to see the scar where the huge limb had broken off the trunk. I wondered how Everett Rawlins had withstood the sight of that tree day after day.

I was jolted from my sad reverie by Tina's voice crackling from the portable radio. "Mike-One to Mike-Fourteen."

Mike-Fourteen had been my radio designator since June of last year. I pulled the radio from my coat pocket. "Go ahead."

"Just a status check. How are you doing down there?"

"Just peachy," I grunted.

There was a moment of silence, and I knew that Tina was complaining to Ash about my improper choice of words for an official police radio transmission. Finally, she said, "Sorry, you were covered by static. Was that *peachy* with a *P* as in *Papa,* or *B* as in *Bravo?*"

When I figured out what Tina meant, I began to laugh. The last thing I'd expected from her was a zinging come-back. Keying the radio microphone, I said, "*B* as in *Bravo.* Sorry about that. How are you two doing?"

"We're about halfway up the hill and haven't seen anything yet."

87

"Copy. I'm done with the photos for now, so I'm going to take a look at the road that leads back to the sand quarry."

"Ten-Four. We'll call when we get to the place where Chet was parked."

I slipped the radio back into my coat pocket and walked over to the rutted lane that the game warden had pointed out last night. The narrow road ran past the barn and then appeared to loop left, around the southern base of the hill. The middle of the road was still dotted with brown puddles and looked muddier than a pre-election hit-piece mailer. I kept to the left shoulder of the lane, taking my time so that I didn't slip on the tall wet grass. I'd covered maybe a third of the distance to the curve when something caught my eye. There were tire impressions in the mud that suggested some sort of vehicle had driven down this road from the direction of the sand quarry and then made a U-turn to go back in the direction from which it had come. The marks also signified that at least one person had been on the road sometime after it began raining yesterday afternoon.

Just what we need — another piece of anomalous evidence, I thought.

I took a closer look at the tracks. It didn't look as if a full-sized car or truck had caused the muddy marks; the wheelbase track was too narrow. This indicated that a quad-runner or similar all-terrain vehicle might have left the tracks.

I pulled out the radio. "Mike-Fourteen to Mike-One, I think I've found something interesting."

"What's that?" Tina replied.

"ATV tracks in the mud, maybe fifty yards or so from the yard. They look like they came from the direction of the quarry and then go back the same way."

"Copy. I'm glad *you* found something, because we came up dry. We'll be there in a few minutes."

While waiting for the women to make their way down the hill, I took overview photos of the tire impressions. Then I checked the underbrush beside the road for other signs of evidence, but didn't find any.

The radio crackled again, and this time it was the day-shift dispatcher. "Mike-Control to Mike-One, we just got a call from the Massanutten Crest Lodge. Some lady staying there wants to report that her Saab was stolen from the hotel parking lot sometime last night."

"What's the victim's name?" Tina asked.

"Sherri Driggs. She's visiting here from Atlanta, and the car is an oh-eight Saab,

Nine-Five model, with Georgia plates of Three-Bravo-Juliet-Oscar-Zero-Zero-Six."

I knew Ash had to be relieved to know that her information about the hit-and-run vehicle's license plate was correct. The alphanumeric had indeed begun with the Three-Bravo-Juliet sequence. Furthermore, Georgia license plates had dark letters and numbers against a white background.

Tina said, "Got it. Send Mike-Three ASAP and tell him that I want a complete report and photographs of where the car was parked."

"Ten-Four."

"And call me immediately if the victim has any information about who might have taken the vehicle."

"Ten-Four."

We finally had a lead on the Saab, but the information merely added several more *whys* to an already baffling mix of unanswered questions. Around here, vehicle theft was still a rare crime, so why had someone stolen the Saab? Why had he gone to Rawlins's farm contemporaneous to the murder? And if you needed some hot wheels for a getaway car, why boost them from the Massanutten Crest Lodge, where the security was tight? It was the most luxurious hotel in the central Shenandoah Valley and only about six miles away, high on the eastern slope of Massanutten Mountain. In fact, Ash and Tina probably could have seen the castle-like upper ramparts of the hotel from the top of the hill they'd been searching.

A few moments later, I heard the rustling sound of footfalls coming through the underbrush. Ash and Tina emerged from the trees about thirty feet from where I stood. It was obvious they hadn't had an easy time of it on the hill. Both women had mud-stained knees, and their boots were caked with large wads of the claylike soil. They paused to scrape the worst of the mud from their boot soles on an old log and then joined me.

I said, "Well, here I am working my fingers to the bone, while you gals are out enjoying a mud bath at the spa."

Tina kicked another chunk of mud free from her boot. "You're a laugh riot, Brad. I should have let you go up there."

"I'd have *mud*dled through. I take it you didn't find any evidence?"

"Not a darn thing. But if someone *was* wandering around up there in the dark, I don't know how he did it without falling and breaking his neck."

Ash said, "You heard that last radio transmission?"

"Yeah, your Saab was a rollin' stolen," I replied. The expression was a California cop colloquialism.

"That explains why it took off the way it did," said Tina.

"But not why it was here last night in the first place. And here's some more confusing evidence." I pointed to the tire impressions.

Tina squinted at the tracks. "So, whoever was on the quad-runner came here after it was raining."

"Yeah, but since I can't find any shoe impressions, we can't say for sure that he ever got off the ATV."

"Still, that means there was someone else on Everett's land besides Chet and whoever was driving the Saab," said Ash.

"That's how it looks," I said.

"I think we should see where the tracks lead," said Tina.

"Me, too. But you should probably also contact the state crime lab and have one of their techs come up here to make plaster castings of the tire impressions."

Tina frowned, and I knew she didn't like the idea of asking for help from another agency. "Can't we do that ourselves?"

I shook my head. "We want an expert for this. I haven't poured a casting in over seven years and I'm not even certain I remember the exact formula to make the stuff."

Tina used her phone to call the sheriff's dispatcher and told her to notify the crime lab that we needed an evidence tech ASAP. Snapping the phone shut, she said, "She'll call us once the lab gives her an ETA on the tech."

"I'll go get the tape," said Ash, as she turned and headed back toward the house. She returned a minute later with the roll of yellow tape and wearing a look of concern. "Tina, there's a reporter from the Harrisonburg newspaper out there."

"Oh, great," Tina muttered.

"And if the paper has found out about this, then you can bet the TV news will be here any minute," I said.

"I guess I'd better go talk to them." Tina sounded as if she were agreeing to undergo a root canal without anesthetic.

"And we'll tape off the road and try to follow the ATV tracks," said Ash. "You can catch up when you're done."

Tina trudged back to the house along the edge of the road while Ash and I blocked off the road with crime scene tape. We began to follow the road toward the quarry. It was a slow journey. I stopped every few feet to take another photo of the tracks in the mud.

The road curved around the base of the hill and then seemed to head straight for the Blue Ridge Mountains. I heard what sounded like rushing water from somewhere ahead. It was still fairly breezy, so my first thought was that it was simply the wind blowing through the pine forest. Then we saw the abandoned sand quarry ahead, and I realized I was wrong.

Ash gasped. "Lord, this is beautiful."

Even allowing for the rusting metal derrick and the ancient vegetation-covered bulldozer, the place *was* beautiful. The quarry had been located at the bottom of the Blue Ridge, right next to a rushing mountain stream that looked as if it belonged in a beer commercial. You could still faintly see where the digging equipment had hacked into the side of the mountain, but over the intervening fifty years since the plant had ceased operation, trees and other vegetation had reclaimed the slopes. The forest was slowly erasing the obscenity.

"Why would you put a freaking quarry here?" I asked.

"Because Everett's daddy could make money selling sand. Folks had a different attitude about the land back then," Ash replied.

"Well, thank goodness times have

changed."

I took some photographs of the quarry, and then we resumed our pursuit of the muddy tracks. The dirt road ended abruptly at a large patch of gravel near the base of the metal platform, but Ash found where the tracks resumed close to the hill. It looked as if the ATV had gone up a narrow and rugged trail that climbed the hill while paralleling the stream.

"I think you'd better let me go on from here," said Ash.

"I'm afraid you're right, honey. One false step — and that happens to me about every seven seconds — and I'd be whitewater rafting without the raft," I said. "Here. Take the camera and be careful."

"I will. Don't worry." Ash gave me a quick kiss on the cheek and then scrambled up the slope.

She disappeared into the forest, yet I continued to look up the hill for another minute or two. Finally, I decided that searching the quarry for any further signs of evidence would be a better use of my time. I headed back over to the derrick and then took a look at the vine-choked bulldozer, which also seemed to have a cedar sapling growing up out of the left set of treads. Then I wandered over to the stream. That was when I heard a throaty grunt immediately followed by what I hoped wasn't the clack of teeth.

The sound had come from my left. I slowly turned in that direction and then froze as a large example of *Ursus americanus,* AKA the black bear, emerged from the undergrowth about twenty-five yards away. Even though I've collected teddy bears for years and used to take my kids to the San Francisco Zoo to look at the bears, I'd never been so close to the genuine article, especially without an intervening fence and moat.

I was terrified, but only for a moment. Then I realized the bear was swiftly lumbering on all fours toward the stream. He — well, I guess it was a he, and I wasn't going to get closer to check — seemed more frightened of me than I was of him. That was only natural, I suppose. Bears don't hunt humans and cut out *their* gallbladders. Anyway, I watched in rapt fascination as the bear splashed through the brook and vanished into the woods. It was a bright and life-affirming moment in an otherwise grim morning spent investigating a violent death.

I was still staring across the stream when Ash returned from the trail. She asked, "Brad, honey, are you all right?"

"I'm fine. No, I'm great. I just saw a black bear," I replied.

"What?"

"I guess I spooked it." I pointed toward the foliage where I'd first seen the bear. "It was hiding over there and then it ran across the stream. My God, he was magnificent."

Ash peered into the forest in the same direction I'd been looking a moment before. "I'm sorry I missed him."

"So am I. And you know something? I've never been interested in making a realistic-looking teddy bear, but now . . ."

"I understand exactly what you mean," said Ash. Years ago, she'd been inspired to create soft-sculpture big cats after we'd spent the better part of two hours in the Tiger River exhibit at the San Diego Zoo.

"So, what happened with the ATV tracks?" I asked.

"The trail dead-ends at a gravel road up on the ridge, and there's no way to tell which direction the ATV went after that. But I found something else that was a little interesting."

"What's that?"

Ash glanced back up at the hill. "Someone recently marked what I think is the property line."

"How can you tell it's recent?"

"The markers are wooden pegs with strips of pink plastic ribbon tied around them. The wood still looks brand-new and the ribbon isn't frayed or sun-faded."

"Good obs. Is it possible the guy riding the ATV was marking the property line?"

Ash shook her head. "I don't think so, sweetheart. There are some places where the wooden markers have been snapped off and it's obvious how it happened. The ATV drove right over them."

"Sending a message, you think? I mean, why do you mark a property line?"

"If you're going to build a fence?"

"Exactly. And it looks as if the guy on the ATV was annoyed over that prospect." I looked toward the spot where the bear had vanished. "I wonder if that bear is living on borrowed time, because it appears Chet wasn't the only one poaching on Everett Rawlins's land."

SEVEN

We started back to the farmhouse and met the sheriff as she came up the road. Ash and I took turns briefing her on what little we'd actually learned.

When we finished, Tina asked, "So, if those property line markers weren't placed by the guy on the ATV, did Mr. Rawlins do it?"

"It's possible," I said. "But I don't remember seeing any wooden pegs or plastic tape in the house or barn."

"One man couldn't install a fence on that hill. That's a big job. I'll bet Everett contacted a fencing company," said Ash.

"But I don't see that as something we need to track down right this minute," said Tina.

"I agree," I said.

Ash checked her watch. "Brad, honey, I have to go. I need to take a shower before I leave for Dulles to pick up Martha."

"And lucky you, you'll get a sneak peek at that Woodland Father Christmas bear of hers that you saw on her website," Tina said enviously. "I'd love to add him to my collection, but with Christmas coming I don't see how I can get him for myself."

I knew the bear she was referring to; Ash had shown me the photo the last time she'd visited Martha Burch's website. The Woodland Father Christmas, about two feet tall, was attired in a gorgeous embroidered cloak and trousers, had miniature snowshoes, and carried a Christmas tree slung over his shoulder. I'd have ordered it that instant for Ash, but she informed me that she'd already engaged in a little tactical hinting and that it was going to be Sergei's Christmas gift to Tina.

Ash said, "I wouldn't worry about it. A certain Russian Santa has already marked you down as a very good girl this year."

The sheriff beamed, and I asked, "Tina, can I catch a ride back to the station with you?"

"Of course."

We walked back to Rawlins's house, where I handed Ash our car keys, gave her a kiss, and told her to be careful. High-speed vehicle pursuits and handling savage dogs were child's play when compared to contending with the kamikaze-like traffic in the D.C. metro area, particularly around the airport.

As Ash drove off, I said to Tina, "I know you've got to leave for the autopsy in Roanoke soon, which will leave me without any transport. If you want me to keep working this case while you're gone, I'm going to need some wheels."

"The only car I have available is the Cannabis Comet." Tina gave me a sly grin.

She was referring to the sheriff department's "new" unmarked car, a silver-colored 2001 Pontiac Aztek. The ugly hunchbacked SUV was what was known as a "drug asset vehicle," which meant that a dope dealer had owned it before it was converted to law enforcement use. Clearly, the former owner had used the vehicle to transport loads of marijuana. The one time I'd driven the Aztek, I'd almost gotten a contact high from the persistent scent of ganja; hence the vehicle's nickname.

I said, "You've got to have *something* else."

"Sorry, but with Ash's patrol car at the crime lab, we're down to a bare minimum of vehicles."

"Fine. I'll drive it, but you'll have to explain to Ash why I came home smelling like a Grateful Dead concert."

I'd just opened the door to get into Tina's police cruiser when a fire engine–red Lexus SC coupe sped down the driveway and skidded to a stop near the house. A large man in his late twenties jumped from the high-end sports car, and I recognized him from the pictures inside the house. It was Kurt Rawlins, and I didn't need any great deductive skills to realize that the medical examiner's office had already notified him of his father's death.

His clothing was as upscale as his car. Kurt wore an obviously expensive camel's-hair sports jacket over an oxford cloth twill shirt. Even his slacks looked pricey, and his shoes had that unmistakable buttery look of fine leather. You could take it to the bank that he hadn't bought those shoes in a discount department store.

I didn't notice much of a facial resemblance between Kurt and his father, but that might have been because Mr. Rawlins had been clean-shaven, while his son sported a full goatee. His sunglasses further concealed his facial features, but from the bulldog set of his jaw, I could tell that he was a man who was used to having things his way.

Yanking his sunglasses off, Kurt demanded of Tina, "Are you in charge here?"

"I'm Sheriff Tina Barron. You're Kurt

Rawlins, aren't you? I'm sorry for your loss."

"Thank you. Who killed my dad?"

"We don't know yet."

Kurt scanned the yard. "Where are the state police detectives? Have they already finished?"

"We didn't call for the state police. My department is investigating your father's death."

"Your department? I don't mean to be rude, Sheriff, but I grew up here, and as I recall the only thing your department was good at was running an illegal speed trap on Coggins Spring Road."

Tina stiffened a little. "Things have changed a lot since then."

"Maybe, but I want an experienced detective on the case," said Kurt as he pulled off his brown leather driving gloves.

"And you've got one." Tina inclined her head in my direction. "This is Brad Lyon. He used to be a homicide inspector with the San Francisco Police Department and has worked hundreds of murders. Now he works for me as an investigative consultant."

I said, "And I promise you, we are going to find out who did this to your father."

Kurt suddenly hung his head, and his chin began to quiver slightly. When he spoke, his voice was thick with emotion. "Look, I'm sorry if I came across as a flaming jerk. It's just that I've been beating myself up all the way over here. I kept promising Dad that I'd be out *next* weekend, but something always got in the way."

"It's pretty common for people to react that way. We didn't take it personally," I said, and Tina nodded.

"And then I get a call from some woman at five-thirty in the morning, telling me he's dead. I still can't make myself believe it." Kurt looked up at me. "How did Dad die?"

I glanced at Tina, who nodded at me to continue. I said, "We found him out here in the yard. He was shot in the chest with an arrow."

"What kind of arrow?"

"According to the game warden who was here, it was a hunting arrow."

In a flash, Kurt's face was contorted with rage. "That son of a bitch! That scum-sucking, mother —"

"Who are you talking about?"

"That white trash bastard, Wade Tice! He owns the next farm over." Kurt jabbed a meaty hand southward and in the general direction of the sand quarry.

I was surprised and felt a little chastened. We'd been focusing exclusively on Chet Lincoln and the driver of the Saab as potential suspects and in doing so had overlooked the fact that murder victims often know their assailant. I'd jumped to conclusions without adequate information and investigation. It was mortifying.

"Why do you think it was Mr. Tice?" Tina asked.

"I *know* it was him. He's been a bow hunter for longer than I've been alive."

"Unfortunately, we're going to need a little bit more than that to charge him. Why would he kill your dad?" I asked.

"Because they've been feuding. Earlier this year, our old water well went dry, and Dad had to have a new one drilled. It was damned expensive."

Tina turned to me to explain. "Depending on how deep the drillers have to go, it can cost thousands."

"Which is exactly what happened," said Kurt. "Then, about a month or so ago, Wade showed up at the house saying that *his* well was going dry and that it was Dad's fault."

"I don't know much about wells, but I'm guessing Mr. Tice thought the new one had caused his to dry up?"

"That's right, but there's no way to prove that. Anyway, Wade said that *he* was going to have to drill a new well and then had the nerve to say he expected Dad to foot half the bill."

"What did your dad say?" Tina asked.

"He told Wade to go to hell. They were never what you'd call friends, but after that, things really went downhill."

"How so?" I asked.

"They stopped talking and then, a couple of weeks ago, Dad bumped into Wade at the Food Lion in Elkton. Dad said that Wade had been drinking and that he started to yell. He called Dad a liar and a backstabbing thief." Kurt's jaw tightened with the memory.

"So what happened then?"

"*Nobody* talks that way to my dad, especially in front of his friends and neighbors. He punched Wade right in the face and knocked him on his butt. Then Dad dared Wade to step outside and say those things again."

"Did Mr. Tice accept?"

Kurt made a dismissive sound. "Of course not. He knew my dad could whip his ass in a fair fight."

"So what did happen?"

"Dad told me that Wade just kept lying there and moaning about how badly he was hurt. But when Dad went to go pay for his groceries, Wade started yelling about how he was going to get even."

Tina and I exchanged meaningful glances. Given the fact that Wade Tice already had a grudge against Everett Rawlins and that he'd just been humiliated in front of a bunch of local townsfolk, the threat to "get even" might have been more than mere bluster. If so, it might explain some of our anomalous evidence.

I asked, "Mr. Rawlins, do you know if Mr. Tice owns an ATV?"

"He used to. I don't know if he still does now. Why?"

"We found what look like some quad-runner tracks in the mud. But it's too early to tell if they mean anything."

"Where did you find them?"

I pointed toward the quarry road. "Back that way."

Kurt's hands tightened into fists. "Which is how you'd get to Wade's farm. I swear to God, I'll —"

Tina cut him off. "You're not going to do anything, Mr. Rawlins, because you might be jumping the gun. We have reason to believe that at least two other people were on your dad's property last night."

"What?"

"That's right. Did your dad ever mention having problems with a poacher trespassing on his land?"

Kurt took a deep breath. "Yeah. Yeah, as a matter of fact, he did. Dad said the guy's name was Chuck Lincoln."

"Could that have been Chet?" Tina asked.

"Maybe. Dad said he swore out a criminal complaint against the guy. Was he here?"

"We can't place him here in the yard, but we do know he was up on the hill."

"What? You think this poacher killed my dad?"

"We don't know," I said. "He took off and we haven't been able to find him."

"I can't believe this!" Kurt threw his hands skyward.

Making a conscious effort to keep my tone congenial, I continued, "What happened was that a deputy was responding to help apprehend Chet Lincoln for that criminal complaint your dad swore out, but as she was passing your dad's farm, a stolen car came blasting out of the driveway and sideswiped her patrol car."

"A stolen car? What the hell was going on here?" Kurt cried.

"That's precisely what we're trying to find out. The car was stolen from the Massanutten Crest Lodge last night."

"None of this makes any sense to me. I can't think of a reason in the world why someone would bring a stolen car here." Kurt turned to give Tina an imploring look. "You knew my dad, right? He was as honest as the day is long."

"That's true," Tina replied. "So maybe you'll understand why we're having such a hard time figuring out what happened."

"What kind of car was it?"

"A new Saab. We don't know who was driving it, and unfortunately it got away."

"You mean the cop let it escape." Kurt was scornful.

Tina jumped in before I could retort. "Mr. Rawlins, the deputy didn't know that your father was dead. She believed she was chasing a low-level offender. But when the Saab almost crashed into another car, the deputy made a good decision and ended the pursuit. Then she came back here and found your dad."

"And if she hadn't gone that extra yard, your dad might have lain out here for days and Longstreet could have starved to death," I added.

"God, I completely forgot about the dog. Where is Longstreet?" asked Kurt.

"At the animal shelter. You can take him home with you, if you'd like," said Tina.

Kurt shook his head. "That's impossible. I live in a townhouse. There isn't room and

I'm almost never home."

"So you're just going to leave him in doggie Gitmo until someone adopts him or they put him to sleep?" I blurted.

"I don't have any other options," Kurt mumbled.

"Well, if you decide to do that, you'll have to go to the animal shelter and fill out some paperwork." Tina made no effort to conceal the disapproval in her voice.

Maybe it was wrong for me to sit in judgment of Kurt. He'd just lost his father, and for all I knew, he really *didn't* have any other options. But his decision to abandon Longstreet to his fate impressed me as being utterly selfish. I decided to drop the subject, however. There was no point in aggravating him and running the risk of derailing the rest of the interview.

I asked, "When was the last time you were out here to see your dad?"

"Three . . . no, four weeks ago," said Kurt.

"Did he mention if he was having problems with anyone besides Mr. Tice and Mr. Lincoln?"

"No."

"And can you think of anyone else who might have a grudge against him?"

"No. He was a good man and didn't

deserve to die with a freaking arrow in his chest."

Tina pulled her notebook from her pocket. "Mr. Rawlins, I have your home address, but can I get your work contact information?"

"Why?"

"Just in case I need to call you during the day."

Kurt removed a business card from his wallet and handed it to Tina. "I'm usually on the road, so call me at the number in the lower right-hand corner."

Tina's eyebrows arched. "You're an executive with Chunky Chuck's Burgers? I'm impressed."

"Thanks. I'm the regional manager for northern Virginia. I supervise twenty-seven stores. I started flipping burgers for them at the Harrisonburg store back when I was sixteen." Kurt looked over at the house and then sighed. "It was tough for Dad when I told him that I wanted to make a career in the restaurant industry. He always thought I'd take over the farm, and I guess I've got to now, but . . . damn, I hate this place."

"Why?" I asked.

"This is going to sound stupid, but sometimes I think it's cursed. My mom died over there." Kurt pointed to the tree. "And now someone has murdered my dad."

In a slightly hesitant voice, I said, "Look, I know you don't want to hear this, but there is a possibility this was a hunting accident."

Kurt seemed to shake himself from his gloomy daze and gave me a steely gaze. "My dad was murdered. You understand? The sheriff says you're a good detective, but I sure haven't seen any proof of that. Why don't you get to work and find out who killed my dad?"

It was easy to imagine him using precisely that same brusque tone of voice with a dull employee who hadn't mastered the intricacies of assembling a triple-decker burger and was on the verge of losing his job. It stung, but at the same time, I had no right to be offended. After all, I'd just spent the better part of ten minutes telling the poor guy all the things I *didn't* know about his father's death.

I said, "Fair enough. You can help me by answering a few more questions."

"What do you want to know?"

"Just how big is this farm?"

"Why is that important?"

I shrugged. "I don't know that it *is* important, but I like to have all the information I can about a victim."

"It's fifty-eight acres." Kurt's tone was a

little less bellicose. "Some of it is used to grow field corn and hay, while the rest is pasture for the longhorns."

"And, correct me if I'm wrong, the property up on the hills is unimproved timberland?"

"That's right."

"Do you know if your dad was thinking about installing a fence up there along the property line?"

Kurt looked a little puzzled. "On the hill? No, he never said anything about that. Why?"

I turned toward the hill. "We were up there a little while ago and noticed that there are new survey pegs along what we think is the property line."

"Huh. That's news to me. Maybe Wade was going to put up a fence."

"I wondered about that, too. But if Mr. Tice was begging your dad for money to help drill a well, he probably didn't have the cash for a new fence."

"Yeah, I see what you mean. I don't know. Maybe Dad *was* considering a fence. I know that he'd had it up to here with the poachers."

"A fence would have been expensive." I looked back at Kurt. "My father-in-law is a farmer, so I have an idea of just how tough

113

it is to turn a profit from a small farm. Was your dad doing okay financially?"

Kurt's features again grew stern. "What does that have to do with anything?"

"Again, I don't know. But, I've got to assume that your dad's death — like most killings — was caused by one of the three eternal *-ances.*"

"The what?"

"The *-ances* are rom*ance,* fin*ance,* and venge*ance.* Maybe I'm jumping the gun, but I don't think romance had anything to do with why your dad was killed. It's obvious he loved and missed your mom."

Kurt swallowed hard. "That's true."

"Which leaves money and revenge as possible motives for murder. That's why I want to know about your dad's finances."

"He wasn't getting rich, but as far as I know, he was doing all right. It wasn't something we talked about."

Tina asked, "How often did you talk?"

"Not as much as we should have. Maybe once a week on the phone," Kurt replied. "Some son I am. I live two and a half hours away, but I could only spare him a phone call a week and a monthly visit."

I said, "Mr. Rawlins, there's no nice way to ask this, but did your dad have a will?"

"Yeah. He finally had one drawn up after

Mom died."

"Do you know where it is?"

"I think he had a copy in his office. I can go in and check if you'd like."

Tina said, "That wouldn't be a good idea, sir."

"What? Do you have some sort of problem with me going into the house?" Kurt demanded as I thought, *Houston, we have ignition.*

"Actually, there is," said Tina. "We're still processing this as an active crime scene, so I'm going to have to ask you to leave for now."

"You're throwing me off my dad's property?"

Keeping my voice serene, I said, "Mr. Rawlins, as far as we can tell, nobody witnessed your dad's death except the person who caused it. That means we have to rely on this scene and the autopsy to tell us what happened. But if you stay here, you might contaminate or destroy vital evidence. I don't think that's what you want."

"Point taken," Kurt grumbled. "But when will you be done? There are arrangements to make and I have to be back at work on Monday."

Tina said, "I understand, and we'll do what we can to expedite the process. Are you going to be staying locally?" She handed him her business card. "I'll let you know when we've released the scene."

"Yes, and I'll expect frequent updates on your investigation."

"I'll call you when I have something to report."

If Kurt realized that Tina's response was fundamentally evasive, he gave no evidence of it. Slipping his sunglasses on, he got back into the Lexus, made a U-turn, and drove toward the road.

As we watched the car leave, Tina kicked at the gravel and said, "I *am* sorry for his loss, but even though I never knew him when he still lived here, I bet that guy was a flaming jerk a long time before his dad died."

Eight

As we drove back to the sheriff's office, Tina radioed to ascertain the status of the deputy sent to the Massanutten Crest Lodge. The dispatcher replied that Mike-Three had just arrived at the station and was completing the auto theft report. We found Deputy Lonnie Bressler hunched over a computer keyboard in the tiny report-writing room.

Tina asked, "What are the details, Lonnie?"

Bressler looked up from the computer monitor. "Not much to report, Sheriff. The victim is a Sherri Driggs and she parked her Saab in the north lot, near the golf course, yesterday afternoon."

"Time?"

"Around eighteen hundred hours. She didn't check her watch, but does remember it was dark. When she came out this morning, the Saab was gone."

"Was the car locked?"

"Yeah, and the alarm was set, but nobody remembers hearing anything."

"What about the hotel security?" Tina asked Bressler. "Did they notice anyone suspicious hanging around the lot?"

"The security director had already called the two guards working last night, and they told him that nothing out of the ordinary happened on their shift."

"How about surveillance video? There are cameras all over the complex."

"But not all of them work," Bressler said with a disdainful chuckle. "The security director asked me to keep this hush-hush, but they had a bad-ass lightning strike back in July during a thunderstorm, and it knocked out a bunch of cameras that they still haven't replaced."

I asked, "Was the car equipped with a GPS theft recovery system?"

"No, just the alarm."

"Did Ms. Driggs show you the exact spot where she parked her car?" Tina asked.

"Yeah, and I got photos." The deputy inclined his head toward a digital camera on the countertop beside the computer. "But there wasn't any physical evidence."

"No broken auto glass?"

"There was *nothing* on the pavement. I made sure of that, Sheriff."

"So the thief probably used a slim-jim to pop the lock."

I said, "What do we know about our victim?"

"Age forty-six, valid Georgia driver's license, and lives in Alpharetta, which she made sure I understood is a ritzy suburb of Atlanta. She checked into the hotel on Tuesday and she's staying in Room Three-Thirty-One. She's scheduled to leave this coming Monday." Bressler looked up from his notebook. "Oh, and Ms. Driggs ain't happy that Deputy Lyon stopped chasing the Saab."

"How did she hear about *that?*" Tina asked.

"It's my fault, Sheriff. I accidentally mentioned it. Sorry," said Bressler.

"Lonnie, what were you thinking? I hope you didn't say anything about the car possibly being connected with the murder."

"No, ma'am. Right after I'd opened my big mouth, I remembered you wanted that kept quiet."

"Good, but I just wish you'd thought of that a little sooner."

I asked, "Is Ms. Driggs traveling alone?"

"Nope. She's on a working vacation and her gofer came along," said Bressler, who sounded relieved with the change in topic.

"His name is Jesse Hauck. Age twenty-three, lives in Atlanta, and drove up here in a Volkswagen Passat."

"Good work, Lonnie. Put your report on my desk and download the photos into the death investigation computer file." Tina looked at the wall clock. "And I've got to get started for the ME's office in Roanoke."

"One other thing, Sheriff," said Bressler. "Ms. Driggs said that she expects to be kept up-to-date on the investigation to recover her car."

Tina rolled her eyes and sighed. "That seems to be a real popular attitude this morning."

As we walked out into the hallway, I asked, "With this bad leg, I'm not very good at genuflecting, but would you like me to roll by the hotel and talk to her?"

"She can wait. I want you to go interview Wade Tice."

"All I need are the keys to the Cannabis Comet and I'll be en route."

"Do you want Lonnie to go along as backup?"

"It's your call, but I don't think that's a good idea." I followed Tina into her office. "If I show up there with a uniform, that's a tacit message we view him as a suspect. I'd like to keep things nice and friendly for now.

120

But if for some reason things go south, I still have Ash's portable radio."

Tina tossed me the keys to the Aztek. "Okay, but be careful."

"I will, and can I ask a big favor? I got all preachy with Kurt over how he was treating Longstreet; meanwhile, my own dog has to stay in his crate all day. Would you mind if I took Kitch with me?"

"I don't know . . ."

"It's just for this morning when I go to Wade Tice's place. I promise I'll vacuum all the dog hair from the backseat."

"And clean up his dog slobber from the windows."

"Think of it as biodegradable window tinting." When Tina didn't reply and raised an eyebrow, I quickly continued, "The windows will be spotless."

"Okay, I guess. But only this once."

"Thanks, Tina. Oh, and one other thing . . . could you assign Kitch a really cool radio call sign like Hellhound-One or Lethal-Woofin'? It'd make his day."

"Good-bye, Brad. I'll see you when I get back from Roanoke," said Tina as she headed for the door.

We went back out to the parking lot. Tina got into her cruiser and headed for the medical examiner's office, while I fired up the Aztek. The vehicle's digital thermometer said the temperature was up to forty-eight degrees, so I rolled all the windows down. That helped clear the air inside the car a little, but it still reeked of Shenandoah Valley sinsemilla.

As I pulled out from the parking lot, I briefly paused to admire the maple tree–lined main street of Remmelkemp Mill. The glorious fall foliage was past its prime, but the street still looked lovely. Instead of making the right turn to go home, I turned left and drove the half-block to Pinckney's Brick Pit. I hadn't seen Sergei in the better part of a week and was hoping to briefly stop at the restaurant to say hi. However, Sergei's big pickup truck wasn't in the lot, so I headed home to get Kitchener.

Fifteen minutes later, Kitch was in the backseat of the Aztek, hanging his head out the open window, savoring the universe of new scents. Before I went to the Tice farm, I made a short detour to the Food Lion supermarket in Elkton, where I went inside to try to confirm one of the bits of information that Kurt Rawlins had given us.

The store manager was puzzled that I was asking questions about a two-week-old event that had never been reported to the sheriff's department. He told me he hadn't seen the encounter, but that one of his cash register operators had. It was obvious that folks still didn't know about Rawlins's death, and I wasn't going to break the news. Witnesses usually feel less compelled to embellish their statements if they think they're describing a minor crime.

The register operator was a middle-aged woman who continued to scan groceries as she talked to me. She told me she knew both Everett Rawlins and Wade Tice and said there was no doubt in her mind that Tice had provoked the fight. Furthermore, she remembered that Tice had shouted words to the effect of that he would get even. I thanked her and the store manager for their help and returned to the Aztek, where Kitch had been busy tinting the passenger windows.

I drove south toward Kobler Hollow Road and, playing a sudden nasty hunch, made a quick stop at the Rawlins farm. I'd half expected to find that the bullheaded Kurt had returned, but he wasn't there. Perhaps I'd misjudged him . . . or simply come by too soon. I continued on to Wade Tice's farm.

Unlike the Rawlins farm, the Tice homestead looked down-at-the-heels and forlorn. The driveway was deeply rutted and could have used about two tons of fresh gravel, the cedar planking on the cabin-style house was in dire need of a fresh coat of stain, and one of the tall grain silos adjoining the ramshackle barn was leaning like the Tower of Pisa. An old International Harvester tractor was parked in the yard. Half of the tractor's engine was missing, and from the metallic clanking coming from the barn, I guessed that Wade was undertaking the motor repairs. I don't know much about agriculture, but it was obvious to me that this farm was in serious financial trouble.

I parked the Aztek and raised the rear windows to prevent Kitch from jumping out and finding some barnyard muck to roll in. Getting out of the car, I caught sight of a bemired four-wheel ATV parked on the other side of the house. However, that didn't necessarily mean it was the vehicle that had left the muddy tracks on the road. A lot of the farmers around here had quad-runners.

A moment later, a middle-aged man with a large flat-head screwdriver in his oil-stained hand emerged from the barn. The man looked to be about five feet, ten inches tall, with a stocky physique, grayish-black hair, and a shaggy iron-colored beard. There was an old brown briar pipe stuck in the right side of his mouth, and a tendril of white smoke rose from the bowl, reminding me of a volcano that was mistakenly thought to be extinct. He wore faded jeans, a sun-bleached blue ball cap, and a ragged old military flight jacket that had about as many holes in it as the plots of the *Star Wars* movies.

"Help you, mister?" asked the man, in a voice that didn't sound particularly helpful.

"Are you Mr. Wade Tice?"

"Look, if you're from the heating oil company, my wife told the woman at your office that I'll have the money to you on Monday." Wade's teeth tightened around the pipe stem.

"No, sir, I'm not from the oil company. I'm Brad Lyon, and I'm an investigative consultant with the sheriff's office." I pulled the badge case from my jacket pocket and showed him my ID card.

Wade glanced from the card to my cane. "You're Lolly's son-in-law that moved here a few years ago from California, right?"

"That's right," I said, hoping the family connection would breed some goodwill.

The pipe sagged slightly as his jaw relaxed and he said, "What can I do for you?"

"If you've got a minute, I'd like to ask you a few questions."

"Is it about that ruckus last night?"

"What ruckus?" I asked, just in case he wasn't referring to the police response to the Rawlins farm.

"All those sirens from out on the road."

"So I take it you haven't heard?"

"Heard what?"

"That Everett Rawlins was killed last night."

Wade Tice folded his arms across his chest. "Huh. That's a damn shame. But what does it have to do with me?"

Tice was cool, I thought, but the body language suggested he was hiding something. However, rather than directly confront him with the potentially damning facts about his conflict with Rawlins and his longtime experience as a bow hunter, I decided on an oblique approach. I said, "You're his neighbor, and I know you want to help. Did you notice any suspicious-looking people or vehicles around here last night?"

"Nope."

"How about a vehicle up on the ridge?" I pointed toward the hill with my cane.

Wade shot a quick disinterested glance at the hill. "Nope. I was in the house with my wife all last night."

"In the past, have you ever noticed any

vehicles up there?"

"Sure. Hunters go up there looking for deer, but it don't bother me none. There's plenty of deer and I figure I can't begrudge a man if he's hungry."

"Getting back to last night, did you hear any strange sounds?"

"Just the sirens. Lots of sirens."

"Is your wife here? Maybe she noticed something."

"Nope, Marilyn is at work."

"And where is that?"

"Why do you want to know that?"

I shrugged, feigning indifference. "I need to ask her these same questions, and I'm just trying to save myself a trip out here later tonight."

Wade removed the pipe from his mouth and used the screwdriver to dig out some ash. Finally, he said, "She works at the lodge as a maid."

"The Massanutten Crest Lodge?" I asked. I found this new link to the lodge mildly intriguing, but after a few seconds of consideration, I was inclined to dismiss it as a coincidence. A farmer's wife usually doesn't have much experience boosting cars.

Wade said, "Yeah. It's a hell of a thing that my wife has to clean up after other folks, but it's been a bad couple of years and we need the money."

"I'm sorry to hear that, and I'll finish up here as quickly as possible so you can get back to work. What was your relationship like with Everett Rawlins?"

"There ain't much to say. We wasn't exactly what you'd call close friends, but we got along okay, I guess." Wade tried to sound casual.

I gave him a long thoughtful look and then gently said, "That isn't what I've heard, Mr. Tice."

"You calling me a liar?"

"No, sir, but I'm confused. You say that you got along okay with Mr. Rawlins, but other folks have told me that you were extremely angry at him for making your well go dry."

With a sudden flick of his wrist, Wade Tice hurled the screwdriver blade-first into the ground. "Oh, I get it! Some rich farmer dies and the law can't move fast enough to falsely accuse a poor man of his murder! Get off my land, you damn rich man's whore!"

"I will, though I'm sorry you feel that way. But nobody is accusing you of murder." I kept my voice calm, while taking note of how quickly and thoroughly Wade was losing his temper.

"Yet. And ain't it amazing? That greedy bastard stole my water and the sheriff's office couldn't spare me the time of day! Civil problem, they said. Can't do nothing. But, you sons of bitches pull out all the stops when a rich man stubs his freaking toe!"

"He didn't stub his toe, Mr. Tice. He was ambushed and shot in the chest with a hunting arrow." I turned as if to go back to the Aztek and then paused to add, "And come to think of it, the other thing I've heard is that you're an expert bow hunter. A regular William Tell. Do you mind if I look at your bow and arrows?"

Wade Tice's face was white with fury. "Screw you!"

"Ouch, that hurt," I sneered. "What happened, Mr. Tice? Couldn't you stand the fact that Mr. Rawlins had mortified you in front of everyone in the Food Lion? Is that why you put a big hunting arrow in his chest?"

"I told you, get off my land! And don't come back!" Wade bent to snatch up the screwdriver.

Even though Tice had armed himself, I made no move to grab my gun. It's a little-known fact, but edged weapons, and that includes screwdrivers, are far more lethal than firearms at distances of less than fifteen feet. If Wade decided to, he could stab me eleven or twelve times before I got the pistol from its holster. I decided not to do anything to further escalate the situation.

"I'm going, but let me offer a word to the wise," I said, my voice suddenly deadly earnest. "At some point I will be back, and you don't want to have that big old screwdriver in your hand when I arrive."

NINE

I deliberately turned my back on the enraged farmer and limped to the Aztek. That was probably a stupid thing to do, considering that Wade Tice's temper tantrum had just turned him into the prime suspect in Everett Rawlins's murder. However, my pride took precedence over caution. I would rather have died than let Tice know he'd spooked me.

When I got to the car, I found Kitch lying on the backseat with his head between his front paws. He'd been frightened by the shouting, but he perked up when he saw me. By the time I was behind the wheel, Tice was gone, and I assumed he'd gone into the house to call his wife. He and Marilyn needed to get their stories straight before I could arrive to interview her.

However, there was a tiny chance that Tice wouldn't be able to contact his wife immediately. The couple was obviously in dire financial straits, which might mean they couldn't afford the additional expense of a cell phone. If so, Tice would have to telephone the hotel housekeeping supervisor and request that a message be passed along to his wife for her to call him back ASAP. That would take time, and I could be at the Massanutten Crest Lodge in less than ten minutes if I ignored the posted speed limits like everyone else around here. I started the Aztek and roared from the farm.

As I drove, I asked Kitch, "So, what do you think, pal? Do we have enough information to get a search warrant for Wade Tice's property?"

Kitch began to pant.

"You're right. Of course we don't," I said. "There's no way to link those muddy tracks to the ATV, because yours truly screwed up and got us thrown off the property before I could get a closer look at the tires. And we both know that his being a bow hunter doesn't translate into a reasonable suspicion that he's the one who fired the arrow."

Kitch yawned and rested his moist chin on my shoulder.

"I agree. Wade *did* lie about his relationship with Everett, but that still isn't enough to get us a search warrant. And it keeps getting better and better."

Kitch smacked his lips.

"How? Well, while I rush over to interview a wife who's undoubtedly going to tell me to go to hell, Wade is probably getting rid of his bow and arrows somewhere on the mountain."

A minute or so later, I was speeding northbound on the Stonewall Jackson Highway and soon approached the turnoff that would take me through Remmelkemp Mill and on to the hotel. However, as I made the left turn, I heard the yelp of a police siren. Glancing at the rearview mirror, I saw the flashing blue lights and muttered a curse. A state police car was behind me, and the trooper wanted me to stop.

I pulled over to the side of the road, shut off the engine, and put my hands on the steering wheel so that they'd be visible. Looking into the side mirror, I watched the trooper get out of her car and slowly approach the Aztek. She was young, but her alert demeanor and officer safety tactics told me that she knew how to conduct a traffic stop. The trooper placed herself just behind the doorpost, so that I had to look over my left shoulder to see her.

"Good morning, sir. I'm Trooper Fuller and I've pulled you over for speeding. I want your driver's . . ." The young cop suddenly paused to take a deep and prolonged sniff of the air coming from inside the Aztek. Then she said, "Sir, just how much marijuana do you have in this vehicle?"

"None. Look, I can explain. I'm a civilian investigator for the Massanutten County Sheriff's Office."

"Riding around with your sheepdog and a load of weed. Right." She was extremely suspicious, and I couldn't blame her. Marijuana cultivators seldom look like Cheech and Chong anymore.

"Yeah, I know it looks strange, but let me show you my department ID." I began to reach for my badge case inside my jacket.

"Keep your hands where I can see them," Fuller commanded.

"Yes, ma'am." There was no need to see the trooper's gun to know it was pointed at my head. I inclined my head slightly toward the walkie-talkie that stood in the center console drink grommet. "I can prove I'm with the sheriff's office. That's a police radio."

"Or a scanner. Every dope dealer I've arrested had one. Now, I want you to get out of the car very slowly."

I grimaced. "Which brings up something else I probably should've mentioned right away. I'm carrying a . . . gun."

Faster than you can say *The French Connection,* I was disarmed and facing the back of the Aztek with my arms outstretched and my legs spread. I told Fuller that my leg really was injured, but she didn't believe me and ordered me to stand still. Again, I couldn't blame her for distrusting me. It's a common ploy for crooks to pretend to be injured. Meanwhile, Kitch jumped into the rear cargo compartment and pressed his nose and slobbery muzzle against the back window to watch the fun.

The cop had radioed for backup and removed my badge case from my jacket when I heard the sound of a big diesel pickup truck slowly pass. The vehicle then pulled over to the side of the road in front of the Aztek. A moment later, I heard a voice I recognized. It was a man with a cultured British Oxbridge accent, and he sounded positively tickled as he said, "Trooper Fuller, I want to thank you from the bottom of my heart. You've given me a moment that I shall treasure for many years to come."

It was ironic that Tina had been worried about me teasing Sergei about the forthcoming trip to Disney World. He was as committed to MAD — mutually assured derision — as I was. Although I couldn't see my smart-mouthed friend, it was easy to envision him with his twinkling blue eyes, steel-gray handlebar moustache, and a wicked grin of delight.

"I need you to stay back, Mr. Zubatov. This man could be dangerous," said the cop.

"Sergei!" I shouted over my shoulder. "You tell this officer who I am or, I swear to God, you will *never* get Ash's white chocolate truffle and Amaretto cake recipe!"

"Steady on, Bradley. Threats like that will only cause me to *dessert* you."

"Do you know this guy?" the trooper asked Sergei.

There was a slight pause, and I knew that Sergei was weighing the loss of a great recipe against a few more moments of devilish amusement. Finally, he said, "Yes, I do. He's Bradley Lyon and he works for Sheriff Barron. I stopped to tell you that . . . and to take a couple of photographs that we can chuckle over later. Right, Bradley?"

"Oh, the fun we'll have," I grumbled. Then I said to the trooper, "May I please stop assuming the position?"

"Yes, of course, and I'm sorry, sir," said Fuller. "I just transferred here from Richmond last month, so I'm still getting to know the local cops."

"And you've met the local greasy-spoon

operator," I said as I turned around and rested my butt against the bumper to take the weight off my left shin.

"Yes, sir, I eat at Mr. Zubatov's place a couple times a week." Fuller bit her lip as I rotated my left ankle and gritted my teeth. She said, "Your leg really is hurt."

"Yep."

"I'm sorry."

"No need to be." I cautiously stood up. "The car does reek of dope and I *was* speeding. I was on my way to the Massanutten Crest Lodge to chase down a hot lead on a potential homicide I'm working."

Fuller radioed her dispatcher to cancel her backup and then handed my badge case and pistol back to me. "Here. No hard feelings?"

"About you drawing down on me? None. If I were in your place, I'd have done exactly the same thing." I turned to Sergei as I slipped the gun back into my shoulder holster. "*You,* however . . . And what exactly did you mean when you said you were taking pictures?"

Sergei held up his cell phone, and his grin grew even broader. "What I wouldn't have given for a tiny telephone that doubled as a camera back during the old days. And just wait until you see the photos. You have this exquisite woebegone look."

"I'm glad I was able to brighten your day and I'd love to hang around and let you torment me some more, but I've got to run," I said, limping toward the driver's door of the Aztek. "I'll see you later tonight."

"Good, but until then, give this some thought: Where can I put a poster-sized framed copy of that picture?" Sergei asked merrily as he followed me.

"Actually, I know the perfect place you can put it. But don't get a frame with glass. It'll just hurt that much more." I shut the car door and resumed my journey to the lodge.

Driving through town, I passed the Remmelkemp Mill Apostolic Assembly, where I saw that the pastor, Terry Richert, and another guy had just finished hanging a banner above the church community center's door. The sign read, TEDDY BEAR SHOW, SATURDAY, 9 A.M.–4 P.M. I honked and waved, while making a mental note that I had to finish Bear-atio's trousers sometime tonight.

The Massanutten Crest Lodge is about five miles west of town and stands high on the east side of the mountain. It's located in an alpine landscape, which is why I guess the resort consortium modeled the place after King Ludwig II of Austria's famous fairytale-like Neuschwanstein Castle. Tourist guidebooks describe the large hotel as looking imposing, but I think the kitschy Sleeping Beauty castle looks as out of place in the Virginia mountains as an ashtray in a hospital room.

The oval-shaped driveway in front of the faux barbican entrance to the hotel was gridlocked with luxury cars and even a couple of limos. Then I remembered it was Friday and the weekend guests were arriving. That likely meant I'd wait for God knows how long for someone to find the hotel's security director for me, and I was already racing the clock to contact Marilyn Tice. Fortunately, I noticed a road sign that read EMPLOYEE SERVICES with an arrow pointing left. I made a left turn and followed the road around the side of the building.

The employee administration offices were located at the back corner of the hotel. I parked the car, and as I got out, Kitch began to jump up and down and whine, indicating that he had to make a potty call. There was no telling how long I'd be in the hotel, so I hooked the leash to his collar and let him out of the car. I figured I'd come back for the police radio, so I grabbed my cane and led Kitch toward a grassy and

139

wooded embankment behind the hotel. There were brown piles of leaves scattered on the slope, and it looked as if the hotel gardeners had been tidying the grounds in the wake of the rain.

I don't know why, but Kitch is pretty particular about where he goes to the bathroom. He wanted to smell every tree and bush, and before long, we were behind the hotel. As Kitch snuffled at one of the piles of leaves, I glanced over at the loading docks. That's when I saw the late-1970s black Dodge pickup truck parked near a short flight of steps that led to a door. I squinted to see the license plate and recognized the alphanumeric sequence from the wanted flyer that hung on the bulletin board at the sheriff's office. It was Chet Lincoln's truck.

There was no time to ponder why Chet was there, because at that same moment, the door opened and a baldheaded man emerged from the building. He was looking downward at something he held together in his hands at about chest height. I couldn't be certain, but the man's posture suggested he was counting currency.

Game Warden Randy Kent was right. Chet *did* look a lot like the cartoon mascot Mr. Clean, but there were a couple of major differences. The poacher wasn't wearing a big gold hoop earring, and instead of Mr. Clean's sparkling white togs, Chet was dressed in grungy jeans and a black sweatshirt that bore the message GOT AMMO? stenciled across his chest in white letters.

When Chet reached the top of the stairs, he finally looked up. That's when he noticed me. We stared at each other for a second or so, and even though I leaned on a cane and had Kitch, I could tell that he somehow knew I was the law. Maybe all those years of hunting had imparted in Chet an instinctive awareness of a fellow predator. And now, recognizing that he was the prey, he darted down the stairs toward the pickup.

I shouted, "Hold it right there, Mr. Lincoln! We need to talk!"

By then, Chet had already thrown the truck door open and dived behind the wheel. I knew there was no way I could get to the truck before it took off, and pulling my gun wasn't an option either. Chet hadn't attacked me, and technically the only reason he was wanted was for a poaching warrant, which wasn't a violent crime . . . at least as far as humans were concerned. The best thing I could do was immediately contact the sheriff's department and get a patrol car rolling in this direction. However, I'd bril-

141

liantly left the police radio in the car.

Chet was just firing up the Dodge's engine as I jammed my right hand into my coat pocket to retrieve the cell phone. With any luck, the day-shift dispatcher wasn't a fan of crossword puzzles and she'd answer the phone quickly. Then things got really interesting. Oblivious to the drama unfolding before him, Kitch had finally selected the piece of greenery he wanted to irrigate. He lunged for the tree just as I began to pull the phone out. Unfortunately, I had the dog leash looped around my right wrist and the sudden jerk caused the phone to catapult from my hand. I watched it sail end over end and disappear into the large mound of leaves.

The Dodge roared away from the loading dock and headed toward the highway at a breakneck speed. Meanwhile, I'd let go of the leash and was on my hands and knees, frantically searching through the wet and slimy leaves for the freaking phone. By the time I found it and called the sheriff's department, Chet was long gone. It was galling. This was the second time in less than twenty-four hours that a member of the Lyon family had allowed a criminal to escape.

All in all, it hadn't been a great moment with Mr. Lincoln.

TEN

I took Kitch back to the Aztek and dried his paws with some fast-food-joint napkins I'd found in the glove compartment. Then backup arrived in the form of a humming white golf cart with a flashing yellow light on its roof. The lodge's security director, Leonard "Linny" Owen, was behind the wheel.

I'd met Linny more than a year earlier while giving his personnel some training on identity theft prevention. Since then, I'd come to both mildly like and pity him. He was the nephew of the hotel's owner and basically a clueless and somewhat rotund nice guy trying to masquerade as a dynamic and hard-nosed security boss. However, the charade wasn't fooling his employees, as evidenced by the nickname they'd given him. Linny thought it was an affectionate diminutive of *Leonard,* but one of the guards had told me the name in fact derived from

Linny the Guinea Pig, a plump, talking rodent from some kids' animated TV series called *The Wonder Pets.*

Linny clambered from the cart. "Hey, Brad, did you see a big black pickup truck speeding through the lot?"

"Yeah, the truck belongs to a guy named Chester Lincoln. He knew that I knew that he has an arrest warrant, so he took off."

"What the heck was he doing here?"

"That's an excellent question, Linny. The truck was parked next to the loading docks and I saw Chet come out the back door."

"His last name is Lincoln? It doesn't ring any bells, but I'll check the employee roster to see if he has any relatives working here. Count on it, I'll get some answers," said Linny as he slammed his fist into the palm of his other hand and jutted his fleshy jaw out, reminding me of an oversized guinea pig *Il Duce.*

I bit my lip to stifle a smile. At the same time, I realized that Linny's idea was a wise one and told him so.

He said, "So, did you come up here about the Saab being stolen? Have you found it? Ms. Driggs is very upset."

"No, we haven't. Sorry. And hey, what was this I heard about the lightning frying your security cameras?"

Even though we were alone, Linny furtively glanced back and forth. "I'd really appreciate it if you kept that under your hat. We lost sixteen cameras, and I don't have the spare twelve grand in my security budget to replace them and all the wiring."

"So ask your manager for some extra money."

"I would, but, well . . . back when I had this new surveillance system installed, he suggested that I add lightning arresters and surge protectors. But that was expensive, and I'd already told my uncle that I was going to come in under budget. So . . ."

"You didn't follow the manager's advice, and you don't want to let him know that."

Linny nodded glumly. "Or my uncle."

"Yeah, you've got a problem. Look, I'll talk to Ms. Driggs if you think it'll help, but right now I need to interview one of your hotel employees."

"Thanks, Brad. Who do you want to talk to?"

"Marilyn Tice. My information is that she's on the housekeeping staff."

"Yeah, the second-floor team. What's this about?"

"It's still kind of confidential. But I can assure you that she isn't a suspect in a crime," I said, adding a silent *For now.*

146

"I'll get her myself," said Linny as he climbed back into the golf cart. "Go ahead and park in one of the handicapped spaces in front of the hotel and I'll meet you in the security office."

"Thanks, but I forgot to bring my handicapped hanging placard."

"Don't worry. I'll advise my people."

Linny drove off. I poured some bottled water into the metal bowl I'd brought along and let Kitch have a drink before I put him back into the car. Then I went around to the main entrance of the hotel, parked, and slowly made my way through the chaotic lobby to the elevators. The security department offices were located in the basement. With its stark cement walls and overhead fluorescent lighting, this part of the medieval-themed hotel was ruthlessly modern.

The door to the security department opened into a small suite of offices. To the left and visible through a large plate-glass window was the security video monitoring room, where a woman sat in semidarkness apparently watching thirty or so color television monitors set in a bank of three even tiers. On the opposite side of the room was a closed door with a sign indicating that it was Linny's personal office. I glanced a

147

second time at the video control booth and had one of those annoying yet unidentifiable feelings that something didn't look quite right.

However, I couldn't give the matter any further thought, because Linny came swaggering into the security office. A weary-looking middle-aged woman wearing a pale blue housekeeping uniform followed him, keeping her gaze aimed at the floor. It was obvious from Marilyn Tice's demeanor that I'd arrived too late. She'd already spoken with her husband.

"Marilyn," Linny began gravely, "this is Brad Lyon from the sheriff's office, and he wants to talk to you."

She barely nodded.

Inclining my head in the direction of his office, I said, "Linny, do you mind if we use your personal office? It might be better if we had a little privacy."

"Be my guest. I'm going over to human resources to check out the employee list." Then Linny pivoted to face Marilyn and pointed a pudgy finger at her. "I want to remind you again of our company policy of cooperating fully with local law enforcement. You do like working here, don't you?"

"Yes, sir," Marilyn whispered.

"Then answer this man's questions. I'll be

148

back in a little while, Brad."

I winced inwardly. The twit thought he was helping me, but ham-handed tactics like that usually backfired. Even if Marilyn provided a statement, she could later recant it, claiming she'd been under duress. So the first order of business was to make sure she understood that the security director hadn't threatened her on my behalf.

Once Linny was gone, I gently said, "Look, Mrs. Tice, ignore what that blowhard just said. As far as I'm concerned, you're here voluntarily. If you've got nothing to say, that's fine. If you want to leave right now, that's fine, too."

For the first time, Marilyn looked up and I saw the distant glitter of fire in her hazel eyes. She replied in a low voice, "And lose my job? I'll bet you'd like that."

"No, I wouldn't. Regardless of what you decide to do, I'll tell Linny that you cooperated fully. But from your cheerful expression, I can tell you don't believe that."

"I don't."

"Fair enough. I don't believe your husband, so I guess that makes us even. By the way, I know he called you."

"What if he did? Is that some sort of crime?"

I raised my shoulders a fraction of an inch.

"Nope, but your neighbor's murder is. You want to go into Linny's office and chat?"

She leaned against the wall and folded her arms. "I can say what I want to say out here. This ain't gonna take long. Wade was with me at home all last night."

"And did he —" I was about to ask if Wade had ridden the ATV the previous evening, but caught myself. If I started asking questions about the quad-runner, it — like the bow and arrows — would likely disappear and we'd never be able to match the plaster castings of the muddy tracks to the ATV's tires. I began again, "And he never once went outside?"

"Not once. We were together all night and went to bed at ten."

"What time did Mr. Tice come in the house yesterday afternoon?"

"He was already inside when I came home from work and that was at five-fifteen."

"Did your husband kill Everett Rawlins?"

I'd deliberately asked a provocative question, but Marilyn didn't rise to the bait. She just lifted her chin a little and said, "How could he? He was in the house all night."

I nodded thoughtfully. "Now, we both know that a wife can't be compelled to testify against her husband, but you need to recognize that she can't lie on his behalf

150

either. That's a crime called Accessory after the Fact."

She gave me a contemptuous look. "*Now* who's doing the threatening?"

"That isn't a threat. I just want you to completely understand the situation."

"I understand. Country don't mean stupid."

"I know. And just because I worked in a big city doesn't mean I'm looking down my nose at you."

"Whatever. Got any other questions?"

"Yeah, could you describe your husband's relationship with Mr. Rawlins?"

"You mean Crawlin' Rawlins, the Kobler Hollow Copperhead? My Wade had a right to be angry with that selfish bastard, but that doesn't mean he killed him."

"Assuming that's true, do you have any idea who did?"

"Nope, and I really don't care." She swatted a strand of hair away from her eyes. "You bootlickers can build some sort of damn altar to Saint Everett, but you'd feel different if you had to live next to him."

"Maybe so. Here's a question out of left field: Do you have any idea who stole a Saab from the hotel last night?"

"No." She sounded crabby at being asked a stupid question. "What does that have to do with anything?"

"To tell the truth, I don't know. Will you humor me and answer another disconnected question? Do you know Chester Lincoln?"

"Never heard of him." Marilyn's face was impassive, and I couldn't get any sense as to whether she was actually telling the truth.

"He drives an old black pickup truck. Maybe Mr. Tice knows him?" I suggested.

"We don't know anybody named Lincoln."

"Funny, he was here at the hotel when I arrived. He ran when he saw me."

She pointedly looked at my cane and smiled maliciously. "I'm guessing he got away."

I smiled back. "He did, so I didn't have the chance to ask him why he'd come here. Was it to talk to you?"

"Of course not. I told you I didn't know him. Why is this important?"

"Chet Lincoln is a hunter who also had a grudge against Mr. Rawlins."

Marilyn slapped the desktop. "If that's so, then why are you trying to frame Wade? You should be talking to this Lincoln fella."

"We're going to. Despite what you think, we aren't trying to railroad your husband. In fact, we're just now putting together a list of possible suspects."

"Uh-huh." Her tone was sarcastically skeptical.

"It's true," I said congenially. "It's way too early in the investigation to accuse anyone. So early, in fact, I probably should have thought to ask Wade if *you* were home all last night."

The mocking smile vanished, and her cheeks began to go pale. "You think I . . . ?"

"I think you're a woman I wouldn't want to cross, and by your own admission, you hated Mr. Rawlins. You're also married to a bow hunter, so that could mean you've been hunting with him, and you look healthy enough to shoot an arrow. I'd be an idiot if I didn't have you in the suspect mix."

She glared at me. "I didn't kill Ev Rawlins, and I was inside the house from the moment I came home yesterday afternoon until this morning, when I left for work. And Wade can vouch for that."

"Mutually supporting alibis. How convenient for both of you."

"We're done." She stalked toward the door.

"I hope for your sake that's true. Thanks for your cooperation."

The seething woman didn't bother to respond and shut the door behind her. While I waited for Linny to return, I sat down at one of the desks to assess the brief interview. The conversation hadn't produced any hard information, but Marilyn had unwittingly provided two significant semantic clues.

First, she hadn't actually denied that her husband had murdered Rawlins. She'd merely asked me how Tice could have committed the crime while inside his house. It was a technically truthful yet nonresponsive answer that gave her ample opportunity for verbal maneuvering if there was a follow-up interrogation. I had to grudgingly respect her. Country definitely didn't mean stupid.

The second important thing that had emerged from the interview was Marilyn's explicit disavowal of killing Rawlins herself, and I was inclined to believe she was telling the truth. That was one of the two times during the interview when I was certain I was receiving an unfiltered and honest answer.

The only other instance of complete candor was when Marilyn expressed her hatred of Everett Rawlins. She had to have known how that sort of naked loathing would look to someone investigating Rawlins's murder, yet she'd been unable to restrain herself. Just like a cancer, hatred that intense took time to grow, and I wondered if the origins of the feud were far deeper than just a water well that had gone dry. But until I had more information, that was useless speculation.

Linny came back into the office. He seemed surprised to find me alone.

I asked, "So, did you come up with anyone connected with Chet Lincoln?"

"No. Not a single Lincoln on the employee roster."

"Well, thanks for trying."

"Are you done with Mrs. Tice already? How did it go?"

"Fine. She told me everything she could," I said, providing an answer that was both strictly accurate and deceptive. "Can I get a little bit more information about her? Is she a good employee?"

"Her supervisor in housekeeping says she's great. Apparently she works hard and doesn't take smoke breaks in the fire stairwells."

"And you said she works on the second floor?"

Linny nodded. "Yeah, but it isn't as if that's the only place she could work. If a maid from one of the other floors calls in sick or — more likely — quits without giving notice, then somebody else has to pick up the slack. Do we need to keep an eye on her?"

"Not at all. Her name just came up as a witness and she isn't suspected of any wrongdoing." Again, I was being a bit economical with the truth, but I'd assured Marilyn that there would be no repercussions to her employment, regardless of the outcome of the interview. Some cops would have viewed that guarantee as nothing more than a piecrust promise — easily made and easily broken, especially after Marilyn's attitude. But I'm old-fashioned and still believe that my word has to mean something.

I glanced over at the security control room and once more tried to identify what wasn't quite right about the scene. The answer finally occurred to me. "Before I go up and talk to Ms. Driggs, can you answer one more question for me, Linny?"

"Sure."

I pointed toward the security control room. "You said that you lost sixteen cameras, but I don't see any blank screens. How can that be?"

Linny went white and began fiddling with one of the gold buttons on his blue blazer.

"Brad, I'm begging you, please don't tell anyone."

"Tell anyone what?"

"Um . . . that we're showing digital recordings on the affected monitors."

"Let me get this straight. That's video footage that was taken *before* the system was fried?" I started to laugh.

"I couldn't let the manager come in and see a bunch of blank monitors."

"It's ingenious, but once the snow comes, somebody is going to notice."

"No, they won't." Linny sounded both miserable and a little proud. "I've got recordings from last winter."

I shook my head in disbelief. "How long are you planning to keep this up?"

"Until spring. Then I can ask for funds to upgrade the surveillance system."

"And your staff has kept this a secret? That's amazing."

"Not really. They know that if I have to come up with that twelve grand, someone is going to lose their job. So, are you going to tell?" He reminded me of a ten-year-old boy who'd just been caught watching the Playboy Channel.

"No, your secret is safe with me. It's none of my business how you run your security department."

Linny heaved a huge sigh of relief. "Thanks, Brad!"

"Just to satisfy my curiosity, which cameras actually *do* work in this hotel?"

"The lobby, the gift shops, the main entrance, and the restaurants." Linny ticked them off on his fingers.

"How about the rear loading dock?"

"Only if you want to see what was there back in April," he said slyly.

I thought for a second and then said, "You know, that gives me an idea. It would be interesting to know how long Chet Lincoln has been coming here. Can you review all the old digital video records from the loading dock camera?"

It would be a time-consuming and eye-wearying task, but Linny knew he owed me big-time. He said, "I'll get right on it."

"Thanks. In the meantime I'll go up to Ms. Driggs's room and listen to her Saab story."

ELEVEN

I hadn't originally planned to interview Sherri Driggs, but I'd told Linny I would. Besides, too many leads seemed to be intersecting at the Massanutten Crest Lodge. I'd initially dismissed the theft of the Saab from Marilyn Tice's place of employment and its subsequent appearance at the murder scene as a twist of fate. But Chet Lincoln's presence at the lodge had strained the whole notion of coincidence. I was convinced there was some sort of connection, and I hoped Ms. Driggs had some information that would help me figure out what it was.

I went to the elevator and pressed the button for the third floor. On the first floor, a room-service deliveryman pushing a food-laden metal trolley joined me in the elevator. We rode upward in silence. I guess my old jeans, boots, and parka told him that I wasn't a guest and that he didn't have to

159

waste any courtesies on me. When the doors slid open, he quickly wheeled the cart out of the elevator and guided it down a hallway that led to the right.

Meanwhile, I stopped to consult a sign on the wall and noted that Room 331 was in the same direction the waiter had gone. I began limping down the corridor, which with its gloomy lighting, stonework, and wrought-iron lanterns looked like a set from a Harry Potter movie.

After a moment, the delivery guy approached from the opposite direction, pushing the now empty trolley back to the elevator. Room 331 was almost at the end of the hallway. I removed my badge case from my jacket and tapped on the door.

It was opened a second later by a handsome and muscular young man wearing a thigh-length white terrycloth robe. He was looking back into the room as he said, "It's a good thing you came back. You forgot our — Uh, you aren't room service."

"Nope. I'm Brad Lyon and I'm an investigator from the sheriff's office." I held up my ID card for his inspection. "Is Ms. Driggs here? I'd like to talk to her about her stolen car."

"Did that idiot come back with the San Pellegrino?" a woman's voice called from a doorway that I assumed led into the bathroom.

"No, Ms. Driggs." The young man was suddenly very formal. "It's a detective. He'd like to speak to you about the Saab."

"Tell him I'll be out in a minute!" she replied. A second later, a hair dryer turned on.

"I heard," I said helpfully. "May I come in?"

"Sure. Of course. No problem with that." He pulled the door open for me.

The doorway opened into a comfortable-looking combination living room and dining nook. There were two extravagant fruit platters on the table. Ahead, the bedroom was visible through another doorway, and I noticed that the bedding was in disarray. Atop the wooden worktable were a laptop computer, a closed briefcase, and a thin stack of paperwork. The suite was as warm as a greenhouse, and the air smelled of fresh citrus, blueberries, and the faint musk of spent passion.

After a couple of moments of uncomfortable silence, the young man said crossly, "Well, it's about time you got here. And what's this we heard about some moron deputy letting the car get away?"

"That deputy is no moron, and she made

a gutsy decision not to put innocent people at risk." I kept my tone serene. "You must be Jesse Hauck."

"Yes. How did you know?"

"It was in Deputy Bressler's report. You're Ms. Driggs's executive assistant, right?" I asked, while silently adding, *and boy toy. Nice work, if you can get it.* At the same time, I was annoyed that this glorified gigolo had presumed to sit in judgment of my wife.

"That's right." Jesse slipped his hands into the robe's pockets. I think he was hoping to appear cool, but the pose only made him look ill at ease.

"Do you enjoy working under her?" My gaze flicked toward the bedroom, and I gave him an innocent smile.

Before he could answer, the hair dryer turned off and Sherri Driggs marched out of the bathroom, wearing a rose-colored silk kimono. Unlike her subordinate, she wasn't the least bit embarrassed by the awkward circumstances of our meeting or her relative state of undress. She asked, "Have you found my car yet?"

With her cornsilk hair in a ponytail and smooth peaches-and-cream complexion, it was hard to believe that Sherri Driggs was forty-six years old. She was slightly taller than average, and she obviously worked out at a gym more times in a week than I will in a year . . . or let's be honest, in my life. However, there was nothing youthful or uncertain about her demeanor. The intensity of her gaze and the set of her jaw vaguely reminded me of Margaret Thatcher in her prime.

I replied, "No, we're still looking for it."

"If your department had done its job properly last night, you wouldn't *have* to be looking for it now."

"Maybe. It's also possible it would have been destroyed in a head-on crash."

"Hmmph." Sherri gave me a once-over and took note of my cane. "And who did you say you are?"

"Brad Lyon. I'm a civilian investigator for the sheriff's office."

"Where's the sheriff? I thought I made it clear to that cop that I wanted to talk to her."

"Sheriff Barron is tied up on a more important case. I'm afraid you'll have to make do with me for now."

Sherri looked affronted. "A more important case? What? Did somebody steal a hay bale or something?"

Jesse grinned, but it looked forced.

I replied, "No, ma'am, we had a murder last night."

"Oh. I see." She sat down at the table. "How can I help you?"

"Look, I don't mean to interrupt your lunch. I can come back later."

"Nonsense. We can talk and eat. Jesse, sit down and eat your lunch," said Sherri, and I knew it wasn't an oversight that I hadn't been invited to sit also.

"But what about the San Pellegrino?" Jesse sounded appalled at the idea of taking a meal without imported sparkling water.

"Later, Jesse."

"Yes, Ms. Driggs." The young man carefully lowered himself into the chair while holding the short robe closed. I appreciated his modesty.

Sweat was beginning to trickle down my back, and I said, "It's awfully warm in here. Would you mind if I took off my jacket?"

The woman took a bite from a strawberry and nodded. I shrugged the coat off and draped it over the arm of the sofa. Sherri glanced at my shoulder holster and then speared a plump blueberry with her fork.

I said, "I just have a few questions. You told Deputy Bressler that you returned to the hotel around six P.M. Where had you been before that?"

"Why do you need to know?" Sherri frowned at a disk of kiwifruit. "Jesse, open that bottle of white zinfandel in the refrigerator."

"Yes, Ms. Driggs." Jesse cautiously slid from the chair and went to the small refrigerator.

I kept my gaze averted from the young man as he bent over to get the bottle of wine, and I replied, "Whoever took your car was probably a pro, and we don't have anybody like that around here. This isn't exactly San Francisco. I'm wondering if someone saw you in the car yesterday, decided they were going to boost it, and followed you back to the hotel."

"San Francisco?"

"Yes, ma'am. I was a homicide inspector with the San Francisco Police Department until this happened." I lifted the cane slightly.

Sherri gave me a reassessing look. "Interesting. And stop calling me *ma'am*. It makes me feel ancient." She took one of the glasses from Jesse as he returned to the table.

"You look anything but ancient," I replied, knowing she'd expect to be flattered. "So, where did you go yesterday?"

Sherri took a sip of the pink wine and said, "Sightseeing. I wanted to see the autumn foliage up on the Blue Ridge."

"It must have been pretty, but you missed

the real show. You should have been here last week."

"That's what everyone tells me. Anyway, we went up into Shenandoah National Park and drove down Skyline Drive. Then we went into . . ." Sherri looked pointedly at Jesse to provide the name that was eluding her.

"Charlottesville," said Jesse.

"That's right. Charlottesville. We had a late lunch and then drove back over the Blue Ridge to —"

"Staunton," Jesse interrupted her. He pronounced the city's name as "*Stawn*-ton," which, though phonetically correct, was nonetheless wrong. Locals refer to the town as "*Stan*-ton."

She gave him a chilly look of reproof. "Yes, Jesse, I knew that."

"Sorry, Ms. Driggs. I was just trying to help."

I asked, "Did you do anything in Staunton?"

Sherri looked back at me. "We did some window shopping downtown, but then it began to rain. That's when we decided to head back here."

"At any point during the day did you notice anyone who might have been paying an inordinate amount of attention to your car?"

She thought for a second and shrugged. "No."

"How about you, Jesse? Did you notice anyone?"

"No." The sulking young man didn't look up from his fruit salad.

"How about here at the hotel? Have you noticed anyone you'd consider suspicious? Anyone eyeballing the car?" I asked.

"Here?" Sherri sounded scornfully amused at the suggestion that riffraff would be guests at a luxury resort, which told me she had an overly narrow definition of just what constituted a criminal.

"You'd be surprised. There are thieves who work nothing but five-star hotels."

"That's fascinating, but as far as I know, nobody at this hotel ever gave my car so much as a second look."

"Even the valet?"

"I don't pay strangers to park my car."

I leaned against the wall to take some of the weight off my now-aching shin. "Okay. You drove back from Staunton. When did you arrive?"

"Around six. Like I told the deputy, I can't be precise as to the time. But it was dark."

"And you came in through the main lobby?"

"Of course. Then we went up to our rooms."

A minor, yet sudden incongruity occurred to me. I asked, "Can we back up just a little bit? The north lot is a fairly long walk from the main entrance, and it was raining pretty steadily by six o'clock. Why did you park so far away?"

"What are you trying to say?" Sherri's eyes narrowed. "That I'm partly to blame for my car being stolen, because the lot was full and I had to park in an isolated spot?"

"That's not what I'm saying at all," I replied, while noting that she'd provided a nonresponsive answer to my original question.

The woman tossed her fork onto the fruit platter. "Look, you seem to be a lot more interested in tracing *my* movements than finding my car. What's going on here?"

"Well, you already know that a deputy chased your Saab last night —"

"And let it get away."

I nodded patiently. "But what you weren't told was that your car was seen fleeing from the scene of that murder I mentioned a few minutes ago."

"What?" Sherri gaped at me. "Are you trying to tell me that a killer might be driving around in my car?"

"That's a possibility."

"Oh my God. Maybe someone *was* stalking us to steal the car." She turned to Jesse. "We're lucky to be alive."

When the boy toy finally looked up from his fruit salad, he no longer appeared sullen. "Excuse me, Detective, but can you tell us who was murdered?"

The victim's name had probably already been on the lunchtime local television news, so I decided that there was no point in continuing to keep it a secret. I said, "He was a local by the name of Everett Rawlins. Why do you ask?"

"Just morbid curiosity, sorry." Jesse reached over to place his palm over Sherri's hand. "It's terribly disturbing to think we were *that* close to a killer."

Suddenly, Sherri Driggs looked her age and maybe a little extra. She nodded and then pressed her free hand against her left eye.

"Is that headache coming back?" Jesse asked solicitously.

"Yes. It's the railroad spike through the eye," she murmured, and then looked at me with her blinking right eye. "I hope that's all you need, because I have to go lie down."

I didn't need to be an air traffic controller to know that something was up. In less than five seconds, the entire interpersonal dynamic between Sherri and Jesse had utterly changed. The problem was, I had no idea why. For all I knew, such mercurial swings in temperament were business as usual in their relationship. On the other hand, the timing was damn fishy. Sherri had been in control and perfectly fine right up until I'd mentioned Everett Rawlins's name. There didn't seem any logical connection between the executive and the dead farmer. Still, her reaction suggested one final and obvious question.

"I'm sorry about your headache and I can let myself out. Thanks for your time." I picked up my coat and made as if to head toward the door. Then I stopped and looked back. "Oh, and Ms. Driggs?"

"What?" she said as Jesse guided her from the chair.

"You didn't know Everett Rawlins, did you?"

"No," she half snapped while massaging her eye.

"How about you, Jesse? Did you know him?"

The boy toy gave me an irate squint. "If I did, don't you think I'd have said something when you told me his name? And it occurs to me that instead of cross-examining us, you should go out and find Ms. Driggs's car."

It wasn't the time or place to point out that Jesse hadn't actually answered my question. I had no legal leverage to continue the interview and still didn't know enough to ask the right questions. So, rather than blunder forward, I make a tactical withdrawal . . . for now.

Slightly dipping the head of my cane toward him in mock salute, I said, "Thank you, Mr. Hauck. That's excellent advice."

A few minutes later, I was back in the security department in the basement. Linny was seated in his office, shoveling chocolate-flavored rice cakes into his mouth and watching a video monitor.

He paused the digital playback and looked up from the screen. "So, how did it go?"

"Okay, I guess. Ms. Driggs is still upset, but not with you or your security guys," I replied. "Did you come up with anything?"

"Not yet." Linny sighed and rubbed his eyelids with his fingers.

"Well, watch just a little at a time. I know you're a busy man, and I don't want you burning your eyes out on my account."

Linny nodded gratefully. "Thanks, Brad,

and I'll call you if I find this Lincoln guy."

Even though I was about dying for lunch, I wanted to check out one other thing before I left. However, I didn't need the blundering security manager mucking things up in his eagerness to help. I returned to the hotel lobby and went over to an illuminated map of the ground floor. Based on the diagram, the doorway through which Chet Lincoln had left the building was located near the lodge's Rathskeller restaurant. I began limping in that direction, while reflecting that the restaurant was misnamed. By definition, the Rathskeller should be in the cellar, next to the security department.

Ash and I had been to the Sunday brunch at the hotel's other restaurant, but we'd never dined at the Rathskeller, even though it was the premier chichi eatery in the Shenandoah Valley and had earned a Michelin star. Maybe it's a matter of financial perspective or that I'm married to a wonderful cook, but the idea of paying more than a hundred and fifty bucks for dinner and drinks seems plain crazy. Call me both frugal and ungodly, but I wouldn't pay that much to attend a repeat seating of the Last Supper.

I arrived in front of the restaurant to find its massive oaken doors closed. A hand-carved wooden sign on one of the doors said the restaurant would reopen at five P.M. for dinner, so I turned my attention to a young woman who stood behind a nearby podium. Considering how overboard the hotel had gone with the bogus medieval trimmings, I was faintly surprised to see that she wasn't dressed as a serving wench.

I showed the woman my ID card and asked her if the restaurant manager was available. She made a brief phone call and afterward told me that Thalia Grady would be out in a moment. Mildly interested in just what sort of food earned a Michelin star, I asked if it was possible for me to look at a menu while I waited. The woman handed me a big leather-bound book.

The old expression "If you have to ask how much something costs, you can't afford it" applied to the Rathskeller. There were no prices listed in the menu. I leafed through the appetizer and salad pages, then noticed a long listing of exotic entrées. However, before I could examine it, I heard the restaurant door creak open. I looked up to see a slightly chubby woman attired in a stylish long-sleeved black dress and calf-length boots emerging from the eatery.

She said, "I'm Thalia Grady, the manager.

Are you the one who asked to speak with me?"

Closing the menu, I said, "Yes, ma'am, I'm from the sheriff's office, and if you've got a moment, I'd like to ask you a couple of questions."

She wore a hint of a frown. "Does hotel security know you're here?"

"They know I'm in the hotel. In fact, I just finished talking to Linny — Mr. Owen — down in his office." All of which was technically accurate, if not the truth. As far as Linny knew, I was already on my way back to Remmelkemp Mill.

"Well, I suppose it's all right then." The woman seemed to relax.

"Ms. Grady, earlier today I saw a man named Chet Lincoln come out the back door of your kitchen area. Do you know him?"

"No. Why?" She looked puzzled.

"He's a fugitive," I intoned, which was more dramatic than saying that Chet had a low-grade warrant out for his arrest.

"No. No, I didn't see him. At least, I don't think so. What did he look like?"

As I gave her the description, she began to shake her head with increasing vigor. I asked, "So, you've never seen this guy around your kitchen?"

"No, and I'd certainly remember someone like him."

"Maybe some of your employees saw him. Would you mind if I talked to them? It would just take a minute or two."

She glanced back toward the restaurant doors. "Actually, now isn't a good time. We're starting prep for dinner."

"And it's Friday, so you're going to be packed tonight. I understand. Could I come back tomorrow, maybe?"

"Weekends are problematic. How about Monday? Oh . . . but then some of the people who were working today will be off." Thalia gave me a bright smile. "Maybe it would be best if you came back *next* Friday."

Thalia was obviously a student of Miss Manners. She'd just very nicely told me to go to hell. It was clear that she didn't want me talking to her kitchen staff, and I knew that come next Friday, she'd have some other reason why I couldn't interview them. Naturally, that made me suspicious, which is exactly what I didn't need: another mental ball to juggle when my brain was already as busy as O'Hare Airport the Wednesday before Thanksgiving. I thanked Thalia for her time, and she slipped back into the Rathskeller.

Before I left, I reopened the menu and

flipped back to the page that had the list of exotic entrées. It could be that I just have plebeian tastes, but it seemed to me that you'd order most of those unusual dishes to brag about them afterward, not because they sounded tasty. There was spicy alligator with tabbouleh, kangaroo strips in a chili and black bean sauce, and grilled rattlesnake Dijon. Then a couple of more regional entrées caught my eye. The Rathskeller also offered fresh venison filet mignon — AKA Bambi — and something called savory bear meatballs with mashed Yukon gold potatoes.

Suddenly, I was no longer hungry for lunch.

TWELVE

"*Bear* meatballs?" Ash demanded.

"The game warden told me there isn't any law against serving it, so long as the meat is obtained legally," I replied.

"Which we know it isn't."

"We *suspect* it isn't. We can't show that Thalia even knows Chet, much less that she's buying poached game from him. And it isn't our job to prove that anyway. We've got a murder to solve."

"I know, but . . . bear meatballs. There's just something wrong about that."

"Look, I share your disgust, but we're also being a little hypocritical. We don't object to eating other kinds of meat." I held up my turkey sandwich to illustrate the point. "What's more, I'll bet when your ancestors first settled in the valley, *they* probably ate bear."

"Because it was either that or go hungry." Ash crunched hard on a tortilla chip.

"That's a whole lot different than some rich tourist at a snooty restaurant eating it for no other reason than it's expensive and he's never had it before."

"You're preaching to the choir, honey."

It was almost three-thirty and we sat in our kitchen eating a light and overdue lunch. Ash had picked up Martha Burch from the airport and managed to escape the D.C. metro region before the onset of the early Friday afternoon commuter gridlock. She'd dropped Martha off at the church community center so that the artist could set up her bears for the following day's show. Other out-of-town teddy artists had already arrived at the church, and Martha had thoughtfully arranged to catch a ride to the motel with one of them so that Ash didn't need to make another trip.

As we ate, I'd brought Ash up to speed on everything I'd learned. Unfortunately, she couldn't make any more sense of the divergent bits of information than I could.

She asked, "So you talked to Randy. Is he going to keep an eye on that restaurant at the lodge?"

"Yeah, but I have a feeling Chet isn't going to be going back there anytime soon. Thalia will tell him that his presence is *problematic.* Please slap me if I ever begin

178

to talk that way."

"I promise."

"So, getting back to Wade Tice. Did you know him back when you were growing up?"

"Not really. He was a kind of a loner and got into lots of fights."

"Whoa. There's a big shock."

"And if I remember correctly, he dropped out of school after ninth grade to work on his dad's farm."

"And that's the same farm where he lives now?"

Ash nodded. "The Tice family has owned that land since before the American Revolution."

"Even if Wade isn't good for the murder, he might be the last Tice to live there. The place had foreclosure written all over it."

"Did you get the chance to tell Tina all this?"

"She didn't have much time to talk." I picked up my plate and hobbled over to put it in the dishwasher. "The moment she got back from Roanoke, the commonwealth's attorney called her in for a closed-door meeting. She said she'd meet us at the Brick Pit around six to debrief."

"Which will leave us plenty of time to make a final inspection of that property for the teddy bear museum and decide on an offer price. It's a big place and I think the location is perfect, but the asking price is way too much." Ash joined me by the sink.

"Especially considering the amount of refurbishing we're going to have to do, and that's just based on the stuff we know about. I say we offer two-thirds, take it or leave it."

"That low? Roger is going to balk," said Ash, referring to Roger Prufrock, the real estate agent listing the house.

"Only because it's a smaller commission for him. But it's time he and the seller got real. It's a buyer's market. That house has been for sale since we moved here over two years ago."

"That's true. And speaking of that, why do you suppose Roger won't tell us who the seller is? He acts as if it's top secret."

"Beats me. But if you're really interested, we can swing by the county offices and look at the tax assessor's files," I replied.

"I'm not *that* interested, but whoever it is should be ashamed of letting that house go to seed."

"That just gives us more bargaining leverage, my love."

Ash took my hand. "I still can't believe we're doing this."

"Same here. Our own teddy bear shop and museum; it's an awfully big step."

"Does that scare you?"

"Not much." I leaned over to kiss her on the forehead. "You see, I'm married to this lovely woman who has a talent for making good dreams come true."

Ash glanced at the microwave clock. "Pastor Terry left a message on the answering machine that we could pick up the key to the church community center this afternoon."

I asked, "When are you going set up our display?"

"If I have the key, I can go back later tonight," said Ash.

"We can go over together later. I like watching you set up the bears."

She gave me a shrewd look. "You just like watching me bend over in tight jeans."

"That too."

"Can we stop there before we meet Roger?"

"Of course. I'll get the key from Terry, while you concentrate on your actual reason for wanting to go over now."

"And what's that, Mr. Smarty Pants?"

"You want a sneak peek at the teddies to see if you want to add any to our collection. That's okay. So would I."

Kitch galloped to the door, ready to resume his duties as an unofficial police canine, and was obviously disappointed when I put him in his crate. We got into the Xterra and drove into town, where Ash parked behind the church community center near the open back doors. There were about a dozen other cars in the parking lot, several of which had out-of-state plates. Our attending bear artists were getting an early start on setting up their furry wares.

The jubilee was set to commence at nine o'clock tomorrow morning, which wouldn't leave much time for prep work tomorrow. As a bear exhibitor, you must have your display finished before the show begins. The attendees who wait in line for the doors to open are always the most avid collectors, and you want to be ready for them.

As we crossed the parking lot, we bumped into our friend Ginger Brame, a popular teddy crafter who specialized in making palm-sized bears. I stood in awe of her talent. Now that I was a bear artist myself, I understood that creating a three-inch-tall and fully jointed teddy was exponentially more difficult than making a large one. Merely *thinking* about the precise hand stitching necessary to make one of those tiny bears made my fingers hurt. Ginger had just driven up from North Carolina and expressed excitement over the upcoming show.

Then we paused in the doorway of the community center, delightfully taken aback by the scene. The L-shaped room ordinarily looked ruthlessly utilitarian, but the combination of teddy bears and the decorating job done by the women's church auxiliary had transformed the church hall into a fall-themed furryland. Just as important, there was that joyous energy in the atmosphere that teddy bears usually seem to generate.

As always, I was humbled when we walked down the main exhibitor aisle. I call myself a teddy bear artist, but the unvarnished truth is that I'm perhaps a competent craftsman. Ash and the people who made these astonishing bears were genuine artists.

As we walked hand in hand, old friends greeted us. We paused to examine the array of sweet bears on MaryAnn Wills's table and then crossed to the other side of the aisle to admire Pat Berkowitch's collection of mohair treasures. Then we came to a dead stop in front of Martha Burch's display and stared at the centerpiece.

"As if I weren't already suffering from an inferiority complex," I said. "That bear is freaking amazing."

"God, he's gorgeous," Ash murmured.

The cinnamon-colored teddy was about twenty inches tall and attired in a robe, a voluminous cloak, and a wizard's peaked hat. Martha had used an opulent yet subtle brown-and-gold variegated fabric for the garments and hat and then lavishly decorated them all with artificial autumnal foliage. And if that weren't enough, the bear held a long wooden staff that had a quartz crystal attached to the top, and he also had an accompanying small and winged fall fairy bear sitting on his shoulder. The bear was such a masterpiece I found it intimidating.

Martha appeared from behind the table. "Hi, you guys! He's the Forest Wizard. Do you like him?"

Ash reached out to lovingly stroke the wizard's cloak. "How do you come up with these ideas? He's just exquisite."

"Yeah, and a reminder that I have no business exhibiting my teddies in the same room where this sort of work is on display," I added.

"Oh, BS, Brad," said Martha. "I like your bears. Ash was telling me about Gil Grizzly, so I don't want to hear any questions about where I get *my* ideas."

Martha was referring to my bear inspired by the character of Gil Grissom, the ironic and introverted crime scene investigator played by actor William Petersen in the original *CSI* TV show. Gil Grizzly was made from silvery-gray mohair, most of which I'd shaved from the bear's upper face with electric clippers to recreate the short beard and moustache that Peterson had sported throughout part of the series. I'd dressed the bear in slacks, a white short-sleeved sport shirt, and a replica of the black Las Vegas PD vest Grissom customarily wore at crime scenes. However, Grizzly's legs were the most authentic and hard-to-achieve element of the entire project. The bear was as bow-legged as the actor.

"Maybe so, but just once I'd like to have an idea like *that*." I inclined my head toward the Forest Wizard. Then, noticing that Ash was still staring in rapture at the bear, I said, "And I've seen this look often enough to know that you might as well go ahead and put a sold sign on it right now."

"But, honey —" Ash began a halfhearted protest.

I cut her off. "Sweetheart, you love that bear and I don't want to put you on suicide watch if we come back tomorrow and it has already been bought by someone else."

"But where will we put him? We're running out of room."

She had a point, but I also knew how much she wanted the bear. For that matter, so did I. Thinking quickly, I said, "He can go into the museum portion of the shop."

Suddenly convinced, Ash kissed me on the cheek. "Thank you, honey."

Then Martha and Ash exchanged hugs and we moved on to the back of the room, where the community center's kitchen was located in a large alcove. Pastor Terry Richert was there and undergoing a Get-thee-behind-me-Satan moment as a church auxiliary lady tempted him with a piece of apple pie. It was a small sample from the array of goodies assembled for the church bake sale, which would run concurrent with the event.

Although Ash had organized the Teddy Jubilee, Richert's Apostolic Assembly was the official sponsor of the event. The women's church auxiliary would run the show, and any profits would be used to help fund the community food bank. Pastor Terry gave Ash the key to the community center and told us that everything was ready. It was clear that he was enthused about the jubilee, too. As we returned to the truck, I reminded myself that I had to find some time tonight to finish Bear-atio's pants.

We drove eastward and over the South

Fork of the Shenandoah River. The house we were interested in was located just out of town, near where Remmelkemp Mill's main street ended at a T intersection with the Stonewall Jackson Highway. With the national park to the east and Massanutten Mountain to the west, it was an ideal location for a business intended to serve both local residents and tourists. We arrived before the real estate agent did, which gave us a final opportunity to walk the grounds and examine the exterior of the building.

The sales literature that Roger Prufrock had given us said that the house reflected the Victorian "Second Empire" style, but considering the shape the place was in, I wondered if the author had been referring to the Holy Roman Empire. The gray three-story house was boxy with a wide front porch, a slate mansard roof, and almost no gingerbread. Even with the fresh light blue paint that Ash envisioned and bright flower baskets hanging from the porch roof, it would never be a cute Victorian home.

However, the property did have some pluses. The electrical wiring was, surprisingly enough, up to code; the oil furnace was in good shape; and the hardwood floors wouldn't require too much restoration work. Another advantage was that the second floor would become the new home of the local teddy bear guild, which met monthly and had nearly outgrown our living room. Furthermore, the yard was big enough to convert a portion of it into customer parking.

Although the cane makes it hard for me to walk while holding Ash's hand, I did so as we took a slow stroll on the brick path that circumscribed the house. The backyard provided a panoramic view to the southeast of the Blue Ridge Mountains and Kobler Hollow. It seemed strange for us to be making plans for a springtime teddy bear garden party when we were only a few minutes away from the site of a murder. However, I didn't say anything to Ash. She was having a wonderful time envisioning our teddy bear shop, and I didn't want to spoil her pleasure with talk of Rawlins's killing.

As we returned to the front yard, I heard the crackle of tires on gravel and saw the real estate agent's BMW pull up beside our SUV. I braced myself. Roger wasn't a bad guy, but with his exaggerated Southern accent, brash folksy persona, and penchant for lame jokes, he reminded me of Foghorn Leghorn, the big rooster from the old Warner Bros. cartoons. He got out of the car, paused to admire his reflection in the car window and smooth the coppery-gray hair on his right temple, and then came through the gate to meet us.

"Bradley, good to see you, old buddy." He vigorously pumped my hand and then turned to my wife. "And Miss Ashleigh, as always you're as pretty as a picture."

I said, "Thanks for coming out, Roger. We're on the verge of making a formal offer for the house, but we'd like to take one more look inside."

"Oh. Well, I have some bad news." Roger's smile became rigid. "The owner has decided to take the house off the market."

"What?" Ash and I asked simultaneously.

Roger showed us his palms in supplication. "Now, don't blame me. This old country boy is only the messenger."

"How did this happen?" Ash asked.

"I truly wish I knew," said Roger. "All I can tell you is that I spoke to the seller a little while ago and mentioned that you were interested in the house. The very next thing she said was that it wasn't for sale anymore."

"And she didn't offer any reason?"

"None at all. It was just 'I've decided not to sell,' and then she hung up. I'm as shocked as you are."

Roger had slipped. In all our past conversations, he'd never referred to the home's

189

owner as anything but "the seller." Yet he'd just revealed that the property owner was a woman. Furthermore, it was a woman who was apparently so financially secure that she felt no need to sell a house during a time when the local real estate market was still in the doldrums. I began to have a nasty suspicion that I knew who the seller was, but wanted some more information before I allowed myself to go ballistic.

I asked, "Roger, did you mention us by name to the seller?"

"Yes, I did. I didn't see any problem with that, Brad, old buddy," the agent said a little defensively.

"And was that the first time our names had come up in your conversations with her?"

Roger thought for a second. "It had to have been, because it's the first time I've talked to her about the property in a month. The seller only wanted contact if there was genuine interest in the house . . . and I assumed you'd be making an offer today. I'm so sorry."

"So are we." I turned at Ash. "We don't need to go to the county offices to find out who the seller is. It's our favorite land baron, Liz Ewell."

Roger confirmed my theory by swallowing

nervously. "Now, you didn't hear that from me."

The set of Ash's jaw told me she'd begun to do a slow simmer. She said, "Of course. That explains why she won't sell the house, the harpy."

Despite being elderly and partially impaired by a stroke, Elizabeth Ewell was the most powerful, wealthy, and despised person in Massanutten County. There was already bad blood between Ashleigh's family and Miss Ewell ever since she'd legally stolen some valuable farmland from the Remmelkemps back in the early 1970s. However, the manipulative old woman had a more recent and personal reason for hating Ash and me. Two years earlier, we'd prevented Liz Ewell from turning the death of her nephew into a million-dollar payday. She'd gotten over the loss of her relative, but not the money.

"You know what they say. Payback is a bitch . . . and so is Liz Ewell," I muttered.

Roger gave me a scandalized look and said, "Now, I don't want y'all to worry. Old Roger has some more listings that he'd like to show you. We can go over right —"

Ash cut him off. "Not today. We're not in the mood."

I added, "Besides which, we both know

191

that there aren't any other properties in Remmelkemp Mill that meet our needs like this place would have."

"Well, I understand you being disappointed, and I just want to assure you that I'm going to stay on the job until you're happy," said Roger.

Ash looked from the house to the real estate agent. "Roger, do you want to know what would make me happy?"

"What's that, Miss Ashleigh?"

"If you'd pass along a message to Liz Ewell from me." Ash's tone was congenial, but the emergence of her usually latent Virginia mountain accent was a subtle clue that she was furious. "Tell that scheming old miser I'll personally go down to South Carolina and buy all the fireworks that we're going to set off when she dies. It'll be the biggest celebration this town has ever seen and loud enough that she'll be able to hear it in hell."

Roger didn't know how to respond. We all knew he wasn't going to transmit any such message, but he couldn't come right out and admit it. So instead, he simply repeated his undeliverable promise to find us the perfect place for our shop. As we walked back to our cars, I began to whistle the tune to "Ding-Dong, the Witch Is Dead." Roger gave us a halfhearted wave and got into his Beemer. A second later, he was on his way back into town.

Ash climbed into the truck, but didn't slam the door shut. Noting my look of surprise, she said, "I'm okay. Oh, I'd still drop a house and Judy Garland on that old shrew if I could, but then I remembered something you used to say. Don't get mad, get even."

I patted her on the knee. "Sweetheart, the law frowns on battering the elderly."

"I've got something quite legal and far worse than assault in mind for her."

"That sounds interesting. Tell me more."

"First, answer a question. What is the one thing that gives Liz Ewell pleasure?"

"That's easy. Knowing that other folks are afraid of her. It makes her feel powerful."

"So, what if we find some place else to put the shop and tell everybody that Liz Ewell assisted us with the purchase, because she wanted to make amends for all her bad behavior over the years?" Ash gave me a mischievous smile.

"You're going to undermine her reputation as a tyrant by painting Attila the Hen as a repentant sinner? That's diabolical. It'll drive her batty."

"I know."

"Talk about killing someone with kindness." I started the truck. "Remind me never to cross you."

THIRTEEN

Although I really liked Ash's proposal to use psychological warfare against Liz Ewell, I had the typical guy urge to retaliate in a more tangible — and let's face it, juvenile — manner. We had just over an hour to spare before we were supposed to meet Tina at the Brick Pit, so I suggested that we had time for a brief errand. I wanted to swing by the hardware store to pick up some cans of obnoxiously bright yellow spray paint that I'd use to draw big pictures of teddy bears on the tall stone wall around Ewell's property, once night fell.

Ash nixed the proposal. She didn't object to the vandalism per se. In fact, she was rather enchanted with the idea of the ursine-themed mural, but she was concerned that I might trip and fall in the dark. Besides, we had some last-minute tasks to complete before the teddy jubilee.

When we got home, Ash went upstairs

while I took Kitch outside and collected the daily half-inch stack of credit card applications and magazine offers from our mailbox. By the time I joined her in the sewing room, Ash was already lost in her work. She was making some final touches on Belinda Banana Split, the newest bear in her "Confection Collection" of teddies that wore incredibly realistic-looking costumes of desserts. I paused to admire the ineffably cute teddy and wonder yet again how my wife could consistently come up with such imaginative designs.

I began to load some of the bears we intended to sell at tomorrow's jubilee into plastic crates and slowly took one of them downstairs to the truck. Then I grabbed a braided rope dog toy and had a fine time playing tug-of-war with Kitch until he almost pulled me off my feet. I regretted that we were about to leave him alone again, but felt some consolation knowing that he'd spend all of the following day with Tina's children. By the time I returned upstairs, not only had Ash completed work on Belinda, but Bear-atio was now wearing the trousers I'd left half-completed the previous evening.

She held up the furry detective and said,

"I hope you don't mind that I finished his pants."

"Not at all. Thank you."

"Bear-atio needs sunglasses."

"And acting lessons."

I reached into a plastic fishing tackle box I'd converted into a bear accessory chest and removed a small pair of wire-rimmed sunglasses that I'd purchased from a doll maker's supply shop. Ash handed me Bear-atio and I slid the shades over the teddy's mohair snout. I adjusted his arms so that they were on his hips, tilted his head over to one side, and was satisfied. Bear-atio looked ready to deliver one of Caruso's eye roll–producing corny one-liners.

"He's perfect," said Ash.

"He'll do," I replied. "But no matter how technically proficient I've become with the sewing and assembly, my bears still look kind of blah next to yours."

"That isn't true."

"Ash, my love, you're sweet but a lousy liar. I'm wondering if I need to try something a little more out of the ordinary."

"Lord, I hope you aren't thinking of making some of those creepy-looking bears with the bug eyes," said Ash, referring to a current and incomprehensibly popular trend among a few artists toward making teddies

197

with oversized heads and distorted facial features.

"Chernobyl bears? I think not. Actually, I've been giving some thought to creating a new collection. But what I have in mind is even less commercially attractive than my cop bears."

"Brad, honey, you can't let your designs be influenced by whether you think people will buy the bears. They've got to come from your heart."

"I agree, in theory," I said, putting Bear-atio on the table. "But with the price of mohair and all the other materials going through the roof, I don't want to waste money on some vanity project."

Ash reached out to rub my arm. "Tell me your idea."

"Well, you know how Gary Nett makes his bears dressed as soldiers from the American Civil War? I'd like to do something like that, but different."

"Go on."

"What I have in mind is making a series of one-of-a-kind teddies to commemorate individuals who've won the Congressional Medal of Honor."

"That's the highest award a soldier can get, right?"

"Yeah, and a lot of times the medal is

given posthumously. My bears would wear historically accurate uniforms, and I'd include a small information card with each one telling the soldier's name and giving a brief account of what he did to win the award." Suddenly diffident, I added, "These bears won't be cute and cuddly, but I'd like to honor some forgotten heroes."

Ash stood up to wrap her arms around my shoulders. "You're right, the bears probably won't turn a profit, but I love the idea. You need to make them and they'll have a special display case at our shop."

We hugged for a while, and I would have been happy to do so for the rest of the evening, except I noticed that it was nearly six o'clock and we had to go meet Tina at the Brick Pit. I put Bear-atio into a plastic crate and carried another load of bears down to the SUV while Ash ran a brush through her hair and fed Kitch his dinner.

When we arrived at the Brick Pit, the restaurant parking lot was misty with smoke and I paused to savor the rich and delicious smell. Unlike many supposed genuine barbecue eateries, Sergei's hadn't made the transition to using a gas oven. He still cooked his meat the old-fashioned way over hardwood charcoal. His customers appreciated the effort, as evidenced by the fact the restaurant parking lot was already two-thirds full.

A moment later, Tina's patrol car rolled into the lot and parked beside our Xterra. The sheriff looked glum as she climbed out of her car to greet us.

"What's wrong?" asked Ash.

Tina glanced across the street in the direction of the county courthouse and shook her head wearily. "Ever since I got back from Roanoke, I've been lectured by the commonwealth's attorney and then three members of the county board of supervisors about how unhappy they are with our lack of progress in finding Mr. Rawlins's killer."

"But we've been investigating less than twenty-four hours," Ash protested.

"And we've made some headway," I said.

"I know, but as far as they're concerned, that isn't good enough," Tina replied. "They want someone arrested by Monday, and the prosecutor is strongly leaning toward charging Chet Lincoln with murder."

"That's crazy. Aside from the fact that we haven't yet proved that Rawlins was even murdered, there isn't enough probable cause to arrest Chet."

"I agree, but the CA doesn't. He says that Chet had motive, means, and opportunity, and that the fact he ran from you at the lodge shows consciousness of guilt."

"Talk about a rush to judgment. Did you tell the prosecutor that we're looking at several other persons of interest?"

"Yes, but he's convinced that Mr. Lincoln is the killer."

"The CA isn't stupid. More likely, he sees Chet as being fairly easy to convict. Our favorite poacher is indigent, already wanted for other crimes, and disliked by the community. He's custom-made to take the fall."

Tina wore a sour expression. "That's what I think, too, but the CA will never admit it."

"What did you say to the prosecutor?" asked Ash.

"That I wasn't going to arrest *anyone* until I was absolutely certain Mr. Rawlins was actually murdered and that we'd identified the right suspect."

"Good for you."

"Thanks," Tina sighed. "But I couldn't very well tell him that and then spend tomorrow running a booth at the teddy jubilee, so it means I'm going to miss the show."

"That's a shame," I said, "but as Ash and I know well, that's the way it is when you're in the middle of a case."

"Can I ask you a huge favor? We were supposed to have adjoining tables at the show, so if I set my bears up tonight, could you guys . . . ?"

"Sell them for you? Of course, we'd be happy to," said Ash.

"Thanks." Tina paused to watch another car pull into the restaurant parking lot. "Maybe we'd better go inside while there are still some tables left."

I held the door open for the women and followed them inside. The Brick Pit was housed in a nineteenth-century cabin with hand-hewn log walls and a flagstone floor; its interior felt like a step back in time to the pioneer era . . . if you could overlook the electric lighting, smoke detectors, modern kitchen equipment, and air-conditioning ducts. Another contemporary touch was Sergei's sound system, which was playing jazz saxophone legend Gerry Mulligan's version of "Waltzing Mathilda." Like me, Sergei was a fan of classic West Coast jazz from the 1950s and 1960s.

We joined the short queue of customers waiting to order food from a young woman behind the counter. Sergei had run the place all by himself up until a couple of months ago, but that wasn't workable any longer. The growing success of his restaurant and his relationship with Tina (which necessitated some free time, after all) had led Sergei to finally hire an apprentice barbecue "pit boss" and a part-time staff.

Tina said, "Okay, you listened to my sad story. What's yours?"

"It's short and sour. We can't buy the Victorian house for our shop," Ash replied.

"Why? Wouldn't they negotiate on the price?"

"We didn't even get that far. It turns out that Liz Ewell owns the place. She took it off the market the moment she found out we were interested in buying it."

"And so it'll just continue to sit there empty and falling apart. Talk about acting like a dog in the manger," Tina grumbled. "What are you guys going to do?"

However, before Ash could answer, something else claimed her attention. On the wall to our left was a bulletin board that usually displayed business cards and yard sale fliers. However, tonight there was an eight-by-ten color photograph thumbtacked to the board, and it showed me facing the rear of the Aztek with my hands outspread on the hatch window while Trooper Fuller frisked me for weapons. Underneath the image was a caption that read, THE LYON TAMER. Both Ash and Tina gaped at the picture, and they had a pretty good reason for being shocked. I hadn't told either of them about the embarrassing episode.

Ash turned to me. "When did *that* happen?"

"This morning. I guess I forgot to mention it." I tried to look innocent.

"You forgot to mention you were arrested?"

"Not arrested. Just stopped and removed from the vehicle at gunpoint."

Ash looked heavenward. "That makes me feel *so* much better."

"How did it happen?" Tina asked.

"I can explain in three words: The Cannabis Comet."

"Oh, no."

"Oh, yes. I got pulled over for speeding, and the trooper didn't believe me when I said there wasn't any marijuana in the car," I said while reaching over to remove the photo from the bulletin board. "Not that I blame her."

"But how did Sergei get a picture of the traffic stop?"

"Your compassionate boyfriend was driving by and thought he'd have some fun before telling the trooper who I was."

By now, we'd arrived at the order counter and could see Sergei hard at work back in the kitchen. He glanced up from the cutting board where he was slicing some baby back ribs and gave me a rascally grin when I held up the picture. I smiled back while trying to figure out some way to sabotage his sound system so that the only thing it would play was "It's a Small World (After All)." As far as I was concerned, my promise not to mercilessly rag Sergei over the impending vacation at the Mouse Empire was now null and void.

We ordered our dinners, filled our plastic tumblers with sweet tea from a pitcher on the counter, and sat down at a picnic table near the back of the restaurant. Keeping an ear cocked for the young woman to call our order number, we began our debriefing. Tina started by telling us about the autopsy.

"Dr. Grice was right." Tina leaned forward and spoke in a low tone so that the nearby diners wouldn't overhear. "The arrow tore out the bottom of Mr. Rawlins's heart and then lodged in his spine. You were also right. The arrow entered his chest at a downward angle. Then we noticed some potentially weird things."

"Oh goody. I was worried that we didn't have enough confusing elements to this investigation," I said with a humorless chuckle.

"Tell me." Tina took a sip of sweet tea and then continued, "Odd item number one: The shaft of the arrow is slightly bent, about five inches above the arrowhead."

"I don't know that much about archery, but it seems to me that would make the arrow unstable in flight."

"That's what I thought, too."

"Maybe Ev tried to pull the arrow out before he died and that's what bent it," Ash suggested.

Tina nodded. "Dr. Grice said that was a strong possibility. She even allowed that it might have happened at some point when they transported the body to Roanoke. Apparently the arrow did bump against the roof of the van as they were pulling the gurney out."

"So maybe the bent shaft isn't important," I said.

"Maybe. But then we have odd item number two: tiny bits of unidentified debris stuck to the four blades of the broadhead."

"Wow. Great obs."

"I can't claim credit for it," said Tina. "Dr. Grice noticed the stuff on the arrowhead when she removed it from Rawlins's spine."

"Could they have been clothing fibers?" Ash asked. "The arrow went through at least one shirt."

"We found that kind of fiber, but it was the other stuff that caught our eye. It was a mixture of minute and irregularly shaped white and brown particles."

I said, "Interesting. I'm assuming you sent it to the crime lab. How long will it be before they get back to you with an answer?"

"Tomorrow."

"Did you sell your soul to the devil? Crime lab technicians don't work on Saturday."

Tina seemed pleased to have surprised me. "I know the criminalist handling the case. We went to the academy together. She was going into the lab to catch up on some paperwork and said she'd bump my evidence to the top of her stack."

Suddenly, we heard the young woman call out our order number. Tina and Ash went to get our dinners. When they returned, the sheriff set a plate with a big wedge of peanut butter pie on it next to my basket of ribs and fries.

I said, "I didn't order this."

"I know," said Tina. "But Sergei insisted."

"He didn't like the look of your smile and said it's a peace offering," Ash added.

"A peace offering? What for? That picture was a funny prank, and I *love* funny pranks. I just hope Sergei enjoys them as much as I do," I said, while the women exchanged worried looks.

Then Tina peered down at her dinner as if seeing it for the first time and said, "My God, I can't believe this. I spent the better part of the morning inside some guy's chest at an autopsy, and now I'm getting ready to eat barbecued ribs."

"Want some ketchup?" I pushed the plastic bottle toward the sheriff.

"Brad!" Ash gave me a scathing look.

"Sorry, Tina. Homicide inspector humor. So, is there an odd item number three?" I asked.

"Yes: you," grumbled Tina as she pushed the basket of food away.

"That's a given. How about odd item number four?"

Tina took a big swallow of tea and then said, "The other strange thing was that we found some tiny bits of what looks like a different kind of brown material stuck to the arrow shaft itself."

"Inside or outside the body?" Ash asked.

"Outside and back toward the feathers or fletching or whatever it's called."

"Maybe it was chili," I offered, and then took a bite of dry-rub-style pork rib.

"Brad, now stop trying to make poor Tina sick."

I chewed and swallowed. "I'm not making a gruesome joke. We know that Rawlins was eating chili just before he was murdered. Maybe he had some on his hands —"

"And it was transferred to the shaft when he tried to pull the arrow out?" Ash finished the thought for me.

"Well, whatever the debris is, I sent it to the lab, too," said Tina as she reached over to snag a French fry from her basket. "Okay, Brad, now it's your turn."

After briefly summarizing the small amount of useful information I'd obtained from my meetings with Wade and Marilyn Tice, I said, "The bottom line is that they both hated the victim's guts and act as if he had it coming, which makes me wonder . . ."

"If Mr. Rawlins wasn't the nice guy we thought he was?" Tina took another fry.

I pushed Tina's basket of ribs back in front of her. "You're hungry. Eat your dinner. I promise there'll be no more sick humor."

"I can't believe that," said Ash.

"What, that I can't behave?"

"Well, yes, that. But mostly I was talking about the idea of Ev having been some sort of secret scoundrel."

"He might not have been," I said. "But if the Tices felt that way about him, then other

209

folks might have, too, and we need to know why."

Tina took a bite of her dinner. Dabbing her lips with a paper napkin, she said, "So we need to investigate Mr. Rawlins's background. We can start with the paperwork we collected from his house."

"In the meantime," said Ash. "Is there any way we can get a closer look at Wade's quad-runner?"

"I don't see how," I replied. "You can take it to the bank that he and Marilyn won't cooperate, and we don't have enough for a search warrant."

"So as long as the quad-runner remains parked on his property, we can't compare its tires against the plaster casting of the tracks."

"That's about the size of it," I said, and then resumed my narrative, covering the mortifying escape of Chet Lincoln and how I'd interrupted the daytime slumber party in Sherri Driggs's hotel room.

Tina's eyebrows arched. "Boffing the employees? That isn't very professional."

"I disagree. Management always screws the hired help. Jesse just gets a more personalized and nicer version of it," I said. "But the most interesting thing about our intimate little visit together was how they both reacted when I mentioned Everett Rawlins's name."

Already knowing what had happened, Ash took up the story. "Sherri suddenly and conveniently developed a bad headache, and Jesse gave some double-talk answer about not knowing who Everett Rawlins was."

"But you think he does?" Tina asked me.

"I don't know. Maybe it's a coincidence that Sherri's Saab showed up at the Rawlins farm. And maybe Sherri really did have a headache. And maybe Jesse just thought he was putting me in my place by answering my question with a rhetorical one of his own."

"But you aren't buying it," said Ash.

"Nope."

"Neither am I," said Tina. "That's an awful lot of *maybe*s."

"But why would *they* have been at Rawlins's farm?" asked Ash.

"We have to assume it's connected with his death. The problem is, there's no obvious link between them and Rawlins. We need more information," I said

"Well, I could call Kurt Rawlins and ask if he's heard of Sherri or Jesse."

"And I could do an Internet search on our erotic executive," said Ash. "Maybe she's in some sort of agriculture-related business."

"Both are good ideas, but I'd rather find the Saab. There's just something so improbable about how the auto theft went down."

"How so?" Tina asked.

"It was raining and chilly, yet Sherri parked her luxury car in about the most isolated portion of the parking lot."

Ash shook her head. "It would have made more sense if her boy toy had dropped her off at the front door and then he parked it."

"Exactly. Or had the valet park it."

We all looked up to see Sergei approaching, carrying a pitcher of sweet tea. He refilled our glasses and then, at Tina's urging, agreed to join for us for a moment. Sergei sat down on the bench beside Tina. Early in their courtship, the sheriff had decided it wasn't appropriate for her to display affection in public while in uniform, so they didn't hold hands. However, I did notice that they sat close enough together so that their knees were touching.

Sergei said to Ash, "Some of your teddy bear artists were in earlier this afternoon. They're nice people."

"Yes, they are. And did you get my message about the lunch tally? I'm going to need twenty-eight lunches for tomorrow."

"I'll deliver them at eleven-thirty." Then

Sergei turned to me. "You didn't eat your pie."

"It's almost too sweet. Kind of like the idea of you riding the carousel at Disney World. But more on that later, my friend." I gave him a beatific grin.

"Brad, you promised," warned Ash.

"But that was before he gave me the post office wanted-poster treatment."

"How in the name of God did he find out?" Sergei asked Tina.

Tina shrugged helplessly. "I don't know. Somehow, he just guessed."

"Look, I'll drop it. I'm sorry, Sergei, and I hope you have a great time," I said remorsefully. "But when you go to the character breakfast, could you get me Mickey's autograph?"

"Getting back to the Saab," Tina interrupted before our male ego melee could get under way in earnest. "We've got a statewide bulletin out, but we haven't heard a word back."

"What Saab are you talking about?" Sergei asked.

"The one that hit Ash's patrol car last night. I told you about it."

"Yes, but you didn't say what kind of car it was. You just said there was a hit-and-run." Sergei suddenly looked pensive. "Was

213

this Saab dark blue with Georgia license plates?"

"You've seen it?" Ash demanded.

"This morning. But I didn't know anyone was looking for it. When I left the house on my way in here, I noticed a Saab Nine-Five sedan parked behind the old Baptist church up in Thermopylae."

Ash, Tina, and I all exchanged eager glances. Thermopylae was a thinly populated and secluded farming community located in a narrow valley between the Blue Ridge Mountains and a range of tall foothills. It was also only a couple of miles east of where Ash had lost sight of the Saab.

I asked, "Didn't that strike you as an odd place for someone to leave a car?"

"Not really," said Sergei. "I've often seen vehicles from out of state parked at the church. As far as old graveyards go, the cemetery is picturesque, and it apparently also attracts people looking for their genealogical roots."

"And what time did you see it?" Tina asked.

"Around nine-thirty this morning."

Ash stood up. "Maybe if we're lucky it'll still be there. Let's go."

"I'll swing by the station and pick up the camera and evidence kit," said Tina. She gave Sergei's hand a surreptitious squeeze as she got up.

I used my cane to pull myself to my feet, and as Sergei and I followed the women, I began to quietly sing, " 'Heigh-ho, heigh-ho, it's off to work we go' . . . C'mon Sergei, you know the words. Or you will soon."

FOURTEEN

Following Tina's patrol car, we headed over to U.S. Route 33, where we turned eastward toward Swift Run Gap and the inky bulk of the Blue Ridge Mountains. We passed the town of Elkton, and not long afterward dense forest lined both sides of the highway. The one-lane road that led into Thermopylae was at the base of the mountains, just before the main highway entered Shenandoah National Park. There were no streetlights, and the quarter moon hanging low in the western sky provided only the weakest of illumination, so it was as dark as the future of good taste in commercial American television.

As I made the right turn onto Thermopylae Road, Ash said, "I hope it's still there."

"We'll know in a couple of minutes," I replied.

I steered the truck through a series of serpentine curves around the bottom of a hill, and then we emerged into the narrow valley. Off in the near distance were the lights of an isolated farmhouse.

Ash pointed to a yellow sign that said the road terminated in five miles. "If you're running from the cops, why do you turn onto a dead-end road in the middle of nowhere? Why dump the car there?"

"At the church? Perhaps he was keeping the Saab-ath holy."

"Or maybe he left it there for service," Ash said solemnly.

"Baby doll, you *have* been hanging around me too much."

Ahead, Tina's patrol car slowed and the vehicle's headlights illuminated the Baptist church. Standing on a foundation of brown stonework, the whitewashed and clapboard building wasn't much larger than a two-car garage. There was a sign by the side of the road that read, THERMOPYLAE FREE WILL BAPTIST CHURCH, ESTABLISHED 1854.

Tina pulled off the road and onto a gravel driveway that looped behind the church. We followed, and Ash inhaled sharply when she saw the dark blue Saab sedan with Georgia license plates. The car was parked parallel to the old cemetery's low stone wall, with the passenger side of the vehicle facing toward the road. The tinted windows pre-

217

vented us from seeing inside the Saab, but it looked empty.

Parking her car so that it faced the Saab, Tina activated her cruiser's high beams and both spotlights, which lit up some grayish-white gravestones in the near distance. I pulled up beside her patrol car and turned my bright lights on, too. Even with all the illumination, the scene looked a little spooky.

Ash jumped from the truck and turned her flashlight on as she joined the sheriff. Tina had her gun hand resting on her holstered weapon as the two women approached the Saab.

Meanwhile, I slowly climbed from the Xterra. It was chilly enough outside that when I exhaled, my breath was a little steamy.

Tina yelled, "It's clear."

"And come over and take a look at this," called Ash.

I walked over to the front of the Saab, and the first thing I noticed was the large and ragged dent in the car's left front quarter panel. I shined my flashlight at the indentation and saw streaks of white paint transfer on the fender that had undoubtedly come from Ash's patrol car. However, I soon realized that Ash had something far more significant for me to look at than the collision damage.

Pointing toward the driver's door, Ash said, "What's wrong with *this* picture?"

I joined her and Tina by the driver's door and saw something that hadn't been visible from the opposite side of the car. The driver's door window was mostly gone. Someone or something had smashed out the window, leaving only some small and fractured chunks of safety glass stuck in the window frame.

Taken at face value, it looked like your typical clumsy car clout. Then I noticed the broken safety glass on the water-stained leather car seat and also on the damp ground beneath the car door.

I said, "Interesting. Didn't you say that you couldn't see the driver because the window was tinted?"

"That's right. I'm absolutely certain the window was up when this thing hit me," Ash replied.

"Add that to the fact we have broken glass on the ground, and it means someone broke the window here. But why?" said Tina.

"To fake a Grand Theft Auto so that the local yokels — that's us, by the way — would buy the story about the car being stolen from the parking lot of the lodge," I said.

"You think Sherri and her boy toy did this?" asked Ash.

"It would explain her unconvincing tale about parking the Saab in a secluded spot and then walking through the rain to the hotel."

"And her sudden and debilitating headache when you mentioned the murder," said Ash.

Tina gave me a puzzled look. "I'm not following. Why?"

"She never parked the car near the golf course on Thursday night. She — and I am inclined to think it was just her in the car — was driving the Saab when it sideswiped Ash's unit."

"Why?"

"Simple logistics," I replied. "We're out here in the middle of nowhere, at least ten miles from the lodge. Sherri looked like she was in pretty good shape —"

"Isn't it amazing you noticed that about a woman," Ash said teasingly.

"I'm a professional observer," I said in a mock earnest tone. "But, as I was saying, she looked fit enough to have done the ten miles on foot, but she couldn't risk being seen."

"But couldn't it have been the other way around? Maybe Jesse Hauck was driving," Tina suggested.

"I doubt it. Based on what I saw of their relationship, Sherri might have shared her bed with him, but not her car."

"How romantic," the sheriff muttered.

"So Sherri must have called Jesse to pick her up, and he came out here in his VW to drive her back to the hotel," Ash said. "Then they realized they needed a cover story and decided to claim the car had been stolen. But why wait until morning to call the cops?"

I said, "For the moment, we have no idea of how long it took them to get back to the lodge. Bottom line: Sherri *had* to say the Saab was parked someplace where no one could have seen it."

Tina nodded. "Okay, I see. So that she could report that it was stolen and not have to worry about anyone saying otherwise."

"It was a decent enough plan in theory, but it was poorly executed." I directed the beam of my flashlight inside the vehicle. "Check *that* out."

A small screwdriver with a yellow-and-black plastic handle jutted from the right side of the steering column where the ignition key slot was located. The crude attack

on the ignition was another bit of proof that a professional car thief hadn't stolen the Saab. I shined my flashlight on the screwdriver, hoping to see some evidence of latent fingerprints. But the handle looked clean. In fact, the tool looked brand-new.

"The ignition has been punched," said Ash.

"Maybe," I said. "But I've never seen an ignition punched with a screwdriver that small. You need one with a flat head big enough to break and then rotate the entire locking mechanism."

Tina said, "But something doesn't add up. This car has to have an antitheft system. Why wouldn't it have gone off when the ignition was punched?"

"Yeah." Ash glanced toward the distant lights of a farm. "Even this far away, someone would have heard a car alarm and called the sheriff's office."

"Which was probably something Sherri wanted to avoid," I said, while perching my butt on the low wall to take some of the weight off my bad leg.

"So, if there was no alarm, it might mean they deactivated the security system before faking the theft," said Tina.

"Makes sense to me."

"How would you do that?" asked Ash.

I shrugged. "I'm no expert, but it seems to me that a security system needs a power source. If they unhooked everything from the battery terminals, it would probably kill the alarm."

"Let's glove up and take some pictures. Then we can take a closer look," said Tina as we all headed back to her patrol car.

"Sounds good. You might also want to get a wrecker en route. We need to have this towed to the crime lab for processing, too." I gestured toward the Saab with my cane.

Before Tina could answer, her cell phone trilled. She pulled the device from her pocket, scrutinized the tiny screen, and said, "It's dispatch."

As the sheriff answered the phone, I said to Ash, "I have to make a call myself, to the security office at the Massanutten Crest Lodge." I retrieved the cell phone from my jacket pocket. "I need them to contact Linny Owen and have him call me ASAP."

However, before I could make the call, we couldn't help but overhear Tina's voice suddenly grow gruff and loud, as she curtly instructed the dispatcher to tell Mr. Rawlins that she was extremely busy and that she would call him with an update later tonight. Then she snapped the phone shut and made as if to hurl it into the darkness.

"Don't tell me. Kurt Rawlins?" I asked.

"It's only the fifth time today he's called demanding to talk to me," Tina grumbled.

"Well, his dad *was* murdered," said Ash.

"Look, I'm genuinely sorry his dad is dead. But between him, the CA, and the supervisors calling me continuously, they're driving me freaking nuts. Do you know why my phone didn't ring during dinner? I turned it off."

"Good idea," I said.

"Not really. I now have six voice-mail messages, all from people who probably want to tell me that I'm not doing my job properly. And for all I know, they're right." Tina sagged, and Ash rubbed her arm.

It upset me to see her so dispirited. I knew how she was feeling; I'd been there. One of the most aggravating parts of being a homicide inspector was dealing with self-important politicians and ambitious police administrators who wanted immediate results in murder cases. Mind you, none of those amateur sleuths could investigate their way out of an open paper sack with instructions written on the inside, but all felt comfortable telling me how to solve a murder.

Furthermore, such interference was a vicious circle. You devoted so much time to

updating people that you couldn't get any work done, which then meant having to tell the kibitzers you hadn't made any progress. It was infuriating and also a battle you could never win . . . if you fought it by their rules. I scanned the sodden ground until I found what I was looking for.

I said, "They're wrong, Tina, and you're tired. But I think I know of a way to help. Is that a department phone?"

"Yes."

"Could I see it for a second?"

"Sure, here." She handed me the device.

I took the phone and limped over to a fairly large puddle of rainwater near the church. The phone began to trill again, and, without checking to see who was calling, I deliberately dropped the device into the water. There was a brief buzzing sound, and the phone's LCD screen got bright for a second and then went blank.

I said, "Oops. I am *such* a butterfingers."

"What the heck did you just do?" Tina demanded while Ash gaped at me.

"Officially, it was an accident. Unofficially, I just removed your electronic dog collar. How does it feel?"

A smile of relief slowly spread across Tina's face. "Officially, I'm very upset because you should have been more careful using

my department phone."

"And unofficially?"

"I'm so damn glad that nobody can call me." Tina bent over and retrieved the cell phone from the puddle. She shook the water from the device, pressed the power button several times, and giggled. "Yes! It's dead. Thank you, Brad."

"My pleasure."

Tina tossed the defunct phone onto the front passenger seat of her patrol car and then used her portable radio to call for a wrecker. When she was done, she said, "Do you guys want to get started with photos?"

I replied, "Actually, I was about to call Linny Owen up at the lodge."

"Why?"

"Before we can confront Sherri and Jesse, we're going to need irrefutable proof that they lied to us."

"Is there a chance we can get fingerprints from the screwdriver?" Ash asked.

"With all the wonderful training that the *CSI* programs have provided folks on how to avoid leaving evidence at crime scenes, I don't think they'd make that mistake."

"So how can Linny help?" asked Tina.

"Sherri said that she and her assistant returned to the lodge around six o'clock Thursday night and didn't go out again."

"Which we now know is a big fat lie," said Ash.

"Agreed, but that can't be proven, yet. We need Linny to review last night's security video footage and hope it will show exactly when they came and went."

"And if Sherri and Jesse were together," Ash added.

"But I thought most of the cameras were inoperative," said Tina.

"Just the ones in the parking lot. Fortunately for us, the lobby cameras are supposedly still working," I replied.

"Then call Linny while Ash and I get started on the photographs."

I flipped the cell phone open but was suddenly lost in thought. All of the talk about establishing a sequence of events and the modus operandi of faking the auto theft had reminded me that I'd almost overlooked a potentially important piece of evidence in the car. I snapped the phone shut again and said, "Ash, honey, would you be comfortable taking the photos yourself and riding back down the mountain with Tina?"

"I suppose. Why?" Ash asked as she pulled the camera case from the backseat of Tina's car.

"Because I just realized that I have to go chase down a time-sensitive lead." I glanced at my watch. It was 7:37, so I might still have time.

"You've lost me," said Ash.

"Me, too," said Tina.

"The screwdriver. It looks brand-new."

"So?" asked Tina.

"We don't know why Sherri went to Rawlins's farm, but I think it's safe to assume that she didn't originally plan to fake the theft of the Saab, since there's no way she could have predicted that Ash was going to show up at Rawlins's farm. However, once Sherri sideswiped Ash, she decided to dump the car. But where did the screwdriver come from?"

"Maybe she has a small toolbox in the trunk," said Tina. "We can look."

"Possibly, but I'll bet you won't find one. People who keep tools in their trunk use them. That screwdriver looks pristine."

"Are you thinking Sherri told Jesse to bring it here?"

I answered, "Yeah, and he probably doesn't have a toolbox in his car trunk either. Maybe I'm being judgmental, but he is such a pretty boy, I don't see him as being a grease-under-the-fingernails sort of guy."

"So he would have had to stop and buy one," said Ash.

I nodded. "Put yourself in his place. You don't know the area and you're driving along Highway Thirty-Three from the lodge toward the Blue Ridge, trying to figure out just where the hell you're going to find a screwdriver at that time of night. You come to Elkton and what do you see on the left side of the road?"

There was a moment of silence and then Tina exclaimed, "Delbert's DIY Emporium!"

I touched the tip of my nose. "And they sell screwdrivers at a hardware store. It seems to fit, but I don't know how late Delbert's is open on Thursday nights."

"Eight o'clock. They're open every night except Sunday until eight."

"And when did the hit-and-run happen?"

"Approximately ten minutes after seven," said Ash.

"That's more than enough time for Sherri to have called her boy toy for help, and then for Jesse to have gotten to Delbert's before it closed." I turned to my wife. "Honey, I need a couple of close-up pictures of the screwdriver, most ricky-tick."

"On it," she replied, grabbing the Fuji Instax camera from the case.

There were two bright flashes of light and Ash returned a moment later, waving two pictures in the air so that the photo emulsion chemicals would dry more quickly. She handed them to me and said, "I assume you're heading down to Delbert's now?"

"Yeah. I need to get there before they close and confirm whether they even carry that brand of screwdriver. If so, maybe we'll catch a break and they'll remember selling one to some guy last night."

"So we can hope that the screwdriver will end up screwing the driver of that Saab." Ash gave us a demure smile.

Tina gave my wife an incredulous look, and I said, "Yep, you've *definitely* been hanging around me too much."

FIFTEEN

I telephoned the Massanutten Crest Lodge while driving down to Elkton. Luckily, I managed to catch one of the nighttime security guards in the office. I explained who I was and gave him my cell phone number, telling him it was imperative that Linny call me. The guard said that he'd try to contact Linny immediately, but couldn't guarantee when I'd receive a callback.

The dashboard clock said it was 7:58 P.M. as I pulled into the almost-vacant parking lot of Delbert's DIY Emporium. Delbert's was an example of an increasingly rare business in the United States: a local, independently owned hardware and building supply store. As I walked toward the cement warehouse-style shop, a middle-aged woman wearing a red vest appeared on the other side of the glass double doors at the entrance. It was obviously the store manager getting ready to close.

If we'd been in an urban area, she'd have probably hurried to lock the doors and then yell through the window for me to come back tomorrow. But thankfully, things are still fairly civilized in the valley. The manager didn't pointedly look at her watch or heave a huge sigh of exasperation. Instead, she held the door open for me.

"Can I help you find something?" the manager asked.

"Yeah, I hope you can." I showed her my sheriff's office ID card and then the photos of the screwdrivers. "Do you sell this kind of tool here?"

Surprisingly, the woman was eager to help. "Sure. They're about the cheapest brand of screwdriver we carry."

"Could you show me where they are?"

"This must be pretty important if you're working on a Friday night."

"It is, but I can't really talk about it."

"That's all right. Everybody else is talking about it. Ev Rawlins was a regular customer and a good man. I hope you catch who killed him."

She led me into the store and down an aisle packed with all sorts of hand tools, including a display of screwdrivers that matched the one in the Saab's ignition.

I then conducted a brief interview of the

manager, whose name was Doris Axford. Doris told me that she'd been at the hardware store on Thursday night, but hadn't been working the cash register and therefore didn't know if anyone had come in to buy a single screwdriver. She went on to say that the person manning the checkout kiosk had been Brianna Stearns, who was off tonight and not expected back at work until Sunday.

Knowing that it was probably against company policy to release an employee's phone number, I asked Doris if she would call Brianna and pass along the message that it was important I speak with her. Doris said she'd do her best, but didn't sound hopeful. She explained that Brianna liked to "party hearty" on the weekends and almost certainly wasn't home.

Glancing at her watch, Doris primly said, "Besides, by now Brianna probably ain't in any condition to know her name, much less remember a customer from last night."

"Do you guys have a security video system?" I asked, while scanning the ceiling for signs of a closed-circuit TV camera.

"No, sir. Never needed one, but I guess times are changing around here."

"And not for the better, unfortunately. Is it possible for us to check the cash register records or credit card transactions?"

"Not tonight. All of that stuff is in Delbert's office, and he's already down in Blacksburg for the Virginia Tech game tomorrow."

Being a fan of Virginia Tech college football is almost an evangelical religion in the Shenandoah Valley, so I knew it wasn't very likely I could persuade the store owner to return tonight, not even to help with a murder investigation. Blacksburg was a three-hour drive to the southwest and Doris told me, in a roundabout way, that Delbert also liked to "party hearty" on the night before a big game, so he'd likely be in no condition to drive. Still, I asked her to call him, too, and pass along the message to contact me at his earliest convenience. I gave her a business card and thanked her for her assistance.

Once I was outside, my cell phone rang.

"Brad, this is Linny returning your call." The director of security spoke loudly so that he could be heard over what sounded like one of the *Shrek* movies in the background.

"Thanks for getting back to me so quickly, Linny. Something has come up, and I need a big favor."

"I hope you don't want an update on Chester Lincoln. I haven't been able to find any security footage on him yet."

"Chet can go on the back burner for now. I need your help with a homicide investigation."

"A what? Is this that murder they were talking about on the six o'clock news?"

"Yep."

"And is that why you were at the lodge today?" The sound of the movie receded and I realized he'd gone into another room.

"Yes, and I'm sorry for not telling you about it, but I wasn't at liberty to talk."

"You could've trusted me." There was an offended tone in Linny's voice.

Actually, I was pretty certain that wasn't true, which was why I hadn't originally told him the real reason for my visit to the lodge. Linny would have promised to remain silent, but he struck me as so desperate to be seen as an important man that he'd have eventually revealed the secret to someone he wanted to impress. However, I needed his assistance, so I had to come up with a plausible and palatable excuse for why I'd kept him out of the information loop.

Does that sound a wee bit callous, duplicitous, and manipulative? Maybe. Call it fibbing, positive spin, white lies, or whatever you'd like, I'll use a falsehood if it helps me find a murderer.

I said soothingly, "It wasn't because I

235

distrusted you, Linny. I was just trying to protect you."

"From what?"

"From the killer. This morning we were looking at Chet Lincoln as possibly being our murder suspect. Now if I'd told you that, what would have happened if you'd seen Chet a little later?"

"I'd have called the sheriff."

"Who are you kidding?" I said with a genuine-sounding disbelieving chuckle. "You and I both know that you'd have probably done something brave and stupid and tried to apprehend him yourself, right?"

"Well, I suppose that's true," Linny said modestly. "But now you don't think Chet is the killer?"

"He's still on our suspect list, but no longer our main focus."

"Then it's Marilyn Tice?"

"There's no evidence that she's committed any crime. However, the same thing can't be said for a couple of your guests."

"At the lodge? Who?"

"Sherri Driggs and Jesse Hauck. It's beginning to look as if Ms. Driggs's car was never stolen from the hotel, or any place else for that matter. That's why I'm calling."

"You mean she made a false report?"

"Yeah, and tried to put you through the

wringer in the process," I said, surreptitiously reminding Linny that he had a personal score to settle with Sherri.

"That's right! How can I help?"

"I need you to go to the lodge and pull the security video from last night. Ms. Driggs said she and Mr. Hauck both returned to the hotel at around six P.M. and neither went out again. We're depending on you to prove that she's a liar."

"You sound as if you want me to come in tonight."

"I do. You've heard of the first forty-eight hours? That's when we solve murders, Linny, and the clock is ticking."

"But I can't come in tonight," Linny was obviously distressed. "I have my kids for the weekend, and there's just no way I can leave them alone. Could I come in first thing tomorrow morning?"

"Of course. I can't find fault with a man who takes good care of his children," I replied, and this time I wasn't trying to butter Linny up. "In fact, get back to your kids right now. I'll send you an email later tonight, with the time parameters and — oh, hell, I just thought of something. Are you going to need photos of Ms. Driggs and Mr. Hauck so you know who to look for on the video?"

"No problem. I met both of them yesterday when Ms. Driggs jumped down my throat over her car being stolen. I'll know them when I see them on the video."

"Excellent. One other thing: You can't let anybody know about this. If Ms. Driggs and Mr. Hauck catch so much as a hint that we're looking at them, they'll sky out for Atlanta and we won't be able to do a thing about it."

"You can count on me, Brad."

"I know. Thanks, and look for that email at your office tomorrow morning."

As I disconnected from the call, I saw a tow truck rolling eastbound on Highway 33. It was probably the wrecker that Tina had summoned for the Saab. I briefly considered following the truck back up to Thermopylae, but concluded it made more sense for me to instead find a computer and do some background research into Sherri Driggs and Jesse Hauck.

I drove to the sheriff's department and waved to the dispatcher as I headed for Tina's office. Suppressing a yawn, I realized that the caffeine buzz from the sweet tea we'd had at dinner was wearing off. There was no telling how much more investigative work had to be done tonight — and after that, Ash and I still had a teddy bear display

238

to assemble — so I put a pot of coffee on to brew.

As the coffeemaker began to gurgle, I emailed Linny the time parameters I wanted him to check on the security video, and then I began my computer search on Sherri Driggs and Jesse Hauck. I was sipping black coffee that was almost as dark as my mood and frowning at the computer monitor when Tina and my wife came in.

Tina pointedly glanced from the coffeemaker to my cane on her desk and then at me seated in her office chair and said, "Gee, I guess you don't need to be told to make yourself at home."

"Yeah, I'm not the only one who might be making myself at home," I said sourly. "And home might never be the same again."

"What's wrong?" Ash asked.

I handed the women some sheets of paper that I'd printed out during my Internet search. "I plugged Sherri Driggs's name into the search engine and look what I came up with."

Tina squinted at the paper. "The Amerriment Corporation? Who are they?"

"A theme park consortium." I looked at Ash. "Do you remember the Sierra Bear Mountain Fair?"

Ash looked up from the paper she held,

and her eyes narrowed. "That cheesy amusement park near Stockton? How could I forget?"

"Well, Amerriment owns it and five other theme parks scattered over the country."

"We got roped into taking Heather and some of her girlfriends to the Bear Fair when she graduated from junior high school," Ash explained to Tina.

"It's a cute name for a park," said Tina.

"That fooled us, too. But the place was awful: dangerous-looking roller coasters, tacky carnival games, and horrible junk food."

"And booze," I added. "It's the only theme park we've ever been to where beer was sold everywhere. It was a warm day and by three o'clock, the place was just full of drunken guys ogling my teenage daughter and her friends."

"We left before Brad could shoot any-body," said Ash.

I nodded. "And when I complained to the manager, he laughed and told me it wasn't nineteen-sixty anymore. So, there's a brief overview on the sort of classy operation you can expect from Amerriment."

"So why is that important?" Tina asked.

"Look down near the bottom of that sheet. Sherri Driggs is Amerriment's executive vice president in charge of operations."

"Are you sure it's the same woman?"

"Here." I handed Tina another sheet of paper. "I printed that out from the Amerriment website. It's an old media release about the opening of the Rocky Mountain Bear Fair near Denver, back in 2006. Even though she's fully dressed, I'm certain the woman in this photo is Sherri Driggs."

Tina put the papers on her desk. "So she's an executive with a theme park company. I still don't understand why you're so upset."

Ash understood and gave me a worried look. "Because she told Deputy Bressler that she was here on a working vacation."

"And I'm wondering if she came here to acquire the land for the Blue Ridge Bear Fair, or whatever it's going to be called."

"Here in Massanutten County?" Tina was incredulous. "I think you're jumping to some huge conclusions. Why would anyone consider building a theme park here?"

"It's an ideal location," I replied. "We're three hours from D.C. and two hours from Richmond, and there's already an established tourist base from the national park and the lodge."

"But they couldn't build an amusement park there. It's zoned as prime agricultural land."

"For the moment. But the board of supervisors can vote to convert the land to commercial purposes . . . and need I remind you that two of our supervisors own ailing construction firms and another has a paving business?"

"All of whom would benefit from the building of the park," Ash added.

Tina thought for a moment and then folded her arms across her chest. "Okay, it could happen. Say you're right. Would a theme park necessarily be a bad thing?"

"Maybe not for the person raking in the profits, but you wouldn't want to live near one."

Ash said, "Tina, a theme park would destroy the soul of this county. This is farm country, but before you knew it we'd have a bunch of junk-food restaurants, motels, and cheap souvenir shops."

I took up the sad litany. "Don't forget the gridlocked traffic, or the litter. And then there's the cherry on top: Amusement parks attract thieves. The crooks will come for the same reason that lions — no pun intended — go to the water hole. That's were the prey is. Tourists have money, credit cards, nice cameras, and cars full of attractive loot like GPS systems and CD players."

Tina now wore a troubled expression. "I

never looked at it that way. But how can you be so certain that she's decided on a location in Massanutten County? I mean, wouldn't it make more sense for her to be looking for a place closer to the interstate?"

"It might, but can you think of a single reason why Sherri would have been at Ev Rawlins's farm last night?"

"No."

"Me either. Except — Ash noticed something very interesting this morning while we were back at the quarry."

Ash's eyes widened. "Oh my! The property line had been recently marked."

"I wonder if Sherri had decided that the Rawlins farm was the perfect location for her newest glorified carnival. And factor in the fact that she took off when Ash saw her and then faked the theft of her own car, and it looks to me as if she *really* didn't want anyone to know she was there."

"But there hasn't been so much as a whisper about some out-of-town company wanting to buy land around here," said Tina.

"That's true, but wouldn't it make sense for Amerriment to try to acquire property secretly?"

"Before the locals got wise and jacked up the prices," said Ash.

"Or got lynch mob–quality pissed that a

respected farmer was contemplating an offer to sell his land and screw his neighbors in the process," I said. "It would have been in Sherri *and* Ev's best interests to keep such negotiations secret."

"I agree, but there isn't any evidence that Mr. Rawlins was considering selling his land," Tina protested.

"Which means now might be an excellent time to call Kurt Rawlins back. Maybe his dad mentioned something about it." I got up from the chair. "Here. I'll even let you sit in your own office chair to make the call."

Heaving a sigh, Tina sat at the desk and telephoned Kurt. We could hear only one side of the conversation, and at first it was like Tina was talking to a windstorm. Nothing she said had any effect, and the gusts got progressively stronger and stronger. But Tina persevered, and eventually Kurt calmed down a little. Yet the burger baron emphatically denied any knowledge that his father might have been considering selling his land.

Hanging up the phone, Tina said, "You probably heard him. He says his dad would never sell the farm."

"Kurt told us himself that his dad never understood why he turned his back on the farm and went into the fast-food business.

Ev might not have figured it was any of his son's business," Ash said.

"You're still convinced that Sherri Driggs was there because she wanted to buy the property?" Tina asked me.

"I'm not one hundred percent certain, but it fits the facts we currently have."

"So are you saying that Sherri Driggs killed Everett Rawlins?" Tina asked. "With a bow and arrow?"

"Yeah, that's where things stop making sense."

"Brad, honey, things haven't made sense since last night when we found the body," said Ash.

"That's true. But consider this final confusing fact." I picked up one of the sheets that the women thus far hadn't seen. "Guess who was a member of the archery team at his alma mater, Cal State Northridge?"

"Jesse Hauck?" asked Ash as Tina snatched the sheet to look at it.

I nodded. "He's listed as having taken second place at an archery competition at UC Irvine back in 2007."

"Are you sure it's the same guy?"

"I can't be absolutely certain, but the Amerriment website has brief bios of the execs, and there was a tiny blip about Jesse. It said he graduated at the top of his class with a BA in business from Cal State Northridge in 2008."

"So, if it is the same Hauck, maybe you were wrong about Driggs and she *did* lend Jesse the Saab," said Tina.

"And run the risk of her car being seen while her boy toy offs some stubborn farmer who won't sell his land? Sorry, Tina, that just doesn't make any sense. More likely, she'd have sent him in his own car with the promise that she'd cover his play if anything went south."

"And then deny knowing anything when the police came calling," Ash added.

"Did you come up with anything at the hardware store?" Tina sounded frustrated and began to rub her forehead.

"Nothing that's going to break the case," I replied. "Delbert's carries that brand of screwdriver, but we probably won't be able to talk to the owner or cash register operator until they return from their respective lost weekends on Sunday."

"So basically we're still at square one," she grumbled.

"Worse. We have five persons of interest instead of just the one we started out with," I said with a weary laugh.

"Five?" asked Ash.

I ticked them off on my fingers. "We've

still got Chet Lincoln, as well as Wade and Marilyn Tice, and now Sherri Driggs and Jesse Hauck."

"Plus the possibility that none of them did it and it actually was a hunting accident."

Tina sounded hopeless. "What's our next move?"

I glanced at my watch. "Look, it's after nine o'clock. It's been a long day, our brains are fried, and everything appears grim. So, there's only one thing left to do."

"When all else fails, hug your teddy bear?" said Ash, quoting a popular arctophile proverb.

"Yep. Ash has the key to the church community center. Let's go over there and set up our teddy bear displays."

"We don't have time," said Tina.

Ash said, "Let's make time. We're in a funk and maybe the best way to recharge our mental batteries is by doing something completely different."

"There is some truth to that," Tina said musingly.

"Absolutely," I said earnestly. "As hard as you've been working, you're entitled to a short *fur*lough."

Sixteen

Spending some time with the teddy bears had been a good idea. It worked as a sort of a spiritual cleansing of the palate after a long and ultimately disappointing day. I have absolutely no talent for posing stuffed animals, so I just sat on a folding chair and watched as the two women chatted and laughed and set up their mohair wares.

Meanwhile, I took a closer look at Tina's collection of teddies. With Ash as our instructor, we'd both taken up bear making a couple of years earlier. However, Tina had far surpassed me as an artist. Her bears were fully poseable and costumed in authentic recreations of the sort of farm clothing worn in the valley in the late nineteenth century. My favorite piece in her collection was of a furry farm wife holding a pie with tiny oven mitts.

Along about 10:30 P.M., Sergei knocked on the community center door. He'd seen the lights on inside and our cars in the parking lot and thought we might enjoy a late-night snack. This time, Tina did hold hands with Sergei, and I ate the decadent apple pie.

Tina gave Sergei a tour of her table, and then they came over to look at our bears. That's when he picked up one of the more obscure pieces from my "Claw and Order Collection." The bear was slightly plump, had a gray distressed wool moustache, and wore a rumpled mackintosh, a woolen scarf, and a herringbone trilby hat.

"I don't need to see the tag to know who this is," said Sergei as he admired the bear. "Inspector Jack Frost was my favorite British TV copper."

He was referring to the unkempt protagonist of the long-running and popular British crime drama *A Touch of Frost*. Sir David Jason played Detective Inspector Jack Frost, and I'd labored for weeks to sculpt a face that somehow reflected the character's doggedness and compassion. In the end, I wasn't certain if I'd succeeded, so it made me feel good that Sergei had recognized the bear.

"Inspector Fur-ost," I corrected him. "And I've got to agree with you. I hate most cop shows, but I enjoyed watching Frost.

The books were excellent, too."

"This, from a man who hates mystery novels," said Ash.

"I hate *unrealistic* mystery novels. Talking Pomeranians and undead aerobic dance instructors don't solve genuine murders."

"You have my sympathies, Bradley. I feel the same way about those foolish espionage thrillers." Sergei put the bear back on the table. "And I hope that Inspector Fur-ost finds a new home tomorrow."

Ash yawned. "I think I need to find my home right now. It's been a long day and I'm beat."

We locked up the church hall and said our good-byes in the parking lot, and then Ash and I drove home. I took Kitch out into the yard while Ash went upstairs to get ready for bed. It was a clear night, and I stared up into the heavens while Kitch snuffled around, probably following the spoor of a rabbit. We're fortunate to live in a place where there's little light pollution, so you can still actually see the nighttime sky. In the Shawnee language, *Shenandoah* means "daughter of the stars." The name was a mystery to me until one night when I noticed that the breathtakingly beautiful stellar river of the Milky Way seemed to be flowing directly above the South Fork of the

Shenandoah River. After that, the name made perfect sense.

I took Kitch inside and went upstairs. Twenty minutes or so later, I kissed Ash good night and turned the nightstand light off. Not long after, I was awakened by the wail of an emergency vehicle's siren traveling along Coggins Spring Road. I turned to look at the clock. The orange numerals read 1:52 A.M. I'd been asleep a little more than two hours.

Fortunately, the racket hadn't woken up Ash. Her breathing was still deep and regular. The past thirty hours had been hectic for her, and I knew she was exhausted. I rolled back over, snuggled up next to my wife, and was vaguely aware that there was now another siren sounding in the distance as I drifted back to sleep.

I was catapulted into wakefulness for the second time when the phone rang. Looking at the clock as I grabbed the phone, I saw it was just 2:16 A.M.

Sounding more alert than I felt, I said, "This is Brad."

"Mr. Lyon? This is the dispatch center. Hang on a second, please." In the background I could hear all sorts of emergency radio traffic, and the dispatcher paused to answer one of the messages. Then she came

251

back on the line. "Sheriff Barron says she needs you to meet her ASAP at Four-Forty-Three Coggins Spring Road."

"What's going on?" I asked dispatch as Ash put her hand on my shoulder. Meanwhile I had the unpleasant feeling that I should recognize the address.

"The hose company responded to a fire at a vacant residence and they're pretty certain it was an arson."

Then it hit me. "Is this that old Victorian house on the south side of the road near the intersection with the Jackson Highway?"

"I believe so."

"Tell Sheriff Barron I'm on my way." I hung up and slowly got out of bed.

"What is it, honey?" Ash sounded groggy.

"It sounds as if someone just torched the Victorian house we wanted to buy," I said as I turned on the nightstand lamp.

Pushing some strands of hair from her face, Ash squinted at me. "Where we were planning to put the teddy bear shop?"

"Yeah, and isn't it just *too* freaking interesting that Liz Ewell took it off the market less than twelve hours before it went up in flames?" I said while pulling the jeans and shirt I'd had on earlier that day from the laundry hamper. Since I was going to a fire scene, it would be foolish to put on clean

252

clothing.

"You think she had the house burned to collect on the insurance?"

"Or Satan came for her early and accidentally went to the wrong address."

"I'm going with you," Ash said wearily as she sat up in bed.

I went over to her and gently pushed her by the shoulders back down onto the mattress.

"No, you're going to stay in bed and go back to sleep."

"But . . ."

"Sweetheart, you're exhausted to the point of almost being punch-drunk, it's after two A.M., and you have a teddy bear show to help run in the morning."

"But . . ."

"So the last thing you need to be doing is tromping around in the dark, breathing smoke, getting soaked and filthy, and then catching a chill."

"What about you? *You're* tired."

"I'm fine. Haven't I always been able to operate on just a few hours of sleep?"

"Well, yes," she grudgingly admitted. "But, Brad, honey, I want to help."

"I know and I appreciate it. But the fact is, you're so tired, it would be dangerous. Even with the fire extinguished, an arson scene is extremely hazardous. It's like a three-dimensional minefield."

Ash pretended to pout. "Okay, I'll stay. But I'm sulking."

Leaning over to kiss her, I said, "And looking beautiful while you do it. Go back to sleep and I'll see you in the morning."

I arrived at the blaze a couple of minutes later and parked behind Tina's patrol car. The air stank of smoke, and the road was jammed with fire trucks. A turbulent sea of fire was swallowing up the old house while a column of flame-lit smoke rose into the dark sky. Hoses snaked across the pavement, and four jets of water were directed at the inferno, but they looked as useless as streams from squirt guns.

As I climbed from the SUV, I heard warning shouts and a loud, ominous creaking sound. Then, like a flaming ship majestically sinking beneath the waves, the upper portions of the home began to collapse into the basement. Geysers of swirling sparks shot high into the air, and the accompanying roar of the collapsing timber and masonry was deafening. Even though I was fifty yards or so from the house, I could feel the pulsing heat.

I headed toward the conflagration and found Tina standing by one of the fire trucks. She was in conversation with a fire department supervisor, and I opted not to interrupt. Another fire truck arrived, and its crew began unrolling a hose. I glanced back at the fire. With the collapse of the structure, it almost appeared as if the firefighters were spraying water into the cone of a miniature volcano.

When Tina joined me, I said, "We've got to stop meeting like this."

She grimaced. "Yeah. As if I didn't already have enough on my plate. Where's Ash?"

"Over there. There'll be a lot more of it by morning." I nodded toward the fire. Tina rolled her eyes and I admitted, "Ashleigh wanted to come, but I had to put my good foot down and tell her no. She's flat exhausted."

"She must have been for you to have won *that* debate."

"Tell me about it. Now, before we go any further, I've got to tell you that if this is arson, I'm out of my league. That's a very specialized field of expertise."

"I know," said Tina. "I've called the state police, but unfortunately, they can't have an investigator here until sometime tomorrow."

"Well, in the meantime we can process everything outside the burn zone. Who made the original fire notification?"

"A big-rig driver going down Route Three-Forty. He called and said the place was burning like a bonfire."

"What made you think arson?"

"When the first fire truck arrived, the engine commander made a quick recon of the exterior of the house to make sure there wasn't anybody here. There wasn't, but he *did* find an empty five-gallon plastic gas can in the backyard."

I glanced toward the blazing ruins of the house. "Unfortunately, now the evidence is gone."

"Brace yourself. We actually caught a break." Tina gave me a weary smile.

"Don't toy with me, Barron," I said in a mock stern tone.

"I'm not kidding. The engine commander recognized that the gas can was evidence and grabbed it. He put it in the cab of his fire truck."

"Hallelujah. The fact that the can was found in the backyard also tells us something about whoever torched this thing — an amateur. A professional would have left the gas can inside the house so that it would be destroyed in the fire. Liz Ewell won't be happy about paying for such sloppy work."

The wind shifted slightly, blowing some smoke in our direction. Tina rubbed her eyes and asked, "Do you really think she's responsible for this?"

"Tina, how many arsons have you had in Massanutten County since you began working for the sheriff's office?"

She shrugged. "This is the first one."

"And it happened just hours after Miss Ewell — who could have given Machiavelli some pointers on treachery — yanked that house off the market, because she couldn't stand the idea of Ash and me owning it."

"Sorry, but I don't see how the two events are connected. She'd already stung you guys by refusing to sell the house. Why burn it down?"

"There you go, injecting logic into the discussion," I said, realizing that my loathing for Liz Ewell might have clouded my ability to objectively weigh the facts. "It's also a damn good point. Okay, maybe I'm *not* the center of the universe. But Liz Ewell is still the natural suspect."

Tina nodded. "Obviously. She's the only one who benefits financially from the house being destroyed."

"Yeah, but that may back*fire* on her. No insurance company will pay if there's evidence of arson."

Tina and I turned to watch the firefighting efforts for a few moments. There were now six hoses on the blaze, and the fire crews seemed to be making some headway. Still, it would be at least a couple of hours before we'd be able to get anywhere near it, so instead we put on some latex gloves and went to examine the recovered gas can. The five-gallon, red plastic jerry can looked new but was missing its screw-on cap. I tilted the jug slightly to the side and noted mud stains on the bottom.

I said, "In the words of the immortal Bugs Bunny: What a maroon. He probably dropped this when things went *whoosh* too quickly. Or . . ." I glanced back at the dying flames and had the disquieting thought that I was looking at a funeral pyre. "Or maybe he *couldn't* carry it away because he was inside when the fire erupted."

Tina was suddenly solemn. "So we might have a victim in there after all."

"And with the house collapsing like that, it'll take days of searching through the rubble before we know for sure."

"Gee, Brad, you sure know how to brighten a girl's night."

I handed Tina the gas container, and we began to walk back to her patrol car. I said, "Let's think this through before we panic. We've got a five-gallon jug that had to have been awfully heavy when it was full of gasoline. How did it get out here?"

"By car, presumably, though the fire chief says that the only vehicles that were here when he arrived were fire trucks."

"So our arsonist didn't park in front of or near the house," I said.

"But he couldn't have parked too far away, because he wouldn't have wanted to carry the heavy gas can very far."

"Or risk being seen lugging it down the road."

"So he would have parked somewhere nearby." Tina opened the back door of her patrol car and put the gas can on the floorboard.

I pointed with my cane to the north. "That's all farmland over there. No roads."

"But Wardlaw Lane is back there." Shutting the car door, Tina then pointed in the opposite direction. "It kind of runs parallel to Coggins Spring Road, which would give him an invisible approach through the field behind the house."

"How about if I cruise over there and see if I can find any suspicious-looking vehicles?"

"I'd appreciate that. I need to stay here." Tina gestured toward the mass of fire trucks.

"I know. And this is one time when I hope we *don't* find the suspect vehicle. It'll mean our firebug is still alive. I'll call you if I come up with anything."

"You can't. You broke my phone, not that I'm complaining. Take the portable and I'll monitor the radio in my unit."

I took the radio from her. "And I might as well take the camera and evidence kit, too."

Returning to the truck, I maneuvered it around some fire hoses and headed toward Wardlaw Lane. Once there, I slowed the SUV down, but there was no sign of any other vehicles. That helped me relax a little. I really hadn't been looking forward to hanging around the wreckage until the cadaver dogs finished playing olfactory Marco Polo with the immolated remains of the arsonist.

There wasn't much to see along the sides of the road; just a lot of wet brown leaves, masses of naked and forlorn-looking honeysuckle vines, and the occasional big bluish-gray rock. Emerging from a dip in the terrain, I suddenly saw the flames and smoke about two hundred yards away across an open field. This was a likely direction for the arsonist to have approached the house.

I was about to head back when something on the side of the road caught my eye. It was a bit of rich burgundy color on an otherwise drab palette. I stopped the truck and got out. Then I grabbed the camera to take several photographs of the unused highway safety flare that lay on the gravel.

Back in the homicide bureau, we used to call that a clue.

SEVENTEEN

Obviously, this was where the arsonist had parked his vehicle, and it was my guess he'd dropped the flare while hurrying to escape. The road flare was another clue that the guy was a rank amateur. Professional torches usually want their handiwork to look accidental; they almost never use that sort of pyrotechnic device to start a fire. Road flares can burn at more than a thousand degrees Fahrenheit, leaving a distinctive scorching pattern and unique chemical signature, both of which will make an arson investigator sit up and take notice.

Once I'd collected the flare as evidence, I began searching to see if our bumbling burn artist had dropped anything else, but came up dry. After that, I turned my attention to the shoulder of the road and was disappointed to see that the ground was too gravelly to have retained any tire impressions. However, I did find the two different spots where the arsonist had crossed over a small and grassy embankment to enter and leave the field. Carefully ascending the bank, I shined my flashlight down at the moist farm soil and admired the most perfect shoe impressions I'd ever seen in my law enforcement career. Indeed, the sole patterns were so distinct that even my untrained eye could tell that they came from athletic shoes.

I reflected that it was kind of a shame there wasn't a Better Business Bureau for crooks that Liz Ewell could complain to about the hapless fool she'd hired. Not only had he flubbed the job of making the fire look like an accident, he'd left all sorts of useful evidence behind. You just can't find good help these days.

"Mike-Fourteen to Mike-One," I called over the radio. "You can relax. There's no car, but I've found where the guy parked. I've also recovered a road flare. Even better, there are two sets of clear foot tracks showing he went toward the house and came back out."

"Copy. Excellent work," Tina replied, and I could hear the relief in her voice. "Are you going to need a roll of crime scene tape to mark the scene? I can have Deputy Paine bring it over."

"That's affirmative. And you're going to have to call the crime lab and have that tech come back up here. We want plaster castings of these pretty shoe impressions."

Deputy Paine arrived just as I was finishing up the pictures of the footprints. After acquainting him with the crime scene, I rejoined Tina. The fire was slowly dying under the assault of thousands of gallons of water, and I noticed that the smoke was now mostly white instead of black. An hour or so later, the fire chief dismissed several of the fire trucks but kept two hoses spraying the debris for flare-ups. Meanwhile, Tina and I cooled our heels and drank some wretched coffee she'd gotten from the only all-night convenience store in the county.

It was nearly six A.M. when the fire chief finally declared the scene safe enough for Tina and me to approach the house to take some photographs and look for evidence in the yard. The smoke hung in the air like fog, so we put on disposable breathing filter masks before proceeding any closer to the still-smoldering wreckage. However, the masks did nothing to protect our eyes, which soon became so red and teary that you'd have thought we'd been watching that old three-hanky film *Somewhere in Time.*

We began our search in the backyard. Tina

used her flashlight to scan the ground while I took photos of the destruction. It was slow and unpleasant work. The house had been sprayed with such a huge volume of water that the backyard was now a quagmire. Before long, my boots were soaked and I could feel my socks becoming cold and wet. Days don't start much better than that. And for all our efforts, we turned up only one useful piece of evidence: Tina located more of the suspect's shoe impressions in the soil on the other side of the backyard fence.

The sun was already above the Blue Ridge when we slogged back to our cars. I glanced at my watch. It was a little after seven o'clock. I was pretty much in a zombie state with fatigue, which kind of shocked me, because back when I was a cop I could work thirty-six hours straight on a murder investigation. Yeah, I'd be a space cadet the day after, but I was capable of that sort of prolonged effort. But that obviously wasn't the case any longer. It sucks getting old. I just hoped that the combination of a shower, lots of good hot coffee, and the kind of breakfast that would give a vegan the shudders would restore my vitality before the teddy bear show opened.

Tina and I were saying good-bye to each other when a big black Ford van pulled up behind my SUV.

"Look who's come out to make sure the job was done properly," I muttered.

"Just when I thought the morning couldn't get any worse," Tina said with a heartfelt sigh.

"You'd better do the talking. I'm liable to say something indelicate."

"You?"

The driver's-side door opened, and a young woman with short-cropped hair and the stern face of a Marine Corps drill instructor climbed out and marched to the back of the vehicle. I heard the rear doors open, then the whine of a small electric motor. A moment later, my favorite local sociopath rolled around the side of the van in her motorized scooter.

It had been more than two years since I'd last seen Elizabeth Ewell. She'd aged badly over that period. Back when we first met, she'd looked sweet and grandmotherly, with plump pink cheeks, white curly hair, and a heartwarming smile that concealed the soul of a robber baron.

Now she looked as hard, shriveled, and sour as a desiccated lemon. She wore a heavy coat and a woolen cap and had a white blanket tucked around her legs. She pretended we didn't exist as she drove the scooter past us.

Tina called, "Miss Ewell, could we speak to you for a moment?"

Liz Ewell stopped the chair and turned it to face Tina. "Unless you can tell me why my house burned down, I don't see why."

"Actually, we *do* know why. That's the reason we want to talk to you." Tina gestured toward the ruins. "This wasn't an accident. We have evidence that someone deliberately set the house on fire."

"I want the name of the person who did this," said Ewell. Meanwhile, her impassive driver jogged up and assumed a position of parade rest behind the scooter.

I kept quiet, but oh how I wanted to say, *Me, too. Can we look in your checkbook?*

Tina said, "We don't know who it is yet, but I'm very confident we're going to identify the suspect."

Miss Ewell's eyes flicked toward me. "Maybe I can help you. Where was *he* when the fire started?"

I hadn't seen that one coming, and I had to admire the scheming old tyrant. By charging me with torching the house, she'd both diverted suspicion from herself and put me on the defensive. Furthermore, it wasn't an outlandish accusation. The real estate agent, Roger Prufrock, had undoubtedly told her of our anger at her refusal to sell us the house. Technically, that constituted motive on our part.

Tina looked thoughtful. "Are you formally accusing Mr. Lyon of arson?"

"Well . . . no."

"Good, because our evidence clearly shows that whoever did this had two good legs. Mr. Lyon only has one."

Liz Ewell gave me a malicious smile. "That's true, but his wife —"

"Don't even go there," I finally spoke. "Look, my hat is off to you. It was an ingenious idea to refuse to sell us the house and then burn it down to frame us for arson. But the guy you hired to do the torch job was literally a flaming idiot."

The old woman's grin vanished. "I didn't have this house set on fire. I was born in that house."

I thought, *You weren't born; you hatched with the other baby cobras.*

Miss Ewell glanced at the wreckage. "Besides, although I detest you and your wife, and certainly would never have sold to the likes of *you,* I wouldn't destroy a quarter-million-dollar house to address the problem. There are far cheaper ways of dealing with self-righteous little crusaders like yourselves. Furthermore, I didn't 'refuse' anything, because I knew nothing about any offer. In fact, up until this morning I hadn't spoken to Roger Prufrock in weeks."

Tina and I exchanged shocked looks. She said, "You talked to Roger Prufrock this morning? When?"

Ewell looked over her shoulder at her attendant, who tonelessly answered, "He called shortly before six-thirty. He said it was extremely important he speak with Miss Ewell immediately."

"And what did he say?" Tina asked.

"Roger the Dodger thinks he's such a smooth operator that it makes me laugh," Ewell replied with a vinegary chuckle. "He called to tell me that my house had burned down and to express his overblown condolences. Then he got to the real reason for the call and offered to buy my now-vacant lot."

"As I recall, Mr. Prufrock lives over in Mount Meridian. That's ten miles from here. Did he say how he found out about the fire so quickly?"

Liz Ewell thought for a moment. "As I recall, he said that someone here in town had called him with the news."

I asked, "How much did Roger offer you for the property?"

"A tenth of what it was worth yesterday

— but he said he'd also absorb the costs of salvage and site cleanup."

"For a three-quarter-acre lot?" My voice was doubtful. "Without the house, even if you don't factor in the cleanup, that's a very generous offer."

"Overly generous, and that's what makes me curious." Ewell pulled the blanket up and tucked her hands beneath it. "Up until this morning, Roger wasn't the least bit interested in the property. Now he can hardly wait to buy the land, and I want to know why."

Although I knew from personal experience that Liz Ewell was a consummate liar, I had the strong sense she was being honest. That, in turn, meant I had to at least consider the fact that she'd also been telling the truth when she denied having spoken with Roger the previous day. And if that was the case, there was only one logical way to explain all the misinformation. Our gazes met, and I think the same infuriating thought occurred to Ewell and me simultaneously.

I smacked the knob of my cane into my palm. "That sneaky son of a bitch conned both of us. Roger used our feud to cover up the fact that *he* wanted the house."

"Not the house. The land." Ewell's eyes

glowed with an unholy light.

"But what I don't understand is the timing. Why burn the house down now?"

"Hang on a second," said Tina. "Are you suggesting that Roger Prufrock is responsible for the arson?"

"It's pure process of elimination. If she didn't pay to have it done" — I hooked a thumb at Ewell, who nodded belligerently — "and since Ash and I didn't do it, then who benefits from the fire?"

Tina's eyebrows arched. "Roger, because he gets the property at a huge discount."

"The only property that two-faced loudmouth is going to get from me is the six feet of earth where I'm going to bury him," intoned Ewell. Usually, when people say things like that, you assume it's intended for dramatic effect, especially when the speaker is an elderly invalid.

However, I suspected that Miss Liz Ewell meant precisely what she said.

I said, "I think we need to roll over to Roger's house right now and have a little chat."

"I agree," said Tina.

"He probably won't be there," said Ewell. "The last thing he told me was that he was leaving immediately for a few days of vacation and going down to Hilton Head to do some golfing. He said he'd call me later in the week."

I said, "How convenient. He disappears, claiming he's going to South Carolina. And who can prove otherwise?"

"You don't think he's actually going to Hilton Head?" Tina asked.

"Call me the original doubting Thomas, but let's try a little experiment." I retrieved my cell phone and found Roger's cell number. The recorded voice said that the phone I was currently trying to call was not in service and that I should try my call again later. I hung up before the call rolled over to voice mail.

Snapping the phone shut, I said, "Old Roger has turned his cell phone off. Now, what real estate agent ever does that?"

"The kind who doesn't want to be found," Tina replied.

"Well, when you find him, I expect you to notify me immediately," Ewell snapped, signaling that our tenuous truce was over. "I'm going home."

I was going to not say a word and just let her roll back to her van. But my conscience was bothering me. Our mutual antipathy had caused Liz Ewell and me to wrongly accuse each other of crimes, and it was mortifying to think that our behavior had

272

been so much alike.

I said, "Miss Ewell, before you go, please accept my apology for having wrongly accused you of arranging the arson."

"An olive branch?" Her voice oozed with disdain. "Don't waste your breath. You and I will always be enemies."

"I understand, but that doesn't mean we *both* have to fight dirty. I'm truly sorry that your house was burned down."

The old woman scowled, spun the scooter around, and whizzed back toward the van with the attendant jogging along after her.

I turned to Tina. "And for that matter, I owe you an apology, too. I'm supposed to be helping you conduct an investigation, not a vendetta."

"Forget it. Up until we found out about Roger's role in this, you had a good reason to suspect her of arson."

"Maybe, but I still feel like an utter ash."

EIGHTEEN

As the van drove away, I said, "Now, getting back to Mr. Roger and this beautiful day in his scorched neighborhood."

Tina tried to stifle a yawn and said, "Why would he have gone into hiding?"

A sudden thought struck me. "Maybe Roger decided to do the torch job himself and got burned. Maybe he was standing too close when he ignited the accelerant. We do have good reasons to believe our arsonist was an amateur."

Tina nodded. "Makes sense. That house was probably full of gasoline fumes when he threw the flare in, which could have caused one hell of a fireball. We need to check the local hospitals to see if anyone was treated for burns sometime early this morning."

"I'm afraid we're going to have to check more than just the local ones — even if he was injured badly enough to require medical attention, I don't think Roger would've gone to a hospital around here. He couldn't take the risk that the emergency room physician would put two and two together when the arson hit the news."

"I suppose you're right. I'll put out a statewide BOL on Roger and his BMW." Tina opened the driver's door of her cruiser and got in. "And even though he probably isn't there, I'm going to roll by his house before I go home."

"Call me if you find him."

"I will. You guys have a good time at the teddy bear show." Tina shut the door and drove off.

It wasn't until I got in my car and shut the door that I realized just how dirty I was and how badly I stank of smoke. When I got home, I went to the back door, which led directly into our tiny laundry room. Leaving my muddy boots on the rear porch, I went inside and began to remove my filthy clothing. I was tired and my left leg was throbbing, but the delicious aromas wafting from the adjoining kitchen offered the promise of revival.

Ash poked her head around the corner from the kitchen and asked, "I was beginning to worry. How are you doing, honey?"

"Tired, but I think the day is already looking up. Is that your pumpkin-cranberry bread I'm smelling?"

"It is. I thought you might like something special after spending most of the night out there. I've also got bacon warming in the oven, and I'll scramble eggs whenever you're ready."

"Thank you, love. With a great breakfast like that in the works and some ibuprofen, I promise I'll catch my second wind," I said, removing my shirt. "Where's Kitch?"

"I already dropped him off at Tina's folks." Her nose wrinkled. "Just put those clothes directly into the washer."

"I'd climb in, too, if there were room."

She came into the laundry room a moment later with a mug of steaming black coffee in one hand and ibuprofen in the other. I took the mug and gave it a look of dewy-eyed affection. "You're *so* beautiful. Do you know how long I've been dreaming of you?"

Ash caressed my cheek. "You can make out with your coffee later, sweetheart. Tell me what happened. So, was it an arson?"

"Yes." I took a sip of coffee and swallowed the pills. "And we're pretty certain that Roger Prufrock torched the house."

"What? Roger? Why?"

"It turns out *he* wants to buy that piece of

property. Not the house, but the land."

"How did you find that out?"

"Liz Ewell showed up just before we cleared the scene. Once we finished falsely accusing each other of arson, we actually had a few moments of civil conversation." I took another drink of coffee and put the mug on the washing machine. "She told us that Roger never said a word to her about us wanting to buy the house. She also never ordered him to take it off the market."

Ash folded her arms across her chest. "And you believe her?"

"I'm as uncomfortable with that concept as you are, my love. But her version of what happened makes sense, so I don't think we have a choice," I said, while removing my jeans and sticking them in the washer.

"That woman would lie to Saint Peter."

"Well, maybe it'll cheer you up a little to hear that Miss Liz is looking bad enough that she might be meeting him soon."

Ash followed me upstairs to the bathroom and stood outside the shower as I continued my story. I told her about the evidence we'd recovered from the scene, Roger's clumsy and preemptive offer to buy the land, and his subsequent disappearance.

As I finished rinsing the spiced apple cider–scented body wash from my hair, I said,

"The one thing that Tina and I can't figure out is the timing. Why did Roger feel he had to rush things?"

"Maybe he knows something we don't."

"Go on." I turned off the water.

"One of the reasons that house was so attractive to us was because it stood near the intersection with the Jackson Highway." She handed me a bath sheet. "But the land might be more valuable without the house there."

I wiped my eyes with the towel. "I see what you're saying. There were only a limited number of ways the house could be used for business purposes."

"Exactly. You could have a specialty shop there, like we'd planned, or maybe professional offices. But if the house was gone, the owner could construct any kind of commercial building, like a gas station or maybe a fast-food restaurant."

"Yeah, but the town isn't big enough to support those kinds of businesses, and you couldn't depend on attracting enough regular customers from the Jackson Highway. There just isn't that much traffic."

"For now." Ash looked a little grim. "That would change if Amerriment built that teddy bear amusement park, wouldn't it?"

My jaw sagged. "Lord, I'm glad that *your*

278

brain is still working. I completely over-looked the fact that Kobler Hollow Road is less than two miles up the highway from where the house was."

"Do you realize what that means? If there is a connection, it means Roger had to have known that Amerriment — or more specifically, Sherri Driggs — wanted to buy property here in the valley."

"Otherwise, he wouldn't have recognized the potential future value of the land that the house was on."

"And the only way he could have known about any of this was if Sherri was using Roger as her real estate agent."

"It fits. Good ol' Roger would be just the one to know whether a farmer was toying with the idea of selling his land."

Ash slapped the bathroom counter. "The part that infuriates me was that he kept quiet and decided to sell his friends and neighbors down the river to make a filthy buck."

"Unfortunately, that seems to be the American way these days. And he may have done more than just betray the folks around here," I said as I went into the bedroom to get dressed.

"You believe Roger might have killed Everett?" Ash followed me and sat down on the bed.

"If he was willing to burn down a building and put a bunch of firefighters' lives at risk, we have to presuppose he's capable of murder."

"I see what you mean."

"So let's assume your theory is correct and Roger was acting as Sherri's real estate agent. We know that Sherri and Jesse arrived on Tuesday. So, what could the new boundary markers you found on Everett's property potentially mean?"

Ash nodded and understood. "That there had already been discussions as early as Tuesday and that Everett might have agreed to sell his land."

I touched the tip of my nose. "But our amusement park pimps *don't* leave, and instead you see Sherri's car at Everett's home on Thursday night. Why are they still here?"

"Because the deal wasn't finalized?"

"That's what I'm wondering, too. Maybe Everett got cold feet at the last second and decided he didn't want to sell. Where does that leave Roger?"

Ash came over to adjust my shirt collar. "Obviously, he doesn't get his commission. But I find it hard to believe he'd kill Everett over that."

"Sweetheart, I've seen a man killed over a four-dollar taco combo plate. Roger was potentially out well over two hundred grand." I sat down on the bed to put on my shoes.

"My Lord! That much?"

"Do the math. Everett would've been selling fifty-eight acres of land to a company that was probably offering top dollar to ensure they got the property quickly and quietly."

Ash looked thoughtful. "A single acre can sell for as much as ten thousand dollars around here. That's five point eight million dollars!"

"But Roger wouldn't get a penny if Everett changed his mind about selling. Plus, you can bet he was going to use that money to scoop up as much of the adjoining property as possible."

"So that he could make a fortune when the land rush began." Ash glanced at the alarm clock. "And speaking of rushing, can we continue this discussion downstairs? We have to eat breakfast and get going, or we'll be late for our own teddy bear show."

As we headed back downstairs, the phone in the kitchen began to ring. Ash rushed ahead to get it while I continued to hobble down the steps. When I arrived in the kitchen, Ash handed me the phone and said it was Tina.

The sheriff said, "Roger definitely isn't the sharpest tool in the shed."

"What did you find?" I asked.

"He wasn't there, but I did locate a plastic garbage bag on the ground outside his garage."

"In plain sight, so you didn't need a search warrant. Sweet."

"Even better, the bag was full of singed clothes that just stink of gasoline."

"Excellent work. That pretty much answers the burning question of our arsonist's identity."

"But not *where* he is."

"I have every faith you'll smoke him out."

Before she could hang up on me, I filled Tina in on Ash's theory about the potential real estate connection between the arson and the murder.

When I finished, Tina said, "Then I guess it's a good thing I put out a BOL on him. I'll call you if we hear anything."

I disconnected from the call and joined Ash at the table. We quickly ate breakfast and then packed up the rest of the coffee and pumpkin-cranberry bread to snack on later at the show.

En route, we both expressed cautious

hope that the absolutely glorious autumn weather would translate into strong attendance at the show. We arrived in town a couple of minutes later and saw that we had good cause for optimism. This was the closest thing to a traffic jam I'd ever seen in Remmelkemp Mill. There had to have been twenty cars idling on the road, all waiting their turn to enter the church parking lot, which already looked jammed to capacity.

Not only that, there was a queue of about thirty people waiting for the community center doors to open. The presence of that many early-bird collectors was a good sign. It meant that people were excited about the show and wanted first crack at the creations inside. More people joined the line, and I gave Ash a sidelong glance. She was beaming. If the early attendance was any indicator, the show was going to be a rousing success.

I stopped to drop Ash off at the curb and told her I'd join her in a few minutes. She gave me a quick kiss and jumped from the car. Then I drove a half block, made a left turn, and headed back toward the county courthouse on a side street. Having parked the SUV, I grabbed my cane and began walking toward the church. As I was about to cross the main highway through town, my cell phone rang. I half expected it would be Tina or Linny calling, but when I glanced at the screen I didn't recognize the number.

When I answered the phone, a groggy-sounding woman with a husky smoker's voice said, "Is this Dandelion?"

"Dandelion? No, this is *Brad* Lyon. Who's this?"

"Brianna Stearns. There's a message on my answering machine from Doris to call Dandelion. She must have given me the wrong number, so —"

Realizing the hardware store clerk was still half blasted and that I'd just confuse her all the more by any further discussion over my name, I said, "Don't hang up! I'm Dandelion. Thanks for calling me back."

"How'd you get a funny name like that?"

"My parents liked gardening."

"Huh. Well, Doris said you're with the law and I want to give my side of the story before you file any charges."

"Actually, I —"

"That skank was coming on to my boy-friend, acting all hornier than the preacher's daughter. That was provocation."

"I'm certain it was, but I don't have the slightest idea of what you're talking about. I need to ask you a few questions about something else entirely."

"Oh. Well . . . never mind."

"Don't worry. It'll be our little secret. Now, Brianna, do you remember working at Delbert's on Thursday night?"

"That's where *I* work."

"Yeah, I know. You were at the cash register. Do you recall that?"

"Sure. You weren't there, though."

"You're right, I wasn't. But do you remember if a man came into the store maybe a little after seven-thirty and bought a screwdriver?"

There was a long pause, and I began to wonder whether Brianna had gone to sleep or, more likely, to seek out some hair of the dog. At last, she said, "That was the cute guy from Georgia."

Bingo, I thought. *Jesse Hauck.* However, keeping my voice calm, I asked, "And how do you know he was from Georgia?"

"He parked his car in the handicapped spot right in front of the doors. I could see the top of the plate."

"Do you remember what kind of car it was?"

"Some sort of new VW. Nice car . . . cute guy." Brianna was sounding drowsy now.

"And I just want to be certain about this: He bought a screwdriver, right?"

"Yeah. He said he liked to screw things."

Brianna chuckled at the witticism.

"He sounds like a classy guy. Do you remember how he paid for the screwdriver?"

"Cash." She yawned and smacked her lips.

"Okay, one final question and then you can go back to sleep. Do you think you could identify that man if you saw him again?"

"Sure. I guess."

I thanked her for the help and left Tina a voice-mail message recounting my conversation with Brianna. Crossing the road, I made my way to the community center and waved at the church ladies seated at the admission table as I went inside. Once inside, I paused to savor both the scene and the palpable atmosphere of goodwill. The hall was full of cheerful people, all chatting and laughing as they searched for the perfect stuffed animal to add to their collections. I don't believe in magic, but I'll allow that teddy bears seem to possess an almost unearthly power to bring out the best in most folks.

It was a good thing I arrived when I did. There was a knot of fur fanatics crowded around both our and Tina's tables, and I noted with satisfaction that a woman was leaving with one of Ash's realistic big cat figures. Meanwhile, my wife was writing up

286

a sales receipt for one of Tina's farmer bears while answering questions about other teddies. I suggested that she let me do the clerical work while she dealt with the collectors. Ash gratefully surrendered the receipt book and pen to me with a thank-you and a kiss on the cheek.

After about ten minutes, there was a lull. As Ash put fresh bears on both tables, I quietly shared with her what Brianna had told me.

Ash said, "Is that enough to arrest Jesse?"

"No. All we can maybe prove is that he bought a screwdriver, which isn't illegal." I took a chunk of pumpkin-cranberry bread from the bag and put it in my mouth.

"But what about lying to the police? Didn't he tell you that he never left the hotel that night?"

"Yeah, but we can't really prove that yet. Our witness from the hardware was sloshed — which makes her statement unreliable at best."

"And Linny apparently hasn't found anything on the security video yet, or he'd have called."

I chewed and swallowed. "Besides, even if Jesse did lie to me, that isn't a crime. I have no peace officer status in Virginia, or anywhere else for that matter. I'm just a civilian consultant. People can lie to me all day, if they want."

Ash picked up McKenzie Macaroon, one of her bears from the "Confection Collection" dressed as a cookie. As she smoothed the fur on the teddy's muzzle, she said, "But Jesse doesn't know that. Couldn't you re-interview him and let him think that he'll be arrested if he doesn't tell the truth?"

"You mean *lie* to him?" I feigned shock. "I'm shocked and saddened that you think your husband would be capable of such underhanded behavior."

"Uh-huh."

"And it's also exactly what I'm going to suggest to Tina that we do."

A trio of women approached the table, so all talk of murder ceased. Curiously, one of the ladies was instantly attracted to Bear-atio Caine. She picked the bear up and began to giggle. As we began to chat, she revealed that she was on vacation from her job in a crime lab in southern Florida. She also said that she and all her peers thought *CSI: Miami* was just about the funniest show on television. I was in the process of showing her all the different ways you could pose Bear-atio when my phone rang. The call was from Tina, so I excused myself as Ash took over for me.

I said, "Hi, Tina, you're missing a great show. We've sold several of your bears."

"I wish I were there. Please tell Ash thanks," said Tina.

"I will. You got my message?"

"Yeah, but I've got other interesting news for you. Game Warden Randy Kent just called, and he's got a lead on where we might find Chet Lincoln. We're heading out to do a stakeout right now."

"Here's a Dick Tracy Crime Stopper tip: Don't take Kitch with you."

Tina chuckled. "I'd already figured that out. And I have some other info. I just got a fax from my friend at the crime lab."

"Already?"

"It seems she stayed late last night to do the analysis. Anyway, we know what the stuff was that we found on the shaft of the arrow, although I don't know how much it helps."

"What is it?"

"The tiny bits of debris we found on the arrow's shaft are dyed and processed cow leather."

"Leather jacket? Boots? A belt?"

"I was thinking more along the lines of an archery glove. Randy told me that most of the bow hunters use them."

"Did your friend have the chance to

analyze the other trace evidence?" I asked.

"Yeah, and unfortunately the stuff on the blades of the broadhead isn't so understandable. It's a mixture of plywood and white plastic fragments." In the background, I heard someone call Tina's name. She said, "Sorry, Brad, we'll talk more later. We've got to roll."

"Be careful."

I snapped the phone shut and saw that Ash had just sold Bear-atio to the criminalist from Florida. Ordinarily, I'd have been overjoyed that the bear was going to a good home, but all I could do was offer the woman a distracted "Thank you." The information about the trace evidence on the arrowhead had given me the unpleasant feeling that I'd overlooked something vitally important at Rawlins's farm.

Plywood and plastic on the blades suggested the arrow had possibly grazed or passed through a structure before skewering Rawlins, but that didn't match what I remembered of the crime scene geography. I mentally replayed our examination of the homicide scene, keenly aware that I wasn't going to be able to enjoy the fur fiesta until I figured out what I'd failed to notice at the crime scene.

Ash touched my shoulder, and I looked

up to see that we were alone again. She said, "Honey, did Tina have bad news?"

"Sort of. The trace evidence on the arrow could mean we missed something at Rawlins's place." I went on to recount what Tina had told me.

When I finished, she said, "I see what you mean. You'd better go back out there and take a second look."

"You wouldn't mind?"

"Not at all. Now that the initial rush is over, I can handle both tables." Ash gestured toward the room, where the collectors were now making a more leisurely inspection of the exhibitors' tables.

"Which I'm afraid you'd be doing anyway." I stood up and gave her a kiss. "I'm going to be a basket case until I figure this out and I don't want to *bruin* your day."

However, my pace slowed as I made my way toward the door. There were hundreds of gorgeous teddy bears on display, and I reminded myself that Christmas was less than two months away. A boy bear and girl bear, posed as if holding hands, caught my eye and I had to stop at MaryAnn Wills's table.

This is probably going to endanger my already shaky reputation as a tough guy, but I didn't need to ask MaryAnn what sort of fabric she'd used for the fur. There's something unmistakably rich about the appearance of alpaca. The boy bear had cinnamon-colored fur with a wide crimson ribbon tied into a bow around his neck, while his ursine girlfriend was composed of golden fur and wore a satin lavender bonnet with a decorative feather on the side. They looked so happy together that I found myself smiling. I knew that Ash would absolutely love the courting couple and decided I'd do a little early Christmas shopping before resuming the murder investigation.

Noticing that I was transfixed by her creations, MaryAnn smiled and said, "The way they hold hands reminds me of you and Ashleigh."

"Which is why they'll make the perfect Christmas present for Ash. I've got to run an important errand right now, but can you hold these two cuties for me until I get back?" I asked.

"I'm sorry, Brad, but I can't. Someone already bought them." MaryAnn didn't sound regretful, however. Indeed, I thought there was a trace of amusement in her voice. "But the buyer will be thrilled to know how much you like them."

As I glanced back down at the teddy bears, the penny dropped. The girl bear's

292

fur was the same color as Ash's hair, and once upon a time, my hair had been cinnamon-colored. I suddenly realized why I'd been particularly drawn to the bears, and why Ash had picked them out as gifts for me.

I chuckled and said, "Apparently, great minds think alike. But please don't tell Ash about this. She likes to surprise me on Christmas morning and I don't want to spoil it for her."

MaryAnn winked. "It'll be our secret."

NINETEEN

Although the sun was shining brightly and the air was as cool and crisp as a freshly picked apple, Rawlins's farm felt gloomy. Maybe it was the deathly stillness; maybe it was the closed-up house; maybe it was just my imagination. Some strands of crime scene tape dangled limply from a couple of tree trunks, and it irrationally reminded me of Tony Orlando and his sappy hit song from so long ago. Nowadays, when you tie a yellow ribbon around a tree, it's usually to seal off a homicide scene.

I knew that I needed to view the homicide scene with fresh eyes, so I decided not to retrace my search path from Thursday night. I still had the evidence camera with me from that morning, so I slipped the camera's strap over my shoulder and limped toward the barn. I was examining one of the building's wooden exterior walls when my cell phone rang. Squinting at the screen,

I saw it was Linny calling.

The security director sounded exuberant. "Sherri Driggs was lying to you and I can prove it! She didn't come back here at six o'clock. In fact, she *left* the lodge at exactly six thirty-two P.M."

"And you have this on video?" I asked.

"I do."

"Excellent work. I knew you'd come through. Was Mr. Hauck with her when she left?"

"No, she was alone. He didn't leave until seven twenty-six, and it looked like he was in a hurry. Then they came back to the lodge together at exactly nine fifty-eight P.M."

"Linny, would you please save all that video footage to CD-ROM? We're going to need it as evidence."

"I've already done that. You can pick it up whenever you're ready. Now, can I ask a question?"

"Sure, so long as you won't be offended if I can't answer it."

"I won't. Do you think they killed Mr. Rawlins? The only reason I'm asking is if they hurt another guest, there might be an implied liability issue that could turn into a lawsuit."

Filing lawsuits against deep-pocket businesses is one of the most popular hobbies in America, so Linny had a valid concern. I replied, "There is no evidence that would lead a reasonable person to conclude that they committed a murder. However, that could change. If it does, I'll notify you. I don't want your other guests exposed to risk any more than you do."

"Thanks, Brad. I can't ask for anything more than that."

"Now if I recall correctly, Ms. Driggs and Mr. Hauck are scheduled to check out on Monday morning."

"That's right."

"We'll need to know if they decide to check out early. Is that a problem?"

"Not at all. I'll contact hotel registration right now and they'll alert me. But there's nothing to stop them from simply leaving. Do you want me to assign someone to watch them?"

"No," I said hurriedly. The very last thing we needed was one of Linny's overeager rent-a-cops screwing the pooch as a consequence of trying to play the role of a secret agent. "If they make your stakeout guy, Sherri and Jesse will bail, and we want them to stay here."

"I understand, Brad. But when this is all over, can I tell my uncle?" Linny asked imploringly.

"Why don't you just invite him to the award ceremony? After I tell Sheriff Barron how much you helped, I'm certain she'll want to give you an official commendation for the great job you did."

I wasn't being patronizing. Linny may have been pretty much clueless, but his heart was in the right place, which is more than you can say for a lot of folks. He deserved to be recognized for his efforts. He'd delivered the goods, which — again — is more than you can say for a lot of folks.

"An official commendation?" Linny sounded almost reverent. "I owe you one, Brad."

"Nonsense. You've earned it. Now, if you'll excuse me, I've got to get back to work."

Once I'd disconnected from the call, I resumed my visual search of the barn and carport, but came up empty. I next headed toward the house. On Thursday night, Ash and I had made a counterclockwise orbit of the residence. Today, I'd circle it by traveling in the opposite direction, which would force me to view the setting differently. I walked around to the east side of the house and stopped so suddenly that I had to catch myself with my cane.

On Thursday night, I'd noticed some

minor damage to the vinyl siding about six-and-a-half feet above the ground. I'd assumed this marked the spot where high winds had torn a flag bracket from the wall, but now I had the unpleasant feeling that I'd been wrong. Retrieving a kitchen chair from the house, I cautiously climbed up on it to get a better look. I could now see that directly beneath the fractured siding was a cross-shaped pair of notches punched into the plywood. It occurred to me that I had no business thinking Linny clueless when I could so blithely overlook the spot where the arrow that killed Rawlins had originally struck.

I took several photographs of the damage and reflected that this discovery didn't merely explain the particles of plastic and plywood found on the blades. It also accounted for the slight bend in the shaft, the impossible ballistics of shooting a bent arrow, and why the projectile hadn't produced a through-and-through wound in Rawlins's abdomen. None of it had made any sense. But now I realized that I'd committed a fundamental error by assuming a bowshot had killed Rawlins. It hadn't. The damage seemed to indicate that someone had yanked the arrow from the wall and used it as an impromptu dagger.

Unfortunately, evidence that answers one question often spawns a host of fresh puzzles: For instance, who'd fired the arrow into the wall? When did it happen? Was it just ahead of the murder or hours or days beforehand? What caused the archer to miss so badly? Who yanked the arrow out of the wall? How did the suspect gain possession of it? And which suspect? All of them, including Roger, could have had access to the yard.

Carefully climbing down from the chair, I telephoned Tina's office and left a voice-mail message telling her what I'd found. I also suggested that she contact the crime lab and request that they come to the farm to seize the evidence. It was too big a job for me, because it would require the removal and collection of the fractured slats of vinyl siding and then cutting out a decent-sized hole in the plywood around the place where the arrow strike had left the scar.

I didn't want to be around when Kurt Rawlins found the hole hacked into his folks' home. He'd undoubtedly blow a gasket and scream that the damage was un-necessary, but he'd be wrong. Merely photo-graphing where the arrow had struck wasn't enough. There was a chance that trace evidence could be recovered from the plywood and vinyl, and the best place to perform that work was in a crime lab, not outside on a ladder.

As I carried the chair around to the front of the house, a red Lexus coupe rolled down the driveway and came to a halt behind my SUV. I thought, *Speak of the devil.* It was Kurt Rawlins's automobile. He got out of the car and walked over to me.

I said, "I'm sorry, Mr. Rawlins, but you're going to have to leave. This is still an active crime scene."

Kurt glowered at me. "I thought you people were finished here."

"Who told you that?"

"Nobody. But you've had almost two days to do whatever it is you do, which is nothing, from the look of it."

I gave him a bland smile. "Processing a murder scene is a little more complicated than assembling combo meals for the lunch rush. We take as much time as we need to get it right."

"My crews work fast *and* get it right."

I was becoming weary of his obsessive need to always be correct. Furthermore, if he'd been anyone but the victim's son, I'd have wisecracked, *Yeah, but they're just cooking hamburger patties. We're working with a much bigger piece of meat.* Instead, I said,

"Then help me get it right. I'll be honest with you, Mr. Rawlins. This is a very complicated case, and we have several potential suspects. That's why we're proceeding so cautiously."

Kurt seemed to deflate a bit and nodded in acceptance. "Then I guess I appreciate that, and I'd better let you get back to work. When can I go in the house? I'm not looking forward to it, but I need to start going through his paperwork."

"We're working as fast as possible," I said, electing not to tell him that we'd already seized several boxes of documents from his father's office. There was no point in firing him up again. "Sheriff Barron will notify you the moment we've released the crime scene."

"And she'll call me when you've found out who killed Dad?"

"Count on it."

I waited until Kurt drove off before I took the chair back into the house. Then I returned to the SUV and headed back to the sheriff's office to upload the new crime scene photos. As I pulled into the parking lot, I saw Tina and Game Warden Randy Kent leading a handcuffed Chet Lincoln from a patrol car toward the building. The only way Lincoln could have looked glummer was if the sign above the door read FORD'S THEATER.

By the time I parked and limped into sheriff's headquarters, the three had already gone inside the department's only interview room. Tina and Randy emerged a moment later, shutting the door behind them. Both law officers looked tired but cheerful.

I waited until they were far enough away from the interview room door so that we wouldn't be overheard and said, "See what you can accomplish if you don't take an Old English sheepdog with an undersized bladder to a stakeout? Where did you find Chet?"

"We grabbed him coming out of the ABC outlet in Elkton," said Tina. ABC stood for Alcoholic Beverage Control. In Virginia, as in many other states, the only place you can purchase hard liquor is at government-operated stores.

"Yeah, and he was so focused on opening his bottle of Yukon Jack that he never saw us," Randy added, referring to an insipidly sweet and potent liqueur made from honey.

"Breakfast of champions," I said.

Tina asked, "What the heck are you doing here?"

I held up the camera. "I'm just getting back from the Rawlins farm. I have to upload these pictures." I went on to explain how I'd come to the worrying conclusion that I'd overlooked something at the crime scene and what had subsequently happened when I went back there for a second look.

Tina said, "Let me get this straight. The arrow hit the side of the house and then someone pulled it out and used it to stab Rawlins?"

"That's the only explanation I can come up with to account for the debris on the arrowhead and the bend in the shaft."

"And for all we know, those two events might have been weeks apart."

"Maybe, but I think the events were relatively contemporaneous."

"How can you tell that?" Tina sounded doubtful.

"Patterns of past behavior. We know that Everett wasn't reluctant about calling the game warden to report poachers." I glanced at Randy, who rolled his eyes and nodded wearily. "In fact, he'd called earlier that evening. So, it's fairly safe to assume that he would have made a 911 call to the sheriff's office if someone had sniped at his house with an arrow."

"Unless things went downhill so quickly that he never had the opportunity to call," said the game warden.

"Which might mean that whoever shot the arrow came into the yard to finish the job, up close and personal," Tina said.

"And the fact that the attack occurred at such close quarters suggests that Rawlins knew his assailant. If it was a stranger, wouldn't it have been natural for him to retreat to the house to grab his shotgun and let Longstreet out?" I asked.

"But if that's true, doesn't it also tend to rule Mr. Lincoln out as a suspect?" Tina nodded in the direction of the interview room door. "They knew each other, but there'd already been one previous violent encounter. I can't see Mr. Rawlins just standing there, waiting for Mr. Lincoln to stab him with an arrow."

Randy said, "Ev may not have known he was in the yard. Remember, Chet makes his living prowling around in the dark and not being seen."

'That's true, too," said Tina. "So I guess he stays in the suspect pool."

"Did you find anything in his truck?" I asked.

"No bow and arrows, if that's what you're asking. I figured we'd need a warrant, so I'm having it towed to the station."

"Yeah, it's more prudent to do it that way. But it seems to me that you're also going to need a search warrant to toss his trailer."

"Which means writing two lengthy affidavits. Meanwhile, in my spare time I can interview Mr. Lincoln, *then* call the crime lab about the new evidence they'll have to collect at the Rawlins place once they finish at the arson scene, and *then* I can run over to the judge's house for him to issue the search warrants." Tina threw her hands skyward in frustration. "Oh, and since I've run out of deputies and the state police don't have any spare troopers, I'll also have to figure out some way I can be in two places at once, so that I can guard the new evidence at the Rawlins farm while *also* freezing the scene at Mr. Lincoln's trailer until we can search it, and —"

I held my hands up signaling her to stop. "Tina, let me help. I can interview Chet."

Randy nodded vigorously. "And I can sit on Chet's trailer until you get there with the warrant."

"Thanks, Randy. I'll take you up on that." Tina turned to me. "You *really* wouldn't mind interviewing him?"

"Tina, at the risk of ruining my reputation as a manly man, I like teddy bears. But I like catching murderers even more. Did Chet agree to talk when you read him his rights?"

305

"He said we could ask him whatever we wanted. He had nothing to hide."

"In fact, he swore on his mama's grave," said Randy.

"When a crook says something like that, it's always wise to demand to see the grave and then dig it up to make sure his mama is actually there," I said with a nasty chuckle. "So, let the digging begin."

TWENTY

I've heard that some hunters deliberately avoid taking showers. Their theory is that when wild animals detect the faint scent of soap and deodorant they recognize it as belonging to a predator — man — and flee the area. Obviously, Chet Lincoln had embraced that concept and taken it to a smelly extreme. The interview room stank so badly of unwashed clothing and flesh that my eyes almost began to water.

Chet was wearing the same attire I'd seen him in yesterday morning . . . and likely the same clothing he'd been wearing last week, and the week before that. He sat at the table looking bored while he cleaned his left ear with his little finger. Removing the digit, he examined the debris he'd pulled from his ear, flicked the stuff onto the table, and then looked up at me.

I set the recorder on the table and leaned over to plug the cord into the electrical socket. Turning the device on and sitting down, I said, "Good morning, Mr. Lincoln. My name is Brad Lyon and I work for Sheriff Barron."

"You're Lolly's son-in-law. You used to be a cop in California." Chet's voice was a gravelly baritone.

"That's true. It's nice to see you again."

"Sorry, mister, but we ain't ever met." He gave me an innocent smile and I suppressed a shudder. His teeth reminded me of the double-decker portion of the Nimitz Freeway after the big San Francisco earthquake of 1989; they were gray, broken, and entirely gone in places.

I said, "Technically, that's true. We've never actually talked, but we did see each other yesterday at the Massanutten Crest Lodge right before you took off like a bat out of hell."

He shrugged slightly. "I'm afraid I don't know what you're talking about. I was at the lodge yesterday, but I never seen you."

It was a fairly clever lie. No one else had witnessed our brief encounter, and even if the security cameras had been working, it was unlikely that we'd both have been in the camera's field of vision. Unwashed obviously didn't mean unintelligent.

I said, "So you don't remember me yelling at you to stop, even though I was less than thirty feet away?"

"You might have yelled, but I didn't hear anything." He pointed at his right ear. "I got hearing loss in both ears from all the shooting I've done over the years."

Or from all the rubbish impacted in your ears, I thought. It was another falsehood disguised as a plausible excuse. Chet gave me a placid smile, and I think he was waiting for me to explode and call him a liar, which might be what many cops would do, but I actually prefer a suspect to fib early and often during an interview. Lying during the course of a police interrogation is like getting rid of the old stuff in your refrigerator's vegetable drawer by running it down the garbage disposal all at once. It's convenient for the moment, but sooner or later you're going to gum up the works.

I asked, "Why were you at the lodge?"

"I was looking to apply for a job."

I sat back in the chair and studied him. "No offense, but you and I both know that the hotel management wouldn't let someone like you within a half mile of their snobby guests."

"And I don't want to be around none of them rich people. It's a part-time gamekeeper job. They have problems with deer eating stuff from the gardens and ground-hogs messing up the golf course."

Again, the answer was reasonable and likely bogus. I suspected that Thalia Grady had told Chet about the vacant gamekeeper position so that he could use the information as an alibi to explain his *problematic* presence at the lodge. What's more, I noticed that Chet appeared to be growing progressively more relaxed. He seemed to think that he was in control of the interview, which is exactly what I wanted.

I said, "Interesting. However, I noticed that you didn't come out of the employee services office."

"I know. I went in the other door by accident. They told me where to go."

"But you didn't go to employee services after that. You drove off."

"I remembered there was someplace else I had to be. I figured to go back on Monday."

"I'm afraid you'll be in court on Monday." I decided it was time to shift gears. "Tell me, what were you doing on Everett Rawlins's land on Thursday night?"

Chet exhaled dismissively and interlaced his fingers across his chest. "I wasn't anywhere near Rawlins's place on Thursday night."

"Game Warden Kent saw you."

"Then he must have damn good eyes, because I was up in the Alleghenies near Reddish Knob, hunting," said Chet, naming a spot about twenty miles west of the Rawlins farm.

"Ev Rawlins saw you, too . . . right before you murdered him."

The attitude of casual indifference vanished in a flicker as Chet's jaw dropped. "What? Rawlins is dead? Nobody said nothing about no murder!"

"With those bad ears of yours, you must not have heard when Sheriff Barron mentioned that we're looking at you for the murder of Ev Rawlins. Oh well, maybe the prison doctor can get you a hearing aid."

"I didn't kill anybody!" said Chet, and for the first time since we'd begun to talk I had the sense that he was providing an unrehearsed and honest answer.

I replied, "Maybe, but before you say another word, let me give you a little advice: Start telling me the truth, because your life may depend on it."

Chet swiped at his suddenly sweaty pate. "I didn't kill Rawlins. Hell, I didn't kill nobody."

"Convince me. But understand this: Right now, the commonwealth's attorney is gathering up the nails and lumber to crucify you. And the *only* thing you accomplished by lying to me was to give him more ammunition to show a jury that you were trying to cover up your crime. He'll have no trouble convicting you of murder."

Chet was growing pale. "Look, Ev and me may have had a little feud going, but that don't make me a killer."

"Actually, as far as the prosecutor is concerned, it does. He'll say that there was bad blood between you two, that you were there the night Everett Rawlins was murdered, and then you ran. And you *were* there, weren't you?"

"Only up on the hill, and I never saw Rawlins. I was just hunting, and I swear to God, I didn't even know that Rawlins was murdered, but —"

"I'm glad you didn't swear on your mother's grave."

"— I can tell you who did it."

I leaned forward. "You have my undivided attention, but this better be good. More importantly, it better be the truth. Otherwise, I'm out of here and you can take your chances with the prosecutor."

"It was that neighbor of his, Tice."

"The husband or wife?"

Chet looked at me as if I were soft in the head. "The man, of course. Wade Tice."

"It was as dark as the inside of a cow on that hill. How could you see anything to hunt, much less the supposed killer?"

"I got me a pair of night-vision goggles like the soldiers wear."

"Of course, because that's how Dan'l Boone used to hunt. Okay, let's start the story at the beginning and you can tell me exactly what you saw."

"I will, once you answer me a question."

"Shoot. Ooh . . ." I held my hands up in mock surrender. "*That* probably isn't the best thing to say to a poacher."

He glowered. "Okay, so I'm white trash. How come *you're* so interested in showing I didn't kill Rawlins?"

"I'm interested in doing the job properly." I paused to collect my thoughts, intrinsically understanding that Chet would reject a Horatio Alger–like explanation of why I was committed to seeing justice done. Finally, I said, "Look, both of us are hunters. You hunt game; I hunt killers. Now, let's say you were up in Alaska and you went out looking to bag a ferocious Kodiak bear. If you couldn't find him, would you feel right about shooting a skunk instead?"

"No."

"I feel the same way. The skunk may smell, but he hasn't really hurt anyone. I want the predator. Does that explain it?"

"I guess."

"Then tell me what happened."

Chet took a deep breath. "I've been hunting on Rawlins's land for a long time."

"Let's be precise. You mean trespassing and *poaching,* right?"

He gave me an aggrieved look. "My people been hunting in those mountains for over two hundred years. It's a family tradition and, hell, I wasn't hurting anyone. Anyway, I was up on the hill above Rawlins's house early Thursday night."

"What time?"

"It was getting dark. It was maybe around five-thirty when I got there. I was out of my truck and walking through the woods toward . . . You been out there?"

I nodded.

"I was kind of prowling toward the road that leads to the sand quarry." Like many of the folks who lived their entire lives in the Blue Ridge Mountains, he pronounced *quarry* to rhyme with *marry.*

"I know the place. You were going down there to hunt bear, weren't you?"

Apparently there was something that changed slightly in my expression. Chet jutted his jaw out a little and said, "Hey, city boy, meat don't just appear magiclike at the market. Someone's gotta kill it. Any meat I eat, I done the killing myself. Can you claim the same?"

Although I strongly suspected that Chet Lincoln was killing bears to harvest their gall bladders and sell the meat to the lodge, I decided not to pursue that line of questioning for the moment. It might derail the interview, and I needed his statement about Wade Tice's actions that night. However, before we finished chatting, we were going to revisit the topic.

I said, "Hey, my wife's family are all hunters. I'm not making a judgment about hunting. Now, getting back to Thursday night. You were armed, right?"

"Right. I use a old Remington Model Seven Hundred. It's bolt-action and three-oh-eight caliber."

"That's a big rifle bullet."

"You need something with some muscle to drop a bear."

"I can imagine. Have you ever hunted with a bow?"

"Nope. Tried it once, because it was more quiet." Chet gave me a swift sheepish look that told me why he'd wanted silence. "But I couldn't hit the damn side of a mountain with it."

"So when the sheriff searches your house,

she isn't going to find a bow and hunting arrows?"

"Depending on how much crap she wants to move, she might find a bow. If she does, I'll thank her, 'cause I got no idea where it went."

"How about the arrows?"

"Hell, I lost them all in the forest. I told you: I ain't no Robin Hood."

"Okay, so you were creeping through the woods on the hill. What happened then?"

"I heard a quad-runner kind of puttin' along that road, real slow." Chet mimed gripping an ATV's handlebars. "It didn't have no lights on, but that actually helped me see it."

"Because night-vision goggles work best in complete darkness. What time was this?"

"Maybe six o'clock. I figured it might have been the game warden. So I hid behind a tree and tried to get a better look."

"And obviously you did."

Chet nodded. "Yeah. That's when I saw it was Wade Tice. He was riding down that dirt road all slowlike toward Rawlins's house."

"And even though it was dark and rainy and you were using those goggles, you're absolutely certain it was Wade Tice?" I quietly demanded.

"I'm positive, mister. At one point, I was maybe ten yards from him. Course, he couldn't see me."

"Would you testify to that under oath in court?"

"If I had to."

"You will." I nodded toward the cassette recorder. "And you realize that if you change your story you might be charged with interfering with a homicide investigation?"

"If I'm swearing by the Holy Book, I tell the truth." Chet sounded a little irate.

Unlike swearing on the grave of your mother, I thought. I said, "And all I want is the truth. Was there any particular reason you continued to hide from Mr. Tice?"

"I hunt on his property, too. Wade never had no problem with it in the past, but I figured there had to be *some* reason he was sneaking around in the dark. I reckoned that things had changed and he was looking for me."

"Did you notice anything else?"

"I'm betting that he has the bow and arrows y'all looking for. He done had a hunting bow slung over his shoulder."

"What happened then?"

"He rode past me and then stopped the quad-runner. I was curious, so I kept watching. Wade got off the motorbike and started tiptoeing toward Rawlins's house. 'Cept I didn't know he was heading toward the house."

"What do you mean?"

Chet locked eyes with me. "Mister, the first I ever heard of Rawlins being dead was when you told me a few minutes ago. So I didn't know where Wade was headed that night. I thought maybe he was hunting."

"What caused you to think that?"

"Wade was carrying his bow like he was ready to shoot." Chet pretended to hold an invisible bow and nocked arrow.

"Did he ever shoot an arrow?"

"Yes, sir, he sure did. I watched him pull that bow back and let rip. Couldn't see the arrow, 'twas too far away. But I know he shot one."

Chet's clarification that he hadn't actually seen the arrow told me that he was still providing a reasonably truthful account of what he'd seen. I asked, "What direction did he shoot?"

"Toward Rawlins's house. But like I done said before, I didn't know that Wade was gunning for Rawlins. I thought he'd spotted a deer or something."

"How many arrows did he fire?"

"Just one . . . that I saw. After that, he

318

started creeping toward the house again."

"What did you think that meant?"

"That he'd hit whatever he was shooting at and was going to collect the carcass." There was a pause and then Chet added meditatively, "Though, if 'twas a deer he shot, I don't know why he didn't drive the quad-runner over. That'd have been easier than lugging it back."

"*Did* he lug it back?" I asked.

"Don't know. It was raining and cold and I had stuff of my own to do. I headed toward the quarry."

"So that's the last time you saw Mr. Tice?"

"Yep, he kind of disappeared through the trees."

"Did you hear him leave on the ATV?"

"Now that you mention it, I did hear the ATV again, call it ten minutes or so after I last saw him. I was up in a notch, so I couldn't see the quad, but it sounded like it was flying back to Wade Tice's farm."

Ten minutes would have been more than enough time for Wade Tice to walk the short distance to the farmhouse, yank the arrow from the wall, and stab Rawlins. Furthermore, I could now prove that both he and his wife had lied to me about him never having left their home on Thursday evening. Add the preexisting feud with Rawlins, the history of violence, and Tice's skill with a hunting bow to the mix, and the surly farmer had once more emerged as the prime suspect.

I asked, "Did you hear any other vehicles that night?"

"There could have been a car or something on the road. Can't say for sure, but I did hear the game warden's truck a while later," Chet replied.

"But before the game warden arrived, you went to the quarry. What happened there?"

"Nothing. If there'd been any game there, Tice's quad scared it all off. I waited awhile, but then the batteries started to go south on my goggles."

"No animals to hunt, no commando night vision, and then the law arrives. All in all, Thursday night was a big bust for you. How could you tell it was the game warden's truck?"

"Out in the woods, you learn to live by your eyes, ears, and nose. I know the sound of that damn Kent's truck."

I almost blurted, *Yeah, and it's a damn shame the bears out there don't recognize the sound of yours.* Instead, I said, "So you took off."

"Yeah. I stopped and got some batteries and headed over to Reddish Knob."

"You must have been luckier there. That's why you were at the lodge yesterday."

The poacher folded his arms across his chest. "Hey, mister, I've told you everything I know about Thursday night. Why I was at the lodge has got nothing to do with any of that."

"I understand, and we can stop talking whenever you want." I reached over and my finger hovered above the stop button on the cassette recorder. "I just wanted to give you the opportunity to tell me your side of the story."

Chet's eyes narrowed. "What are you talking about?"

The comedian George Burns once observed that the secret to success in acting was the ability to fake sincerity. It's also the secret to success in cop work. Sometimes you have to lie, and when you do, you'd better be good at it.

I said in a mildly regretful voice, "I had a long chat with Thalia Grady yesterday and you know what? She threw you under the bus, Chet."

"I'm not saying I know her, but what did she say?"

"She certainly knows you," I said, while slowly withdrawing my hand from the cassette recorder. "Thalia told me that you

321

supply the venison and bear meat for the restaurant. But she had absolutely no idea that you were selling her poached game and was so shocked I thought she was going to faint."

Chet slapped the table. "Shocked, my ass! Why that backstabbing broad-assed bitch! She's lying! She knew *exactly* how and where I was getting that meat!"

"No doubt. But unless you have some sort of proof that she was involved, it's your word against hers."

"Hell, she even called earlier this week and left a message on my answering machine telling me where I could pick up some deer that was hit by a car!"

"No! They serve *roadkill* at the Rathskeller?"

"Mister, you would lose your appetite for all time if you knew some of the things they was dishing up at that place."

"Wait a minute. You said she called earlier this week. Did you delete the message?"

"Nope. I got a real old answering machine and I can't remember the last time I erased the tape." An evil smile began to spread across Chet's face. "And now that I think on it, there are other messages on that machine from her."

"Such as?"

"Well, back in September, Kent nearly caught me. I told her about it and said I had to lay low for a while. She called the next day and left a message, saying she wasn't paying me to hide from the game warden. She was all squawking, 'Go out and get some venison. I got customers to feed.'"

"I think you've found your proof, Chet. If you still have those recordings, Thalia is dead meat," I said. The poacher chuckled at the bad pun as I continued, "By the way, does Thalia also buy the bear gall bladders from you?"

Chet's vengeful smile vanished in a flicker. "I don't know nothing about that."

I understood why he'd instantly reverted to lying-and-denying mode. As Game Warden Randy Kent had told us on Thursday night, the U.S. park rangers had found dead and mutilated black bears inside Shenandoah National Park. So Chet Lincoln couldn't admit to having harvested bear gall bladders without otherwise opening himself up to federal prosecution and the draconian punishments that usually resulted from that process.

I said, "You don't know anything about bears being killed for no other reason than to yank out an organ so that it can be used as a snake-oil cure for impotency?"

"Nope."

"What's the matter, Chet? You're suddenly all tongue-tied. Aren't you going to lecture me about how hunting is a family tradition from the pioneer days? Gee, would Davy Crockett *kill him a bar, just to steal a gland?*" I sang the final few words to the tune of the theme song from the 1950s Disney television program.

"I want my lawyer."

"And I need some fresh air. Everything about you stinks, including your soul. And my fondest hope is that someday a big black bear harvests *your* gall bladder."

TWENTY-ONE

Grabbing the cassette recorder, I left the interview room and went to tell the jail deputy that Chet Lincoln could be booked into custody. After that, I headed down the corridor to Tina's office. I found her seated at her desk. She was so focused on the computer monitor and typing up the affidavit for a search warrant that she didn't hear me come in.

I cleared my throat. "If that's the paperwork for Mr. Lincoln's truck or mobile home, it can go to the bottom of our 'to do' list."

Tina swiveled in her chair to face me. "He actually told you something worthwhile?"

"Yeah, and it's a good thing you didn't let the prosecutor stampede you into arresting Chet. I'm convinced he isn't the killer, though he might just turn out to be our star witness." I went on to briefly recount Chet's statement.

"So he saw Wade Tice shoot an arrow and then head toward Everett Rawlins's house?" Tina asked. "With the other information we have on Mr. Tice, that's pretty damning. Will Mr. Lincoln testify to that in court?"

"He says he will, but even if he changes his mind, we have his statement on tape." I held up the recorder. "But the more important thing is that we now have enough information to get a search warrant for Wade's house and his ATV. It's time to put this case on Tice."

Tina looked heavenward but elected not to acknowledge the dreadful pun. Instead, she said, "Okay, so I'll start writing an affidavit for the Tices' place. Can you have dispatch radio Randy and tell him that he can clear from Chet's mobile home?"

"Absolutely, but first, let me bring you up to speed on something else that I forgot to tell you before I interviewed Chet. Linny has video proof that Sherri and Jesse lied to us about never leaving the hotel on Thursday night." I then told her about how the couple had departed an hour apart from each other and then returned together shortly before 10 P.M.

Tina said, "Huh. It seems to me that if Mr. Hauck didn't leave the hotel until seven-thirty and stopped at Delbert's shortly before it closed, he couldn't have killed Mr. Rawlins."

"That's how I read it, too. Ash had already found the body by then." I went over to the coffeemaker and poured myself a cup. Holding up the carafe, I asked, "Want some?"

Tina shook her head. "Mr. Hauck may be out of the suspect mix, but it still leaves Ms. Driggs as a possible killer."

"More so now than before, I think. Our original theory was that the murderer had to be a skilled archer, and there was no evidence that Sherri had ever handled a bow and arrow in her life." I took a sip of coffee.

"But if you're right about how the arrow shaft got bent, she was as capable of stabbing Mr. Rawlins as anyone else."

"It might also explain the sudden shift in the power dynamic the first time I interviewed them," I said meditatively.

"How do you mean?"

"When I arrived in the suite, she was clearly the boss and he was the pampered and reasonably well-trained pet. However, once I broke the news that Ev had been murdered, Sherri folded up faster than a paper dinner napkin and Jesse started acting like Conan the Toy Boy-barian."

"It almost sounds as if he had her over a barrel."

"Maybe he did. I'm wondering if Sherri didn't tell him the truth about how she ended up in Thermopylae on Thursday night. Maybe I just don't recognize true love when I see it, but I doubt Jesse kept his mouth shut out of loyalty to her." I finished the coffee. "The question is: Which liar do we talk to first? Wade, Sherri, or Jesse?"

"I think we have to follow up on Wade Tice."

"Agreed. We could speculate all day about what Sherri might have done at the murder scene, but we have strong evidence that Wade fired an arrow and was last seen heading toward the victim's home."

"And that could have been because he'd missed and wanted to finish the job."

"It fits both the evidence and timeline. We have to consider him our primary suspect, which means it's time to . . . roll the Tice."

Tina shook her head in disbelief and then turned back to the computer. "I'm going to pretend I didn't hear that and get started on the new search warrant affidavit."

"Fortunately, you can use the same preliminary information for the new warrant."

"I know, but I need a description of the premises."

"It's a two-story cabin-style house made out of brown wood, composite shingle roof,

328

with a red brick chimney on the . . ." I closed my eyes to recall the Tice farm and continued, ". . . north side of the residence."

"Thanks."

"*De nada*. Hey, do you mind if I go over to the teddy bear show for a couple of minutes? I imagine Ash is chomping at the bit for some news."

Tina waved, but didn't look up from the computer screen. "Tell her I said hi, and take your time. This is going to take a little while."

As I approached the church community center, I was happy to see that vehicles still filled the parking lot. Even better, it looked as if there were some fresh attendees arriving. It's been my experience that you can measure the success of a teddy bear show by how dramatically the collector crowd drops off when lunchtime comes. Once inside the hall, I decided to take a few minutes and resume my search for a Christmas gift for Ash.

Most guys view Christmas shopping for their spouse as an experience akin to a tooth extraction — it's a task to be completed as quickly as possible. I'm different. I actually enjoy the process of shopping, especially when I'm hunting for the perfect treasure for Ash at a teddy bear show.

Crossing over to the side of the hall opposite of where Ash sat at our display table, I headed up the aisle, carefully surveying the bear bonanza. I wasn't certain what I was looking for, but would recognize it instantly when I saw it. Often, it's the bear's costume that generates a collector's initial interest in a teddy, but that's a secondary consideration for Ash and me. Costumes are nice, but we're primarily on the lookout for a teddy with a sweet face. And I'd just found one on artist Donna Griffin's table.

It was a panda bear, fashioned from black-and-cocoa-colored mohair. Somehow, Donna had crafted the teddy's expression to express thoughtfulness, serenity, and kindness. It was the face of a loving companion, and I knew Ash would adore it, particularly because our friend Donna had created the bear.

I paid for the bear and asked Donna to give it to Pastor Terry to hold until I could come and collect it. Then I headed back over to meet with Ash. I found my wife standing beside our exhibitor table, which appeared curiously bare of bears.

Ash was holding Edie Éclair, one of her teddies dressed in a delectable-looking chocolate éclair costume, while a woman I recognized as a photographer from the Harrisonburg newspaper interviewed her. Remmelkemp Mill usually didn't generate much news, but between the murder, the fire, and the teddy jubilee, it looked as if the town was going to make the paper three times in a week. I didn't approach the table until the reporter finished with Ash and wandered off to take more photographs of the teddy jubilee.

Ash smiled when she saw me. "Here's something I've never said before: I was beginning to get worried about you."

I kissed her on the cheek. "Sorry, love, but I just couldn't get away."

"And from that uncomfortable look in your eyes, I can tell that you can't stay."

"I don't have to go right this minute. But once Tina finishes typing up the search warrant paperwork and gets the judge to issue it, we'll be heading over to Wade Tice's place."

"Then you have time for lunch." Ash put the teddy bear on the table and led me to a chair. "And while you eat, you can bring me up to date on everything that's happened."

I nodded toward our mostly vacant exhibitor table. "You go first. There was a pretty big bunch of bears here when I left."

"And it stayed that way until around

eleven. Then I suddenly had a crowd at the table and everyone wanted to buy a piece. Brad, it was like nothing I've ever seen." She handed me the plastic foam food box containing my lunch from the Brick Pit.

"It sounds *bear*-ly believable."

"It was amazing." Ash was beaming. "I even sold several of Tina's bears."

I scanned the table. "And Gil Grizzly is gone."

"That's the most exciting news. The lady who bought him wants to talk to you sometime about making a companion piece."

"You're kidding."

"No, she wants you to make Bear-a Sidle." Ash was referring to the character of Sara Sidle from *CSI*, the criminalist who'd been in a relationship with Grissom. "Anyway, I wish you'd been here to see it. It was our best day ever at a show."

"I wish I'd seen it, too." I covered my mouth to conceal a yawn. "Hey, do we have something to drink with caffeine in it?"

"Are you starting to drag?" She retrieved a can of Diet Coke from our lunchbox-sized cooler and opened it.

"A little, but I'll be fine." I took a sip of the soda. Then, between bites of pulled pork sandwich and cold French fries, I told Ash everything that I'd learned since leaving the church hall to make a second inspection of the Rawlins home.

When I finished, she said, "If Tina doesn't finish the paperwork until the show is over, I'd like to come with you when you serve the warrant at Tice's house."

"I'm guessing that Tina would probably welcome your help and not just because we've run out of deputies. You're cool under pressure, which is exactly the kind of cop you want as a member of a high-risk entry team."

Ash patted my hand. "That's about the sweetest thing you've ever said to me."

"It's true." I folded my coat up into a makeshift pillow and placed it between my head and the cinder-block wall.

"But why would we be making a high-risk entry into the house? I thought you said there wasn't enough probable cause to arrest Tice."

"There isn't, but we know he has a potential for violence."

"And he probably has other weapons besides the bow inside his house."

"Exactly. And we have to assume that he might do more than just brandish a screwdriver when we go back there." I closed my eyes.

"Should I call Tina and see if she wants

me to suit up?"

"Good idea." I pulled the phone from my shirt pocket and blindly handed it to her.

"Brad, honey, are you going to sleep?" Ash asked in a low voice.

"Nope. I'm just going to rest my eyes for a minute or two. Then I have to get back over to Tina's office."

A moment later, Ash gently rubbed my shoulder and whispered, "Sweetheart, you need to wake up."

"I'm not asleep," I replied, without opening my eyes. At the same time, I was dimly aware that my chin felt oddly cool.

Ash chuckled. "You've been dead to the world for a couple of hours."

As I sat up and blinked in confusion at the church hall, I realized that I had indeed been sawing logs, and the reason my chin felt cool was that my mouth had been open and I'd been drooling. It was a real *GQ* moment. Wiping my chin with my hand, I said, "You should have woken me up."

"Honey, I figured that if you didn't even stir when I sold our last few bears, you needed the sleep." She handed me a cup of hot coffee that she'd gotten from the church kitchen. "Here. Drink this."

"Thank you." I took a swallow of the coffee, which looked and tasted like furniture varnish. "And I suppose I needed the nap. What's going on?"

"Tina just called. She finished the warrant and is taking it over to the judge to have it issued. We have to go home so I can change into my uniform."

"What about our stuff here?"

"We'll take the cash box and come back for the other things later," Ash replied as she slung her satchel over her shoulder. "I've already talked to Pastor Terry about it."

I pushed myself to my feet and gestured toward the mass of exhibitors' tables. "What about the other bear artists? Won't they be upset that we're cutting out of here early?"

"You're kidding, right?" Ash leaned over to kiss my nose. "I've already spoken with most of them, and right now, I'm the most envied woman in the room. Most people only dream about doing this sort of thing."

As we slowly headed toward the door, some of our fellow artists and friends began to stand and clap. At first, I thought it just a public manifestation of thanks to Ash for the splendid job she'd done organizing the successful show. But as the applause grew, I understood that the crowd was expressing something more than appreciation. The artists and collectors knew that Ash was on her way to do something potentially life-threatening, and they wanted her to know how proud they were of her.

I glanced at my wife and saw that her eyes were shining. She realized the motivation behind the applause, too. With her head ducked low, Ash gave the crowd a jerky wave as we went out the door.

Outside, I asked, "How does it feel to be a hero?"

"I'm not a hero." She wiped her right eye.

"You are to me and to all those women in there." I motioned with my cane back toward the church community center.

We went home and Ash quickly changed into her deputy's uniform while I put my shoulder holster on. Then we drove to the sheriff's office, where we saw a state police car and an Elkton PD cruiser parked in the lot. Tina had obviously called in reinforcements to help serve the search warrant. Inside, we found Tina and four cops in the small roll-call room, and once we took our seats, the briefing began. One of the officers was Trooper Fuller, who'd stopped me the previous day. I waved, and she kind of cringed.

"Is that . . . ?" Ash whispered.

"Yep, the only other woman who's given

me a massage since we got married," I replied.

"Hmm. I don't know if I like the sound of that."

"Relax. If I can stay awake, I'll let you search me for weapons later tonight."

Tina began the briefing. Like most good tactical plans, hers was simple. There'd be no lights and sirens as we approached the house. We'd roll in slowly and quietly. Once we arrived, three of the cops would rush to secure the sides and rear of the house while Tina, Ash, and Deputy Bressler went to the front door to make contact. If, after making knock and notice, there was no response from inside the house, it was Bressler's job to smash the door in with the "Key to the City" — a heavy metal battering ram.

My job was simple, too. Because I wasn't a sworn officer, I'd drive the SUV and follow the small procession of patrol cars into the farmyard and remain by the vehicles until the real cops secured the scene. There was a time when I'd have chafed at the idea of being in the rear with the gear, but not now. I've kicked down doors and it's exciting, but with my bad leg, I had no business being part of an entry team.

A few minutes later, I was driving the last vehicle in a motorcade of police cars. We

337

headed east and were soon approaching the Tice farm. Pulling into the farmyard, I noticed two vehicles parked near the house. There was a mud-spattered red Ford pickup truck, which I assumed was Wade's, and a beat-to-hell gray Ford Tempo, which had to be Marilyn's car. If the vehicles were any indicator, the Tices were home.

By the time I came to a stop behind the cluster of patrol cars, the cops were already scrambling to their assigned posts. Their guns drawn, Ash and Tina were on the left side of the front door, while Bressler stood on the right, holding the battering ram. I got out of the SUV and took up a position of cover at the rear of one of the police cruisers. Meanwhile, Tina pounded on the door and shouted that she was the sheriff, had a search warrant, and was demanding entry. Tina waited perhaps five seconds for someone to answer the door, but when there was no response, she yelled at Bressler, "Do it!"

As Bressler muscled the battering ram into position, Ash held up a hand, then reached over and tried the doorknob. The door was unlocked, and she pushed it open. After a brief exchange of surprised and sheepish looks, Tina and Ash charged into the house, shouting over and over again that they were with the sheriff's office. Bressler dropped the ram onto the wooden porch with a crash and followed the two women inside.

I was so focused on the dangers Ash might be facing as she searched the house for a possible killer, and so on edge, dreading the sound of gunfire, that I broke one of the cardinal rules of a police tactical operation. My head wasn't in the game. That's why I didn't hear the rapid footfalls coming from around the corner of the barn until just before the person burst into the yard. It was Marilyn. She was charging toward the house, and it looked like she was carrying a rifle.

Yanking my gun from the holster, I pointed it at her and yelled, "Marilyn, stop and drop the gun or I'm going to kill you!"

Taken by surprise, Marilyn turned to look at me and stumbled to a halt. "I don't have a gun!" she snarled.

That's when I noticed that the item in her hands wasn't a rifle. It was a pitchfork — a lethal weapon in its own right.

"You don't have any hay to bale either, so drop the pitchfork."

She glared hatefully at me for a moment and then threw the tool to the ground.

Fortunately, one of the cops on the perimeter noticed our little standoff, and I heard him call Tina on the radio. Ash and Tina emerged from the house a moment later and trotted over to where Marilyn stood. My wife grabbed the pitchfork while Tina ordered Marilyn to put her hands behind her head. Marilyn refused and made as if to walk away, a move she undoubtedly and instantly regretted. In a flash, Tina had the woman in a rear wristlock control hold that made my arm ache with pain just to witness it being applied. Holstering my gun, I hobbled over to where Marilyn now stood wearing handcuffs.

Once Tina had made the formal notification that we were there serving a search warrant, she asked, "Where is your husband?"

Marilyn tossed her head to move some strands of hair that had fallen across her face. "Figure it out for yourself, you cow!"

Tina's jaw tightened a little, but she remained otherwise impassive. "Mrs. Tice, I don't think you realize how serious this situation is. We're investigating a murder, and we have solid proof that you and your husband lied to us."

"My Wade said he didn't kill that miserable old son of a bitch, and I believe him. But I'll tell you one damned thing: I wish he had, because Rawlins had it coming."

"Why?" Ash asked.

340

"Because Rawlins sold us out like Judas Iscariot sold our Savior. The only difference was that Crawlin' Rawlins was going to get six million bucks instead of thirty pieces of silver," Marilyn hotly replied.

As two pivotal puzzle pieces came together, I sighed and added, "Meanwhile, you and Wade were going to be left trying to run a farm next to a freaking amusement park. You're right. Rawlins did betray you."

Marilyn turned to stare at me. "How . . . ?"

"That isn't important, right now," I said. "But I think it's time you told us what you saw when you were cleaning that hotel room up on the third floor of the lodge."

TWENTY-TWO

"Sherri Driggs's room?" Tina asked.

"Yes. Marilyn usually works on the second floor, but Linny told me that the dependable members of the housekeeping staff routinely have to cover for the flakes." I glanced at Marilyn. "That's why you were up on the third floor, right?"

She nodded.

"Which is how you learned that Rawlins was going to sell his farm," I said. "Why didn't you tell me about this yesterday?"

Marilyn sagged and said despairingly, "How could I? The deck was already stacked against Wade, and I figured it would only make him look guiltier."

"You're right, it would have. I imagine your husband was madder than a hornet when you told him that it wasn't enough that Rawlins had cost you thousands of dollars by running your well dry, but now he planned to sell his farm to an amusement park company."

"Is that the reason Wade went over there on Thursday night?" Tina asked.

"Wade was home —"

I cut her off. "Marilyn, the very worst thing you can do for Wade and yourself is to provide another false statement. I'm pretty certain that Sheriff Barron is willing to give you a second chance to tell the truth."

"That's true," said Tina. "So don't spoil this opportunity by lying to us."

Marilyn twisted her arms around. Rattling the handcuff chain, she added, "Am I under arrest?"

"Not for the moment. The only reason I cuffed you was for officer safety. You weren't following instructions."

"Well, I am now. Could we take these off?"

Tina shook her head. "They'll stay on until I'm certain I can trust you."

"And here's the first test of how willing you are to be truthful: Where is Wade?" I asked.

"He's off hunting." Marilyn motioned with her head toward the mountains.

"Did he take his quad-runner?" said Tina, scanning the yard for the vehicle.

Marilyn nodded.

"How about his hunting bow and arrows?"

"No, his rifle."

"Where are his bow and arrows now?" I asked.

She looked at the ground. "I don't know. They used to be in our closet upstairs, but they were gone when I got home from work yesterday afternoon."

I gave a disbelieving laugh. "And you didn't think there was anything suspicious about him getting rid of the possible murder weapon?"

"No, because I know Wade didn't kill that man." Then Marilyn sighed and added, "And even if I didn't, I knew better than to ask Wade about it. He was mad enough already."

"When will Mr. Tice be back?" Tina asked.

"Probably suppertime. We eat at five-thirty."

"So we've got an hour or so to talk." I pointed toward the house. "Let's go."

Tina began dismissing the cops as Ash and I escorted Marilyn inside the house and into the gloomy little living room. With its cocoa-brown paneling, beige carpeting, and taupe-colored furniture, it seemed to me that a Three Musketeers candy bar had been the inspiration for the décor. Ash helped

344

Marilyn sit down on the couch and then took up a standing position near the front window so that she could keep an eye on the yard.

I briefly considered sitting in the big recliner, but decided that wouldn't be wise; it was obviously Wade's chair, and though we'd taken some valuable baby steps toward securing Marilyn's cooperation, that fragile truce would be broken in an instant if she thought we were being disrespectful of her husband or home. I went into the kitchen and returned carrying a wooden chair, which I set opposite the sofa.

Tina came into the living room a moment later and gave us an inquiring look that clearly said, *Has she been behaving?* Ash nodded.

"All right, Mrs. Tice, stand up and let me take those handcuffs off." Tina pulled her key ring from her gun belt. Once she'd removed the restraints, she said, "Now, while Mr. Lyon listens to your new and improved statement, his wife and I are going to search your house for evidence. Here's your copy of the search warrant. Do you have any problems with that?"

"No, ma'am." Marilyn didn't bother to look at the papers as she sat back down on the sofa.

"Glad to hear it. Brad, she's all yours."

As Tina and Ash went upstairs, Marilyn grumbled, "Who died and crowned her queen?"

"She's the sheriff. Cut her some slack," I said, while sitting down on the kitchen chair. "She's basically been working around the clock since Thursday morning. Besides, you probably could have avoided all of this if you and Wade had told me the truth in the first place."

"I suppose."

"And as long as we're discussing really bad decisions, I've got to ask. What in the name of God were you thinking about, charging a bunch of armed cops with a pitchfork?"

"I didn't know it was the law until I came around the side of the barn and you stopped me."

"Still, you were armed and ready for a fight. Who did you think was there?"

"Some of Rawlins's friends. Lots of folks around here have already decided that Wade killed him, and they're mad. I found that out this morning when I went to the Food Lion."

"What happened?"

"I was treated like a damn leper while I was shopping — people scurrying away from me and muttering under their breath. Then, when I came out, I saw that some coward had slashed one of my car's tires." Marilyn's lips compressed with rage. "So when I heard that big crash, I thought someone was smashing up our house."

"I'm not defending that sort of vile behavior, but there *is* a reason why people suspect your husband."

"Because of the feud. But people only heard one side of it — Rawlins's side."

I leaned forward in the chair. "Then tell me your side. What happened at the lodge?"

Marilyn sighed and slumped into the corner of the couch. "You were right about me being sent up to help the housekeeping team on the third floor. I do good work and I'm fast, so I get sent up there a lot, which is a pain."

"More work."

"For the same pay and no tips. By the time I get up there, the third-floor housekeepers have already collected all the tips from the rooms."

"Even though you're doing their jobs? That isn't exactly fair."

"As Wade says: Welcome to Planet Earth. Anyway, I got sent up there on Thursday at around eleven-thirty and started vacuuming and cleaning rooms."

"And you saw something in one of the rooms that attracted your attention?"

"Yeah, Room Three-Thirty-One. I want to make something real clear." Marilyn sat up straight. "I didn't go up there to snoop around — why would I? I didn't know anything about the people in that room. I didn't touch anything either."

"I understand."

"Well, I sure hope my boss at the lodge does, because she fires housekeepers who mess with a guest's stuff. I can't afford to lose this job."

"If what you saw was in plain sight, I don't think you have anything to worry about."

"It *was* in plain sight. Right there on the table."

I nodded. "Okay, before we cover that, let's back up a little. When you arrived in front of the door to Room Three-Thirty-One, what did you do?"

"I knocked and said, 'Housekeeping,' like always. I didn't hear anything, so I used my key card and went right on in. There was nobody in the living room part of the suite, but . . ." Marilyn's cheeks began to turn pink.

"Was there someone in the bedroom?"

"The bedroom door was shut, but from the sound of it, there was a man and a woman in there and they weren't playing Scrabble, if you know what I mean."

"Actually, I do. I just missed their matinee performance yesterday."

Marilyn recoiled with surprise. "You were in that room? But why —"

"That isn't important. Please continue. You're in the living room, they're . . . preoccupied in the bedroom, and . . . ?"

"I decided I'd come back later. But I thought I'd grab their breakfast dishes before I left. I was just trying to make less work for myself later."

"Makes sense."

"Well, there was a coffee cup on the desk along with a bunch of papers and what looked like a land survey map. When I picked up the cup, I just happened to look down at the map." As Marilyn spoke, she placed her hand in front of her eyes, ostensibly to rub the bridge of her nose.

The gesture would have appeared meaningless to someone who hadn't studied body language or interviewed thousands of liars. Yet I recognized its true significance: What she'd actually done was subconsciously block my view of her eyes, which told me that she was probably lying about the supposedly accidental circumstances of the discovery. More than likely, Marilyn routinely snooped on guests to relieve the boredom of a dead-end job cleaning up after rich folks.

Ordinarily, I'd have braced her over the falsehood, but there was no point. Looking at someone else's possessions wasn't a crime, so I really didn't care how she'd ended up noticing the map. I just wanted to know what she'd seen.

"What drew your attention to the map?" I asked.

"It had an information box at the top that read, KOBLER HOLLOW AGRICULTURAL DISTRICT."

"Which you recognized as being where you live. That would have made me curious." I deliberately phrased the statement to subtly suggest to Marilyn that, given the circumstances, her decision to inspect the paperwork more closely was perfectly understandable.

Marilyn nodded. "I didn't figure there was any harm in taking a closer look. Then I saw a stack of official-looking papers next to the map. They were escrow papers that said Rawlins was selling his farm to some company."

"For six million dollars?"

"It was a little more than six million, but I don't remember the exact number."

"Was there anything on the paperwork that said who was handling the transaction?"

She thought for a second. "Yes. Swift Run Gap Realty."

The penny dropped. "Swift Run Gap Realty," I muttered, "owned and operated by Roger Prufrock."

"I don't know anything about that."

"Don't worry about it. Now, was it the fact that Rawlins was selling that made you angry?"

"Not at first. There was always the chance he was selling out to an agribusiness combine that would continue to farm the land. Things wouldn't have really changed much. But then I found the other map."

I raised my eyebrows slightly. "Found?"

Marilyn gave me a challenging look. "So what if I moved some papers? If you were worried about your home, you would have, too."

"You're right. What was on this other map?"

"A drawing of the amusement park they were going to put on Rawlins's land. The Blue Ridge Mountain Bear Fair, they called it. It about made me sick. We work hard and it doesn't always pay, but Wade and me love our life out here in the country. It's quiet and we live close to nature. All we want is to be left alone."

"And that was all going to change if they built a carnival next door. Noise, trash, people using your driveway for a turn-around, and probably fireworks every Friday and Saturday night in the summer." I sighed. "I understand why you felt sick."

Marilyn glanced out the window, and I had the impression she was viewing a dismal future. In a bleak voice, she said, "It's going to be worse than that. It's going to destroy us."

"How so?"

She looked back at me. "Some of the rides they planned to put in were on that map. One of them is a big log flume ride with a waterfall."

Suddenly, I understood. "Which means they'll have to drill more and bigger water wells to fill up the fake river, and your well will go dry again. And, of course, a big company like that has high-priced lawyers, so it won't be the amusement park's fault."

"Of course not," Marilyn agreed. "So there I was. I'm looking down at those papers, the headboard is banging against the wall, and I realized that Wade and me was about to get the same treatment as the folks in the other room."

"Screwed?"

"Without so much as a kiss. That's when I got mad and poured the cold coffee from that cup all over the escrow paperwork," she said warily.

"As an official representative of the sheriff's office, I'm obligated to tell you that what you did was wrong." I paused for a second and then continued, "But as someone who loves the Shenandoah Valley and doesn't want to see it turned into more urban sprawl, I've got to say: Bravo. What happened then?"

My reply drew a cautious smile from her. "From the sound of it, that couple in the bedroom still didn't know I was there. So I left the dishes behind and got out. When I came back later to clean the room, they were gone, along with all the paperwork."

We were interrupted by the sound of Tina and Ash coming back downstairs. Tina paused at the front door and said, "We couldn't find any archery gear upstairs, so we're going out to check the barn. How are things going here?"

"We're getting a lot of our questions answered. Marilyn has been very co-operative," I replied.

"Good. We'll be outside if you need us."

Ash gave me a smile and then followed

Tina outside.

Once the women were gone, I resumed my line of questioning. "When did you tell your husband about what you'd found in the hotel room? Did you call him?"

Marilyn said, "No. We don't have a cell phone and he's usually out in the fields or in the barn. I told him when I got home that night."

"And having seen your husband melt down like the Chernobyl reactor, I can guess how he took the news."

She suddenly looked despondent. "Wade isn't a bad man. He just has a temper and wants to be treated with some respect."

"Maybe. But it's hard to respect someone who's constantly looking to be the victim of an insult, even if none is intended."

"I know. He's got a thin skin."

"So, what happened when you told him about Mr. Rawlins and the amusement park company?"

"He got blistering mad and . . ." She shrugged and looked down, obviously reluctant to say anything more.

I said in what I hoped was an empathetic tone, "I understand this is hard. But we know for a fact that Mr. Tice wasn't much more than thirty or forty yards from Mr. Rawlins's house on the night of the murder.

We also know that he was armed with a bow and arrow. So, if you really want to convince me that your husband didn't kill your neighbor, you have to tell the entire story."

She looked up at me with eyes that were feverish with fear and said in a hushed tone, "Look, mister, if I didn't know what was going to happen when Wade went out on Thursday night, and all he ever told me was that he didn't kill Rawlins, can I be arrested for murder if . . . ?"

"If it turns out he did it? No. The only way you could be looking at charges is if he tries to claim that you helped him."

"He'd never do that. Never."

"Are you trying to convince me or yourself?" I asked gently.

Marilyn lowered her head and began to softly cry. I suddenly felt very sad for her. It was clear that she loved her husband and wanted to be loyal to him. But Wade's volcanic temper, propensity for violence, and uncanny skill at making bad decisions had placed her in an untenable position.

After a moment, I said, "Did your husband go out on Thursday night with his bow and arrow?"

She wiped some tears from her cheek. "Yes."

"Did he say what he was going to do?"

"Just that he was going to pay Crawlin' Rawlins a visit."

"How long was he gone?"

"Maybe forty-five minutes."

"When he came home, did he tell you what had happened?"

"What you mean is, did Wade tell me that he'd killed Rawlins?" Marilyn snuffled and then glowered at me. "No, he just put the bow away and said that if the sheriff came asking about any stray arrows, that we don't know nothing about nothing."

"And the next day he went out to ditch his bow and arrows." I leaned over in her direction and asked in a stage whisper, "Mrs. Tice, just between you and me, are you still certain your husband didn't kill Ev Rawlins?"

She looked down again. "I . . . I don't —"

Before she could answer, we both heard the throaty whine of the quad-runner as it rolled into the yard. Then Ash and Tina began shouting at Wade to stop the ATV. As I pushed myself clumsily from the chair, I heard the ATV's engine roar as Wade gave it the gas, more shouts to stop, and then the crack of a gun being fired.

TWENTY-THREE

I yelled at Marilyn to remain where she was, but I don't think she even heard me. Wailing with terror, she almost knocked me down as she barreled past on her way to the front door. I hurried to catch up.

However, Marilyn came to a sudden halt on the front porch and screeched, "Wade! You pull your head out of your butt *right now* and turn that damn quad-runner off!"

I joined her on the porch and saw Wade seated on the stationary quad-runner while Tina and Ash pointed their guns at him. The women had good reason to be cautious, as Wade had a hunting rifle slung over his right shoulder. The ATV was facing away from the house, and it was obvious what had happened. Wade had driven into the yard, seen the patrol car, and tried to flee. However, I could also see why Wade had elected to stop: The front wheel of the quad-runner closest to Tina was flat, which told me that she'd put a bullet into the tire.

Wade looked over at his wife and then reached down to shut off the engine. As he slowly climbed from the ATV, Tina holstered her pistol and yanked the rifle from his shoulder. Then the farmer stuck his jaw out and began to spout insults and noisy self-pity. He was so busy running his smart mouth that he didn't notice Marilyn, who was marching across the yard toward him with her hands balled up into fists.

Arriving in front of her husband, Marilyn delivered a powerful roundhouse sucker punch that Wade never saw coming. The blow connected solidly and he tumbled backward against the ATV and then fell to his knees. Wade massaged his jaw and stared up at his wife in confusion.

Marilyn stood over the farmer and pointed an accusing finger at him. "Damn you! I have flat had enough of you feeling sorry for yourself and losing your temper. This time it's got us both in real trouble. Now, Wade, I love you, but a husband shouldn't do things that make his wife think she has to lie for him. Did you kill Ev Rawlins?"

Wade was looking at Marilyn as if this were the first time he'd ever seen her. "No, baby, I didn't kill him. I told you that."

"No, you didn't, you worthless excuse for

a man. You let me think you might have done it and put me in an awful spot."

"I'm . . . I'm sorry, Marilyn."

It was both too late and too soon for apologies. The only thing that the request for forgiveness accomplished was to make Marilyn that much more angry. She made as if to take another swing at her husband, but Ash restrained her. Meanwhile, I watched in quiet amazement as the belligerent farmer who'd threatened me with a screwdriver yesterday now knelt and quailed before his wife's long overdue eruption of fury.

Marilyn shouted over Ash's shoulder, "Wade, you tell these people exactly what you did on Thursday night or we're done! I'll be out of here before you can blink twice!"

Wade now wore a look of panic. In a pleading voice he said, "Marilyn, I know I've been a damn fool, but please don't go. Please! I promise I'll tell them the truth."

"You'd better!"

"I think it might be best if I took Mrs. Tice in the house," said Ash.

"While we get a *voluntary* statement from her husband," I added. "And you *do* want to talk to us, Mr. Tice, don't you?"

"Yes, sir." Wade climbed to his feet and

watched Ash and Marilyn as they went inside the house.

Tina said, "But before we get into that, I have to ask, do you want to press charges on your wife?"

"For what?"

"Domestic violence. It's against the law for her to hit you like that."

"And what happens if I do?"

"We'll take her to jail when we're done here."

Wade reached into his mouth to experimentally wiggle a tooth and then said, "No, I don't want to press charges. I reckon I've had that slug coming for a while."

I thought, *Oh, you think?*

"Fine, but remember that I gave you the chance." Tina removed the ammunition magazine from the hunting rifle, snapped open the bolt, and peered into the breech to ensure that there weren't any bullets in the weapon. Then she held up the rifle and said, "This isn't what you usually hunt with. Where is your hunting bow?"

"Gone."

Tina frowned at him. "Look, Mr. Tice, I'm tired, I've got a headache, and I've got a prosecutor who's in a hurry to put *some-one* on trial for murder. If you don't want to be that person, stop playing twenty questions. Where are your bow and arrows?"

Wade rubbed the spot where his wife had slugged him. "I threw them in the river, yesterday."

"Why?"

"Because after I got done talking to him" — he nodded in my direction — "I got afraid that I was going to be blamed for Rawlins's murder."

"But not because you did it, of course." Tina made no effort to conceal her disbelief.

"Hey, I keep telling you I didn't kill Rawlins. You've got to believe me."

Tina carefully leaned the rifle against the side of the ATV and then folded her arms across her chest. "No, I don't, considering you lied your butt off to Mr. Lyon. Didn't you tell him that you never left your home on Thursday night?"

"Yes, ma'am." Wade hung his head. "That was a lie. But I'm telling the truth now."

"We'll see about that." Tina glanced at me.

I nodded. "Mr. Tice, what happened on Thursday afternoon when your wife came home?"

He took a deep breath. "She told me that Rawlins was selling his land to some amusement park company . . . said she'd seen the paperwork and it was a done deal."

"How'd that make you feel?"

361

"Flaming mad. He was going to collect six million bucks while we had to deal with Six Flags over Hell."

"That's an understandable reaction. What did you do next?"

There was a long pause before he said, "I acted like a damn moron. I went over to Rawlins's place to send him a message about how pissed I was."

"What kind of message? Flowers? Greeting card? Singing telegram?"

Wade gave me an irritated look, but maintained his temper. "No, it's stupid but I decided to shoot a hunting arrow into the side of his house."

"Why?"

"He'd know it was from me, but wouldn't be able to prove it."

"So . . . would it be fair to say that you meant to frighten Mr. Rawlins?"

"Yep. There was nothing I could do to stop him from selling his land, but I *could* make the time he had left on that farm miserable."

"Nasty. Every time he went outside he'd worry that there was another arrow inbound."

He made no effort to sound penitent. "That was the idea. So I grabbed my bow and arrows and rode my quad over most of the way to his house. Then I walked the rest of the way."

"Did Marilyn go over there with you?" I asked, giving him the opportunity to mitigate his guilt by spreading some of the blame onto his wife.

He shook his head vigorously. "No! She stayed home and told me that I should, too."

"You should have listened to her."

"I know. Anyway, I got close enough to see the house, but not so close that his man-eating dog would know I was out there." He shrugged. "And then I took aim at the side of the house and let loose with an arrow. But I made sure I didn't aim close to a window. Like I said, I just wanted to scare him."

I rolled my eyes. "Then you should have bought a fright mask. You don't do it by firing a razor-sharp broadhead hunting arrow at an occupied dwelling. That's reckless endangerment, even if you don't intend to hit anyone."

"But it was the only kind of arrow I had."

"And you were in a hurry to do something mind-numbingly idiotic. Okay, what happened after that?"

"I moved a little closer toward the house. I wanted to see him crap his britches when he saw the arrow sticking out of the wall."

"Even though Mr. Rawlins might have released his man-eating dog?" Tina asked suspiciously. "That doesn't make any sense."

"I'd . . . well, I'd nocked another arrow." Wade stuck his hands into his jeans pockets. "No brag, but I hit what I shoot at with a bow. If he'd set Longstreet on me, I'd have dropped that big old dog like a sack of wheat."

"So you were willing to kill his pet, just to satisfy your evil curiosity?" I asked. "For God's sake, *the dog* wasn't responsible for Mr. Rawlins selling his farm to the theme park company."

He smoothed his beard and gave me an uncomfortable look. "I guess I didn't think that part through all the way."

"No kidding. *Did* Mr. Rawlins come out of the house?"

"Yep. At first, he just stood on the porch looking around. Then he kind of wandered around the house. But . . ." There was the faintest trace of exasperation in Wade's voice.

"What happened?"

He grumbled, "He walked right past the arrow and never saw it. I mean, he was so close to the damn thing that I wanted to shout, *Stop and look up, you goggle-eyed old miser!*"

364

"So you went through all that commando low-crawling and Rambo sniper action in the dark for nothing. That must have been frustrating."

"Frustrating ain't half the word."

"Did that make you mad enough to shoot another arrow at the house?" Tina asked.

It was an excellent question. We'd been assuming that the same arrow that had killed Everett Rawlins had left the hole in the wall. However, there was the chance that Wade had used the bow more than once.

"And maybe *by accident* that second arrow hit Mr. Rawlins? It wouldn't be murder, if you didn't mean to hit him." Tina pressed the point, while offering Wade room to minimize his responsibility for the act.

"I'll say it again: I didn't kill Rawlins! Not on purpose and not by accident! I only fired one arrow and it hit the house *exactly* where I aimed."

I said, "But he never saw the arrow, which, by your own admission, made you even more angry. Is that why you came out from your hiding place to deliver your message to Mr. Rawlins in person?"

"I didn't do any such thing."

"So, how'd Mr. Rawlins end up with an arrow in him?"

"Beats the hell out of me! I stayed in that

365

thicket until I went back to the quad. I never went near him and he was alive when I left."

"So you say. But you'd made nothing but terrible decisions up to that point, so why should we presume that you'd suddenly wised up?"

Tina jumped back in. "Mr. Tice, do you use a glove when you go bow hunting?"

"Yeah. So what?"

"What kind of glove?"

"A three-finger release glove," he replied.

I noticed that he involuntarily clenched and unclenched his right hand, which suggested he wore the glove on that hand.

"What's the glove made out of?" Tina asked.

"Leather. Bison leather, I think."

"And what color is it?"

"It was brown. It's pretty stained now." Wade obviously felt the questions were foolish and gave her an impatient look.

"You didn't throw that glove in the river, too, did you?"

"No. No reason."

"Good. Where is that glove? I want it."

"It's upstairs with my hunting gear. But why?" Wade huffed.

Tina gave him a hard stare. "Because the crime lab found tiny bits of brown leather on the shaft of your arrow."

His jaw worked for several seconds before the words came out. "And you think they came from *my* glove?"

She nodded. "Right now, the evidence says that you were the only person out there wearing gloves."

Wade drew himself up to his full height. "Listen good, Sheriff: I don't know nothing about any leather on that arrow. Maybe it happened when I pulled it from the quiver. And even if I'd thought about going over and getting in his face — and I ain't saying I did — I couldn't have, because of that car coming down his driveway."

I hated to admit it, but it sounded as if he was telling the truth. I asked, "What kind of car?"

"I don't know. All I saw was headlights. I thought maybe he'd called the law and it was a sheriff's car. That's when I lit out of there."

Tina and I exchanged quick glances, and I could tell we were both thinking the same thing. There was a good chance that Wade Tice had witnessed the arrival of Sherri Driggs's Saab. If so, the amusement park exec had just taken the brass ring as our most likely suspect.

"I know things look bad for me, but it seems to me that you might want to talk to whoever it was in that car before you try to ramrod me for murder," Tice grumbled.

"You're absolutely right, Mr. Tice," Tina said thoughtfully. "But in the meantime, I'm going to want to send that glove to the crime lab."

"Okay. But before that, will you do me a favor, Sheriff?"

"That depends on the favor."

Wade fixed her with an earnest gaze. "I'd be obliged if you told Marilyn that I co-operated with you and told the truth . . . even when it made me look like a dummy."

"Yeah, I can do that," said Tina. After a moment, she added, "And if it does turn out that you lied to us, I'm thinking maybe I should just call and tell Mrs. Tice. It would save the county the cost of a trial."

Wade gave her a hangdog look and nodded.

As Tina and Wade headed for the house, I limped over to the Xterra and leaned against the hood in an effort to take some of the weight off my throbbing shin. I was suddenly exhausted. I'd been running on adrenaline, strong coffee, and willpower for almost two days now, but I could tell that I was coming very close to my limit. The knowledge that I could no longer do the things I'd been capable of as a young man left me feeling both discouraged and a little frightened.

The police radio inside the patrol car crackled and I heard Tina pick up, but couldn't make out what they were saying and didn't really care, as I was too busy having a self-pity party. A few moments later, I heard the clatter of rapid footfalls on the wooden porch steps and looked up. Ash and Tina had come out of the house and were trotting across the yard toward the sheriff's cruiser. Both women looked excited.

Ash yelled, "Follow us to the station, so that you can ride over with us! We're going to New Market! The local cops just found Roger Prufrock's car at a motel!"

"Did you get the glove?" I asked.

Tina raised her right fist and waved the brown archery glove at me. "It's right here! Now let's go!"

Their eagerness was infectious, and I suddenly felt a little less weary and sore. I knew this sense of rejuvenation was artificial. It was born of an adrenaline rush, and once those drugs had worked their magic, the fatigue and pain would come back with a vengeance. But that didn't matter right now. We had a murder to solve. I hopped into the SUV and almost beat the patrol car back to the sheriff's station.

Twenty-Four

At the sheriff's department, we all bundled into a cruiser and headed out again. As we drove past the church community center, I noticed that the parking lot was now mostly empty. There were only a few teddy bear artists left, packing up their stuff.

Turning to speak through the Plexiglas barrier separating the front and back seats, I said, "You did a great job of organizing the show, honey. I'm just sorry I missed so much of it and that we had to leave early."

Ash, who was sitting in the backseat, replied, "I know, but you can look forward to staying all day next year. Hopefully, we won't be investigating a murder then."

Tina called over her shoulder. "So you've decided there's going to *be* a next year?"

"Everybody at the show seemed to really enjoy themselves, and lots of the out-of-town artists told me that they'd come back next year, if we did it again. It's a lot of work, but . . ."

"It's great that you're going to make this an annual event," I said. "But who are you kidding, honey? It's not just a lot of work. It's a s-teddy job."

Because Ash was on the other side of the plastic barrier, I couldn't hear her. But I was pretty certain that she'd groaned in unison with Tina.

The town of New Market isn't much more than fifteen miles to the northwest of Remmelkemp Mill . . . as the crow flies. However, we aren't crows and there is no direct route between the two communities, so Tina and I had plenty of time along the way to recount to Ash what Marilyn and Wade Tice had told us during their interviews.

Ash said sadly, "So Everett was really going to sell out? That just makes me sick."

"I know it's disappointing, but there isn't much room for doubt," I replied. "Ev Rawlins was going to take the money and run."

Tina kept her eyes locked on the interstate traffic ahead and said, "And with Swift Run Gap Realty handling the real estate transaction, Roger Prufrock knew the amusement park was going to be built."

"Which gives him a motive for arson," Ash said.

"And maybe even murder," Tina added.

371

"All Mr. Tice saw were headlights. For all we know, it might have been Roger's BMW."

"True enough. What's your plan for when we get to the motel?" I asked.

"Beats me. We don't have probable cause to arrest him."

"Even though you found those burned clothes at his house?" Ash asked.

"All he'd have to say is that it happened when he used some gasoline to burn a bunch of raked leaves. We can't prove otherwise until the lab analyzes his clothing," Tina replied.

I said, "And we won't even be able to ask him that, if he doesn't open the door. We don't have a search warrant, so we have no legal right to force entry into his motel room."

"And he won't open up if he knows it's us," said Ash.

"So we've got to come up with some way to trick him into coming outside. Gee, is there anyone in this car capable of that sort of deviousness?" I said innocently.

Tina chuckled as we turned onto the off-ramp for New Market. For most people, New Market is just a blur seen from the interstate, but it's a secular shrine for those who honor Southern heritage. The town was the site of a Civil War battle back in 1864 that featured an attack by the teenaged cadets of the Virginia Military Institute, which is now a cherished component of Confederate military myth. The community really hasn't changed all that much since then . . . if you can overlook the gas stations, convenience stores, and fast-food restaurants, and the ten-foot-tall painted fiberglass statue of Johnny Appleseed that belongs in some kitsch hall of fame.

The motel was on the west side of the freeway and stood on the crest of a low hill. Tina turned into the motel parking lot and stopped in front of the office. A young-looking New Market cop and a Shenandoah County deputy sheriff leaned against their patrol cars, waiting for us. We got out of the cruiser, and the cop told us that he'd found Roger's BMW parked at the rear of the motel. The cop stressed that he hadn't stopped to take a closer look at the Beemer, but had retreated and called for backup. After that, he'd spoken with the motel manager who'd reported that Roger was in Room 115, which was on the ground floor. The young cop had done an excellent job, and if we were lucky, our renegade real estate agent was still unaware that we'd discovered his hiding place.

As Tina, Ash, and the two lawmen went

to conduct a quick reconnaissance of the rear of the motel, an idea of how we might entice Roger from the room occurred to me. The ploy would require a prop, so I began to search for something made out of metal that would make plenty of noise when I walloped it with my cane. I found what I was looking for next to the soda machines and carried it back to the front of the motel. Ash, Tina, and the cops had already returned from their scouting mission, and they made no effort to conceal their looks of mystification.

Ash said, "Honey . . . uh . . . why are you carrying that big trash can?"

"This is going to get Roger out of his room." I raised the weathered galvanized steel canister. It was easy to lift because it was empty. I'd removed the trash-filled plastic liner bag and left it next to the soda machines.

"How?" Tina asked.

"The magic of special effects. We're going to wreck his BMW."

Tina looked at me as if I'd lost my marbles. "What? Brad, we can't damage his car."

"You're right, but we can make him *think* it happened. Now, here's how we're going to work this . . ."

A few minutes later, we were in position and ready. Tina and Ash stood on opposite sides of the door to Room 115, with their backs pressed against the wall so that Roger couldn't observe them though the fish-eye peephole. Meanwhile I was hiding to the rear of a big Dodge Durango SUV, which was parked next to Roger's BMW. The New Market cop was about forty yards away, sitting in his idling patrol car and waiting for Tina's signal. She waved for him to begin, and it was showtime.

The cop slammed his foot down on the gas pedal, and his car laid down a smoky trail of acceleration skid. Then, as the officer approached my location, he stood on his brakes. That was my cue. Once the car skidded to a stop, I smashed my cane against the side of the trash can, to replicate the sound of a traffic collision. Then I pointed to the cop. He hit the gas again and roared around the corner.

Not wanting Roger to recognize my voice, I tried to disguise it. Hoping I sounded like someone from the urban Northeast, I shouted, "Hey! Get dat freakin' guy's license plate! He just hit dis freakin' Beemer!"

There were a couple of tense seconds as we waited to see if Roger would take the bait. Then the door to Room 115 swung open, and Roger came reeling outside. I think we all winced at the sight. The agent had a mixture of first- and second-degree burns on his face and scalp, and his pink and blistered skin reminded me unpleasantly of a fat Louisiana hot-link sausage that had spent too much time on the barbecue grill.

Still oblivious to Tina and Ash, who were following in his wake, Roger lurched toward the rear of the BMW. That's when I stepped out from behind the SUV and said, "Hi, Roger. Man, you got one hell of a sunburn while you were golfing down in South Carolina earlier today. Is that why you came back so soon?"

Roger looked from the back of his undamaged Beemer to the dented trash can and realized he'd been duped. Then he gave me a nervous grin and said, "What are you talking about, Brad, old buddy? I wasn't in South Carolina."

"I know, and those burns weren't caused by the sun. You were too close to the house when the gasoline ignited. And don't bother to lie. We found your gas can, a road flare that is going to have your fingerprints on it, and your burned clothes."

Roger nodded glumly. "I guess you've got me."

"What are you doing here? You need to be in a hospital." Then I smelled the strong odor of hard liquor on Roger's breath. "Or a detox facility."

"I'm fine. Just fine," Roger replied in a slightly slurred voice. He dismissively waved his right hand. The gesture revealed that his hand was also burned.

Even though Roger had declined medical attention, I was pretty certain he was too intoxicated to know just how badly he was injured. Therefore, we had a moral duty to call for the EMTs, even if that meant an abbreviated interview. I glanced at Ash, who nodded and went over to ask the New Market cop to contact his dispatcher and have paramedics sent to the motel. Meanwhile, the state trooper gave us a wave and returned to his cruiser.

Tina said, "Mr. Prufrock, we have a few minutes, so we'd like to ask you some questions."

The real estate agent slowly wheeled to face Tina. "Sheriff! How good to see you. Perhaps we could . . . uh . . . set up a time to chat on Monday?"

"I think *now* would be best."

"Especially for you," I added. "Look

Roger, you're a wheeler-dealer, so let me put this in terms you'll understand. Now's the time to cooperate and buy yourself some goodwill that can be redeemed later at your trial."

"Where you might be charged with arson *and* murder, if you don't tell us the truth," said Tina, playing some verbal hardball.

Roger gave Tina a bleary-eyed look of amazement and fear. "Murder? Oh my God, was someone in that house? You've got to believe me, ol' Roger didn't know that there was anybody inside."

"There was nobody in the house that we know of," said Tina. "We're talking about the murder of Everett Rawlins."

"Ev? I didn't kill Ev. Everybody says that Wade Tice did it."

Roger was far too drunk to skillfully dissemble, so I was inclined to believe he was telling the truth, as he knew it. I said, "Everybody might be wrong. So let me get this straight, you weren't at Ev Rawlins's house on Thursday night?"

"No! No. I was at my office and then I was home." The agent began to lose his balance but steadied himself at the last moment.

Ash came back and murmured, "The rescue squad has been notified, but there's going to be a slight delay. They're just clearing from a car crash."

"Okay, then we have a few minutes before the medics get here and transport Roger to the hospital. We'll see what we can get from him before they arrive," I muttered to my wife and Tina. "Let's move him back inside the room and sit him down. There'll be fewer distractions."

"And he won't be as likely to fall over," Tina added.

We led Roger back inside the motel room, where I discovered what he'd been using as an anesthetic. On the nightstand was an amber-colored plastic prescription bottle of oxycodone pills and beside it a large bottle of rum. Roger had been watching a college football game before we'd interrupted him with our bogus car crash. The real estate agent sat down in the chair while I found the TV remote and shut off the set.

"Hey, I was watching that!" Roger complained.

I sat down on the bed opposite the chair and said, "I think it's more important that you focus on us for a few minutes."

Roger eyed the liquor bottle on the nightstand. "Could I have some more rum while we talk?"

"That's probably not a good idea. Now,

we already know about Ev Rawlins selling his farm to Amerriment so they can turn the farm into a theme park. We also know that you were the agent handling the transaction. So, what happened on Thursday?"

"Thursday . . ." Momentarily forgetting that his brow was scorched, Roger reached up to rub his forehead and then jerked his hand away in pain. "Thursday . . . we were supposed to sign the final paperwork on Thursday right around suppertime."

"You mean the sale hadn't been finalized?" Tina asked.

"No. We'd been dickering since Tuesday, but Ev was dragging his heels. It was making Friggin' Driggs crazy . . . that's my little nickname for that foul-mouthed Amerriment lady, by the way."

Tina wrinkled her nose. "That's sweet."

"She certainly *isn't* sweet," said Roger, oblivious to Tina's barb. "That woman belongs in a kennel."

Tina shook her head with frustration. It was obvious she didn't have any patience with drunks. I, however, had learned to deal with other people's booze-impaired brain functions while I was still a child, as both my mother and father had been alcoholics.

I said, "Where were you going to meet to sign the papers?"

"Rawlins's house," he replied. "But I got a call from Driggs that afternoon. She was all upset and said the paperwork was ruined."

"Because someone had poured coffee all over it," I said.

Roger gave me a wary look of surprise. "How'd you know that?"

"Don't worry about how we found out. Just keep in mind that if we know something that insignificant, we'll also know if you start lying. Now, what else did she say?"

"She said she needed a fresh batch of sales documents as soon as possible. I told her that was going to take some time, and she jumped down my throat and said that I'd better get my hillbilly ass in gear." The agent sounded angry and with good reason. Despite its wide usage in American culture, the word *hillbilly* is extraordinarily offensive to folks who live around here and throughout the rest of Appalachia.

"What happened after that?" Ash asked.

"Her Majesty had spoken, so I started putting together a new bunch of escrow paperwork. I had the documents saved on my computer, but it was a lot of work."

"I can imagine," I said.

"Brad, old buddy, are you sure I can't have something to wet my whistle?" Roger made a big production out of smacking his lips. "All this talking has flat dried me out."

"Sure. How about some water?"

"How about just a tiny sip of that rum?"

"If you don't want water, you can't be that thirsty."

"But I'm hurting."

"No doubt, but whose fault is that? You set the fire."

"I know, but I want a drink."

"Not on top of God knows how many of those oxycodone pills you've taken. Fire-water with opiates is a lethal combo. And no offense, but I don't think any of us feel like giving you CPR."

Roger's tone became petulant. "Look here, that's my bottle. I bought it with my own money and *I want a drink*. Otherwise, I'm going to stop talking."

We didn't have time to waste arguing over booze, so I leaned back and gave him a cold smile. "If that's supposed to be a threat, you're a lot drunker than I thought. Here's a reality check, Roger: You have no leverage. We don't need your help to find out who killed Ev Rawlins, so don't try to haggle with us."

The agent gave me a shrewd look. "Oh yeah . . . ? What if I told you it was Sherri Driggs and maybe her assistant, too, at Ev's house on Thursday night?"

"We already know that," I lied. "We'd be mildly interested in hearing your version of the story, of course. But whether you talk or not, you aren't getting any more rum. That's the deal, take it or leave it."

Twenty-Five

Roger sagged against one of the chair's armrests. "I'll take it."

"Wise choice. And just to make sure that old demon rum doesn't tempt you any more, I'm going to ask my wife to pour the rest of it down the sink."

"My pleasure." Ash gave the real estate agent a disgusted look as she grabbed the bottle and headed for the bathroom.

"A few minutes ago, you told us that you weren't at Mr. Rawlins's place Thursday night, so how could you possibly know who was?" Tina did a fine job of sounding as if she already knew the answer and couldn't care less what Roger had to say.

"Oh now, Sheriff, everybody in town knows that Miss Ashleigh chased a Saab from Ev's place on Thursday night. Now, that's the same kind of car that Ms. Driggs drives."

"We've known that for days," said Ash as

she came back into the room.

"But you don't know *why* Driggs was there," Roger said in an almost childish smug tone.

I leaned over and fixed him with a hard stare. "Roger, would you please get to the point before I regret not allowing you to overdose?"

The agent looked a little miffed. "Okay, remember I said that I had to print out all that new paperwork? Well, I thought I should call up Ev and tell him that we'd be a little later at his house than we'd planned."

"And what did he say?"

"He said he was sorry and told me that he'd been reconsidering and had changed his mind. He didn't want to sell his farm."

"What did you say?"

"I asked him why. Asked him if it was a problem of not enough money."

"Was it?"

"No. He said that it had been his family's land for over two hundred years and that it just felt wrong to turn it into an amusement park."

Tina said, "There went your big commission right down the drain. That must have been upsetting for you."

"I was disappointed. Very disappointed."

"And scared about having to break the

bad news to Ms. Driggs, I'll bet," I said.

Roger nodded. "I called Her Majesty and she about had a meltdown. She cursed so hard and so long I thought she was having a crazy fit."

"What did you do?"

"When she finally stopped calling everyone and everything a motherf—" He glanced up at Ash and caught himself in time. "Sorry. Well, I was still trying to salvage the deal, so I asked Ms. Gutter Mouth if she'd consider upping the offer price."

"Even though Everett made it clear that it wasn't a matter of how much money was being offered?" Ash asked.

"Lots of people tell me things like that, Miss Ashleigh. But it *always* boils down to folks wanting more money." Roger looked away from my wife.

I said, "So you didn't really honor his decision. You just figured there was no point in talking any further until you could put more money on the table."

"That's about the size of it," said Roger. "Anyway, Driggs told me to up the offer to seven million dollars even for the land, but that was as high as she would go."

"Did you call Mr. Rawlins back with the new offer?" I asked. Off in the distance I heard a siren begin to wail and knew it was the rescue squad on their way to the motel. We were running out of time.

"No. I just printed out a fresh stack of paperwork with the new sales figure and decided to go over and see Ev in person."

"And what time was that?"

"I got there around three-thirty, but it was a waste of time. Ev told me that his mind was made up. He wasn't going to sell, no matter what the price." Roger shook his head in disbelief. "Seven million dollars and he turned it down."

"Where is that paperwork now?" Ash asked.

Roger said, "I left it on his kitchen counter. I thought maybe he might look at all those zeroes after that seven and change his mind . . . and I was right."

The siren was growing very close now, and I could hear the rumble of the diesel engine as the ambulance came up the low hill. A moment later, the siren stopped and the ambulance turned into the motel parking lot. We had perhaps a minute left to get all the answers we so desperately needed.

"How do you know that?" Tina demanded. "Did you go back out there that night?"

Roger shook his head vigorously. "No. I

didn't hear anything from anyone that night, so I assumed the deal was dead. I went home."

I said, "But clearly, at some point, you learned the deal wasn't dead."

"That's true. Just before I met with you two at the house yesterday, I got a call from Driggs's assistant, Jason . . . Jesse . . . Jason, whatever." Roger waved his hand listlessly. "He started crowing about how he'd gone out to Ev's place on Thursday afternoon and convinced him to sell his farm."

"Why would Mr. Hauck be calling you? Had you ever spoken with him before?"

"No, so I asked to talk to Driggs. But he told me that from now on I'd be dealing with him. And you know what?"

"What?" I asked.

"He was just as big a jerk as she was!"

"Forgive me if I don't react with shock. But something puzzles me, Roger. Everyone around here — including Jesse Hauck and Sherri Driggs, for that matter — knew that Ev Rawlins had been killed early on Thursday evening."

"So?"

"So . . . didn't you wonder about Mr. Hauck admitting to having been at the house so close to the time of the murder?"

Roger shrugged. "Hey, I'm not a detective."

Before I could respond, Ash jumped in. "Oh, now, Brad, I can understand why good ol' Roger didn't give it any thought. He was too busy getting ready to burn down a hundred-year-old Victorian mansion."

The real estate agent tried to look both remorseful and dignified. "I'm not proud of what I did. But you can't stop progress, Miss Ashleigh. That theme park was coming, no matter who handled the transaction. So *somebody* was going to get that money. Why not me?" Roger said defensively.

"You call traffic, litter, and urban sprawl *progress?* And God only knows how many real bears would be killed to make room for your trashy Bear Fair." Ash's hands balled up into fists, and I thought she might take a swing at the agent. "Roger Prufrock, you are a mealymouthed, nickel-plated scumbag, and I hope those burns you have are just a preview of the place you're going someday."

The ambulance stopped outside the room, the truck doors slammed, and the EMTs came in, carrying their medical gear. We went outside as the medics worked. It was twilight now, and a chilly breeze blew down from the Allegheny Mountains. I zipped up

389

my jacket and leaned on the hood of the Beemer.

Stifling a yawn, I said, "So Jesse is apparently running the show now. What does that tell us?"

"That he knows Driggs killed Rawlins," said Tina.

I nodded. "And he's blackmailing his boss. She keeps her freedom by boosting her former boy toy up the corporate ladder."

"But I don't understand. If Everett signed the documents, why kill him?" Ash asked.

"We only have Jesse's word, via Roger, that Ev actually did sign the documents. Has anybody seen those escrow papers?" I asked. "When a house is sold, there are multiple copies of the transaction documents. One bunch for the buyer, one bunch for the real estate agent —"

Ash cut in excitedly, "And one for the seller. But we didn't find any escrow paperwork in Ev's house."

"We didn't really look. So we're going to have to go through that mountain of paperwork we recovered from his office to make sure they aren't there before we talk to Sherri," I said.

The EMTs led Roger from the room and out to the ambulance. It seemed the alcohol and opiates he'd been taking for the pain were wearing off. Roger moaned as he climbed into the back of the ambulance.

Tina said, "I guess I should go over and tell him he's under arrest for arson."

"I'd get his car keys before they go." I rapped my knuckles on the hood of the BMW. "But I can't see any point in arresting him right this minute."

"Maybe I'm missing something. Didn't he confess to the arson?"

"Yeah, but Roger isn't going anywhere, and if you take him into custody now, you'll just saddle the county with his medical bills. So why not wait until he's out of the hospital and then file charges on him? There's just something obscene about the idea of our tax dollars being spent on his medical treatment." I nodded toward the ambulance, where Roger was now being strapped to a gurney.

Tina gave me a weary smile and went to get Roger's car keys before the EMTs took off. She called a tow truck for the Beemer and made sure the tow operator knew how to get to the state crime lab in Roanoke, and then we were free to head back to Remmelkemp Mill.

A half hour later, we sat in Tina's office eating spicy Thai takeout for dinner and starting in on the mass of paperwork collected from Rawlins's den. We each took a thick stack of papers and discovered we had a long night ahead of us. The documents weren't in any particular order, which meant we had to examine each individual sheet.

Despite the good food, or maybe because of it, I could feel myself becoming sleepy and my vision began to blur, so I went down the hall to make some more coffee. The last thing I wanted was another cup of mud, but I wasn't going to be able to stay awake unless I got some caffeine into my system. Thank God for legal stimulants.

When I came back to the office, Tina was on the phone, and I saw that Ash had temporarily abandoned her search of the paperwork and was instead watching her intently. Clearly, the sheriff was in the process of receiving important news.

"Don't touch anything else. We'll be there in a few minutes," Tina commanded before hanging up. Turning to us she said, "It looks like our paper chase is going to have to wait for now. That was the EMT from our rescue squad. They're up at the Massanutten Crest Lodge. Jesse Hauck is dead."

Twenty-Six

"Apparently, he fell from his balcony into the middle of a wedding reception," said Tina, as she stood up and grabbed her uniform jacket from the back of her chair.

"Talk about dropping in unannounced," I said. "And if Jesse *was* blackmailing Sherri, how convenient for her that he's dead."

"Didn't you say they were staying on the third floor?" Ash sounded doubtful. "That isn't *that* far a fall."

"He fell way more than three floors," said Tina. "That side of the hotel is built on the edge of like a forty- or fifty-foot cliff. There's a big château at the bottom that the hotel rents out for special events."

"Like weddings or . . . *fall* festivals. Did the —" My cell phone rang and I glanced at the screen.

It was Linny, and the security director's tone was grim. He seemed to be making an effort not to be overheard. "Brad, we need you and the sheriff to come to the lodge right away."

"I know. The rescue squad already called to tell us that Jesse Hauck is dead."

"That's right, and he fell from Ms. Driggs's balcony. I'm up in the room right now. She says that she was in the bathtub when it happened, but I'm suspicious."

"Good work, but don't ask her anything else, Linny. We're on our way." I hung up and said to the women, "Let me grab a Coke on the way out the door, and then we need to get up to the lodge, Code Three. Linny is in the room right now and on the verge of going Inspector Clouseau on us."

"Oh Lord," said Tina. "Let's go."

A couple of minutes later, we were speeding through the darkness in Tina's patrol car, headed for the lodge. Meanwhile, I was trying to get the caffeine into my system as fast as possible. I chugalugged the Coke so quickly that I gave myself a painful dose of temporary brain freeze.

"Brad, we need to get someone up to Ms. Driggs's room ASAP, so why don't I drop you off at the main entrance and then you can head up while Ash and I go down the hill to where the body is," Tina said. "I'm going to have my hands full trying to control that madhouse down there, and we potentially have two separate crime scenes."

"Good idea," I said.

Tina added, "And while Brad talks to Ms. Driggs, I'm going to need you to process the body, Ash."

"But I've never handled a scene by my-self," said Ash.

"I know, but I think you're ready," said Tina.

"I agree," I said. "You're observant, you've got good instincts, and —"

"And I had a good teacher," Ash inter-rupted. "Okay, I'll do my best."

"Of course you will, and don't hesitate to call me if you have any questions," I said. "And be prepared. Jesse is probably going to be a mess." I felt guilty that my wife was going to handle the undoubtedly gory scene while I chatted with Sherri up in the luxuri-ous hotel suite.

"I can handle it."

"I know you can. I just don't want you to be caught off guard," I replied.

We rounded a bend in the highway, and the lodge lay just ahead. As always, I thought the place looked even sillier by night. Bathed in the glow of pink spotlights, the faux fairy-tale castle reminded me of the My Little Pony toy palace our daughter had played with as a young girl. When the patrol car skidded to a stop in front of the main entrance, I got out of the car, limped inside the hotel, and rode the elevator to the third floor. Linny was waiting for me in the corridor outside Room 331. The door was open, and I peeked inside the room. Sherri Driggs was sitting at the dining nook table. She wore a stunned expression and the same silk kimono I'd seen her in yesterday. She didn't seem to be aware that I was present. But that might have been a subterfuge.

Linny pulled me aside and said in a hushed voice, "Thanks for getting here so quickly. She's kind of falling apart."

"That's always useful when you know the cops are going to want to ask uncomfortable questions," I whispered in reply. "What's her story?"

"Just that she was taking a bath while Mr. Hauck was out on the balcony having a martini and a cigar."

"Out on the balcony? It's a little chilly for that, isn't it?"

"No, we have portable propane heaters out there. It keeps things pretty warm."

Liquor and a cigar sounded like the ingredients for a man's victory celebration, so I was inclined to rule out the already slight possibility of suicide. That left accident and murder as the potential reasons for Jesse's death. I asked, "Who got here first?"

"I did. I was down in the security office, watching the old video recordings and looking for that Lincoln guy, when one of my security officers called about the accident. I went over to the château and the body was . . ." Linny blanched and swallowed hard. "I'm sorry."

I touched him on the shoulder. "No need to apologize. It can be a pretty horrifying sight."

"But I forced myself to look and I saw that it was Mr. Hauck. I came upstairs and knocked on her door, and was getting ready to use the passkey when she opened up."

My phone rang; it was Ash. There was a cacophony of voices in the background, so it was a little hard to hear her. She said, "Brad, I wanted to update you on what's happening down here."

"Hang on a second." I limped down the hall about ten yards, so that I wouldn't be overheard by Sherri, and quietly said, "Okay, I'm clear to talk now. What's going on?"

"Here's what we've been able to find out, so far. There was a bluegrass band playing at the wedding reception and when they finished a song, a man from up at the hotel yelled something about knocking off the *Deliverance* music." Ash's voice betrayed irritation. A sarcastic allusion to the movie is just as offensive as *hillbilly* to the people around here.

"So how many people were going to go up and kick Jesse's ass?"

"Lots. They yelled at him to shut up, and he shouted something back about how brothers and sisters shouldn't get married."

"The inevitable hillbilly incest joke. Man, I'll bet the crowd was ready to get torches and pitchforks and storm the castle à la *Frankenstein.*"

"They were. But here's the interesting part: Some of the guests swear they heard a woman from about the same location as the man. Supposedly she yelled at him to shut his GD mouth. Hang on a sec, honey." Ash lowered the phone, and I heard Tina tell her that the medical examiner was en route. Then she came back on the line. "Okay, I'm back. Anyway, he began to heckle the crowd again and then he started to scream."

"And arrived with a splat a couple of seconds later?"

"I don't even want to think about what it sounded like when he hit. But I guess what I'm trying to tell you in this roundabout way is that we're pretty certain Jesse was the one doing the shouting."

"It also might mean that the woman those guests heard was on the balcony with Jesse."

"Sherri Driggs?"

"Maybe she's a pushover."

Ash chuckled uneasily. "Sometimes I wish I could be as detached as you are about this sort of thing. Jesse looks . . . really bad."

"I'm sorry you had to see it, honey."

"I'll be okay. I wanted to do police work, and this is part of it."

"Unfortunately, that's true. I just hope you never see so many murder victims that you have to develop my kind of gallows humor as a defense mechanism." Disconnecting from the call, I turned back to Linny. "Sorry. You were about to tell me what happened when Ms. Driggs opened the door."

"She seemed surprised and angry to see me," the security director quietly replied.

"How so?"

"The first thing she said was that she couldn't believe I was bothering her at that hour."

"Was she dressed like that?"

"Yeah, but she also had a towel wrapped around the top of her head like a turban. She said that she'd just gotten out of the

Jacuzzi and the bathroom door had been shut."

"Which is also a convenient alibi to explain why she didn't hear her assistant screaming as he fell to his death," I said. "What happened when you broke the news that Mr. Hauck had literally crashed the wedding reception?"

Linny gave me an indecisive look that told me he didn't know whether to laugh or be nauseated at the macabre one-liner. "She told me I was crazy and that Mr. Hauck was out on the balcony."

"Interesting that she could be so certain of that while she was incommunicado in the whirlpool bath."

"That didn't occur to me," Linny admitted. "Anyway, Ms. Driggs said she could prove I was wrong and led me out to the balcony."

"And of course, Mr. Hauck wasn't there. How'd she react when she realized you'd been telling the truth?"

"She still insisted I was wrong, and then she went up to the balcony railing and looked down."

"And saw the pandemonium down at the château?"

Linny nodded. "I think that's what finally convinced her."

And I think you witnessed nothing more than an elaborate dog-and-pony show, I thought, but kept my own counsel. I said, "You said she began to fall apart?"

"At first, she kind of screamed and began to cry. But now she's getting more and more withdrawn. It's like she's catatonic or something."

"That's always useful when you don't want to answer troublesome questions," I replied. "Linny, I need your help. First of all, may I have your permission, as a duly authorized representative of the lodge, to search her room?"

"Of course."

"Thanks. Now, when we go in there, I need you to keep her occupied for a little while, but I want her to think we believe this is an accident. Meanwhile, I'll take a quick look around the suite."

"I could tell her we're very sorry Mr. Hauck fell and that the lodge is going to pick up their bill."

"Good thinking. I'd also like you to stay in the room while I question her. I need an independent witness to our little chat."

Linny threw his shoulders back and sucked in his gut. "I'm ready whenever you are."

I followed Linny into the suite, and he

began by expressing his condolences. Sherri was still sitting at the table, and she turned her bleak gaze on Linny, who'd begun to nervously yammer about how the hotel was going to comp the bill. However, I noticed her eyes flick in my direction as I passed her and went into the bathroom.

The room was a wilderness of stark white tile and smelled faintly of raspberry. Leaning over the tub, I saw that the bottom of the Jacuzzi was wet and there were water droplets on the sides. However, that didn't actually mean Sherri had been bathing. The lag time between the identification of Jesse's body and Linny's arrival at the room could have provided her with plenty of time to stage the scene.

As I emerged from the bathroom and headed for the bedroom, Sherri asked Linny, "What is he doing here?"

"It doesn't happen very often, but when a guest . . . dies we have to notify the sheriff's office," said Linny.

"But what is he looking for?"

Shutting the bedroom door behind me, I couldn't hear the rest of the exchange. I paused briefly to scan the room. The bed was made, but a shallow concave depression on one of the pillows and the wrinkles in the bedspread told me that someone had been lying down there. A large sliding glass door on the far wall led out onto the balcony.

I pulled the glass door open and went outside. Linny had been right; the propane heater did keep things warm and cozy on the veranda. From below, I could hear the distant buzz of many voices. The balcony was rectangular, about ten feet deep and fifteen feet wide, with a four-foot-tall crenellated stone wall surrounding the enclosure. With its series of regular square gaps, the barrier reminded me of a jack-o'-lantern's teeth.

It was dark, so I pulled out my flashlight. I swung the beam to the left and saw two wooden patio chairs and a small table. On the tabletop I noted a stainless-steel cocktail shaker, a ceramic ashtray littered with small gray cylinders of what appeared to be cigar ash, and a box of matches. However, there was no sign of a martini glass or cigar, and I wondered if the adult pacifiers had still been in Jesse's hands when he'd taken the plunge, as it were.

I checked the other side of the balcony, where the large metal heater was located, and then walked over to the wall. Standing before one of the square gaps in the wall and looking down at the château, I realized how easy it would be to push someone from the castle. All it would require was surprise and a little swift application of leverage to send the victim plummeting to the ground below.

Checking each gap in the wall, I shined the flashlight beam obliquely against the uneven surfaces of the stones. I was looking for trace evidence such as clothing fibers, a tiny smear of brown shoe polish, or even fragments of broken fingernails . . . anything to show that Hauck had struggled to prevent himself from going over the side. But I came up with a big fat zero.

Next, I turned the flashlight and my attention to the flagstone floor. There was a burnt wooden match beside one of the chairs and a crumpled cellophane cigar wrapper near the door. Then something else caught my eye. It was brown and partially concealed beneath the metal lip at the base of the heater, on the side facing the sliding glass door. I slowly knelt and shined my light at the object. It looked like a tiny leather hula skirt.

Pulling the phone from my pocket, I called Tina. "Was our vic wearing brown slip-on shoes?"

"Hang on and let me see." A moment later, she came back on the line. "That's affirmative. Though he's only wearing one on his left foot. The other shoe must've come off during the fall."

"Can you tell me if the shoe you have there has tassels on it?"

"Yes, there are two tassels on the shoe."

"Does it look like there were ever any more?"

"No. A man's shoe would look silly with more than two tassels on it."

"Agreed. It also means that the tassel I just found up here came from the missing shoe. Tina, you and Ash have to find that other loafer, ASAP. I think the tassel came off when Sherri shoved her boy toy from the hotel balcony. Maybe the top of his shoe scraped against the stone block. However it happened, it was dark, she didn't see the tassel, and it somehow ended up several feet away from the wall, beneath the propane heater."

"I see what you mean. If Jesse had accidentally fallen, you'd have found the tassel close to where he went over the wall."

"Yep. It shows that someone — probably Sherri — was out here on the balcony with Jesse, which demolishes her story that she was in the Jacuzzi when this happened."

"We'll get busy looking for the shoe," said Tina.

"And I'm going to interview Sherri. Wish me luck."

"Call me when she's confessed."

"I will." I tried to sound more hopeful than I felt.

In truth, I *was* pessimistic. I was simultaneously fatigued and jittery from too many infusions of caffeine, going up against a woman who'd risen to the top rungs of the ladder in the cutthroat and male-dominated world of big business. Her success in that ruthless arena told me that she was tough and difficult to intimidate. She had absolutely nothing to gain by admitting to the two murders and everything to lose.

Then I had an odd thought. Sherri was in the amusement park industry, which meant that her business was creating fantasies for other people. Perhaps she was good at it because she understood the thought patterns of her customers. Maybe she was susceptible to fantasy herself. The old adage "You can't con a con" is utter nonsense. The reason why swindlers succeed is because they're credulous themselves. They understand how to make an attractive pitch.

The solution was suddenly obvious. I'd weave a plausible yet imaginary version of the murders that seemingly offered Sherri an escape route from her present predicament. The goal was to lure her into fantasyland and then spring the trap. I just hoped I was enough of a con man to fool her.

Twenty-Seven

I left the tassel where I found it. The piece of leather's precise location on the flagstone floor beneath the heater would be pivotal to the case. Therefore, we'd need to photograph and take measurements of the evidence before we collected it.

Pushing myself to my feet, I went back inside the suite. Sherri Driggs was still sitting in the chair, while Linny stood near the doorway looking uncomfortable. It looked as if the security manager had run out of things to say. I just hoped he'd stopped talking before inadvertently revealing that I didn't think Jesse's death was an accident.

Opening the miniature refrigerator, I removed a can of Coke. I didn't particularly want another soda, but it was vital that I subliminally demonstrate I felt sufficiently in control of the circumstances that I didn't need to ask her permission to take things from her minibar. If Sherri was going to buy my misleading tale, she had to believe I was fairly confident that I'd solved the riddle of Rawlins's murder. At the same time, I knew she'd suspect something if I came across as too cocksure. I wanted her to help me solve the puzzle to her advantage.

Sitting down opposite Sherri, I set my cane on the table and said, "Ms. Driggs, I'm sorry for your loss. I know this is difficult, but I have to ask a few questions and I hope you'll be patient if you've answered some of them previously."

"I've already told him that I don't know what happened." Sherri nodded in Linny's direction. "I was in the bathtub when Jesse fell."

"I understand that, but maybe you can provide me with some background information. For starters, were you two alone this evening? Did you have any guests?"

"While I was taking a bath? I think not."

"Maybe Mr. Hauck invited someone in and you didn't hear?"

"I suppose that's remotely possible, but I can't think of who it would be. Jesse didn't know anyone around here."

I turned to Linny. "Mr. Owen, could you tell me something? A lot of luxury hotels maintain a computerized database on when guest room doors are opened and shut. Do you do that?"

Linny looked flustered, like an actor who'd forgotten his line. Finally, he said, "Why . . . yes, we do."

"Is it possible for you to find out when the last time the door to this suite was opened, prior to your arrival?"

"I'll get on that right away," said the security director.

Linny pulled his portable radio from his coat pocket and requested the information. A moment later, he received his answer. The last instance anyone went in or out of the suite was at 5:52 P.M. The time coincided with a room-service delivery of two dinners and a fifth of gin. I kept a poker face but was jubilant. It meant that Sherri couldn't use the ever-popular SODDI defense: Some Other Dude Done It. She and Jesse had been the only ones in the suite.

"Thanks, Mr. Owen." Turning back to Sherri, I said, "Sorry for the interruption. Now, can you tell me why Mr. Hauck was out there drinking alone?"

"Because I can't stand the smell of cigars."

"Me either. How much did Mr. Hauck have to drink today?"

Sherri looked pensive. "I wasn't keeping tabs on him, but it seemed to me that it was quite a bit."

410

"Did he normally drink a lot?"

"No, but . . . Wait, are you suggesting that he might have been drunk and fallen from the balcony?"

"It's too early to tell, but let's not get ahead of ourselves. I don't want to put words in your mouth," I said, hoping to do precisely that, "but were you about to tell me that Jesse had been drinking more than usual?"

"That's true." She grimaced, seemingly troubled over revealing something negative about her deceased lover.

"Well, that wouldn't surprise me."

"Why?

"Because he was in a world of trouble — trouble of his own making." I gave her a sad smile. "It's my guess he was trying to drag you down, too."

There was a long pause and she finally said, "I don't know what you're expecting me to say."

"Then I'll say it: Mr. Hauck was on the verge of ruining everything you'd been working for. You see, Ms. Driggs, we've been very busy since I was here yesterday, and I know all about the Blue Ridge Mountain Bear Fair. Why didn't you tell me that you were in negotiations to purchase Everett Rawlins's land?"

She looked down. "Because I knew there wasn't any connection between the transaction and him getting killed."

"Knew or hoped? Anyway, I also imagine you weren't eager to have Amerriment sucked into a public relations crap storm. Murder and amusement parks are a bad mix."

"Family entertainment complexes," she corrected. "And yes, the bad publicity was a major consideration."

"Especially since it looks as if your assistant made Mr. Rawlins a deal he couldn't refuse."

She sat up straight in the chair. "Wait a minute. Are you accusing Jesse of having something to do with Mr. Rawlins's murder?"

"C'mon, Ms. Driggs, let's cut the crap," I rebuked her. "You drove Mr. Hauck out there. You saw what happened. Look, we know that Mr. Rawlins was threatening to scuttle the deal unless you came up with a lot more money. Was Mr. Hauck just supposed to scare the old guy?"

"I don't know what you're talking about. And I told you that —"

"Do yourself a favor and stop lying," I said, hoping she'd ignore the advice and tell me even bigger and more damning false-

412

hoods. "Your Saab was recovered last night and we can prove it wasn't stolen. That means you were there on Thursday night."

"No, it doesn't. I loaned my car to Jesse. He said he was thinking about getting a Saab and wanted to test-drive mine on some mountain roads. I didn't know where he was going that night."

"Right."

"I'm telling the truth. I wasn't there and I'd like to know how you're so certain that Jesse killed that poor man."

"Because a bow and arrow were used to murder Mr. Rawlins, and all our evidence points to the killer being an expert archer," I said, not ready to reveal the secret that Mr. Rawlins had actually been stabbed with the arrow.

"So?"

"He may not have mentioned it to you, but we did some digging and found out that Mr. Hauck was a member of the archery team when he was in college." I gave her a complacent smile. "I know we're just a bunch of rubes out here in the country, but we *can* connect the dots."

Sherri did a splendid job of looking awestruck. "I had no idea he was into archery."

"Just like you didn't know he killed Mr. Rawlins?"

"I didn't!"

"Prove it. Tell me a story I'll believe."

"I have no control over what you'll believe or won't believe," she said primly. "All I can tell you is the truth."

"I'm all ears."

"For starters, Jesse may have been an expert archer, but I never saw him with a bow and arrows."

"Today?"

"Ever. But you were right about Mr. Rawlins playing hardball with us. We'd already come to an agreement in principle on the sale of his land. Then, on Thursday, he said he'd changed his mind and didn't want to sell."

Sherri crossed her legs, and her robe slipped open to reveal an almost indecent amount of tanned thigh. I knew it wasn't an accident. She was preparing to blame everything on Jesse and wanted to distract my attention from the interview. I glanced at Linny, who was staring slack-jawed at Sherri's legs as if he were a Knight of the Round Table having a vision of the Holy Grail.

"Did that make you angry?" I asked.

"Of course not. It was just a tactic to get more money. I'm used to that sort of thing, but it infuriated Jesse."

414

"Why?"

"Because he felt the old guy was playing us for a couple of chumps. Those were Jesse's exact words."

"Go on."

"Sometimes Jesse could be so juvenile."

"That could be said about most twenty-something men."

"I know. Anyway, he was sulking and then, out of the blue, he asked to test-drive my car. If it improved his mood, I couldn't see any harm in that, so I let him. But you've got to understand: I didn't know where he was going that night."

"And what time was this?"

"He left around six P.M."

"While you stayed here?"

"I had absolutely no desire to go out driving in the rain at night," Sherri replied.

I noted that she hadn't actually answered my question, but decided to let her think she'd fooled me. I asked, "Was he gone for very long?"

"Yes. As a matter of fact, it got to be so late that I was getting ready to call the state police to see if Jesse had been involved in a traffic accident."

"And then?"

Her jaw tightened. "Sometime around ten he showed up here, soaking wet, scared, and

415

telling me that he had to ditch my car."

"And naturally you wanted to know why."

"He said he'd stopped for a couple of drinks and then, on the way back to the lodge, had sideswiped a police car. It was an accident, but he knew he'd be arrested for DUI if he stopped." She locked eyes with me. "He didn't say a word about this happening at or near Mr. Rawlins's place."

"Even if that's true, you helped him conceal his involvement in the hit-and-run by falsely reporting your car stolen."

"I made a bad decision and I'll admit it. It's going to sound selfish, but I did it to protect my reputation," she said with a heartfelt sigh. "If Jesse had been arrested for DUI while driving my car, it would have reflected very unfavorably on me with Amerriment's board of directors. I've worked too hard to get where I am to lose it all over a fender-bender."

I was impressed. Sherri had done a pretty amazing job reinterpreting the facts of the case in a way that pointed to her being guilty of nothing more than bad judgment.

I said, "Okay, that was Thursday night. But during our talk on Friday morning, you learned that your car had been seen at the Rawlins farm. Why didn't you say something to me then?"

"I wanted to talk to Jesse first . . . and find out whether we needed to get him a lawyer."

"So you developed a sudden headache to break off the interview."

She nodded.

"Once I was gone, what did he tell you?" I asked.

"He admitted that he'd been at the farm, but swore that he hadn't seen Mr. Rawlins or killed him."

"Why did he go there?"

"Jesse said that he was just going to talk to the old man, but that he changed his mind once he arrived."

"You believed him?" I made no effort to disguise my amusement.

She locked eyes with me again. "I didn't know anything about how Mr. Rawlins died or that Jesse knew how to use a bow and arrows, so I had no reason not to believe him."

"Even it that's true, you had a duty as a *good citizen*" — I paused to give her an ironic smile — "to come forward and tell us that Mr. Hauck was there."

She raised a warning finger. "Don't be a wiseass. I'm trying to cooperate, and this is hard enough as it is."

There was a tap on the door. Linny opened it just a crack, saw it was Ash, and

417

swung the door open. She had a brown paper evidence sack in her hand, and she looked pleased. Assuming that she'd found Jesse's missing shoe, I gave her a wave, signaling her to come into the suite. It had been a very long day and I thought she might enjoy what was going to happen next. Sherri feigned disinterest as Ash handed me the bag.

Looking inside the sack, I said, "You found it. Excellent work, honey."

"And it's exactly the way you thought it would look," Ash replied, obliquely telling me that a tassel was missing from the shoe.

Continuing to peer into the bag, I hooked a thumb at the amusement park executive and said, "Honey, I want you to meet Ms. Sherri Driggs. She was driving the Saab that hit you on Thursday night."

"Hi! Nice to finally meet you," Ash said in a mock cheerful tone.

Sherri's face grew hard. "Wait just a damn minute! I told you that Jesse had my car."

I looked up from the paper sack. "Yeah, I know. You told me lots of things, but most of them were lies. Which is only fair, I suppose. I was lying to you, too. But now it's time for some hard truths. I think I know why Jesse Hauck died and how it happened."

"Oh, really? Enlighten me," Sherri said in a mocking tone.

"Actually, I'm hoping you can enlighten me. Was he blackmailing you? Is that why you killed him?"

"That's ridiculous."

"That's also a nonanswer. You see, we *know* that you were at Everett Rawlins's farm on Thursday evening."

"Jesse had my car. He —"

"Mr. Hauck couldn't have been driving your Saab, because we have security video of you leaving the lodge at around six-thirty. He didn't leave until an hour later, and we have a witness who saw him in his VW."

"As if somebody around here would recognize him."

"To a certain extent that's true. But your boy toy had a one-track mind. The clerk at the hardware store remembers him because he flirted with her when he paid for the screwdriver."

"That you needed to make it look as if your car had been stolen," Ash added.

I said, "And then, here's what I think happened: You told Mr. Hauck that you were just trying to cover up a hit-and-run. You didn't tell him that you'd killed Mr. Rawlins —"

Sherri slapped the table. "Because I didn't!"

"But when I showed up yesterday and mentioned Mr. Rawlins's death, Mr. Hauck put two and two together. Being a good young businessman, he decided to turn the tragedy into a profit . . . at your expense. What did he want, your money or your job?"

"Both." She was trembling with anger. "All right, I was there on Thursday night, but *I didn't kill Rawlins.* I'll take a polygraph test to prove it. The old man had an arrow sticking out of his chest when I got to the farm. I was terrified and I panicked."

"Why?"

"*Why?* For all I knew, the person who'd shot that arrow was still out there. I didn't want to be the next target."

"Did you think about calling the sheriff?"

Sherri squinted at me as if I'd lost my mind. "And end up in the middle of a murder investigation that would delay or even derail my project? Thanks, but I can think of easier ways to waste millions of dollars."

"But if you didn't kill him, why would you be worried about that?" I asked.

Ash cleared her throat. "Because she was hoping to secretly buy the land and get the board of supervisors to rezone the property

420

before anyone knew there was a theme park coming. Right?"

Sherri gave her a sour look.

Ash continued, "She realized that once the local folks knew the truth, there'd be an uproar and the politicians probably wouldn't have stayed bought."

"We didn't bribe anyone, but yes, we wanted to keep the project confidential," Sherri replied. "Look, I conduct tough business negotiations for a living, and I win them. There was no reason for me to kill Everett Rawlins."

I said, "In light of the fact that you've repeatedly lied in two separate interviews, we're going to need more than just your word before we believe that."

"Then I'd suggest you talk to Kurt Rawlins, Everett Rawlins's son."

I kept a poker face. "How do you know him?"

"I've dealt with him for a few years. We have Chunky Chuck's Burgers restaurants in our theme parks."

I wanted to say, *Don't you mean family entertainment complexes?* Instead, I asked, "And how is Kurt involved in all of this?"

"He knew that we were interested in putting a park in the mid-Atlantic region and suggested we look at the Shenandoah Valley," she replied. "We did some checking and the idea appeared promising. A few weeks later Kurt called and told me that his father would consider selling his farm to Amerriment."

I said, "I hate to sound cynical, but we do live in a quid pro quo world. What was Kurt going to get out of the deal?"

"An executive VP position at Amerriment in charge of all food and beverage concessions."

"What kind of salary would that entail?"

"We were still negotiating that."

"But it's safe to say it would be a lot more money than what he was making with Chunky Chuck's."

"That's a fair statement. So, you see?" Sherri gave us a confident smile. "Why would I ruin everything by murdering his father? Furthermore, if you had any proof that I killed him, you'd have arrested me already."

I nodded. "That's true. Unfortunately for you, we *do* have strong evidence that you murdered Jesse."

"While I was in the Jacuzzi?" Her tone was scornful. "I'd like to see you prove that."

"Well, sure. I can do that."

"Beware of the things you ask for," Ash muttered.

I carefully slid the brown slip-on shoe from the paper sack and onto the tabletop. "You probably recognize this, don't you?"

Sherri glanced at the loafer for a nanosecond and then looked up at me. "It's Jesse's shoe."

"Yup. My wife found it on the ground in the vicinity of Mr. Hauck's corpse. Notice anything peculiar about the shoe?"

"No."

"You didn't really look, but that's okay. I'll cut to the chase. One of the tassels has been torn from the shoe." I pointed to the damaged leatherwork. "And I found that tassel on the balcony floor. It was ripped off when you shoved Mr. Hauck over the wall."

"Aren't you jumping to conclusions?" She smirked at me. "As I told you, Jesse had been drinking a lot. He was probably tipsy, lost his balance, and this damage you're talking about with the tassel happened when he accidentally fell."

"That would be a plausible theory, except for one thing. The tassel was nowhere near the base of the wall. It was several feet away, beneath the rim of the propane heater."

"So what?"

"The only way it could have gotten so far from the wall was if someone kicked it. Mr. Hauck couldn't, because he was plummeting to his death. That leaves you." I gave her a gentle smile. "It was dark, and you never saw the tassel. Who could? It was a tiny bit of leather and you were probably stressed to the max after pushing your back-stabbing boy toy to his death. But in your hurry to get to the bathroom and establish your bubble bath alibi, you unwittingly kicked it under the heater."

"What makes you think that I was even out there?" Sherri engaged me in a stare-down contest. She tried to look confident, but I detected a dim flicker of fear in her eyes.

"For heaven's sake, that's the easiest part to establish. You heard the security director." I inclined my head toward Linny. "The computer records show that nobody entered or left the suite after five fifty-two this afternoon. You were the only other person here."

Sherri's face became an expressionless mask. "I'm not saying another thing. I want my lawyer."

I glanced at Ash. "That's your cue, Deputy Lyon."

Ash pulled her handcuffs from her gun belt. "You can call your attorney from the station. You're under arrest for the murder of Jesse Hauck."

"Wait a minute. I can't go dressed like this." Sherri gestured toward the flimsy kimono. "At least let me put on some real clothes."

"Oh, I don't think so," Ash replied as she pulled the other woman to her feet. "If you were comfortable being dressed like that while talking to my husband yesterday and again today, then you can't be *that* modest."

"But it's cold."

"So is shoving your boyfriend from a balcony." Ash handcuffed Sherri. "Let's go."

TWENTY-EIGHT

Linny held the door open and Ash guided the still-protesting Sherri from the suite. I knew the security director craved being seen escorting my wife and her handcuffed prisoner through the hotel lobby. It would be as close as Linny would ever come to conducting a perp walk, and I didn't want to deny him that harmless pleasure. However, I had to talk with him for a moment and called to him to wait.

"What do you need, Brad?" Linny glanced nervously toward the receding sound of Sherri's voice.

I replied, "I'm going to go downstairs and get the camera, so I can photograph that tassel and collect it as evidence. But that's all we can legally do tonight. Any other searching of paperwork and possessions is going to require a search warrant. So, once I finish, could you please change the digital locking codes on this room?"

"Sure. Just give me a call when you want it done. Here's the passkey to get back into the room." Linny handed me a plastic key card.

"Thanks. And nobody comes in or out of the room — including housekeeping and security — until we come back with the warrant. That will probably be tomorrow. Any problem with that?"

"None. You can count on me."

"I know, Linny. Thanks for the backup." I patted him on the bicep. "Now go and catch up."

Linny bolted from the room and jogged down the hall. I hoped he'd overtake Ash before she and Sherri got to the elevator. Grabbing my cane from the table, I shut the suite's door and headed for the elevators at a far more sedate pace. I rode the elevator to the lobby and then hitched a lift down the hill to the château on one of the hotel's electric golf carts.

As we pulled up in front of the large wooden building, the bluegrass band began playing "Orange Blossom Special." The crowd inside the building began to applaud and shout their approval. Apparently, the bridal couple wasn't going to let a murder interfere with their wedding celebration.

Tina was on the lawn beside the château,

standing just inside the crime scene tape perimeter. Jesse's body was concealed beneath a blue plastic tarp and lying on the grass, behind the sheriff. Joining her, I briefed Tina on what Sherri had told me and concluded my update by telling her that Ash had arrested the executive for the murder of her assistant.

When I finished, Tina said, "Let me get this straight. Sherri Driggs has been lying to you continuously *and* we can prove that she murdered her lover, yet you believe her when she says she didn't kill Everett Rawlins?"

I replied, "Look, I'm not ruling her out as the killer. And for that matter, Wade Tice, Chet Lincoln, and Roger Prufrock are still in the mix, too. None of them has an ironclad alibi."

"And isn't it interesting that our favorite grieving son Kurt Rawlins flat-out lied about knowing anything about the real estate deal when I talked to him on Friday night? That's mighty peculiar, because if Roger Prufrock was telling the truth about Mr. Hauck's phone call to him on Friday afternoon, the deal had already been finalized. Or is it possible Mr. Rawlins signed before he died?"

"More likely that Jesse decided to forge

the old guy's name on the documents and figured that Kurt wouldn't complain."

"We've got to find that escrow paperwork."

"I'm assuming there are copies up in the suite," I said, stifling a yawn. "But we won't be able to go through her possessions until we get a search warrant."

Tina rubbed the back of her neck and grumbled, "Which means tomorrow at the earliest."

"In the meantime, I think I should go talk to Kurt."

"Right now?"

"Why not? You've got everything under control here and I'll bet he won't be expecting someone from the sheriff's office to show up unannounced at his hotel . . . ?"

"The Madison Inn. It's near the university."

"Maybe I can parlay the surprise into some honest answers."

"I guess it's worth a shot." Tina tossed me her car keys. "Take my unit back to the office to pick up your car. I'll catch a ride back when I'm done, which I'm afraid isn't going to be anytime soon."

"Thanks. Hey, before I go, let me try to brighten your night with a riddle." Hooking a thumb toward the body, I asked, "How are Jesse Hauck and Hills Bros. Coffee alike?"

Tina shook her head and sighed. "I know I'm going to regret this, but how?"

"They're both good to the last drop."

She chuckled wearily. "That's sick, so why do I think it's funny?"

"Because the best homicide investigators I ever knew were the ones who learned to laugh at tragedy. Welcome to the club, Tina."

I drove Tina's patrol car back to the station and went inside to drop off the keys with the dispatcher. As I left the communications center, Ash emerged from the report-writing room with a booking sheet in her hand. We met in the hall and, not caring about on-duty decorum, gave each other an encompassing hug.

After a while, I heaved a huge sigh and whispered, "Hey, I feel as if I've hardly seen you over the past couple of days."

"God, I know," she quietly groaned. "What are you doing back here already?"

"I'm going to take a run over to Harrisonburg and interview Kurt Rawlins," I replied.

Ash gave me a suspicious look. "Are you going to talk to him alone?"

"No way. The burger bully has a temper, and I'm too tired to put up with his crap. I'm going to have the Harrisonburg cops meet me at the hotel where he's staying."

"Good."

"Deputy Lyon," came the tinny sound of a man's voice from the station's public address system. "Please come back to the jail. Your prisoner says that she wants to talk to you."

"I wonder what she wants *now,*" Ash grumbled. Then she gave me a kiss and said, "Be careful, and I'll see you a little later tonight. Love you, Brad."

"Love you, too, my darling," I said, reluctantly releasing her.

As I drove toward Harrisonburg, I mentally role-played the interview, trying to decide which interrogation tactics would work best against the aggressive and often argumentative Kurt.

I'd traveled perhaps a mile when something occurred to me. So far as I knew, Tina hadn't gotten any calls or messages from Kurt Rawlins for hours. That was damn odd in light of how frequently he'd called her on Thursday and Friday. Maybe there was a good reason why he hadn't called tonight, but the thought struck me that Kurt had repeatedly made it clear that he wanted inside the house as soon as possible to begin going through his father's papers. Although Tina still hadn't released the evidence hold on Rawlins's farmhouse, the impatient and assertive Kurt didn't impress me as the sort of guy who took no for an answer. So I wondered if the reason why he'd suddenly stopped pestering Tina was that he was otherwise engaged in an activity that required his full attention . . . such as disobeying the sheriff's orders and searching his dad's house.

It seemed to me that there was no point in driving all the way into Harrisonburg when Kurt might be just a couple of miles away. I turned the truck around and headed back toward the dark bulk of the Blue Ridge Mountains. As I passed the ruins of Liz Ewell's old childhood home, the moonlight revealed faint, thin, and misty tendrils of smoke still curling upward from the low mounds of wreckage. I arrived on Kobler Hollow Road about five minutes later and tried to imagine the narrow forest lane converted into the entrance to an amusement park. The idea was obscene.

One of my personality faults is that I often believe the worst about other people. I'm not proud of that trait, but it does have an upside. I'm never really astonished when folks do stupid things; it's what I expect from them. Therefore, it didn't come as a shock when I saw a light on inside the farmhouse and Kurt's Lexus parked by the front porch. I pulled out my cell phone, speed-dialed sheriff's dispatch, and told her that instead of Harrisonburg, I was out at the Rawlins farm and making contact with Kurt.

I parked behind the sports car and climbed from the truck. As I did, the house suddenly went dark and Kurt's large silhouette emerged onto the porch. Pushing the front door shut, he tucked his hands inside his coat pockets. He stood on the porch for a second, obviously watching me, and then abruptly walked down the steps toward the Lexus.

With a dry chuckle, I said, "Oh, now don't run off on my account, Mr. Rawlins. In fact, let's talk."

"About what?" Kurt replied while reaching for the car's door handle. "I have every right to be here. This was my home."

"You mind if I ask what you were looking for?"

Kurt slowly turned to face me, but the dim moonlight made it difficult for me to read the expression on his face. He said, "Nothing in particular. I just wanted to walk through the house and say good-bye."

"You sound awfully sentimental for someone who was trying to sell his family's farm to a corporation that specializes in building cheesy theme parks."

His posture stiffened. "I don't know what you're talking about."

"Please, Mr. Rawlins. I'm tired, it's cold, and for a businessman, you aren't a very effective liar." I took a step closer to him. "And who knows? Maybe if you had told me the whole truth, we might be that much closer to figuring out who killed your dad. Besides, Sherri Driggs just finished telling me most of the story."

"I'll bet she didn't tell you that *she* killed my dad."

"You're right, she didn't. As a matter of fact, she claims she doesn't know who did it."

"Well, I *know* she did it. She told her assistant that it was an accident . . . an accident, my ass," Kurt snarled. Then in a more somber voice, he continued, "She said she'd gone over and tried to talk to Dad while he was having his supper and that he threatened her with the arrow. Sherri tried to take it away from him, they wrestled, and he got stabbed."

I was so weary that it took a couple of seconds for me to appreciate the full import of what Kurt had just said. It was ironic. During our investigation, we'd diligently photographed and processed several crime scenes; collected all sorts of potential physical evidence, including four motor vehicles and an ATV; submitted evidence to the crime lab for analysis; interviewed more than a dozen possible witnesses and suspects; and in general burned the candle at both ends for three days, laboring without success to positively identify Rawlins's killer. All that work, and as it turned out, none of our whiz-bang CSI procedures were as pivotal to cracking the puzzle as Kurt's verbal slip. Only four people knew or even suspected that Everett Rawlins had been actually stabbed with the arrow: Tina, Ash, the medical examiner, and me. We hadn't shared this information with anyone, so there was only one way Kurt could have known what actually happened.

Finally, I said, "And you don't believe that?"

"No." Kurt shook his head vigorously.

"Neither do I. You know why?"

"Why?"

"Because you are the only person in the world besides me and the three other cops who processed the murder scene who knew that your dad was stabbed with the arrow. Everyone else thinks the arrow was shot from a bow," I said, fumbling to open my jacket and get to my gun. "I'll be a son of a bitch. *You* drove down here from northern Virginia on Thursday evening and killed your dad."

Maybe it was because I was so tired, but Kurt was faster on the draw. He yanked a small stainless-steel revolver from his coat and pointed the weapon at me. His right hand looked dark against the silvery metal of the gun, and I realized he was wearing the same brown leather driving gloves he'd had on when we'd first met yesterday morning. I suddenly knew the origin of the trace evidence on the arrow's shaft. Kurt had been wearing the gloves when he'd plunged the arrow into his father's chest.

"Get your hands up or you're a dead man!" Kurt was suddenly so panicky that his voice squeaked.

I let go of my cane and raised my arms. Then, as if there weren't enough to occupy my attention, my cell phone began to ring. I was terrified, but also knew that my only chance for survival rested on my ability to make Kurt understand that there was no chance of escape and also no profit in killing me.

Trying to keep my voice calm, I said, "You hear that phone?"

"Don't answer it!"

"I don't need to. That's the sheriff's office, and they already know that you and I are here. I called and told them that just before I got out of my truck."

"That's a lie." He took some shuffling steps closer to me and paused. It was obvious that he was a novice at taking hostages and was trying to figure out how to grab the gun from my shoulder holster without getting too close to me.

"When you start hearing sirens in a little bit, you'll realize I'm telling the truth." My bad leg buckled and I nearly lost my balance, but I quickly regained my footing.

He retreated a couple of steps but kept the revolver shakily pointed at my chest. "Stand still and keep your hands up!"

"Dude, with only one good pin, this is the best I can do," I said, hoping the fact that I hadn't gotten a bullet for the sudden move meant he wasn't eager to kill me. My cell phone stopped ringing and I added, "They'll be coming soon."

"You are so full of crap your eyes are brown." Kurt did his best to sound scoffing. Then, in the distance, a siren began to yelp and he shot a nervous and fleeting look in that direction.

I heaved a weary sigh. "So, what's the plan? Sherri Driggs is already in jail and charged with murder, so you can't blame her for *my* death."

"In jail? But you said that —"

"Oh, she's not under arrest for your dad's murder. Sherri killed Jesse Hauck earlier this evening by pushing him over the hotel balcony." I briefly glanced to the west, where two more sirens had begun wailing. "Her incentive to kill was pretty clear-cut. She murdered her assistant because he was blackmailing her. But I don't understand your motive."

"Just shut up!" His hand trembled as he brandished the gun.

"I've got to know. What in the name of God did your dad do to deserve to be skewered like a butterfly on a display board?"

"It was an accident. He changed his mind about selling the farm and we argued, but I didn't mean to kill him."

"That's kind of hard to believe, considering our present situation." I nodded toward the jiggling gun. "For instance, how'd you even end up with the arrow in your hand?"

"It was stuck in the side of the house when I got here. Dad never even saw it, until I yanked it from the wall."

"And that happened while you were fighting?"

"I swear to God, we weren't fighting! It

438

was just an argument."

"And you lost your temper because his decision not to sell the farm meant that all your big career plans with Amerriment were ruined." My arms were beginning to become sore and quivery from the effort of keeping them elevated. "That's disappointing, but not much of a reason to off your old man."

"It didn't happen like that," Kurt said through clenched teeth. "Dad was standing there in the yard, spouting some crazy crap about how it just wouldn't be right for him to hurt his friends and neighbors by selling his land. I had my back turned to him . . ."

"And?"

"Then he said that there was something almost sinful about the idea of putting an amusement park where my mother died." There was a pause and when Kurt resumed speaking, his tone became both soft and more frightening. "Imagine that. My mother died because that old bastard kept her out here in the middle of nowhere, and then he has the freaking gall to use his crime as an excuse not to sell the farm."

"I can see how that would have made you angry. What happened?"

"I spun around to scream at him, but he'd moved. He was a lot closer to me than I thought . . . right behind me. I was holding the arrow by the shaft . . . and it just went into his chest." Kurt now sounded slightly nauseated.

"So it was a tragic accident." I allowed my arms to drop a millimeter or so.

"You don't believe me." He glanced toward the driveway.

The first siren was very close now — perhaps a half mile away — and I suspected Ash was driving the patrol car. Situated as we were in the darkness between the house and vehicles, she wouldn't be able to see Kurt and me when she pulled into the yard. That meant she was driving into a potential ambush, and I couldn't let that happen.

I needed to come up with some magical combination of words to defuse the situation; otherwise I'd be forced to launch a suicidal attack on Kurt. However, that wasn't much of an option. The odds were that he'd shoot me, and the very best outcome I could hope for was that Ash would kill Kurt and that I might stay alive long enough for the paramedics to arrive.

Trying to keep my tone casual, I said, "It doesn't matter what I believe, and the fact is, I can't disprove your story. All you have to do is sell your version of the tale to one member of the jury and you'll be a free man. But the only way you can make that happen is if you do the smart thing right now."

"And surrender? So that I can be sent to prison? I don't think so," Kurt snarled. "Shut up and give me your gun. I'll take my chances —"

Kurt stopped midsentence, interrupted by the sound of something crashing through the brushwood that hemmed the driveway. We both turned to look, and I saw a dark and large figure on all fours burst from the undergrowth and quickly lumber across the yard. It was the biggest black bear I'd ever seen. Obviously frightened by the earsplitting howl of the approaching siren, the animal was running for the safety of the abandoned quarry.

As the bear drew abreast of our vehicles, its head swiveled in our direction and it half stumbled, surprised by our presence. The bear growled, and Kurt pivoted his upper body to point the revolver at the creature. That was all the opportunity I needed. I jerked my pistol from the shoulder holster just as Kurt snapped off a wild shot at the bear. There was a deafening crack and the yellowish-white geyser of muzzle flash from the revolver was blinding.

Closing the short distance between us in

two large and very painful strides, I pointed the business end of my gun right between Kurt's terrified eyes and said, "Throw down the gun, young man, or I'm going to give you a forty-caliber lobotomy."

Kurt dropped the revolver. It bounced off the trunk of his Lexus and fell to the ground, where it would be relatively safe for now. I glanced to my right and couldn't see the bear, so I backed away from Kurt and ordered him to raise his hands and slowly walk out into the yard. Meanwhile, the siren stopped and bright flashing lights suddenly illuminated the driveway as the patrol car arrived. The cruiser slid to a stop on the gravel, its headlights shining on a now-quaking Kurt.

Ash shouted, "Brad, are you all right?"

"I'm Code Four, honey. I'll cover him while you take him into custody," I replied, as I limped toward her. "And be careful. This desperado murdered his daddy and was ready to do the same thing to me."

I made a point of ensuring that Kurt could see my pistol pointed at his noggin as Ash searched him for weapons and handcuffed him. We squeezed him into the narrow back-seat of the cruiser and slammed the door shut, and then Ash used her portable radio to notify the other responding units that everything was all right. Tina acknowledged the message and in another rare breach of radio discipline said it was a good thing that *someone* was fine, because she was on the verge of having a heart attack.

As we walked back over to the Lexus to retrieve my cane and Kurt's gun, I asked, "So, how did you know to come here Code Three?"

"Sherri Driggs changed her mind about not talking and told me that she'd telephoned Kurt Rawlins on Thursday afternoon when the real estate deal went south. Kurt told her he'd drive down and promised that he'd get his father to sign the papers," said Ash, shining her flashlight on the ground as she searched for the revolver.

"Which means that this was the car Wade Tice saw pull up in front of the house, after he shot the arrow," I said, pointing to the Lexus.

"That's what I thought, too." She stooped to pick up the gun. "And then I realized you'd gone off to meet the killer alone. Thank God you called dispatch and told them where you were."

I slowly knelt to grab my cane. "And thank God you came as fast as you did."

"Why?"

"Because he had the drop on me. He was

443

on the verge of killing me and then ambushing you," I said, taking her hand.

Ash inhaled sharply. "But how did you get the gun away from him?"

"With a lot of luck and a little help from an oversized teddy bear. You may not believe the rest of this story, but it's the *bear*-faced truth . . ."

TWENTY-NINE

In crime fiction and cop TV shows, nobody ever sits for hours writing paperwork. Real life is very different. We had arrest reports to complete and evidence to log, not to mention the search warrant affidavits that still had to be written. It was after eleven P.M. when Tina called it a night and said it was time for all of us to go home. There was still at least a full day's worth of investigative work in front of us, but after the last few days we were almost dazed with fatigue and it would have to wait. Work would resume tomorrow, after lunch.

We drove by Tina's folks' house, picked up Kitch, went home, and were snug between the flannel sheets of our bed not long after. My last sensation before going to sleep was the faint yet delicious smell of Ash's cinnamon bun–scented lip emollient.

The following morning we woke up late and had a leisurely time over coffee and hot cocoa in our living room. Kitch was obviously glad to be home. By both breed and personality he isn't a lap dog, but he'd climbed up into my easy chair with me. Meanwhile, Ash was on the sofa, curled up beneath a quilt.

She said, "With all the craziness yesterday, I think I forgot to tell you something."

"What's that?" I asked.

"Come tomorrow morning, Ev Rawlins's dog Longstreet is going to be released from doggy jail. Tina told Sergei about him, and he's decided he needs a dog."

"That's good news. I don't mind locking up people, but pets? That's a whole other kettle of fish."

"I know. So who actually forged Everett's signature on the escrow papers?"

"We won't know for certain until the questioned-document specialist examines the paperwork, but my money is on Kurt," I replied, while scratching Kitch between his shoulder blades. "It was thoughtful of him to have the documents in his car."

Ash nodded. "It's creepy to think that he took the documents from the house after he killed his dad."

"He won't cop to it, but that seems to be the only way the papers could have been removed from the house."

"And if the escrow documents were forged, that means the real estate transaction is null and void. Amerriment doesn't own Everett's farm."

I nodded. "That's the silver lining to this entire sordid spectacle. What's more, with the PR nightmare of two murders linked to their theme park project, I don't think Amerriment will try to build one of their carnivals around here."

Ash drank the last of her hot cocoa. "And could Kurt actually convince a jury that killing his dad was an accident?"

"Unlikely. He's going to have a huge problem selling the 'oops' defense to a jury. Kurt's big problem is that he never called the paramedics. That's hard to explain if skewering his papa was just an accident. Add the subsequent forgery, the false information he gave us —"

"And his attempt to kill you."

"All of which contribute to showing consciousness of guilt. Bottom line: Kurt is going to be flipping burgers in the prison chow hall for a long, long time."

"Good," said Ash, as she got up from the sofa. "I'm going to make myself some more hot cocoa. Can I refill your coffee?"

"Please."

As I held out my cup, the telephone began

to ring. We exchanged looks of dread. Folks don't customarily telephone on Sundays before noon, so we both feared it was Tina inviting us to respond to a fresh calamity.

The receiver was on the end table beside my chair, and I picked it up. The tiny ID screen showed that the caller was a J. Janovich, and I allowed myself to relax a little. I had no idea of who he was, but I could be reasonably certain he wasn't calling to ask us if we'd like to get dressed and come look at a corpse.

I said, "Hello, this is Brad."

"Mr. Lyon? I'm Jeff Janovich from Hawksbill Creek Realty. You don't know me and I hope I'm not calling too early, but I left several messages on your phone yesterday."

"We were out all day and most of last night, and frankly we haven't been in a hurry to listen to our messages. Why is it so important that you talk to me?" I sat up in the chair and pushed Kitch from my lap.

"Because Miss Ewell's instructions were that I was to contact you immediately."

"About?" I signaled Ash to come closer and listen in on the conversation.

"About a home she might be interested in selling to you."

"And I'm supposed to believe that Elizabeth Ewell wants to do *us* a good turn?

448

Look, Mr. Janovich, it's been nice, but I'm going to hang up now and have another cup of coffee."

"Wait! Please!" Janovich implored. "It's her understanding that you are looking for an older residence in or close to Remmelkemp Mill that could be renovated and converted into a teddy bear shop."

"I never mentioned that to her, so how'd she know?" I asked.

"She didn't say and, well, if you've talked to Miss Ewell . . ." Janovich laughed nervously. "Well, then you know that mostly means listening, agreeing to her instructions, and not asking questions."

"That's true."

"Anyway, she has instructed me to inform you that a Queen Anne–style Victorian home on Coggins Spring Road is available for sale. You may know the house. It's across the street from the church."

Ash's eyes widened and she blurted, "Oh my God, the old Dwyer house?"

Janovich replied, "I assume that's your wife I just heard? Yes, we are talking about the Dwyer property. Would you like to look at it?"

Ash nodded eagerly and mouthed the words, *It's perfect.*

I said, "Yes. Give us a call back tomorrow

morning and we'll set up a time."

"Sounds good. I look forward to meeting you and Mrs. Lyon and showing you this very special property."

"Just one final question: Did Miss Ewell explain this sudden goodwill? It's no secret around here that she doesn't like us. She'd have to know we'd be suspicious."

"As a matter of fact, she said you'd ask something like that. I'm supposed to tell you that she still thinks you're a pain in the . . . backside —"

"I'll bet that isn't the word she used."

"But at least you're an honorable pain in the backside and man enough to admit when you're wrong."

"Tell her thanks, and that I'm *not* looking forward to doing business with her."

"I actually think she'll enjoy hearing that," said Janovich. "Talk to you tomorrow."

I hung up and there was perhaps ten seconds of silence as we exchanged joyous looks and large Christmas morning–style grins. Neither of us wanted to speak for fear of jinxing the unexpected good news. Meanwhile, Kitch sensed our happiness and decided to celebrate, too. He bounded over to his toy basket, picked up his favorite plastic squeaky toy, and began squeezing it between his jaws.

Ash started up the stairs, and I asked, "Where the heck are you going?"

"I'm going to get dressed. C'mon, let's go look at the house," she replied excitedly. "Call Mr. Janovich back and ask him to meet us there."

Janovich agreed to meet us there at noon. We loaded Kitch into the SUV and drove into town. It was easy to find the Dwyer house. Even though it was in need of a good pressure washing, the three-storied, pale yellow Queen Anne Victorian home was still the prettiest house in Remmelkemp Mill. Leaving Kitch in the Xterra, we got out and went to the front porch to look through the windows.

After a while, Ash asked, "So . . . could we be open by the first week of December?"

I squinted at her. "Honey, I'm as thrilled over this as you are. So, please don't take this wrong, but are you nuts? That's just over three weeks from now, and even if we agree on a price, it'll take a month for escrow to close."

She waved at the air dismissively. "Escrow can close faster than that if both parties agree to it. Besides, I'll bet we could get permission to start work as soon as we have a deal."

"That could be a really big project."

451

"I don't think so. If the inside is in as good a shape as the outside, it won't take that much work." Ash pointed through the window. "The hardwood floors look fine, and there's plenty of wall space to install nice wooden shelves."

"Okay, but what about the tiny issues of getting insurance, registering with the state tax board, and securing a county business license?" I asked.

"I can handle those things while you work with Daddy to get the shop ready. And Tina told me that Sergei would help out in his free time."

"All right, *maybe* it's possible we could open the shop in three or four weeks. Maybe. But why the rush?"

"Because I want the shop open and running before Heather and Colin come here for Christmas," said Ash, referring to our daughter and her fiancé. "I need to have the business startup out of the way so that we can start planning Heather's wedding."

"Whoa! I didn't know they'd set a date."

"I guess I've got to spoil a surprise. They've scheduled it for the end of May, and they plan to get married here. They were going to officially announce it to the family over the holidays."

I squeezed her hand. "Well, then I guess

we've got our work cut out for us."

Ash looked up at me and fixed me with her Delft China blue eyes. "So, you think we can do it?"

"I'm *certain* we can do it." I leaned over to kiss her lightly on the forehead. "Hey, if there's any one thing I've learned over our years together, it's this: Once we put our minds to making something happen, nothing can stop us."

A TEDDY BEAR ARTISAN
PROFILE
MARTHA D. BURCH

My wife, Joyce, and I have long loved Martha D. Burch's teddy bears. Whether it's one of her traditional mohair teddies, a girl bear attired in a Victorian dress, or a costumed furry tribute to Theodore Roosevelt, we're captivated by her creations. But back in the summer of 2007 Martha took her work to a new and incredible level of imaginative excellence. She began crafting exquisitely costumed and accessorized wizard-themed teddy bears, among them the Ice King mentioned in Chapter Five.

The Ice King is real and stands with a handful of other bears on permanent display in our library. It was a one-of-a-kind teddy bear and one of my Christmas gifts to Joyce that year. In 2008, the Ice King received the Teddy Bear of the Year (TOBY) award for Best in Show. The prize was an enormous honor, but what makes the Ice King truly special is that our dear friend Martha created this gorgeous teddy.

Martha lives with her husband, Jim, in Wisconsin, and she is a renaissance woman. She not only makes teddy bears, she plays guitar and sings in a popular bluegrass band, is a much-sought-after master of ceremonies for teddy bear conventions across the country, is a skilled auctioneer, and — of special import to a retired cop — even cooks homemade doughnuts. However, there's a good reason why Martha is best known for her teddy bears. She's been making stuffed animals for more than a quarter century and is one of the pioneers who helped make artisan teddy bears such a popular American collectible.

Martha's ursine odyssey began in 1983 when she wanted to give handmade Christmas gifts to friends and family. At the time, she didn't know anything about the world of artisan bears, but she was drawn to the idea of making teddies. Using old coats and quilts from her mother's antiques shop and employing a Steiff bear as a model, she taught herself to craft simple bears that pleased both her and the lucky people who received them.

"Those early bears were *really* unsophisticated," Martha recalled with a chuckle. "They had button eyes, no noses or mouths, and strings as joints for the limbs. For quite a while, I wasn't aware that there was an artisan teddy bear community or shops that sold bear-making supplies. That was a good thing, however. It forced me to innovate and experiment."

Martha's work soon became far more sophisticated, and she discovered the world of collectible teddy bears. She enjoyed being around other artists, loved the attitude of bear collectors, and soon established herself as one of the preeminent teddy artists in North America. Martha also became a fixture at bear shows across the country, and over the years she has had some touching experiences.

For instance, a collector whose mother had recently died appeared at an Illinois teddy bear show and provided Martha with her mom's photograph, old woolen coat, and eyeglasses. Her request was as simple as it was challenging: She wanted Martha to create a teddy bear to commemorate her mom. A month later, Martha took the completed bear to a Wisconsin teddy bear show, where the collector would pick it up.

"I'd done my best, but I was worried, because I was trying to recreate her mom and you can never really be certain of how well you've realized someone else's vision," said Martha. "But I realized that I'd succeeded when I saw the lady. She was standing at the end of the aisle crying, because the bear really looked like her mom. It was a humbling moment. That's the real payoff and what keeps me still excited about making teddy bears after all these years."

I'm glad to hear that. We live in a world that often seems pretty jaded. Yet Martha's bears provide a spark of enchantment in our otherwise mundane lives. As she said, "We've lost a sense of 'awe' and 'ahh,' but we can bring magic into our lives if we just focus on the beauties around us."

Another way, I might add, is to have a few of Martha's sweet bears in your home.

Martha attends teddy bear shows throughout the United States. If you'd like to learn more about her wonderful bears and her event schedule, I invite you to visit her website at www.marthasbears.com.

AFTERWORD

I regret to report that there isn't any such event as the Massanutten Mountain Teddy Jubilee. However, one of the benefits of creating an imaginary bear show is that I can populate it with some of our favorite artists. Donna Nielsen, Pam Kisner, Darlene Allen, Ginger Brame, Gary Nett, MaryAnn Wills, Pat Berkowitch, and Donna Griffin are genuine bear makers, and we love their creations. I want to thank them both for allowing me to use their names and making the world a better place with their teddy bears.

Furthermore, I want to offer personal thanks to our dear friend teddy bear artist Penny French for her gracious guidance and assistance. Although I write books set in the world of bear making, I'm merely a collector and couldn't make a teddy if my life depended on it. That's why I depend on

Penny to ensure that I have my facts and nomenclature straight.

ABOUT THE AUTHOR

John J. Lamb is a retired homicide detective and hostage negotiator. He and his wife collect teddy bears, and at last count had over 700. His first book in the popular Bear Collector's Mysteries, *The Mournful Teddy,* was a finalist for the prestigious Dilys Award. For more information, please visit: www.johnjlamb.net.

We hope you have enjoyed this Large Print book. Other Thorndike, Wheeler, Kennebec, and Chivers Press Large Print books are available at your library or directly from the publishers.

For information about current and upcoming titles, please call or write, without obligation, to:

Publisher
Thorndike Press
295 Kennedy Memorial Drive
Waterville, ME 04901
Tel. (800) 223-1244

or visit our Web site at:

http://gale.cengage.com/thorndike

OR

Chivers Large Print
published by BBC Audiobooks Ltd
St James House, The Square
Lower Bristol Road
Bath BA2 3SB
England
Tel. +44(0) 800 136919
email: bbcaudiobooks@bbc.co.uk
www.bbcaudiobooks.co.uk

All our Large Print titles are designed for easy reading, and all our books are made to last.